# id

A Novel
By
Kevin Spark

STORY MERCHANT BOOKS
LOS ANGELES
2022

ISBN: 978-1-970157-35-2
Story Merchant Books
400 S. Burnside Avenue #11B
Los Angeles, CA 90036

www.storymerchantbooks.com

Interior format by IndieDesignz.com

FOR MY FAMILY.

# Part 1

# 1.

"Thunk, thunk, thunk," the soft wet beat of muffled drum filters into the dream of a little girl asleep. Alison Shelly is riding a blue horse with a rainbow mane. A mother she never knew rides next to her through a landscape only imagined. The rhythmic cadence of her breathing syncs to the pulse beyond sleep, still distant enough for slumber but drawing closer with every stroke.

"Thunk." Louder, closer, clearer, it becomes a gnawing intrusion once noticed. She looks to her mother for an answer, who, frowning, shakes her head, telling her to ignore it, but the sound penetrates and wipes away the last vestiges of sleep and pulls her into the waking world.

"Thunk," the sound made real. Alison, struggling to free herself from the tendrils of sleep, opens her eyes beneath the covers, wary of what lurks above. Knowing, the way children do, that some things only come to life when seen. But she is a brave child and breaks the surface as her eyes carefully move from one corner to the next, bedsheets clutched under her chin. Stuffed toys stare blankly back from glassy eyes, everyone, and everything in their proper place, just as she left them. The only movement comes from the gentle sway of her curtains catching the night breeze. She gets out of bed and shuts the window.

"Thunk."

Without bothering to switch on the light, knowing she shouldn't, she follows the sound downstairs.

"Thunk."

Louder in the kitchen but still one room away, she stops to run her finger over the tiny table already set for two. Syrup and salt, knives and forks, a day-old flower picked for her father, beginning to wilt. In the quiet of the night, drained from the color of the day, the room looks somber, false even, as if set for a play.

"Thunk."

*It's coming from the cellar. Dad must be working downstairs,* thinks Alison, her eye drawn to the blade of yellow light spilling from the open door, slicing the kitchen in two. The door that never shuts, constantly bouncing open, *too much damp in the wood*, her father once told her. To prove him right, Alison gently pushes the door shut, only to watch it bounce open once more, the light blinking in the dark. She licks her lips, her mouth is dry, and her throat parched and pads over to the sink. Taking a clean glass from the draining board, she fills it with cold water from the tap and takes a large swallow. It's good and cold. She's sure her father would like one. She is, after all, Daddy's little girl.

"Thunk."

She makes her way down the narrow stairway, careful not to make a sound. He'll *be surprised*, she thinks, but pleased to see her, he always is. A naked bulb hangs over her father's head. He has his back to her, diligently working at his bench. The chest freezer is open. A meat cleaver clasped in his right hand is raised above his head, ready to slice into whatever is on the bench. Alison weighs just over twenty kilos, light for a girl her age but heavy enough to creak the central stair. She screws her nose, surprise gone. Father stops mid-swing, caught in the moment. A moment she will remember. A moment she could have avoided, why couldn't she have just stayed in bed? Something tells her to turn away, go back, an echo from the dream, screaming to be heard, but Father is working, and like a good girl, she wonders if he's thirsty.

He turns to face her, lit up by her presence. She was right. He *is* pleased to see her. He always is. She is his life, after all.

"Hi honey, did I wake you?" He notices the glass, "Is that for me?"

His voice is chirpy, slightly higher than most of the dads she's met, making him sound permanently happy, as if ready to burst into song. She'd almost forgotten about the glass in her hand. Looking down she briefly wonders how it got there.

"Uh-huh." Her voice is thin, almost a whisper, "the window was open."

"I'm sorry, honey," he tells her gently, glancing at the bench, his smile breaks into a grin. There's a dark enthusiasm she's never seen before twinkling behind his eyes. "Hey, you wanna see what daddy's working on?"

She most certainly does not want to see what Daddy is working on, nor does she want to know. Daddies should have secrets. She wants to turn back re-join the dream, but her feet move her forward. She can see how much blood has soaked into his shirt sleeves and the tiny crimson dots that speckle his face. The rubber apron offers only partial protection. He wipes the sweat from his brow, leaving a red smear. Alison feels her lips tremble, eyes widen, she doesn't want her father to know that sometimes he scares her. She knows how much he loves her. His world is her, just the two of them, that's how it's always been, always will be, he's told her many times. There has never been room for anyone else. She knows he would never do anything to hurt her and would protect her with his life or someone else's. But he still scares her, something in the sing-song voice and the shadow she sometimes sees behind his eyes. She was sure once she had seen something lurking in there, hidden in the dark, something that wasn't as agreeable as her father, something that scurried away when the light shone. Sometimes she wondered if he was pretending to be the man he is, and if pretending, then what kind of man was he?

He followed her gaze and looked down at his shirt. "I guess this ain't ever coming out," he says, grinning in his sing-song voice. "Well, come on over here honey, why don't cha' take a look and see what's in the freezer?"

Every part of Alison's young brain screams, NO DO NOT LOOK, DO NOT LOOK AT WHAT'S IN THE FREEZER, YOU WON'T LIKE WHAT YOU SEE, AND IT WILL HURT YOU AND SCAR YOU. BECAUSE ONCE YOU PEEK BEHIND THE CURTAIN, YOU'LL NEVER BE THE SAME AGAIN. But she can't help it. She takes one last look at the father she knows before becoming the man known by a different name. Alison bends her head for a peek, and the world she knows disappears.

# 2.

The animal inside is a hungry beast patiently biding its time in the belly of the man, watching the world through periscopic eyes, waiting for the opportunity to strike. They share the same body, it, and the man, but they are not the same. The man is weak; easy prey always has been, long before *it* appeared. But *it* is different, *it* takes what *it* wants, does what *it* wants, comes, and goes as *it* pleases. The beast knows the man tries to keep him away. His attempts are laughable; made-up symbols cut into the skin; an amalgam of religious iconography and wishful thinking designed to ward *it* off. Those were simpler, more shameful days when a crucifix was enough to strike terror into the soul of any child unfortunate to be left in the caring hands of the church.

The man wakes to find the girl in what is supposed to be his sanctuary. Intricate patterns born from a language known only to him cover the walls in crude daubs and smears, matching the scars on his skin, they have been designed to ward off the beast, and he feels the shame of his ignorance. The constant pounding of the drum, the watchful eye, and the nagging pain remind him, *it* lives beneath the veil, always scratching at the surface. *It* never sleeps, always there urging him on, lurking in the dark. It was the animal that caught her, not him— graduating to something more substantial, always hungry, an insatiable appetite. Always room for one more. The man knows what he's become, the animal inside frightens him, yet he owes it a debt of gratitude that cannot be repaid, he knows it cannot, will not stop, and God help him, he's beginning to like it. The rise and surge of something deep inside, the abandonment of responsibility, and the joy of the tide that grips and pulls him under suffocated in a black embrace as *it* takes his place. But there is the girl.

Naked, bound, and gagged on her side, knees to her chin. The man had tried, truly he had, but there was no stopping it; the animal was coming whether he liked it or not, and like it, he did. The whites of her eyes shone like twin moons through the grime and muck on her face. He tries not to look at her, to make contact, he knows it will bring the animal racing quicker to the surface like a rabid dog.

She didn't know, how could she? The animal doesn't understand pity, only want. If she knew what the man was trying to do for her, he knew how grateful she would be. He slides closer and places his hands on her shoulders, gently stroking as if to say, *there, there, it will be all right,* knowing it won't. *It will soon be over,* knowing it will. She recoils at his touch, too terrified to see the truth, he nods, he understands. It's not her fault, nor is it his. Neither of them is where they want to be. The animal has done this to them both.

# 3.

Jack Hopper hates the heat, the kind that traps the mind and body in the glue of day. He needs to stay alert. When someone is taken on the street, the end can be messy and permanent. These people are not kidnappers. Their goal is self-satisfaction, not avarice. Driven by a craving so utterly consuming, they are transformed into the monsters they grow into. Morality rejected over relief, just like any other addict and just like any other addict, when interrupted, the penalty can be severe.

This one had started small, killing rats and pigeons in the park. Hell, he had been doing the city a favor ridding it of vermin, but a few vagrants had gone missing also. No one had reported them, no one would, but he knew. He knew the signs. He had seen it before; an acquired taste once developed wasn't easily given up. The girl had been stupid, walking in the park at night! No doubt she wanted to enjoy the eerie cast of a silvery moon, maybe a Twilight fan or just another crazy. Not the sanest, safest thing to do, *but why the fuck not? What was wrong with that? It's a free country, isn't it?* Thankfully it had been a full moon, bright enough to light the night, and they had been seen.

He swallowed hard, dry mouth, wet skin. Ironic. Contradictions everywhere; freedom comes with a hefty price tag, a big lock and a big gun, and a tiny little room with bars for a door. Keep your precious things hidden out of sight. *Safe* rooms the size of a cell, locking in the freedom we cherish.

Hopper had picked up the trail quickly thanks to an anonymous call from a well-intentioned witness, refusing to give their name. Predictably, as they closed in, no one had seen anything since. A common equation in his line of work. And why not? Why get involved? *Not my problem, I saw nothin' I know nothin'.* Not their world, insulated by ignorance. But Jack Hopper had a unique way of stripping the walls bare. It hadn't taken him long to figure out which part of the city the girl had been taken. A swift search of the shitholes, going by the name of social housing, eventually led them to where they were now.

The building should have been condemned years ago, held together by grease and grime and the stink of poverty. It was hard to believe families still thrived or at least continued to populate. Forgotten souls slung out to rot in the wreckage of a *progressive* society. Every floor a sensory experience, as Jack and his team sucked in the detritus of human garbage.

*Should have gotten everyone gloves, maybe even Hazmat suits,* thought Hopper as they slowly made their way forward, ignoring the muffled crimes of tomorrow behind closed doors if they were lucky to see sunrise. The fourteenth floor, unremarkable as the previous thirteen, in the same way serial killers are considered, *unremarkable* until they're not. Intermittent flickering from antiquated ready-to-blow strip lights brought the wallpaper to life, clouds of mold advancing from corners, staking, and claiming what was now theirs. The sticky threadbare carpet sucked at Hoppers' shoes like quicksand revealing black rotten floorboards wet with moisture. Had the place seen better days? He doubted it. Cleaner? Perhaps. Better? Open to interpretation.

Breathing hard, Hopper was trying to stay calm. He could feel the building invading him from the outside in. Closing his eyes to focus, he needed to think of the task ahead. *Save the girl, kill the psycho, save the girl, kill the psycho, save the girl, kill the psycho, save the girl, kill the psycho,* his mantra repeated over and over again. When adrift in a sea of violent insanity, everyone needs an anchor. Mother's boiling babies, gang's killing gangs, pimp's beating whores. Rapists, child molesters, pornographers, abusers, junkies, he wanted to set a match to it all and watch it burn, an ache so powerful it felt like a teenager's crush. He wanted to be the fire starter. Even the *respectable* suburbs weren't immune, just better hidden. Violence was everywhere, permeating airwaves and digital bandwidths, desensitizing our brains. Maybe the psychos were right, give in, let go, let the currents take you, offer no resistance, and suck it in. Someone looks at you the wrong way, punch them in the face. Cut up in traffic, follow the son-of-a-bitch and teach them some fucking manners. Road rage, life rage. Why stifle it? The effort to keep it in, to bottle it up, was sometimes more than he could handle, more than anyone could handle. Want something? Take it. Life was a rare and bloodied steak, and he wanted to take a bite. He could feel himself starting to grin. *Careful, Jack, don't let the others see you like this.* He knew what they thought of him, and if they didn't, they should. He wanted to chew on the gristle and howl at the moon, just like the rest of the bat-shit crazies. The fury inside was ready to blow, and someone was going to get hurt. Thank fuck he'd found a psycho to do the hurting. Hopper pulled at his collar; he could feel his animal waking up.

*Save the girl, kill the psycho.* Hopper's mantra snaps him out of his reverie, and he takes a moment to check his team. Strong, capable men, they've seen and been through a lot, more than most, yet they still keep showing up for work. Over the years, the faces may have changed, but moments like this remain the same; everyone tense, high on anticipation, adrenaline coursing through your body so fast you can hear your neighbor's heartbeat. This shit makes you feel alive, and you'll either live for it or die trying. There are junkies on both sides of the door, but only one has a badge. Hopper, as lead detective, knows he's not well-liked, he doesn't care, in cases like these, he also knows they'd rather have him on their side than anyone else. He's one of the top addicts in the force, always first in, keen for a hit. Hopper takes a deep breath and gives the signal. One swing of a battering ram is all it takes, and the door splinters.

The man hears the crash, and he knows the animal heard it too, too late to stop, the animal is coming, and there is nothing he can do. He tried and failed, but maybe it was for the best. Taking one last look at the girl, he leans in to kiss her gently on the forehead, a sign of affection, but she squirms away. She heard it too, the noise of rescue, of relief. Saved, ordeal over, pervert caught, locked away, justice delivered. Sometimes the system worked. Hopefully, the police will teach him a lesson or two on the way back. She smiles at that; it's something she would have liked to see.

Her captor pats the bandage he applied to her leg where the beast had bitten and drew blood; she winces and scuttles further back. For the first time, she sees him through his lank dirty hair. He looks different; he's not the man she thought he was. The man in front is young, no older than her, she recognizes the fear in his eyes and is glad, *it's your turn now,* she thinks. She doesn't know it's her he's scared for. He nods, resigned, he understands her revulsion, but he wasn't the one that took her, bit her, the animal had. Did she think this was her rescue? In the nick of time, just like the movies? He offers a weak consolatory smile, this was life, not fantasy. He knew what was coming; he could feel it. The girl blinks back her doubt, *I'm going to be saved, and you'll get yours, they shoot wild dogs like you,* she matches his stare, but he's already gone instead something else stares back and takes a bite.

The scream announces the urgency. Almost there is still a chasm away. Flashlights cut the gloom like lightsabres. Greasy rags heavy with filth cover broken windows, keeping the night breeze at bay, filtering clean air too bad. The smell hits Hopper like a wall, an acrid burning musk of discharge, bad in and bad out. Hopper hears someone retch and thinks, *you get used to it,* realizing you never should. Powerful torch beams section the room spotlights picking out details the team wished they hadn't. A grotesque tableau covers the wall; dead animals opened, entrails stretched and pinned, creating a mockery of Da Vinci's last supper. More have been nailed to tiny crucifixes on the road to Golgotha. It makes Hopper want to laugh, and he suppresses a giggle, *not the time or place*, a cruel parody of his Sunday school education, how disappointed the brothers would be. He shakes the thought from his mind, stay focused; *save the girl, kill the psycho*. They're just rats, that's all, just rats he smiles.

The team moves quickly towards the cry, one last room to check. No one wants to go in; no one wants to shake hands with madness behind in case it sticks. Sometimes it does. Sometimes it leaves a stain so bad it won't wash out. It might fade with time, but it's always there, a reminder of how ruined and bruised the world is. Will she be dead? Will she be like the rodents nailed to the wall? Hopper can feel them getting ready, preparing the worst their imagination can muster. *It's never enough*, he thinks, *sane people do not think like crazy people, it's why we lock them up*, and keeps his dark secret to himself. He's often proven right thinking about what lies behind the door. Maybe he should be locked up too!

Behind the door, the animal waits, the man inside too weak to act, to keep its prey safe, so it had come. So little resistance, welcoming, the man had done the right thing giving himself over. It could feel them on the other side, hear their breath, smell their fear, their hesitation. They didn't know, couldn't know what it was like to be fully alive, to be the animal, to take and deny yourself nothing. To live in truth was to really live. A connection to impulse, to act without hesitation, no rhyme nor reason, just him.

The air was hot, and time was slow. Hopper was sweating. He felt a drop of perspiration run down his spine, settling into his belt, leaving a trail of ice to cut through the fever. Moving quickly, his team had cleared every space, nook, and cranny and were awaiting his signal to advance. Steady and by the book, Hopper took a deep breath; he'd shaken hands so many times with the devil it no longer mattered. He wanted to smile and promised himself a thick steak after this, rare and bloodied, he needed something to chow down on, to begin tearing. *Save the girl, kill the psycho, save the girl kill the psycho*, one last look at his team, and Hopper waved sanity goodbye.

A swift kick was enough. Hopper leading with his gun, an extension to his arm, tracked the room by the beam of his torch. He hears her first, before his searchlight lands upon her, the soft whimpering of a wounded animal, bound and gagged in the corner, blood pumping in rhythm to an accelerated heartbeat.

Hopper bent double, crab walks to where she lies as the team file into the room, their lights chasing shadows back into the corners. Hopper signals them to stop. The one they're after is still here, hiding. They know the drill and take cover, safety, above all else, comes first.

Hopper can see the terror in the girl's eyes, he hates it because he likes it, understanding only too well the intoxication of power and wishes he didn't. Cutting her hands and feet free, he turns his head to catch a breath. She stinks. Whoever took her debased and marked her as his own, smearing her body in the same medium that paint the walls, but she is alive, for the moment. She'll never be the same again, but she is alive. Hopper can see the fresh wound above her clavicle, an inch higher, and her artery would have been torn. Still thick with blood, he sees it for what it is, a bite. He isn't shocked, just curious and doesn't think, *poor girl.* Instead wonders about the taste. She wants to scream, to let go, give in to the hysteria of the moment, but Hopper needs her calm and takes out a handkerchief she can press against the love bite on her neck. Gently placing a hand over her mouth, he lifts a finger to his own. Her eyes wider now, look behind him, she's screaming inside trying to warn him, he wants to smirk, how many times do you get to say, *He's behind you,* and mean it? Hopper turns slowly, no sudden movements, no surprises, nothing too fast, and sees him for the first time; a young man, early twenties, smeared in matching symbols and patterns like the girl. His eyes, clear and bright, shine through a thatch of thick, unkempt hair. He looks like he's grinning, a shared joke caught in the moment. Saliva runs down his chin because the stained animal teeth clamped inside his mouth are too big. Hopper doesn't feel the same sense of disgust as the girl at his feet, his mind is clear, but he has a question burning in his brain. Why? What happened to turn a young man into this? What is the world when this is the result? He knows he will have to shoot the young man but doesn't want to. He sees a reflection of his own madness and feels a pang of sympathy?

The animal is looking at Hopper. Why doesn't he do something? What is he waiting for? He isn't scared like the rest of them. The animal circles the man, *I am the animal, I do what I want, I live free without regret or remorse,* so why doesn't he shoot? He needs to know and looks deep into the man for an answer and finds something familiar looking back. It's a bolt to the head, a lightning strike that lingers, and he understands. He's never met another like himself, but there it is, deep in the belly of the man lives a beast looking back. The man has his own animal and wonders if he even knows. He suspects he already does.

*What does it want this beast inside?* They both think.

There is a moment when Hopper feels a connection, eyes locked together binding them, and they know each other; theirs is the only communication that's needed. A fleeting moment that will last forever, a shadow cast on the walls of memory, a reminder of what lies below. But sympathy and understanding are foreign bedfellows to the beast. He has lived long enough without them and feels the sliver of a new emotion, fear. Fear of being found out, fear of revelation, is the antithesis to what he has become, and the fear turns to anger.

Inside, the young man wakes, wanting to look out, but the window is small, he struggles to be free and rise to the surface, he wants to explain, but the animal pushes him down. Looking at Hopper once more, he knows there can only be one. Kings don't share. The connection breaks, and he feels only hatred. The moment is gone as quickly as it came but never forgotten as he leaps. In here, the animal is king; he takes what he wants, he lives in truth, never again will his vulnerability be exposed.

The sound is deafening, the spark blinding as Hopper reacts instantly, and the animal falls like a dead weight, but not quite dead. His teeth slide from a mouth no longer there, in a pool of saliva, blood, and bone. The bullet took away part of his face; his tongue lolls where his right cheek should be, his jaw, now dislocated, hangs at an odd angle to his face. Breath comes in short sharp gurgles. Hopper is beside him, trying to hold his face together, blood seeping through his fingers, he wanted to understand. The animal is gone, and the young man blinks up at Hopper. If he could laugh, he would, but his mouth is gone. Hopper can see the lie he's living and knows it's only a matter of time before his animal swims to the surface and takes control, one last gurgle one last breath, and the man closes his eyes and slips away.

# 4.

Shelly woke with a jolt. Did she scream? Sometimes she does. Previous partners had told her so. They had tried to help, she'd had lots of help, well-meaning, well-intentioned help, but none of it *helped; it* couldn't. Once peeked behind the curtain, you can't un-know or un-see the truth. A bitter carousel of foster families had tried. The cute little blond girl with the sorrowful face carrying a secret so savage it could wrench the heart from the most charitable of chests. Failure was inevitable. A dirty little secret that was hers alone, if shared, at worst would scare them, at best unnerved. Keeping their children apart, a safe distance, not so far away she would notice, but not so close either. She buried herself in books. Knowledge became power; she would know what the rest of the world cannot, keeping the answers safe, her answer safe. Was she her father's daughter after all?

Shelly drew her long limbs to her chin and reached the pack of cigarettes kept within arm's reach. She drew hard, holding the smoke inside for a moment longer before exhaling. Catching her reflection in the mirror at the foot of her bed, she let the sheets drop as the smoke swirled around her head. She was still an attractive woman, her body kept in almost perfect condition, save for the smoking. Exercising fanatically, swimming three times a week, sometimes four, constantly running on the treadmill, bought to exhaust and relax her so that fatigue and tiredness would eventually overtake and lead to sleep. Weekends were the hardest to fill, spent at the gym or hospital. What few friends she had, urged her to go out, socialize, have fun, meet a man, meet a woman if that's what it took, *but have some fucking fun!* Constantly set up on blind dates she didn't ask for or want, but as she had gotten older, so had her *dates,* along with the accompanying baggage and enthusiasm of her friends. She didn't mind the emotional excess, provided it didn't get in the way of a one-night stand. A fuck, is a fuck after all, and a girl has needs. Her only difficulty was a quick exit before they opened their mouths, feeling the need to unload and swap sad stories.

Over the years, she had developed quite a reputation, fantasies shared between the sex-hungry, sex desperate, and sex curious at the hospital. Conveniently placed, she used them as distractions, before they became too tedious, too demanding, too feeble, and easily bruised. Finding them shallow and lacking. Their failures, never theirs, always the fault of others, misunderstood and mistaken, claiming still waters that ran deep in ponds she had no desire to fish in. Of course, her detachment did nothing to help, nor did her habit of psychoanalyzing those around her. Most didn't want or appreciated her off-the-cuff diagnosis.

5.15 am. Too early to go back to sleep, too early to start the day. A quick run to clear the head, she extinguished her half-smoked cigarette, it was a filthy habit after all, but we all need a vice and took a large swallow from her water bottle. After thirty minutes on the treadmill, she was coated with a light sheen of sweat and had begun to feel better, lungs purged, head clear, and made her way to the bathroom. After a quick shower, she toweled herself dry, pausing to stare at herself in the mirror, looking deep into her eyes as she had done a thousand times before. What was it she looking for? Did she even know? Would she recognize it in herself? She shook her head, today was special. He would help. It had taken her years to find someone like him. Thank God he hadn't murdered anyone or at least no one anyone knew about; he was a rare treasure. Most psychopaths were either shot and killed on capture or perpetrated crimes so hideous they were either confined to solitary or locked down in high-security facilities heavily sedated. In any case, they were most certainly not handed over for research.

He was different. Young, good looking, at least *as* good looking, before the policeman had shot off half his face. As a product of the state, they were obliged to be held accountable for his state of mind. Were we responsible for what he had become? Compassion and hope, credible currency to a liberal ear. We would learn from him, find out what made him, *him*, she told them. Nature vs nurture. She would finally get to meet the animal inside for the first time. Only it wasn't.

She had met the animal once before, long ago when she was a little girl in her father's basement. He had told her so many times he only wanted what was best for her and, in many ways, lived up to his promise. It was because of him she had excelled. He was her motivation, the fuel for her fire and her need to know, the fear she may eventually turn out like him. Daddy's little girl. It was a secret she'd kept safe for so many years, only a select few of her trusted colleagues knew, a secret shared when it suited her. How could she connect with her peers when she had so little in common with them, and what if she was a danger to them. Was she risking their lives, by mingling them with hers?

This was her moment, a chance to peek once more behind the curtain, but on her terms. Virtual reality had been the key she had been waiting for. The ability to present a world without repercussion or judgment, to determine the learned morality of the superego, how it governed our actions or if the mediation between real and imagined was enough to keep the id in check. Were we products of our upbringing, or were our personalities genetically coded into us, relinquishing choice? I did it, because it's who I am. And what of her? The thought literally kept her up at night, she had taken a bite from both worlds.

She had become interested in 'gamers' and how easily they shed the social constraints of right and wrong, actively engaging in some alarming and horrific acts. She had even come across several games that included the ability to rape, torture, and murder non-player characters or NPC's just for *fun*, as these actions neither advanced nor prevented any progression within the game itself. Players believed that if it didn't happen, it didn't matter; she knew different. She had witnessed a steady increase in demand first-hand and how normalized violence had become. Without consequence, nothing, it seemed, was off-limits. But there was a problem. An external third party designed the constructed environments. Subjects were living through someone else's fantasy by proxy, which meant it limited its scope and therefore wasn't a true reflection on the subject's own morality. By combining neuroplasticity mapping and VR, she found a way for subjects to visualize their own environment, pulling assets from an expanding library stitching together an appropriate setting through a simulator. Basic at first, but as more subjects used the *game*, the more extensive the library, and the more sophisticated the result. It became a matter of; *think it, build it.* The results had been interesting but still inconclusive. When faced with a realistic echo of their lives, their impulses were dialed down until they made the cognitive leap that it was still a game. They were still making conscious decisions based on a simulation that hadn't happened. She wanted to know how we wanted to act before the superego took over and to what extent our nature was governed by the inherited or the acquired. Were we products of our environments, or do we shape to fit, and if so, was there a trigger?

# 5.

The building was surprisingly ordinary, withstanding every attempt to modernize, it retained a practical municipal governmental look. It looked like the architects had gone to great lengths to make sure paying taxpayers wouldn't be offended by an overspend on the less desirable elements of society, resulting in a simple whitewashed concrete box with a mezzanine! Floor to ceiling windows carefully manicured lawns with sharp, clean lines hinted at something that could have been, but wasn't, and although large, remained none threatening, contrary to what it contained. Shelly had been informed the transfer could take place without her direct involvement but insisted on taking possession first-hand, ensuring no accidents were about to happen. Male nurses at high-security psychiatric prisons didn't have a reputation for compassion and consideration. Since arriving, Shelly was eager to meet her patient zero, listed as a John Doe. She named him herself, Adam.

Shelly's guide, Dr. Conner, the resident in charge, took her through the entry procedures designed to minimize risk and maximize containment in the event of a security breach. One gate after another slid open using a key card or digital number pad, each more secure than the last. The internal structure had been designed around a cube of cells as a square spiral, the more dangerous inmates being closer to the center. Conner explained it was for security reasons as another door slid open. Each section could be isolated in the unlikely event one of the inmates managed to get out,

"That way, we can contain them in the corridor," he continued helpfully, "plus, it also means that no one cell faces another, so they can't excite each other."

"Or communicate."

"Or plan."

"Which keeps them completely isolated?"

"Exactly."

"Not much in the way of stimulation then?"

Shelly noticed the two accompanying male nurses exchange glances as they wheeled the gurney alongside, confirming she made the right decision to come along.

"You don't have this area staffed?" Shelly asked as they continued turning right.

"CCTV, motion sensors..." replied Dr. Conner, pointing to the security cameras, "everything's rigged to an alarm... no-one comes down here voluntarily."

Shelly counted approximately two lights in-between each cell as they walked, measuring the width to be approximately five feet, giving them less than two meters of liveable space. If you weren't crazy when you arrived, you were when you left. They walked on in silence.

Dr. Conner eventually stopped in front of door 271, unremarkable except for the number. Shelly guessed they would be close to the center. Conner told her otherwise. They were only on floor 3 of 8, each floor could house up to forty-eight inmates, and, although her subject was past the halfway mark, which was impressive, he was by no means considered the worst. Shelly thought about the other one hundred and thirteen and wondered if she might get access to them later if her experiment proved successful. Conner slid back the viewing plate on the heavy metal door, through which Shelly was able to get her first look at 'Adam.' The room was a windowless white box matching the outside corridor. The only 'furniture', a raised platform from the same material as the floor. A thin mattress, previously glued to the top, was in pieces strewn across the room, the acrylic stuffing scattered like snow. The sterility of the white was punctuated by blood and shit smeared over the floor and walls. Shelly recognized the intricate patterns from the photographs in his file. 'Adam,' freshly painted, remained squatting in the corner. His restraints torn and discarded with the mattress. Shelly could hear him growl, she knows he can't see her face but he can read the enthusiasm and curiosity in her eyes through the letterbox window. He lunges hard and fast at the glass, his head connecting with a crack leaving a bloodied smear as he slides to the floor.

"I thought you said everything was monitored?" Shelly asked without taking her eyes off Adam.

Conner cleared his throat, "It is. He was cleaned up for your visit. We don't know how he does that... you know, the jacket. We can have him hosed down if you need." An icy glare from Shelly told him no.

Adam, heavily panting back in his corner, his face still raw and poorly stitched from the gunshot, now carries a fresh wound above the eye. "What about his face, can't you bandage it?"

"We've tried, he pulls them off… look, I, I know this looks bad," stammered Conner, "but, you have to understand… it's a question of funding, lack of support … I… we do our best for them. They do get to go outside."

"Have you managed to learn anything about him?"

"In cases like this, it's impossible to…"

"Of course, I understand," Shelly cut him off, and she does understand. She understands the dehumanization of patients, that cruelty comes easier than kindness, that sensory deprivation is more cost-effective than stimulation. She understands it's far easier to lock the door and forget the thing behind was once a person. Yes, she understands but not in the way Dr. Conner and the system understand. She smiles back, she would like to lock him in the room with the patient and watch, but wouldn't, because she also knows there's a very real possibility, she could end up in a tiny, molded room for herself and her foster carers would have been right after all.

"Then let's get this open," she says instead, smiling as if it's just another day at the office. Dr. Conner nods to the nurses, who exchange a quick look. The bigger one takes out a baton as the other unlocks the heavy door, the patient inside stiffens at the sound of the lock. Dr. Conner takes a step behind Shelly. The nurse by the door unclips a tazer from his belt and slides the door open. The movement is sudden, catching them unaware. Adam leaps, he's quick, far quicker than them, making a bid for freedom, although he has nowhere to run. Shelly stands her ground, hand tightening on the pepper spray in her pocket, Conner squeals and shifts further back. Feigning left, darting right, Adam almost reaches them before he's caught and knocked to the floor. He struggles until something heavy hits him on the head, the back, the legs, the head again. Clean white pain lights up his body and shoots through his brain, pressing reset. A head full of static gives him the reprieve he craves, there is nothing else, and he feels alive. The tazer is jammed into the back of his neck and delivers its charge as Adam floats away into unconscious.

"Fuck, that was way intense," says Conner, grinning with more enthusiasm than intended. Shelly glanced back and smiled. He misinterprets it as recognition of a shared experience. "Hey, you know, once we're finished, if you're sticking around, I thought maybe we could…"

"No," Shelly replied without looking up, "we couldn't." The orderlies finished strapping the patient onto the stretcher and grinned at each other as Shelly took out a pre-prepared syringe from her bag and stuck it deep into Adams' neck. "It's a sedative for the journey, it won't last forever, and I'd rather not repeat today." Conner isn't sure if she's talking to him or the patient, but after being slammed down so quickly and abruptly, he'd rather not ask, preferring to stay silent. Shelly knows she probably hasn't made any friends during her visit. She doesn't care. She has what she wants.

# 6.

The operating theatre is prepped and ready to go, the surgeon standing by. It has taken Shelly four months, several favors, and an exchange of services to arrange complete reconstructive surgery for Adam. A beginning they both needed. The connection between self-image and actuality is a profound one, the inside connected to the outside physically just as much as mentally. Dysmorphia. The mind plays tricks, reinforcing a lack of self-esteem promoting a steady erosion of confidence. To see bumps, lumps, and blemishes where there were none. Shelly should know, she had treated her fair share of patients, referring them to the gentleman below, ready to reshape her patient's face. Sometimes, the act itself was important, not the result. An exercise in control. A new face represented a rebirth that was both actual and symbolic. We don't choose the face we're born with; instead, we often grow into the one we have. Shelly wanted to replicate the opportunity for Adam. He would become manufactured by her. Angelic and flawless, his scars on the inside would provide the blueprint for his playground. The topography of his psyche. His would be a face of purity the vainest would die to claim as their own.

"That's him, is it?"

The voice startled her as the surgeon made his first cut. Professor Donahue had joined her in the viewing gantry, the man responsible for her funding. She had known the professor for years, ever since medical school. He was one of the few who knew why she devoted so much time to her work. He gently placed a hand on her shoulder, reminding her the property below wasn't hers alone. Shelly flinched as Donahue let it slide off. She was, of course, grateful to the older man for his help but resented the intrusion, claiming her work as his own, riding her coattails. Still, there had to be concessions. For the most part, Donahue was well-intentioned, supporting her when others wouldn't. Hadn't he been the one to offer her her first research post? So what if she showed a little more leg during their *meetings*? She got what she wanted. He'd tried to act like a surrogate father figure, urging her to make friends, go out, have fun, get laid. She just hadn't realized he'd meant with him.

"We were lucky to find him," Shelly replied.

"I hear he's in a bit of a mess… won't recognize himself by the time they've finished. He's a good man Wainright." Donahue waved at the surgeon below, who glanced up and gave a curt nod. The old boy network, useful but odious. Donahue wasn't the only *mentor* ready to provide young, eager students a leg up!

*God, you're pathetic, checking in on me, making sure you get the recognition for doing fuck all*, she wanted to say, choosing instead to pander to his ego, "I couldn't have done it without you, Michael. I trust you."

"And I you," he smiled back, revealing a set of cosmetically whitened teeth, reminding her there were expectations to fulfill, "I'm always here when you need me. Favours are like good wine; they need to be shared amongst those who appreciate them." Donahue resisted the temptation to squeeze her buttocks. He was sure his time would come. He never forgot a favor owed.

# 7.

The patient, known as Adam to all but himself, was healing. It wasn't because his arms, for the most part, remained bound to his bed and therefore was unable to tear and scratch at his new face, but more so because of the hood. Constructed from a fine mesh, it was bound to his shoulders by molded fastenings, making it impossible to remove. Twin lenses welded to the mesh offered dual portholes to peak, tinted windows to a world of perpetual twilight. Combined with the steady flow of drugs, it had the disorientating effect of being in two places simultaneously, detached from his own body as if he were a visitor peeking through twin portholes.

He had no concept of time or how long he had been there. The routine was always the same; the lights would blink on, and he would wake fastened to the bed, struggle to the point of exhaustion until *they* came. Figures in one-piece surgical suits, hoods were drawn so tightly over a face hidden behind mirrored glasses. Whenever Adam looked at them, he looked at himself. He knew they were different by size and counted four visitors in all. The drugs were never the same and offered a range of experiences from hallucinogenic to the more sedentary, desensitizing to the point of coma. Given a choice of menu, he would have preferred the more psychotropic. A dislocating experience where he could feel himself pass through the confines of his body, drifting upwards to look down at himself before slipping unseen through the walls and out into the vastness that lay beyond. In truth, he had no idea if these moments were symptoms of the drugs or real. Unlike other effects, he felt in control, flying through meadows, woodlands, wherever his mind would take him, his body skimming the earth. Sometimes he would visit the city with unlimited access to places he had been previously chased from. He felt like a ghost without connection, unable to participate, inevitably ending up back in his sterile room with a deep sense of longing.

Today is different. Today, his arms are free. He is thinner and no longer has the strength of the animal that once lived inside. His face feels unfamiliar.

Working his jaw, he opens and closes his mouth, running his tongue over his teeth. They are sharp and strong, and he feels like biting something. He gently pulls at the hood, testing the mesh, teasing for an opening when the alarm sounds and his head feels like it might split. The noise is piercing, and his hands instinctively cover his ears as he crouches. The door opens, and one of *them* enters, carrying a food tray. It's the shortest of the four, by the way it moves, Adam guesses female. He may be weak but he's sure he's still stronger than her. Struggling to his feet, intent clear, he wants to share the hurt and pain and feels the animal rising, now awake, now here. He tries to jump but trips and falls. His ankle is shackled to the bed by a chain, the metal rim cuts into his flesh, and he bleeds a little, feeling like an attack dog snarling at the intruder. The woman in white places the tray on the floor and removes what looks like a pistol from a white leather pouch attached to her belt, Adam can't recall seeing it there before. Raising her arm, she fires. The dart hits Adam in the shoulder, and the pain spreads like a fire from the burning point of contact. Inside, he collapses, no longer the vicious attack dog, now so much less so, and in one last final act of humiliation, his bowels empty as his body shudders. The woman in white picks up the tray, Adam watches her leave as the shadows in his peripheral vision close, and he gives in to the dark once more, and the voice inside sniggers.

He is awake again, but cannot be sure because he cannot see. His world is black. His breath, stiff and labored, is reflected from the walls of a tomb, but his arms and legs are free, and it takes him a moment to realize only his head is imprisoned. Instinctively he reaches out, but his limbs are secured by wires he cannot see, movements restricted and controlled. He understands that the freedom he feels is an illusion, wrists, elbows, torso, knees, and ankles all tethered and tied. Whatever movement there can be is not his. He is a puppet. Inside his imagination, where he has learned to live these past few months, he thinks of his head as separate, elsewhere, perhaps boxed and labeled, put away in storage for a later date to be experimented on. He hopes his body will be safe, and whoever pulls strings will be careful.

A faint hum fills the dark as the soft glow of a red light brings the inside of the helmet to life. He has become a living filament. Paralyzed, he cannot look to the left, right, nor up nor down. A metal halo bolted to his head secures him in place so that only his eyes can move. He can see wires and circuitry cover the interior from his limited vision, snaking behind, out of sight like worms underground. Some, he knows, have attached themselves to his head, paratrophic mouths milking his thoughts, sucking his brain, the animal drawn out like poison.

"Adam, this is Dr. Shelly. There is no need to be scared. You're in good hands."

The voice startles him; *Adam? Who the fuck is Adam? Is that me?* It fills the void like a benign God, a woman's voice, soft and gentle. He does not believe himself to be in *good hands*. He knows he is a puppet for those hands and will do what they will, good or bad. He growls at the voice, telling it to *fuck off*, his voice is small and weak by comparison, and he remains quiet.

"Adam, I'm about to give you an injection. You will feel a burning sensation, but try not to fight it. It will help you relax."

*Adam? Am I supposed to be Adam? Is that my name?* He doesn't think so but can't remember what it once was. More drugs. He readies himself to fight the effects; what else is there for him to do? He is not prepared to give in so easily. *Click, hiss, jab*, a needle penetrates his skin. The pain isn't slight, nor is it quick. The movement is slow, continuous, and methodical, the way only a machine can be. The burn of the needle is nothing to what follows, a lit cigarette to the skin, a passing childhood memory never far away. Spreading like wildfire, radiating from the base of his neck, through his jaw, behind his eyes to the top of his head where the sucking worms greedily draw him in. It moves through his body, shoulders, arms, chest, torso, groin, thighs, and legs. He is filled with searing lava and wants to scream, his voice empty, arms and legs no longer his, separated from all he knows and all that he is.

Telescopic fingers descend from the inner casing towards his eyes, he tries to blink them shut, but the claws reach out and nip at the tender skin of the lids, peeling them back. Twin plastic tubes fastened to his temples feed a steady drip of liquid into his opened eyes, keeping them moist. The only place he can look to the front, a screen bursts to life, a brightness that is total and blinding. Transfixed and hypnotized, he is consumed by the light and begins to forget the pain.

"Adam, your name is Adam. Do you understand?"

The voice again, but this time different. It feels like it's coming from within himself. Warmer and softer, he wants to please it, make it happy. *Does he understand?* How nice to be asked. He can't remember his name. He's heard the name *Adam*. It must be his. The voice would know. It doesn't sound familiar, but then again, what's in a name?

It's hard to form a word when your tongue doesn't work. It takes all his energy and focus, the voice deserves it, and he wants, above all else, to please the voice, and repeats the name that must be his.

"Adam," he slurs, "Adam," this time better, "Adam," he repeats, and it finally begins to sound like his own.

The screen begins to change. The static fades to become a single block of color, with a pinprick of concentrated light in the center.

"You see the white light, Adam. I want you to move it."

How can he move it when he can't touch it? He concentrates hard, he wants the light to move so badly, and it does, directionless he slides the light across the screen in sync with his eyeballs. He is happy and if he could cry, he would.

"Good Adam, that's very good. Now I want you to move the light to the left."

The voice is pleased, and so is he. It wasn't so hard. He moves the light to the left. It's easier this time. More connected, he becomes the light.

"To the right." The voice tells him.

Adam does as he's told, although he wants to do more, to show the voice what he can do, move it in circles, dance around the screen. Nothing is too much effort for the voice.

"That's good, Adam. I want you to move the light back. Take it back to the room at the hospital."

Adam moves the light to the room he was in before. He is surprised at how easy it is. He is on the bed, bandages removed, though his face is blurred, censored by a memory he doesn't have. He enters his body. Able to see through his eyes once more, he is both man and audience at the same time. The orderly comes with a tray of food. He can feel the anger and hatred of the young man on the bed, but these are no longer his thoughts and feelings, only echoes. He lunges towards the orderly, the chain pulls, and he falls. The woman in white takes out her gun and fires. The omnipresent Adam of the room wants to take control of the light, take revenge, and act out what Adam of the bed could not. The chains dissolve, and his fingers stretch into claws, but the voice distracts him.

"Adam." The image fades, returning to the block of red with an idling light, "I want you to go back, back to when you first began. I want you to show me who you are."

The red on the screen changes as Adam's mind drifts, slowly at first, accelerating as the memories fly past in reverse, a pinball of his past bouncing between events until he comes to rest at the point of his birth, ready to be born.

Dr. Shelly observes Adam's progress from her control platform. Every aspect of her subject was monitored and recorded. Twin screens positioned side by side relay imagery from inside the helmet; one fed by a micro camera shows the slack-jawed face of Adam, unconscious but awake, eyes held open by clamps. The other linked to the screen inside the helmet projects images from his subconscious.

Inside a giant tank of reinforced glass, thick enough to withstand an earthquake and filled with dense salt water, allowing for maximum conductivity,

Adam floats, suspended by a series of wires, designed for limited movement feigning free will. His head encased in what could be mistaken for a deep-sea diver's helmet from the shoulders up. Cables spread outwards and upwards, coiling around support wires like black snakes. A giant proboscis protrudes from the front of the helmet, curling over the lip of the tank as it connects to a compressor below, where it greedily sucks in oxygen with just a hint of sedative. Heat lamps warm the tank beneath, casting an eerie glow across the room, maintaining a consistent temperature as Adam reverts to his embryonic state.

"Congratulations, Dr. Shelly, looks like you're about to become a mum. You feel like celebrating?"

The technician to her left, Mike Dean, is grinning and holds up what looks like a cheap bottle of wine he's been hiding in his bag. Simon Callow, the second assistant, looks up expectantly from his workstation, knowing better. She knows he's breached security protocols by bringing alcohol to a restricted area but also knows, for most, this would be a time to celebrate. She also knows that social norms would welcome a blind eye. Achieve something of significance, mark the occasion by blotting out the accomplishment with alcohol. Maybe they're hoping they'll see another side of her, a warmer side, or take bets to see if one of them can get into her panties? The thought makes her shudder, and the phrase, *it's not you, it's me*, pops into her head. She disagrees; she knows it's them. They annoy and irritate her. Yes, she would like to celebrate, yes, it's a milestone, yes, this could be one of the most critical moments in her career, so why celebrate with people she cares nothing for? How could they possibly know what it's taken to get here or why? In truth, she has no one to share her success with, no one she has become close to or understands the part of her that's still standing in the basement holding a glass of water. It would be an injustice and an insult to her father to celebrate with them.

Instead, she smiles back and hopes she can hide the irritation she feels. They have the look of expectation, and she can feel her mask slipping, the paint wearing thin on the smile, freshly painted this morning. She's never felt comfortable in situations like these, even when she graduated med school, years of hard work and late nights exorcized by the popping of a cork. For her, it was an interruption. A hiatus of a life's dream, why stop now?

"Maybe later, Mike. We still have a long way to go before we begin congratulating each other. We've only just started." She watched their faces crash as they exchanged disappointed glances, knowing, *later*, will never come. They'll talk about her later, and they'll talk about how cold and detached she is, and when they're drunk enough, they talk about how she doesn't recognize their contribution and how ungrateful she is. She doesn't care. They've done what they were paid to do and have become victims of their success in many ways, rendering themselves superfluous to her needs. But it's all she can manage to say without sounding rude.

But they are wrong; she will celebrate and mark the occasion with Adam when they're gone. She's eager to record the id, to walk in the maze of his memories and understand that which drives us, the originator of desire. A glimpse isn't enough for her, there are no shortcuts. She will feel what he feels, know what he knows, and meet the beast within. What better way to celebrate? She leans into the microphone, eager to start. "Show me," she whispers, and it begins.

# 8.

Inside, not outside, upside down.

The light burns bright; there is a sharpness too acute to be understood by a brain not yet formed. Desperate, wanting, hungry, all needs ignored. The first lesson learned: *you're on your own.* You once belonged to another, fed from inside, and you cry and scream for her. The one that kept you safe and warm. You took everything she had to give and more, now brutally ejected, spat into a cruel world. She was the one that should have loved you, wanted you, held you, but there is no warm embrace for you. Instinct takes over; hungry: eat. Tired: sleep. Hurt: endure and accept. Pain is the life you lead, get to know it because it knows you.

There will be moments when the darkness is swept away by a simple kindness, a drunken hug or a kiss, a tender sweep of the hair, or a stumbled upon treat. Brief moments too quickly chased away by the reality of life. Fighting tooth and nail, to claw through the day and survive to the next. You learn how not to be noticed, too small to protect the one you yearn for. Love swapped for a chemical affection—the adoration of spoon and needle, the passion of a higher power. You feel the day she died living it once more, the clammy white face with unseeing eyes. You know she's dead. You've seen death before, but you still cry and pull her hair and scratch her face. She abandoned you long ago, but you take her warmth and sleep curled on her chest, breathing her scent, wishing her alive.

Her lifeless body turns grey. She starts to smell, and the rats come. You fight them at first. They nip and bite, hungry as you are. You see her move, but it's the rats inside. You wait to die, having never lived, a mercy for the lonely. But you are found, no mercy here. Washed and scrubbed until you bleed. Dressed, pushed, and pulled, there are beatings to endure. The man on the cross looks down, tears in his eyes. It's you he cries for, but he cannot help. Nailed to a tree, he's in a worse state than you.

There are bigger boys than you. Mean, and cruel, and violent, but honest. The priests and brothers are different; disguised as men of God, they come at night, hidden under a cloak of darkness. You fight and struggle because it's all you know, but size wins out. They hold you down, and the pain is unbearable, invasive, and brutal. You learn to hide; when they find you, you hide within yourself. When it's over, the smell is sickening. It disgusts you. You feel like the rubbish discarded at the end of the day left to rot, stinking and unclean it contaminates and fills you.

The beatings become predictable, a way of life. You endure, and you grow. You get strong, take the lessons learned and show them what they taught you. The smallest one first. You remember the shock, the terror, and the exhilaration that went with it. Chasing the thrill, you find the second, the third, and fourth, each one easier than the last. Their screams and pain help wash away the grime, cleansing you for a moment, but the dirt still sticks on the inside. You yearn to be clean again, and so it begins.

The man in the flowing black robe, worse than the rest, gives no respite. He comes when he likes. You remember the silver crucifix around his waist, always at eye level, the light blinking as you choke, gag and retch. You wait, the trap laid, excitement brimming. Believing the bell tower is safe to hide, he cowers as you swing the trap door shut. The shock and surprise are almost enough to reward you, almost. He's angry at first, spitting obscenities, but you smell his fear through the threats and taunts. He pleads and begs for his life, telling you how sorry he is, that mercy is a sacrament, as you kick and punch and bite. It isn't enough. You cannot retrieve what was so brutally taken. He is old and weak; his limbs no longer have the power they once had. You break a rib, then another and another. You break an arm. You bite on an eye, ripping it out with your teeth. You tear at his face devouring him. It still isn't enough. You puncture him with his crucifix for the times he pierced you and show him the cross you made. He understands; he will die for his sins. His begging shrieks and cries quickly turn to curses and the promise of eternal pain. But you have this already.

They are at the door, banging, pushing, they can't save him. You drag him and his cross to the ledge. He's heavy, much heavier nailed to the wood, but your strength comes from somewhere deep inside. He knows what's coming, *time to make the final sacrifice* you say, and push. The scream follows him down, splintering with the wood on impact. He is alive. You hear him moaning. He will never be the same again, but neither will you. Old *habits* die hard.

You're alone and cold. The needle in your hand is the most precious thing you own. The glint and sparkle from the candle intoxicate as the light shimmers off the syringe. You know the promise of oblivion only too well, learned from your love lost, like mother like son. The tourniquet is tight, the ridges of your vein rise and pulse, parts collapsed you find an open channel to plunge the needle in and watch a cloud of blood mix with the piss-yellow liquid, and you press. The effect is instantaneous: warmth floods your body. Colors change, becoming more explicit, red is redder, blue is bluer, and you slip into a different time zone. The world is yours to control, to slow down, or speed up on a whim. The squalor becomes a palace. The roaches, subjects, and you know what it is to be present. But the world changes on a dime and the warmth begins to burn, heart quickening as you struggle to regain control, but the darkness creeps in, and the visions come. Through the swirling mist, shadows nip at your feet and take shape. Nightmares spun from the depths of your soul: a face known but not, familiar unfamiliar. Bullies and demons come to visit, grins wide and wet and dripping. You want to run, but your feet are frozen, glued to where you lie in the muck and the dirt and the grime of your life. They overpower and fill you up. You tear at yourself to exorcise the demons, and she comes. Your hope, your salvation, back to claim you. You are a figment she ignores, slumping down, she pulls out her needle. The pain of her is too much to bear, her long-dead eyes match your own, and you see the rats.

The rats come streaming from the inside, her thin T-shirt stained and worn clings to the outline of her breasts. There is movement from her belly, a mockery of birth as one chews its way out. Her mouth gapes, pushed open by wet spiky hair, beady red eyes, and twitching nose, scratching past her swollen tongue, widening her jaw until it cracks. Desperate to turn, run, look away, but you cannot. The rats turn their attention to you, nibbling toes soon they will be inside, and you will be gone, like mother, like son.

You sense its presence; it was there in the bell tower. It knows you and feels for you, understands your anguish, crying as it rushes to the surface. It will be your protector because no one else can or will. You need never be alone again. You are submerged as the animal surfaces, a relief to give in. Far below, the deep is warm, soft, and gentle; floating in the dark, the animal takes over. It will never hurt you because it loves you, and for a very long time, you know what it is to be cared for. The animal, inside out, inside outside upside down, open and free, it will do what you cannot and take what you cannot, and spare the pain. Free. You are free, but freedom comes at a price.

It does what it likes this animal of yours. You have almost forgotten what it was like to be the one in control, unsure what came first, you or the animal. You struggle, but the animal is strong, far stronger than you ever were. On the days you are the man, you know it is still there, sleeping, ready to wake, sometimes watching, stalking, ready to pounce? When it comes, it comes at speed. You hide as it takes over, hiding in the corridors of your mind. Does it know you are there? The animal does what you cannot; desire is absolute and consuming. When it sleeps, when you are back and see the debris of what it's done, tiny bodies litter the place you call home. You can taste them on your tongue, fear mingling with blood. Then you see it. A body so twisted and bent no longer resembling a real person. A discarded mannequin. You've seen them in alleyways; limbs twisted like the body before you. You don't know him, a vagrant like you, and like you, will not be missed. You cry a little, not because you're sad but because there is no one to weep for the human rubbish on the streets and know your fate will be the same.

You hide the body as best you can, sneaking it away from prying eyes, it doesn't matter, no one looks, no one cares. It gurgles to the bottom of the lake in the park, weighed down by rocks. There have been more, many more. That's when you see her. Was she watching? You doubt it but worry because of the animal. You feel it stir, it will do what it needs to survive, and you fear for her safety. She reminds you of someone's face you can no longer see and the warmth of an embrace too brief, before the rats came, before the animal.

The animal doesn't know right or wrong. The animal only knows how to survive, but there is a new struggle. The passenger it carries. It can feel him trying to take control to ride its back like a master. The animal has no master. It does what it wants because it can. The animal saw her first. It felt the desire as it slumbered, always one eye open, the passenger too stupid to know, too weak to act. Darting forward, the girl is too slow, fragile, weak, and scared. The animal takes her not because it wants to, but because it can, and inside you scream.

You wake and see the girl. It's not too late. You use the symbols remembered from childhood to keep the animal at bay. Painting her naked body, you try to cover what you can with the rags you have. The girl is scared, terrified out of her wits. You want her to understand that it's not you. You would never hurt her. You intend to keep her safe, that she mustn't scream, or fuss or make any loud noises because the animal will hear, and it will come. You pat her head and stroke her hair, you smile and try to speak, it's been so long, your voice sounds harsh and alien to your ears. Embarrassed by what you have become. You wish the animal had kept silent. You wish it were gone. You wish the animal had never been born. You wish so hard; it hears you and wakes up.

There is a crash as the door splinters and breaks, someone is coming, inside you begin to laugh as the animal rushes to the surface and drags you back down.

The animal is in control and will not, is not, ever going to let go again. There is someone here, someone to save the girl, your girl, the one you took. The air is thick with fear. You are strong and will survive, born from violence. The door opens, a beam of light cuts the gloom like a sword. A man is behind the blade, and a man can be killed, so you wait, the darkness your hunting ground, the shadows your lair. The man with the gun sees the girl. He raises an arm, ready to shoot. You brace for death, a welcomed reprieve from the life you've lived. It doesn't come. The man hesitates, looking at you, into you, and for a moment, you see yourself looking back. He has his own animal, this man; inside, looking out.

'*What does it want, this beast inside?*' A moment of calm before the storm. He sees you this man, and you see him, a connection, a shared understanding of the pain you once felt. It doesn't offer comfort this animal, this brother of yours, instead, a reminder of what you once were, and it strips you bare. The fear spills out in a flow of hatred. You are not the lie. You are the truth. The animal takes what it wants without remorse, and you leap. There is a flash, and the world ceases to exist, but in the blackness, the animal knows there is another, and is no longer alone.

The body inside the tank knows what it is to be alive with sensation, synapses firing, new pathways laid as muscles spasm and tense, an alarm clock to the sleeping beast that opens one eye and begins to stir, and Shelly sees the other.

# 9.

Hopper had lived in the city his whole life and couldn't remember a time when the suburb of 'Angel Heights' didn't deserve the reputation it was known for. Built fucked, using pre-fucked materials by opportunistic developers, houses were old before they were new. Corpses of broken cars populated front yards of single-story homes. He hated and despised the area, a lingering shame from a progressive 1970's housing plan, ripe for exploitation, abandoned and ignored, left to rot. Unfixed and unfixable, a haven for undesirables, considered a no-go area by most of the force, but not Hopper. Hopper felt drawn to it. Lawless and unforgiving, he had, on occasion, found himself smashing a suspect's head against the tarmac in the hope of shaking loose a piece of information, but sometimes, just because he could, and there was no-one to complain.

Currently partnered with Bernie Hyde, an ok cop but lazy, a little too keen to take the easy bust. Avoidance was his strategy, place yourself in the wrong place at the right time. Don't dirty your hands when someone else is willing. *Fuck it*, why not? The job didn't pay enough to go out there and risk life and limb. Some guys were made for the uniform, but not the work. Tall, square-jawed, blond hair, a regular jock and poster boy. Hopper resented him, but then again, he resented the rest of the world.

Michael Watts was an ugly stain on the street, habitual user, and abuser of everything and anything he could get his hands on. He was in and out of institutions his whole life, starting with juvie and migrating to the big house as he matured. Watts had never made it past the first rung on the corporate ladder as a career criminal, preferring to lurk in the less challenging areas, scavenging his way through life, randomly moving from one crime to another. His favorite, little girls; easy prey. He was known as an opportunistic snatcher, taking kids from *decent* suburbs on their way to or from school. Acting on the spur of the moment, snatch first ask later, but not before he'd had his fun; only then would he send in his greasy ransom note. All parents paid, not always the full amount, but they paid, and Watts would take what he could, and for the ones that didn't or couldn't pay—well... everyone paid one way or another.

Being a certified schizophrenic, once apprehended it was always the same. Watts was swept up in a cycle of social liberalism, given the opportunity to clean up in a court-appointed detox center, fresh meds and an overworked caseworker with a piss week promise to keep him on the straight and narrow. Hopper hated a system that knowingly put repeat offenders back on the streets destined to repeat, and Watts was a seasoned offender, he knew how to work the system better than anyone. With an overstretched parole system and an overcrowded prison, there was no room for the likes of Watts, it was easier and more convenient for him to become someone else's problem, if only for a short time. Hopper did what he could to help, beating up a recently returned suspect, reminding them that although the system may have failed, he wouldn't.

A child had gone missing on her way to school. The family wasn't wealthy, working hard to afford their piece of the pie, the privilege of a good suburb, one that was considered safe and had featured as the backdrop to several family soaps, every cent accounted for. They wanted to pay but couldn't. At least not while the banks weren't open. They called the police as soon as the letter slipped through their door. It had Watts's MO all over it. He had been back for only six months!

Hopper knew he could be wrong, but people were nothing if not predictable. So here they were, Hopper and Hyde, outside the last known address of Michael Watts in the early hours of the morning. The day after the night before, already promising to be a hot one. Hopper thumped his fist against the front door as Hyde made his way around the back. Reluctant to separate, he's soon back. "Doesn't look like anyone's home," the relief palpable in his voice.

"He's in there; he just has to know we're serious." Hopper raised a boot ready to smash the door, which opened a fraction too soon. Missed opportunity!

"What the fuck do you want, you know what time it is?" Screeched Tanya Watts, the lawful wife of Michael and fellow addict, as she opened the door, just enough to give Hopper a good lungful of fetid morning junkie breath. She spat a glob of brown mucus on the porch next to Hopper, who could feel the muscle in his eye twitch, he'd like nothing better than to bring his boot crashing down on her skinny pale neck so he could listen to it crack.

"I've got a few questions for Michael. Is he in?"

"No, he fucking isn't, I..." Hopper, without waiting, pushes past, gun drawn, safety off, not bothering to wait for an answer. "Oi! You can't just barge in. We ain't done nothing wrong."

"You were born wrong," Hopper shouts over his shoulder as he scans each room, gun first. He hears a window slide open in the backroom and kicks the door open in time to see Michael Watts climbing out the window as he makes a bid for freedom. "Back yard", Hopper yells out, hoping Hyde has the sense to act before squeezing through the window after him, "he's making a run for it."

Heartbeat up, pulse racing, lungs burning, his breath comes in hard and sharp pants. Hopper loves it; the game is on, although always careful not to enjoy the chase too much; it's his job, not his hobby, and thank God for that. Watts is moving fast, ducking in and out of alleyways, grabbing any obstacle he can to throw at Hopper, a broken trike, clean washing that smells dirty, garbage, empty bottles, anything, until he takes a wrong turn. Watts has cornered himself in dead end at the back of a Chinese restaurant. He could try and make it over the wire fence, but the big cop with the mean face would probably catch him and give him a beating for making him sweat. *Give in now, spare yourself the pain, cut a deal.* He knows what they want and knows the drill, dropping to his knees, hands behind his head ready to be cuffed. Gulping for breath, Watts is relieved to stop. Maybe he can go back to the hospital, take it easy, get cleaned up, three meals a day, get fit. God knows it's hard on the outside. What else was he going to do? Who the fuck is going to give him a job with his rep?

"Ok Ok" Watts pants, "I 'ain't done nuthin' wrong, what you after me fur? I got my rights. I got me a diagnosis."

Hopper doesn't move; he hates everything about Watts, the sound, the look, and the smell of him. He thinks of the little girl and how many more little girls there have been and will be, and for a moment, stops him from ramming the business end of his gun in Watts's open mouth and pulling the trigger. He still needs to know where the little girl is.

*There's something wrong with this one,* thinks Watts. He can see it in Hopper's face. It's a look he's seen before, but never on a cop. It's a look he doesn't like, it means something bad is going to happen. "Ok cop, I give up. Just a little chase is all. You got me. I'm giving up. We can talk."

But Hopper doesn't want to talk, at least not yet, he's still thinking of the little girl and how scared she must be. "Too bad you resisted arrest though!" Hopper says calmly before smashing his gun into the side of Watts's face.

Hyde is running down the streets; *Hopper should have caught him by now, where the hell is he?* He thinks when he hears a cry behind the Chinese restaurant. Not Jack Hopper, he can take care of himself, but junkies are dangerous. They have Aids and knives and needles, and a death wish, which makes them unpredictable. *Best be careful.* He tells himself, slowing down, tentatively making his way down the side of the restaurant to the rear, amongst the discarded boxes loaded with grease and leftovers from last night's dinner. The smell makes his stomach turn. But nothing prepares him for the alley.

"Holy fuck Jack!" Hyde can't help noticing some of Watts' blood has speckled Hopper's face. He must have got some in his mouth. *Aids, Hep C,* he thinks and throws up.

"Resisted arrest, can you believe it?" Grins Hopper, the red stain of Watts's blood on his teeth.

# 10.

The tears collect at the end of Michael Watts's nose and drip onto the Formica table bolted to the floor. His face is bloodied, cut, and swollen. He can barely see through his left eye and his ribs hurt enough to be worried, really worried, but he hates hospitals. He knows they do things to you in hospitals, so he stays quiet. Last time he was there, they put a microchip in his brain, he doesn't know why, he just knows it's there, they tried to tell him different, but he knows a lie when he hears one. He also knows there's no profit in honesty. He's heard the stories; people waking up minus a kidney or a lung or worse. Keep calm, use it; take the pain, it only hurts when you breathe!

"It's police, fucking, brutality, is what it is," sniffed Watts, "I want a lawyer, I got rights same as anyone else. I 'ain't no piece of rubbish to be trampled on. He's a fuckin' psycho. I want to make a complaint."

Detective Richardson had heard it all before, from both sides; *he fell down the stairs, he tripped, hit his face, resisted arrest*, but it was hard to make any excuse stick after the violent beating Hopper dished out. Sure, Watts was one sick puppy, but there was still the girl. God damn Hyde, where was he? He was supposed to keep an eye on him. They'd been worried about Hopper for some time, ever since the psycho took a bite out of the girl, but he was a cop, and we look after our own. Who doesn't go a little crazy occasionally? When you see what we see, it would be crazy not to.

Richardson sighed, trying to look as benevolent as he could, nodding gently, brow furrowed, all empathy and understanding, but doesn't take his eyes off Watts for a moment. He hates him as much as Hopper and would like to jam his pencil in his eye but doesn't because right now, a little girl's life depends on them. And he's not Jack Hopper. "It's OK Michael. You'll get your lawyer, of course, you've got rights. You're just the same as anyone else, innocent until proven guilty. It's how it works." Richardson reassured him, smiling as best he could. It's a good move using his first name, establishing trust, and all the rest of the shit. He hopes it was worth it for Hopper. It sure as shit wasn't worth it for the little girl.

"But here's the thing Michael," Richardson continued, in the best *friendly uncle* voice he could muster, "if the girl dies... well... you'll be fucked then. And then you won't have any rights anymore, will you? I understand about your diagnosis." It's a struggle to keep his voice calm; he manages it, just. "But if this goes south.... you'd be liable for the injection and not the kind you like – I mean the nasty kind. You know they say it's not supposed to hurt, but that's a lie, it does. Hurts like shit. I've seen it happen. Just make it easy for yourself, give it up, it'll soon be over, and then you'll be free to go home. You'd like that, right? Course you would."

"Not with that psycho on the loose. I know him. He'll just come back and finish what he started, I seen his eyes, he was real liking it. You 'ain't getting' nothin' from me without my lawyer." Watts wiped the nose that Richardson wanted to break. Instead, ever the diplomat and optimist, he nods and excuses himself. A few more moments and he'll talk, he's sure of it, has to be. He'll promise him a restraining order on Hopper, get him to start thinking about his little crack pipe, make him sweat.

"Ok, Ok. You've been through a lot. Why don't we take a break? I'll be back in five, and you'll get your lawyer. Think about what I said Michael. You could back home, snuggling up to the missus. You've got five minutes to think about it." Richardson gives him a big grin and a sly little wink, just one of the boys. *I get you, we could be friends, you and I*, and Richardson leaves.

Watts is left on his own. *Five minutes* the cop said. *He didn't seem too bad, knew the score, what's up and what's down, besides how long will he have to wait for a lawyer?* It could be tomorrow by the time he's out. What were the choices? Back home, him and Tanya cooking' up a hit or two, always looking behind to see what's coming, or doing it cold in the sweat tank? Not much of a choice, least that cop will have to sweat some too. Besides, the girl's too skinny to be worth much, not much fun when they're bony. He likes the ones with more meat, puppy fat, they call it, pre-bleeds he calls them. *Fuck it; she's not worth it*, he thinks.

# 11.

The midday sun feels angry on the skin and blasts through the windows like the aftermath of a nuclear bomb and stops dead, picking out little specks of dust floating in the air, winking in the light, impossible to catch, easy to inhale. Hopper waves an arm and watches them swirl. Dust from decay, the dead skin cells of colleagues. How many times a day does he suck in someone else? It's the waiting that's the hard part; he feels it more than his colleagues. If Hyde had been five minutes longer or had the decency to take a walk, he would have gotten what he needed from the stink rat. That's the trouble with today's younger detectives, no stomach for the job. To do what it takes. What it really takes. The good old days when being a cop meant something. You didn't just enforce the law; you were the law. Respect *was* the badge. He could see the change on the older guys, their enthusiasm for the job drained by too many pencil pushers concerned over rights. The right to remain silent, the right to an attorney, the right to have the living shit kicked out of you.

The room stirs as Richardson walks in. They're all keen for news, but one look at the man's face was enough to tell them it's bad. "The little cock sucker wants a lawyer. He knows his rights better than we do." Richardson tells them, making his way to the coffee machine.

Hopper shakes his head in mock disbelief. He always knew the outcome; the law skewed to service scum like him. "And how long's that going to take? Un-fucking-believable. Rights? What about the girl's rights?"

Richardson doesn't bother to turn. "Tell me, Jack, when you were busy beating him up," he continues quietly adding sugar, "was it her rights that you were thinking of? Because right now, Watts loves you. As low as he is, as much of a degenerate as he is, he *does* have rights and knows it. Whereas you, my friend, may have given him his get out of jail free card. It was an asshole move and a dangerous one, if that girl gets hurt...," he lets his voice trail off, but Hopper knows what he's thinking, *if she gets hurt, this is on you,* a glance around the room tells him it's what they all think. *Asshole, idiot, liability, psycho.* Richardson is probably right, but it doesn't make it right. Too much dead skin sucked in. Is that what's wrong with the world? Did Richardson breath in too much of Watts?

"You should have tried harder," Hopper hears himself say, and wished he'd only thought it.

"Look at my face Hopper, you look at me," Growls Richardson. He's in the perfect mood for a fight, especially for one that won't jeopardize an important outcome like Watts. Hopper lifts his eyes and can see the anger and hate living in the creases of the old cop's face. *Let it go* Hopper wants to tell him, *we all feel it, give in, and smash the door down no one would blame you, hell, I'll even join in and hold him down for you,* but he doesn't. "You think I don't want to do what you do? Like some crazy mother fucker who thinks he's on the side of right?" Richardson barks at Hopper, spitting out each word, "I'd like nothing better than to tear that scum a new one. But I don't, you know why? Because I have restraint Jack. It's something you should learn. Because right now my restraint is helping me not punch you in the face. Maybe you should have tried harder when you had the chance." He glances over at Hyde, spreading the blame, before turning sharply on his heel, "I'm taking five minutes, I need some fresh air, this place stinks."

Hopper was right, too much dead skin in the old man's lungs. He knows the rest of the room agrees with Richardson; *asshole, idiot, liability, psycho,* sadly he doesn't disagree. How many times has he looked in the mirror and promised himself, *today will be the day I really, really try not to be an asshole?* But how long does it last? Maybe he should be the one to go with the flow and see where the current takes him. He thinks back to the young man with the animal teeth, never too far away, and thinks, *why not?*

"I'm sick of this shit. Give me five minutes with *Mr make me fucking puke* in there. I'll get what we need," Hopper stands, intention clear, Hyde steps in front of him.

"Don't. Don't do this Jack... think about it." Stammers Hyde, a half-hearted attempt to block his way.

"You heard him Hyde. Five minutes. It takes Richardson that long to wipe his ass. Just keep an eye out. Be a partner for once. Have my back, that's all I ask." Hopper pushes past him. It's what they want, it's what they all want. They know what's coming to Watts, they trust him enough for that. He'll get the information because that's what he does. Hoppers can feel his smile spread like a warm glow through his loins, thank God he has his back to them. He's going to enjoy this. It's about time someone had some fun around here.

Feeling better about life, Watts is still sniffing when Hopper opens the door.

"Hey party pal, we never got to finish our conversation." The sniffing stops as Hopper quietly shut the door.

"Get away from me .. you're, you're not supposed to be here. I was gonna tell, I was, I swear I was." The fear is palpable in his voice as he involuntary tests the cuffs fastened to the table. There's nowhere for him to go, and he knows what's coming. Hopper knows he's scared, no scratch that, terrified as he gets a whiff of urine and watches a puddle form under the chair. It disgusts him. It makes him angry. Someone will have to clean that up. Someone decent. Someone who works hard. Someone who doesn't fuck kids, lowered to cleaning up the stain of _him_. His piss. HIS. The filth, the scum. Hopper's head throbs with pounding blood, his teeth ache, and muscles tense. God only knows he needs a release.

"I know that Watts. You were always going to tell." Hopper smiles, rolling up his shirt sleeves and winks back, unlocking the cuffs. "Looks like someone got free."

"Please... Don't."

Hopper can barely hear the words under the drums. He's pleading, begging, desperate. _Just like a little girl_, he thinks.

# 12.

The drums have stopped. How long has it been? Was it five minutes? Hopper can't remember. He knows where the girl is. There's a houseboat along the river, past where the old smelting plant used to be. Hopper knows it well, home to water rats of both kinds. A choking rasp gurgles from what's left of Watts takes Hopper by surprise, his body hangs limply off the chair like a discarded jacket with legs and a head. His face, a rare and bloodied steak, almost featureless. *Alive!* Is he disappointed or relieved? He's not so sure and is finding it hard to care.

When did he find out where the girl was? Watts must have still been able to speak, to spill as it were. He really spilled this time, he spilled everywhere. He can't remember much after that. He heard the drums. No. Felt the drums. Pounding, relentless drowning out everything else.

Where did it all go wrong for Watts? The man was once a boy, and the boy a child, and the child had a mother. When did it break? When did Watts become the monster and start preying on little girls? He must have known the difference between right and wrong at some point, or did this vital piece of knowledge pass him by? Looking at the broken body of what used to be a man, it's not sympathy Hopper feels, just curiosity. The door opens; it's Richardson. Hopper hopes he washed his hands, hygiene isn't always a priority for some. He's seen them, leaving the stalls without so much as a handshake under the tap, going straight back to work. They let the dirt stain them.

"Jack. What have you done?" Shock and concern register on Richardson, but for who? Watts, or the girl.

"A houseboat, down from the smelting plant. You'll find her there, under the floorboards. Let's hope she hasn't drowned." Richardson blinks back, his mouth opening and closing like a goldfish, continuing to stare. *What's wrong with you, you dumb fuck?* Hopper wants to scream, *are you still confused?* "The smelting plant," he repeats, this time a little louder, feeling the drums starting up again. "You know it?"

It's hard for Richardson to turn away, ask any rubbernecker drawn to an accident. "I.. Yeah, I know it... Jack, what the fuck... what happened?"

*I beat the living shit outta' him what does it look like? I thought that was pretty fucking obvious,* Hopper thinks, amazed Richardson had to ask considering how obvious it all is, instead, telling him; "He got free and went for me, he was like a crazed animal, something about his rights, said he was going to make us all sweat. I was acting in self-defense… so…" The drums quieten and he changes the subject back to the matter at hand. "…the houseboat then."

# 13.

Like everyone else, Adam is waiting in line at the cafeteria in the hospital dining room. Same, same, but different. All totally normal, doing what normal people do, although what passes for *normal* in here doesn't necessarily pass for *normal* out there, because Adam and his friends are most definitely not *normal*. *Normal* people don't end up here. But that doesn't bother Adam, he's still part of the crowd, blending in, being as normal as normal can be.

The patients shuffle along. It's Thursday, Adam knows it's Thursday because on Thursday, Spaghetti Bolognese is on the menu with sponge and custard. This is how some of the *guests* define the days of the week, predictable routine, God help them if they change the menu or chef. The *guest* in front of Adam seems agitated, irritated at how long it's taking, the line is slower than it should be. It's ok thinks Adam. Be calm, we have nowhere else to be and nowhere else to go. Just be here and concentrate on something else. He begins to do the exercises Dr. Shelly told him to do. Breath slowly. Reconnect to your surroundings. Be present. Look at the plastic tray, see how it curves up at the edges, the pattern, a light speckle, like the markings on an egg.

*Plop,* his sponge and custard are generously dropped into his plastic bowl. He hadn't even been aware of moving that's how good Shelly's exercises are. *I must be getting better,* he thinks as he smiles at the orderly serving food, who surprisingly smiles back, today is a good day. But not for all.

"What the fuck are you smiling for? You like the slop in here?" The agitated man in front asks.

Adam does like the *slop* in here and is about to say so when the *guest* leans over and grabs Adam's sponge cake with his fat dirty hand, and jams it into his own mouth. Custard and sponge dribble onto his clean white jumpsuit as he waits for Adam to respond. He needs a release from his tension.

"Not so fucking smiley now, are you?" The young man spits the words out through a mouthful of food. Flecks of sponge and custard fly out of his cakehole much easier than the words as he struggles to swallow the handful.

No. Adam is most definitely not smiley anymore. He glances at the plastic spork on his tray, and although the material has been designed to buckle under force, rendering it useless as a weapon, Adam still manages to jam it into the other patient's eye. It yields immediately, bursting with a mixture of blood and fluid. The man instinctively covers the wound as Adam reaches out and grabs the back of his fellow patient's head, bringing it down hard against the steel rods that make up the serving bench, once twice, three times for luck. His skull cracks, Adam can feel the fragments move and slide under the skin in his hands. Leaning forward, he takes a bite below the ear. More blood, more pain. The tension is gone, and Adam spits out a sizeable chunk of flesh. People are running, screaming, the man is dying, chaos reigns, the animal is awake.

"I said. What the fuck are you grinning at, idiot?"

The man still has his eye in place and head intact. *Idiot?* Thinks Adam, *surely, we're all idiots in here!* The security guards have already taken an interest and are no longer leaning against the wall, waiting for the inevitable, ready to break up the usual outcome of a patient altercation. Adam pushes the animal back down; he's the one in control, he's where he wants to be, connected to his environment, and it's still a good day. There's always another bowl of sponge and custard, it's not like they'll ever run out. The animal, back in the shadows, sulks and goes back to sleep with one eye open.

"Nothing, I wasn't grinning about anything." It's the wrong thing to say and the man becomes more irritated. Adam doesn't want any trouble, he would have liked to have said; *you I'm grinning at you, you fat greasy fuck, and how easy it would be to take a bite out of you, you're a real piece of cake.* The pun makes Adam laugh.

"You think I'm funny now, do you?" The man inches closer to Adam, he can smell his breath and notices the pock-marked skin on his cheeks, it reminds him of an orange. He's larger than Adam, but that doesn't matter. "I could take you apart with one hand tied behind my back. You think that's funny?" The man asks.

"Like a real piece of cake," Adam replies, still smiling.

The man pauses for a moment before his brain registers it as a joke, *a piece of cake, and he just ate a piece of cake.* He puts two and two together and bursts out laughing, pleased at his ability to recognize a joke when he hears one. Maybe he's not so far gone after all.

Adam glances over to the orderly, who has his hand lightly resting on his telescopic baton and winks. The orderly removes his hand and goes back to leaning against the wall, and winks back. It's a shared moment, recognizing that the threat has passed, a sure sign that Adam is more normal than most. He's getting better. After all, he's the only one who can hear the animal grumbling in the dark.

# 14.

Adam leaps at the camera in his room, face full screen, but without purchase, drops to the floor. Frustrated, he tears at the bandages covering his face revealing a patchwork quilt of stitched wounds, he tries once more, splattering the lens with a light speckle of blood. An orderly enters and fires a dart. Disorientated and dizzy from the sedative, Adam makes one last desperate attempt before collapsing. Dr. Shelly freezes the image on the TV screen in her office.

Adam and Shelly are sitting together on the couch, the blinds half closed to avoid the glare from the midday sun casting parallel lines on the wall opposite. Shelly opens them before taking a seat behind her desk. Sunlight spills into the room. Adam in the office is different from Adam on the screen. On screen, Adam is smaller, thinner, and doesn't have much of a face. For all the anger and the venom, his presence is less. Adam absently touches the light scar running just below his hairline and meets Dr. Shelly's gaze. Her face is a puzzle, impossible to read. He's known fear, disgust, and anger, but she betrays nothing, a one-way street framed by glasses. Everything in, nothing out. But Adam knows not to be fooled by her. Cold, emotionless eyes search and scan like a laser. Lie, and she'll know. She always knows. She's expecting a response from him, but looking at a cold echo that isn't him, what else is there to say? He clears his throat. "It's hard to believe it's me. I don't remember it, any of it... being like that." Shelly's eyes squint a fraction, a barely perceptible movement in the corner, but Adam sees it, "I know it is me, I get that," he quickly adds, the eyes relax, "but... it's not. I don't know that version of me." He hopes it's the answer she's looking for; he hates it when he disappoints her.

She smiles back; his relief is palpable. She knows Adam tells her what he thinks she wants to hear; it's good that he wants to please her, to keep her happy, it doesn't matter, she has her, *access all areas* pass, and can use it whenever she likes. There are no lies between them, not anymore, the tank has seen to that. The little game they play is harmless, she should throw him a bone now and then, a small smile, a pat on the knee. Maybe a biscuit if he's been a really good boy, *roll over and Mommy will rub your tum tum.*

"I heard about the dining hall. I was impressed." Shelly absently tells him, flipping open a file in front of her. Informal couch time is all well and good, but let's not forget who's in charge.

"It wasn't a big deal," Adam tells her, pleased she knows as he twists to face her; he'd been trying to think of a way to drop it into their conversation, although he's a little disappointed she doesn't make a big thing of it and wonders if he should. He decides not to and does his best to appear casual, "he's sick, right? He wouldn't be here if he wasn't," he continues, "I know he didn't mean anything by it, just letting off steam."

"Interesting. It's good you see it that way. I see it differently, but it tells me how far you've come." She gestures to the frozen image on the screen before flicking it off. "Sit down Adam," nodding to the seat opposite in front of her desk. He obediently obliges. "You didn't feel like letting off steam?"

Adam tries to maintain eye contact with her, as he remembers how much he would have liked to tear a hole in the man's neck but looks away in case she gets a glimpse of the animal way down there in the dark. "Of course not!" He does his best to sound indignant. She smiles at that. Does she know it's a lie? He feels genuinely insulted and ashamed that she could still think of him as the man he once was.

She lets out a little laugh. "Don't look so alarmed, it's only natural to get angry in that situation, the difference is how we act, how we control our anger and to what degree. Actions have consequences."

He hates it when she does this, never asking him a question directly, far better to leave a statement hanging in the air like bait. "Which would have been wrong," Adam tentatively answers, without conviction, knowing they would have sent him back. He hopes it's what she wants to hear. Shelly frowns. *Shit.*

"What else Adam? Remember, no secrets. I know you know. Stop trying to tell me what you think is right and just tell me what you think. Remember, here is a safe space."

"Because," his answer is slow and guarded, full of doubt, but she nods encouragingly. "Because," he continues, "because boredom can be frustrating. I knew he was picking a fight just for the hell of it. Anything to make the day go quicker, and if I joined in, it makes me just like him, which I'm not. It's not just because I know it's wrong, any idiot knows that. It's because I knew why. Frustration leads to anger, isn't that what you always say?" He loves it when he has a chance to reflect her own words back at her, it shows he's been listening. She smiles back at him, thank God.

"Exactly right, anger is often a symptom of something else, and it's up to us to find out what that is, it's how we read people. It's our first step towards empathy. Knowing we can't do what we want is a big step, understanding why is bigger. It's an important distinction."

Adam looks back confused, she doesn't care, she has what she wants and wants more, "Imagine you're working outside for the city, in a park for example…"

"Like a job?" Adam interrupts.

"Yes, just like a job." *Christ it's like talking to a two-year-old* she thinks, "your job is to look after the grass, to keep it clean, you've spent all morning raking the leaves, the grass looks beautiful, all nice and clean and tidy when some kids come along and kick your pile of leaves over, spreading them back over the grass, you'd be angry right?"

"I guess so."

"I guess so!? All that hard work for nothing, and they're laughing at you, calling you names, like retard and moron. They think it's fun to mess with the idiot in the park. Wasting your time so that you don't get your lunch. Trying to get you in trouble, maybe even fired." Shelly squints her eyes, "I think you'd be angry, wouldn't you?"

Adam is getting a headache, he'd like to take the rake and smash it over their heads and jam the splintered end into their stupid smug faces, but he knows that's the wrong answer. It's ok to be angry, she just said so, because what they did was wrong. After all, he did spend all morning raking, which means that if he started at eight and stopped for lunch at twelve, that's four hours! Then again, he's out in the open and has a job in a park which would be fun, so if he had to do it all again, it wouldn't be too bad, in fact, he wouldn't mind too much at all. "Maybe just try to ignore them. I'm the one who's going to come off worse in the end," *I'm not,* he secretly thinks. "So, I guess I'd just have to rake them up again. They'll get bored eventually."

Shelly leans back in her chair, hands clasped together in front of her. "Very good Adam, that's really very good," and it is good, even though he sounds suspiciously like someone intellectually impaired. "Let's try another." She sees that he doesn't like this game, he's getting twitchy which is what she wants.

"You remember you're in charge of the grass, it's a very responsible job, only this time there's a man walking his dog. He lets the dog off the leash, and it runs off." Adam is smiling, my God she thinks, he probably knows what sort of dog it is, "but the dog runs onto the grass and squats down" she continues, "and takes a shit." Adam is visibly shocked. Her deliberate use of the word *shit* spoils his fantasy, making it crude and vulgar. She knows he doesn't like it when she uses bad language. "There's a sign that says, dog must be kept on the leash at all times. You know this because you put the sign up, dog's aren't allowed on the grass, and to make matters worse, the man walks away, ignoring it. He's supposed to pick after his dog and put it in the bins provided. But because he hasn't, that means you have to! You have to pick up his dog shit, and he knows that, but he does it anyway because he thinks it's beneath him, but he doesn't think it's beneath you. It's ok for you to pick up his dog shit. What would you do?" Shelly watches Adam's frown grow.

*I'd get the son of a bitch and make him eat that shit, hold him down until every last little bit has been swallowed up. Then I'd get him to eat my shit. That's what I'd do*, thinks Adam, but then again, what if he was a big man, and he made him eat the shit? Besides, he'd most likely lose his job. He can guess that feeding shit to the public would most certainly be a fireable offense, and he wouldn't want to end up back here, answering stupid questions like this one. "I would report him, and then I guess I'd just have to clean it up anyway. It doesn't matter what he thinks, it's what I think that matters." He shrugs, "it could be worse. It's not like I have to use my bare hands." Adam looks up expectantly.

Shelly resists the urge to clap her hands and throw him a treat. Adam is a success. Or at least he's a success in the artificial environment of the hospital, which is why he'll soon be forgoing structure for something a little more random, chaotic, and real. "I have a surprise for you Adam," she tells him, beaming like the proud mother she is.

Adam doesn't really like surprises, but he knows people like to give them. "Great," he smiles back, feigning enthusiasm, and notices some movement in the garden outside her office window. A woman dressed in her nightshirt is spinning and dancing, she looks blissfully happy.

"Because you're doing so well, I've organized something a little more challenging for you, something that I feel we'll both get a great deal out of," Shelly tells him excitedly.

The woman in the garden is engaged in a dance to a rhythm only she can hear, Adam has lost track of what Shelly is saying, preferring instead to concentrate on the woman's movements in the nightshirt.

"Do you know what I mean when I say we are as much of a product of our environment as it is of us?"

Four orderlies have surrounded the woman; her attitude has changed, no longer the carefree and happy dancer, she begins to recoil, lashing out. Adam turns from the window, "I'm not sure I understand."

"Life in an institution isn't life. It's predictable. What will you have for dinner on Monday?"

"Sausages," Blurts Adam a little too quickly, knowing how he sounds, but he does like sausages.

Shelly raises her eyebrows. "There is no free will with an expected outcome. I need to see how much you've really changed... out there," she gestures towards the window, noticing the woman for the first time as the four orderlies overpower her.

"I still don't understand."

"Outside in the real world. Beyond the gates. It's something I think you're going to love." Shelly closes the blinds and adds, "I think we both will."

# 15.

It's been over four months. Four months of waiting, four months of mind-numbing boredom, of tedious day time TV. Drinking too much and picking fights. Watching porn and getting laid, but not nearly enough. God knows Hopper tried to keep his mind and body occupied. Even moonlighting as a security guard now and then, cash in hand, every little bit helps after all. But if ever there was a spirit-crushing, coma-inducing pointless job, it was the night watch security guard for the empty car parks around the city or unlet office buildings and warehouses, hard-wired and fully monitored by closed-circuit cameras and motion detectors. But for reasons Jack couldn't fully understand, there was still the need for a human being. Insurance he assumed. Blame more likely. Everyone needs someone to point the finger at when things go wrong, even the machines.

He'd enjoyed his stint freelancing as a private dick for some ex-colleagues who'd set up an investigative business. Providing the extra muscle to pressure some poor fool into paying up. Pain is a genuine and honest currency exchanged for time; take a beating, get a week. But don't forget the interest, interest always gets paid in the end. Hopper didn't even mind the surveillance. People were interesting after all, and he could watch, he could watch for hours. Grubby liaisons dressed up to be something more, white lies turned grey, then black with age and practice, pathetic apologies when caught. Hopper often found a quick punch in the face was far easier and quicker than having to listen to the excuses he didn't care about, or the bribes so often offered.

*No-one needs to know. We weren't hurting anyone,* they'd plead. Then there were the indignant, taking the moral high ground, *I suppose you feel good about this, do you, ruining people's lives?* Curiously, he did. *Is this how you get your kicks?* Yes. Or simply, *don't you know who I am?* No, and I don't care.

Jack's personal favorite, *whatever they're paying you, I'll double it, all you have to do is walk away.* The lack of accountability was staggering, a litmus to a moral compass gone haywire. Even if he could walk away, he wouldn't, and the offer always angered him, the arrogance he could be bought off so easily. But in the end, it was too much; it made him feel sleazy. The husbands who would slip him an extra fifty to hurt the guy cheating on their wife, the salacious attempts from wives to win him over, or the smug lover offering money. All poison to an already darkened soul.

But the girl had been found alive. And to Hopper that was all that mattered. Watts had slowly come out of his coma but would never be the same again. It was doubtful he would ever eat solids, let alone bother another child, and in Hopper's eyes, that was a result. As it was for the parents, who put together their own social media campaign heralding him as a hero, dispensing justice when the system wouldn't. The department saw it differently and placed him on suspension with reduced pay while they figured out what to do with him. The last thing they needed was a PR disaster. They couldn't afford to get rid of him, nor could they condone his actions, like some kind of vigilante cop hero operating under his own rules. Instead, they played along, downplaying Hopper's part, giving Hyde credit for the arrest, fast-tracking his career. In the meantime, Hopper had to agree to therapy or that would be the end of his career. After several months, he would undergo a full psychiatric evaluation to determine his state of mind and ability to resume his duties.

He had to laugh. It was a move Bobby Fisher would have been proud of. He reluctantly agreed, what else could he do? It wasn't much of a choice. It was either that or resign, in which case he would be subject to a potential lawsuit from Watts' lawyer. The real kicker: he was to be placed on administrative duties during this time. Missing Persons. No investigations, filing, or data entry as it was now known. As Blake pointed out, they recently acquired a new system, and for it to work effectively, they needed previous files and caseloads entered manually. Plus it would give him an additional line on his CV *Nice touch*, Hopper thought, considerate. They wanted to give him a chance at least. He figured it would give them just enough time to allow things to die down before they established enough of an excuse to absolve them of responsibility and get rid of him permanently. During which time he was to be deconstructed and evaluated. For what? He was already halfway out the door. He pitied the poor fool who had the job of poking around in his head.

# 16.

When Hopper wasn't busy throwing himself a pity party, he ended up spending most of his days and nights at his old partner, Arthur Acton's place. A skate ring imaginatively named *'The Circle.'* After much persuasion to leave the force, he'd opened it with his young wife. Hopper could never understand Art's reasons for the move; most ex-cops bought a bar or a restaurant with a guaranteed client base of colleagues past and present, ready to offer support. Not Art. His reasons were as fluid as the skating, depending on which day you asked him. He would tell you; *when you make a break, you made it clean otherwise, you're never truly free. Who wants to hang around with ghosts?* Hopper suspected something deeper. The notion of going round and round getting nowhere, he always liked that, a gentle dig at the constabulary—Art the philosopher. Although the real reason, Hopper suspected, was more straightforward, Jade loved to skate. He'd bought it for her.

Jade had been an anxious police wife, most of them are. Waiting at home for the unexpected call or knock at the door, the one you dread. *No life for a wife,* she would say backed up by *a happy wife means a happy life,* and Art would have done anything to keep her happy. So, he left the force. They'd even promised him a desk job if safety was all he was worried about, but for Art, it was all in or not, a clean break. Ironically, Hopper, alongside Art's wife Jade, encouraged his decision, yes, he'd be losing his best friend, yes, he'd be losing the only man he ever looked up to, yes, he'd be losing the best and only partner he would ever have. But far better to lose him from the job than to lose him from life. Like Jade, Hopper had started to worry about Art. The man had become too precious to let go. Besides, marriage had softened him, he wasn't as young as the men he was hunting down anymore. Jack would take on the extra workload, putting himself in harm's way making sure Art stayed protected. Eventually, enough had been enough, and Art quit, *having one anxious wife at home was enough,* he'd said. He didn't need another at work.

Art set up *'The Circle'* shortly after. Never popular, but that was hardly the point. You only needed to spend five minutes with Art and Jade to see how blissfully happy they were. Hours spent arm in arm, going round and round in circles. They'd even managed to persuade Hopper, against his better judgment, to learn to skate. He'd surprised himself, and them, by being good at it. For him, it became his go-to place for thinking. Besides, the buzz of wiping the smile from their faces was almost equal to the thrill he could get at top speed. Something Jade thought hilarious; watching the big man whizzing round and round, grinning like an idiot, his trench coat flapping behind him. But it all changed, as things do, when someone gets shot.

Art was packing away the roller skates when Hopper walked in. *Everything has a place everything in its place,* he thinks and hopes, no, prays that Jack will one day find his. Hopper reached under the counter for the size elevens Art puts to one side for his friend and grunts a basic hello. It doesn't take long until Hopper is doing circles, one, two, three, four, building up speed. Art grabs a six-pack of beers from the fridge before taking a seat in the spectator's gallery, reserved for mums and dads who no longer come. The place is old, outdated, and out of sync with the world, just like its owner and favorite patron. *Bad day,* he can judge Hopper's mood by the number and speed of the revolutions he does, *definitely a bad day.*

Hopper finished his last rotation and coasted to the barrier where Arts is waiting with a beer, after quickly gulping it down, takes a seat next to his friend. Their silence is comfortable. Art knows he'll talk when ready as they watch the stragglers on the floor. A teenage couple still courteous polite, most likely on a first or second date. Time travelers from a different age. An awkward dad with his teenage daughter almost too old for him and the ring, nervously glancing over her shoulders, making sure her friends aren't around to watch. *You're safe, sweetheart, just enjoy it while you can,* Hopper thinks. Her friends, if they were typical teenagers, wouldn't be seen dead in a place like this, and would most likely be at home, transfixed and hypnotised by screens of all shapes and sizes with better things to do.

"I don't know why you don't just sell up." Hopper asked, still looking at the young couple, "There must be developers who'd be interested."

"You know why."

They let the ghost of Arts wife gently settle over them. Art thinks about the time he spent with her, Hopper thinks of the day they found her.

"You gonna' ask me how it went, or are we just gonna sit here and enjoy the view?"

Art smiles to himself and takes a drink, "I enjoy the view when I have one. People are interesting. They do interesting things when you take the time to look."

"I see people everyday Art. They 'ain't that interesting. Dangerous yes. Disappointing yes. Predictable yes. Interesting… not a word I'd use."

"No? What about them?" Art nods to the young couple still going around arm in arm, "What do you see when you look at them?"

Hopper shakes his head smiling, "I know what you see, some bullshit like, the potential of young love and how warm and fuzzy it makes you feel, and who knows they could grow up to be like the fucking Waltons, and that gives you hope… something like that? Sorry to burst your bubble, but my guess is he's all nice and polite because he hasn't been able to get past first base… that'll change in time… when that kid gets a home run… well, I doubt he'll be so gentlemanly anymore." Hopper takes a swig of his beer and glances at his old friend. "You disagree?"

"I'm guessing it didn't go too well today." Art grins back. "You're wrong, all I see are two kids having fun. That's the difference Jack. I agree, he probably hasn't gotten past first base, and boy does he want to, but when he does get that home run… who knows." Art shrugs his shoulders, "maybe he will, maybe he won't. You could be right. He may have a shitty home. Be a violent little prick. Maybe his dad hits him and his old lady so that's what he'll do, 'cos that's all he knows. Sure, he'll be all sorry and regretful just like the times before, until he's not. But. Maybe he won't. You don't always have to take the cards you're given. When you see some shitty future, you're the one that's making a choice. You're choosing to see the world that way. I just choose to see it differently, and I think my way is better. They have a chance to write their own story Jack, same as you used to."

"Used to?"

"When you see the world as a shit-hole, it is a shit-hole. Maybe it is time to get out, do something different. I worry about you Jack."

"You amaze me Art. You of all people."

"Why? Because of what happened to Jade? It's because of what happened I think like this."

"And what the fuck would I do? The world sure as hell doesn't need another skate ring, maybe I'll come and work for you."

"No chance. I'm not having your sorry ass hanging around here, I don't have enough customers as it is without you scaring them away with your unbridled optimism." Art pulls out another beer and hands one to Hopper. "So, what happened, they can your ass?"

"Psychiatric evaluation."

Art can barely contain himself, even the teenagers stop for a moment to look at the shaking body of the old man, as Art laughed himself into convulsions.

"Jesus Christ, Art, you're gonna give yourself a heart attack calm the fuck down. It's not that funny." Hopper can't help it, against his better judgment he starts to laugh along, what the hell! It is kinda' funny after all. Him, Jack Hopper, the original bad ass having to go for therapy. Whatever they find isn't going to be pretty.

"I'm sorry, I shouldn't laugh." Sobs Art, dabbing at his eyes, "you of all people. But you know what Jack? This could be the best thing that's ever happened to you, seriously. Look around and tell me how many of us make old bones? I'm glad I got out when I did. It took the love of a good woman to show me the way, and as sure as shit' ain't Shinola, you can't do it on your own. I know there are those amongst us that deserve to have their balls cut off, and rightly so. But there are some out there doing good work, trying hard, making it happen. Who knows, if you stop being such a miserable prick long enough, you might even get laid! You can't save everyone Jack."

"I guess not, but I'm not so sure it's the best thing that's ever happened to me. You remember those twin hookers I told you about – now that was the best thing that ever happened to me. And you're right, I know we can't save everyone, but I thought we got paid to at least try."

# 17.

Inside, outside, upside down! The animal is awake. The animal is dreaming. The animal floats adrift in a sea of its own making. The images are real but reflect a past that never happened, an imprint of an echo, something wanted not had. The desire is as genuine as the need for satisfaction, an itch that cannot be scratched. In this place, the animal is king. In this place, the animal is free to roam and do as it pleases. No longer held by the body, the mind, free to wander, conjures up what it wants and takes it. Satisfaction guaranteed.

The girl is there too, bound and gagged, the man is gone, only you remain. You see the marks on the girl's body, primitive childlike daubs designed to keep you away, pathetic, like the man you once were. There's a noise, ever alert, your senses in overdrive, you lick your teeth. Now real and feel them taper to a point, your jaw muscles ache, you want to, need to, bite so badly. They have come, you knew they would. The door breaks, and you retreat to the shadows to watch the intruder from the dark.

The intruder is with the girl, crouching down, his torch cuts the darkness as he swings the beam. You see him, eyes wide and darting scared. There is something else, not fear, not for him, coiled like a spring, the man is ready. There is something familiar. You move closer to look him in the eye and say what? *Do you know me? Do you understand me? I know you do because I recognize you brother. I have been waiting,* Cain to your Able. You growl and look into his eyes while you catch your breath. He isn't a man, any more than you are. He knows you in an instant, a reflection looking back. You see the glint of recognition in his eyes, you are the same, and you pounce. There is a blinding flash. Only this time he misses. This time the bullet doesn't take away your face, this time it is your turn. You fall on him; razor-sharp teeth plunge into his neck. Flesh yields as you tear and gnash. Bathed in blood, you howl. The other men enter the room, slow and clumsy, eyes unaccustomed to the dark. In full flight, you pounce from one to another, ripping, tearing, and biting, crimson fountains paint the room. The metallic coppery taste of them quenches your thirst and fans the fire in your heart.

The body in the tank relaxes, more than just energy spent, and you know there is another just like you. Your twin brother, as the sticky red blood pools at your feet.

# PART 2

# 18.

Hopper is waiting. Hopper is bored. Hopper is being watched. He doesn't like it. It makes him feel uneasy. It makes him feel like a suspect. When he first came in, he noticed the camera mounted in the far corner of the waiting room, where the wall meets the ceiling. He assumed it was for security reasons, but now not so sure, like a rat in a cage under observation. He'd heard of behavioral tests, often used by top-level companies when hiring executives or managers. The aim: to observe a potential applicants to find out how suited they were for the position. Under the scrutiny of a watchful psychologist, every choice made would be recorded and analyzed to gain an insight into their personality. What magazine they choose to read, did they do the crossword, look out the window, make polite conversation with a convenient plant, sit on their hands, fidget or shit in the trash can? All used to build a profile.

Was he just another guinea pig? Of course he was. He was there to be studied. The room is deliberately sparse, devoid of personality and comfort. A two-seater couch and single armchair with a coffee table between them overflowing with the usual out-of-date magazines one might find at a doctors or dentists. If he did nothing, would that be a black mark against him? Would the tabloid and magazine selection make him frivolous and superficial? The broadsheet, serious, intellectual? What if he made a paper hat from the crossword page? Would that indicate a disregard for other people's property or show him as a clown? He decided to stare back. He wanted them to know he knew. He wouldn't play along. Too smart for their games, and if he were wrong, they would be left with a very peculiar and boring security tape. That alone would be enough to question his sanity if it ever fell into the wrong hands. Damned if you do, damned if you don't!

Dr. Shelly was far from bored, watching Hopper was akin to watching flames in a fireplace or fish in a glass tank. Fascinating and hypnotic. She knew he knew, otherwise why stare back so intensely, but did he know she knew he knew? Most likely, she shook her head and smiled. He was going to be fun, she was glad he wouldn't disappoint, after all, it had taken her a while to secure him as her patient. It hadn't been easy. She had watched him through the eyes of Adam repeatedly, experiencing the same moment thing over and over, until there was nothing left to uncover, other than the understanding, she needed to see the world through his eyes to add balance. Adam and Jack Hopper were two sides of the same coin. Although another officer had been credited with the arrest of Adam, it hadn't taken her long to find out who he was. It hadn't come as a surprise that Hopper's mental health had deteriorated but it was a stroke of luck that he had been placed on administrative duties pending the results of his psychiatric evaluation to determine whether he was fit for duty. Apparently, he had a problem with authority—who would have thought! She had quietly pulled a few strings in the background so as not to make a noise, making sure he appeared as a referral, not a request.

How long had he been staring back, five minutes? No longer, more like ten. He had kept her attention for all that time by doing nothing, always the promise of something. When would he break? How would he break? Did she really want to find out? She had been looking forward to this moment ever since she had known him, albeit in a different reality. She took a moment to compose herself, first impressions were crucial, she couldn't afford to come across as a giddy registrar or fangirl. She had to appear professionally distant, containing her excitement at the possibility of a reunion between her Cain and Able. How would it be for them to meet, would they still recognize one another? The Adam of today was very different to the one Hopper had shot half his face off. And what of the beast inside? Shelly took a deep breath and exhaled before leaning forward and speaking into the intercom on her desk.

"Would you mind sending Detective Hopper in," she watched her receptionist enter the waiting room to let him know his time was up. Hopper took one last look at the camera and winked. *This may actually be fun*, she thought.

Meeting the man of your dreams was always going to be a nerve-wracking experience, but meeting the man of someone else's? Intoxicating for a voyeur, compelling for a participant. How often had it been said, don't meet your heroes in the flesh, they can only ever disappoint? She would play their first meeting as casual, she needed him to trust her, to know she was on his side, which would take time. Morality or ethics were a blurred line in the heat of the moment. Do the actions outweigh the result? Terrible deeds have been done in the name of what's right, good, and holy, read the history books, check the papers. She needed him to know she understood.

Hopper opened the door, he was bigger than she imagined or, rather Adam imagined, but then again, the mind does play tricks. "Detective Hopper, please come in. May I call you Jack." Shelly extended her hand with a warm smile. Little things count, who shakes whose hand first can make or break a meeting, take control, take charge.

"Jack's fine," Hopper replied, unsmiling, "Shelly, right?"

Not doctor, just Shelly, *interesting*, she thought and made a mental note. "Shelly will be fine."

Hopper took in her office, the same beige decor as the waiting room, walls lined with bookshelves stacked with heavy leather-bound volumes, a couple of framed prints of inkblots. He'd heard about those. Something about the patterns that revealed the sort of person you were. All he saw were inkblots and wondered what that meant. The far side of the room had been dressed to be warmer and housed the obligatory couch and armchair, a setup one might come to expect in any mental health professional's office. The sight depressed him; it was a place he never thought he'd end up. The shrinks couch, babbling about his childhood. Others yes, him no. *Stay alert Jack*, he told himself, *you tell them what you really think, and they'll lock you up for sure.* He took the seat in front of her desk, deciding to keep it business like. The large window behind her overlooked the grounds of the hospital; he noticed a couple of what he assumed to be patients shuffling about the rose garden.

"Nice view, keeping an eye on the nut jobs?" He nodded towards the window.

"We prefer not to use the term *nut job*. I prefer the more clinical terms like *fruit loop, basket case* or just plain *loony.*" Shelly kept her tone as deadpan as she could muster, it almost raised a smile from Hopper.

"Maybe they're the ones who've got it right, and it's everyone else who's crazy." He replied, trying to sound nonchalant.

"Not sure I share your point of view. Usually, if I see someone shitting in their own hand I don't tend to think, *hey, now that's a good idea*! Why don't we make ourselves more comfortable Jack, it's not an interview?" Shelly moved to the opposite side of the room, taking a seat in the armchair and flipped open a notebook gesturing to the couch. Jack winced, it wasn't where he wanted to be. *Did she just smile*, he thought? *She's enjoying this, playing games.* He couldn't help himself, against his better judgment he found himself smiling. That was a funny crack about *shitting in your hand*, besides, she was a lot easier on the eye than expected which was a pleasant bonus. Hopper took a seat on the couch.

"What happens now? I tell you about my childhood?" He asked

"If you like. Although I thought maybe we could get to know each other a little better first before we get into the really heavy stuff."

Hopper folded his arms. "What do you want to know?"

*Defensive.* "Ok, let's start with: why do you think you're here?"

"Come on Doc, we both know why I'm here."

"I'm not sure *we* do. I assume you think it's because of what happened with Michael Watts?"

Hopper shrugged, resigned to his fate. Shelly smiled; she was used to patient hostility. Most didn't necessarily agree with their diagnosis or the reasons why they were there in the first place: *It wasn't me, it was them. I was driven to it. It's not my fault, they had it coming, I just did what anyone would have done in my situation,* were often the overarching sentiments. She had hoped Hopper was different and felt a little twang of disappointment. Still, early days. *Give a little, get a lot more back,* she knew the tricks of the trade on how to gain a patient's trust. Appear open, stay closed. Be objective but empathize. She decided to change track. "I understand how this might appear to you; I get it I really do. You saved the little girl, yet here you are. Knowing what could have happened, the tragedy you prevented, and this..." she took a moment to indicate her room, "this is how they repay you?"

Questioning the authority that sent him here helped position Shelly closer to his side of the fence, Hopper shifted in his seat and changed his body posture as she continued, "I don't blame you. I wouldn't want to be here either. Honestly, I'd be feeling pretty resentful if I was in your shoes." Her performance was bang on target; an off-hand criticism of the department provided her with just enough of an *'in'*. Hopper: tough, misunderstood, the end outweighs the means. The man clearly had a moral code of his own, did it matter there were casualties? Most probably not, collateral damage was part of life. It hadn't hurt either that she had allowed the top button of her blouse to pop open. "I'll tell you what Jack, let's even it up a little. There must be things you'd like to know about me?"

Hopper was concentrating on looking at her eyes, he was aware of the gape in her blouse and could make out just the slightest hint of lace behind. *Stay in control remain focused* he told himself, *but she was right, he had saved the girl, and this is how they repaid him, what if she'd died, what then?* He knew he made them look bad. But he got results, hence why he was here. Had they fired him, the press would have had a field day. Instead, they saw him as a dinosaur, police brutality, excessive force, all unspoken traits of the job once considered fair game, now no longer tolerated. Yes, he was old school, but *what the fuck did any of them know? Tell that to the victims and the victim's families. What would he like to know? Does she have a boyfriend? Did she fuck on a first date? Does she really think she can handle him, prod around in the places he's been, and still sleep at night? Can she handle it, him?* He doubted it. "Ok." He smiled back, *let's see.* "How long have you been doing this?"

"Almost twenty years."

"And what makes you think you're suited for this."

*Because my father chopped up fifteen people and stitched them together in different ways, because I'm worried, I might be just like him, because I've spent a lot of time inside Adam's head and I really want to get to know the real you, not what Adam thinks about you,* was what she wanted to say, but didn't. "Because I'm a fully trained medical doctor as well as psychiatric clinician and have over sixteen years' experience in the field. I recognize our actions are often symptomatic of something deeper. And, if we're lucky, that's what I'm hoping to find."

*My actions are symptomatic!! Holy shit, I'll tell you what they're symptomatic of, I see a grown man wanting to rape a little kid. My symptoms are I want to tear that sick fuck a new one.* "Maybe it's the system and not me. Have you considered that?"

*Oh, it's you alright.* "It's a possibility. Why not?" Shelly smiled back.

*You really think I'm that easy?* "So, blame it on the system. Does that go for everyone?"

*Smart.* "Do you think so?"

"And what if I told you, my twenty-five years' experience tells me, a sick fuck's a sick fuck. If it's the system, then the system doesn't work. Sometimes it's a kindness to put them down." Hopper, being deliberately controversial, waited for a reaction he didn't get. Shelly stared back impassively, waiting for him to continue. "You think I was wrong. Doing what I did?"

*Straight to the point.* "You think you were doing Watt's a kindness?"

Hopper shrugged, "Maybe, he's never going to stop. Sure, it's a kindness of sorts, maybe deep down he wants to but can't, and has to rely on someone like me. You thought about that? Or are you going to keep answering a question with another question?"

Shelly paused to take stock, she wanted to make sure he knows she's considering her answer, even if it's a predictable thing to say, "I have thought about that, but it doesn't matter what I think, what matters is what you think."

"It matters to me."

He was smart, does the end justify the means? He wanted her to be definitive. *Yes,* she was just like the rest of them. *No,* maybe worse. Goading her into a confrontation, knowing if they started diametrically opposed to each other, future sessions would be a waste of time.

Shelly narrowed her eyes and leaned towards him. "And if I say no? No, you were wrong to do what you did. What then? I'm just another cog in the machine that doesn't understand you, that will never understand what it's like to get your hands dirty. And I mean *really dirty*. To wade through that sort of pain and despair every single day? To know that people like Watts will keep doing what they do, because that's not who they are but what, and they will never ever stop. We save one girl today, but what about tomorrow, and the next day and the day after that? That I'm ignorant to the needs of the victims, championing the rights of people like Watts over theirs. And if I say yes? What does that make me? Complicit? Will you feel vindicated? At ease with yourself? Or will you see it as patronizing, telling you what you want to hear or what I think you want to hear, which is by far much worse since it indicates I'm arrogant enough to assume I know what makes you tick before even saying hello? Saying yes, doesn't get me on your side Jack, it just makes me look shallow. I don't think it's that simple."

Hopper leaned back. "That's the problem right there. What would you have done doc? Tried to reason with him? Talk him to death and lay some psychobabble bullshit on him, by which time the girl would be dead?"

"You're asking me to condone torture."

Hopper swung his legs of the couch. "I'm asking you to recognize it for what it is. I'm asking you, do you think me beating up that sick fuck was the right thing to do? Knowing that time was running out and he knows how to play the system? Was a beating worth saving the girls life for?"

The answer was obvious, of course she considered a little girl's life was worth more than Watts. Who in their right mind wouldn't? That wasn't the point. Shelly was going to lose him unless she could create some common ground, but refused to be corralled into moralizing the situation. She needed to remain objective. It was clear that for Jack Hopper, the world was black or white. You were with him or against him, he was intent on driving a wedge between them, creating a gulf so deep it would be impossible to cross, self-sabotaging before they even had a chance to begin.

"Just so we're clear. What you're saying is; you know Watts so well you can predict his actions and that in no way would he be prepared to compromise himself, because that would mean be admitting his guilt, right?"

"It's a simple question doc, you're being evasive. There's no argument. It's a simple yes or no answer. We could have played twenty questions all night. Eventually, we would have to let him go, by which time she'd be dead, if you can't see that I doubt we have much to talk about."

The wedge was going in deeper, no compromise. She felt stupid allowing herself to be so easily boxed in but knew she could turn it to her advantage. If she wanted to get to know him, develop a relationship and see the same world from his perspective, he needed to trust her. This was far bigger than just him. Take your time, he can wait, build, she already had her answer. It was obvious, who in their right mind would say no, the least she could do was build the tension.

"Then I suppose the answer would have to be. Yes."

"Yes?" Hopper wasn't sure he'd heard her right, this was the first time that anyone had been prepared to listen, to understand his point of view, maybe this wasn't going to be so bad after all. "To be clear, you're saying Yes. Yes, you don't think what I did was wrong or, yes, what I did was wrong?"

"I want to be quite explicit on this Jack, no grey areas. In this case, yes, I believe the end justified the means. With the right kind of provocation and given how much time you had. Yes, as you say, there was little choice. Extreme circumstances require us to behave in extreme ways."

Hopper had been convinced that this was going to be a waste of time, a precursor to him being fired. *Rip the Band-Aid off, let's just get it over with.* Perhaps he'd been too hasty. "So, you're saying, you think what I did was ok?"

"I'm not saying it was ok, I'm saying I understand the situation you were in, coupled with your experience and knowledge of the man, you made a decision. The only way to get the information you needed in the shortest amount of time, especially as you say, time was running out, was through violence and intimidation. You needed Watts to believe that there was a real possibility of being beaten to death unless he told you what you wanted. He needed to be in fear for his life, otherwise, he wouldn't have given up information that would prove his guilt. In this situation, yes, I think your actions were justified. Was it ok? Questionable. Ethical? Absolutely not. But I understand there are times when ethics must take a back seat. The end justifies the means, right?" She took note of Hopper's change in posture and expression, he was beginning to listen, to open up. "But I do have one question… more of an observation really."

"Go on."

"You didn't stop."

Hopper knitted his eyebrows together. "What do you mean? You already said yes."

"And I believe that." Shelly crossed her legs, allowing a little more thigh to show. "You needed him to believe he was in fear for his life, yes? That whatever he would face by admitting his guilt wasn't worth dying for, and as you pointed out, he knew the system." She waited for Hopper to nod. "But you beat him unconscious," Shelly glanced down at her notes for effect, "it says he was unconscious when…" *turn the page, heighten the tension.* She loved to be dramatic when she had the opportunity, "…Richardson walked in. Unless Watts fainted at that exact moment, I'm assuming he lost consciousness as a result of what happened."

"So?" Hopper felt uncomfortable, the couch was too low, the room too hot and what the fuck was her point, he had felt for a moment she understood him.

"Let's agree your actions were entirely justified in order to get the information, right, we agree on that?"

"Yes."

"Which you got. And as a result, were able to save the girl's life?"

"Yes, so, so?" Hopper could feel himself becoming irritated by her line of questions.

"My point is Detective. Watts told you what he knew whilst he was still conscious, yet he was unconscious." Shelly waited for her point to sink in, "you had the information whilst he could still speak, yet you continued to beat him," *turn the page, pause,* "until he was unconscious," *refer to notes, pause for more effect,* "suffering severe facial injuries, broken jaw, nose, fractured cheekbone, eye socket, missing teeth, top and lower," *pause, look up continue,* "there's more if you like?"

"I was there. I think you've made your point." Hopper stood; he didn't like being manipulated. "It's easy for people like you, high up in your tower looking down on the poor fucks out there passing judgment, writing up your little theories, you have no idea what's really happening, in here." Hopper tapped the side of his head. Art was wrong. This was always going to be a waste of time. He should have bailed and let things take their natural course. He'd get a job in security, do some private work. He'd get by. Who gives a shit! Watts was off the streets for good, if that was his legacy, then it wasn't a bad one. He would be just one more casualty of an ever-expanding broken system favoring criminals. Why not do them a favor and get it over with. "You know what doc? You write what you want to write. For a moment there, I thought you could see things from my perspective, but you go ahead. You tell them what they want to hear. I'm just as bad as them, let's not waste any more tax dollars. I don't want to be here any more than you do. You want to know if I regret what I did? Not a chance, when I think back to smashing his face in, I don't regret it, I think, *good fucking job*, he got what he deserved, and you know what else? I'd do it again.'

Hopper was on a roll, and it felt good, what did he really have to lose? He was out anyway so why not take the opportunity to say what he really thought.

"You want to know about human behavior? What makes us, us? Our imagination that's what, our ability to get creative. You think you know me; people like me? You have no idea how far down I go. Or are you one of those weak-kneed liberals that lights a candle for some sick fuck on death row? What about the victim? Who lights a candle for them? We've become so caught up in making sure we're doing the right thing we end up with murderers and rapists on TV as God dammed fucking celebs! Oooh, don't offend anyone lest we step on their rights. Rights! There are some out there that don't deserve to be treated like the rest of us, because they're not like the rest of us. I know what side of the line I stand. You go ahead. Write your bullshit report, I haven't got time for this."

Hopper could feel his heart beating faster, pulse racing, proud and exhilarated by his rant, he looked back at Shelly expecting… what? She remained seated, staring at her notepad. Hopper's outburst had been impressive, he was right, there was nothing more creative than cruelty. Humanity's capacity to continuously re-invent methods to deliver pain was genuinely inventive. You only had to think of the number one religion in the world to know that.

Shelly calmly closed her notebook and spoke in calm, quiet tones. "We have a man here, an investment broker…" Shelly looked up briefly to make sure Hopper was listening, "ex-investment broker," she corrected, "good job, six-figure salary, probably felt invincible, living in his tower as you might say. Predictably, he lost his job during the GFC. Familiar story. Mounting debts. Expensive wife. House, private schools. It's a boring, repetitive story. I'm sure you can imagine. Eventually, the strain was too much, a failed marriage, house on the market, kids taken out of school. He felt ashamed. Of course, it wasn't his fault, but that didn't matter, should have kept a little back, planned for a rainy day! However, his luck was about to change, he got a phone call, or rather _the_ phone call. All his problems were about to go away, but his four-year-old son whom he'd just picked up from the overpriced kinder-garden he could no longer afford was screaming so loudly in the car when he took the call, he was unable to hear or talk, instead of calling back he pulled his son from the back seat and threw him off the bridge they had stopped on." _Don't look up continue, remain impartial,_ "A woman, forty-two, who, in front of her children, smashed her ninety-year-old mother's head in with an iron. She used to make a clicking sound with her false teeth had been doing it for years until one day she complained her daughter was making too much noise whilst eating. We have a young man who kept the severed heads of his sexual conquests in the fridge so that he could continue to engage in fellatio with them. Whilst another preferred to cut out and eat the vaginas of his victims…" *Good story to pause on. Shocking. Ugly. The use of the word vagina coming from a woman, especially to someone like Hopper. Look up, remain calm, stay objective, give him a little smile and continue.* "We have a young man who'd been systematically abused by foster parents in whose care he'd been placed. When he was old enough, he shot them both with the gun they used to terrorize… sorry sodomize him. He cut up their bodies and fed them to the family dog. A Labrador. They'll literally eat anything. The foster parents could only be identified through the dog's stool samples!" Shelly met his gaze. "Are they all undeserving of our understanding? The trouble with lines Jack, is they become too easy to cross and then what?"

"Ok I get it. Congratulations, you get to deal with the shit of humanity as well."

Shelly kept her tone quiet and controlled. "What interests me Jack, is for Watts to tell you what you needed to know," *bring him back, keep him on track,* "he had to believe you were capable of inflicting such terrible pain… even within the walls of the police station, so much so he was prepared to confess. You asked me, did I think it was the right thing to do, or would I do the same thing if I were you? Given the situation, your knowledge of the man and the limited options available. Yes, I do. Would I have done it? In my experience, thinking and doing are two different things. But let me ask you a question. Do you think anyone else <u>could</u> have done what you did? Watts is a deluded schizophrenic and seasoned criminal who knows the system inside and out. It's fair to say that he would most likely see through any good cop bad cop pantomime and no doubt would have worked things to his advantage. Not you, he was genuinely terrified enough to admit what he did. It's because of who you are, not in spite of, that you were able to save the girl. But what's interesting to me, is, you didn't stop. That's why you're here. Not because of what you did, but because of what you didn't. He told you, but you wouldn't or were unable to stop. I'd like to know why, wouldn't you?"

# 19.

The zoo wasn't what Adam thought it would be. A sad and lonely place for visitors and animals alike, separated by bars. Bars on the inside. Bars on the outside. Adam was finding the free world was just a bigger prison and felt intimidated by the scale. He had started out with good intentions, hoping to make friends, but found being considered 'normal' was a bigger challenge than anticipated. He had initially been introduced to Fisher, the man who ran the zoo, by Shelly when she first took him there on his first day. *We'll look after him, don't you worry*, he'd said, patting him on the head as if it were his first day at school, and like so many other first-timers had wanted to run after Shelly when she'd left, screaming for her not to abandon him. But time has a way or normalizing. Fisher largely ignored him from the moment Shelly left, giving him menial jobs to do, *scrub this, wash that, pick that up, put that down*, the list was endless, but Adam was happy with the work. He had started to know the animals and they him and had begun to understand their personalities. The chimpanzees at first seemed like cheeky exhibitionists, clowns always ready to entertain, but after time, Adam had discovered they were far smarter than the crowd gave them credit for. They knew how to manipulate an audience, to get what they wanted, carefully marshaled by the alpha male in the group. Adam, always careful to acknowledge him first, had developed a kind of mutual respect between them.

The Hyenas, curious and sociable, always ready for a laugh, were something of a surprise, highly excitable and vicious their laughter hid a quiet anger. The cougar, solitary and moody, seldom ventured out of its lair, secretive in nature, it avoided the gawping strangers that stopped outside its cage, Adam made sure to give it the privacy it craved. However, Adam had his favourite. The Canadian timber wolf, the largest of its kind, intimidating to workers and visitors alike, even behind bars. Dressed in a heavy black coat, flecked with orange and grey the fashion-conscious would kill for and had, she radiated a grace and dignity that was lost on her audience. A careful snarl, the baring of her teeth was enough to remind them who she was, and had it not been for the bars between, she would be only too willing to show. While most would avoid eye contact, fearing the intensity of her stare would linger beyond the waking hours fuelling nightmares for days after, Adam was captivated by her. Her unblinking yellow eyes made brighter by the contrast of her black coat would hold him in their stare until they were no longer separate. Joined by an invisible thread, Adam could feel her loneliness, knowing what it was to be displaced, a common bond suggesting she knew more about him than Shelly. She could look beyond the outside and deep within. She didn't judge, didn't recoil, a quiet acknowledgment and a shared secret they were both quiet on the outside, raging on the in.

Adam had made it part of his daily routine to stop by her cage and feed her the scraps he managed to steal from the kitchens. Their friendship had grown so much that she had, on occasion, granted him permission to stroke the soft hair under her jowl. It was a thrill to feel her warm breath and the weight of her broad head, knowing that within less than a second, she could tear his arm from its socket but chose not to. It was the only time when Adam felt truly alive, his heartbeat matching hers.

Leanne Bonelle felt the confinement of her circumstance: single mum, zero education, zero work experience, zero references, zero skills, and zero paychecks. Feeling the wrong side of thirty-nine, she was too close to her sell-by date to turn a profit for a pimp and had been cut loose years ago. She took up too much real estate reserved for a profitable younger, firmer, fitter, and tighter models, it was a buyer's market after all. Her only option was an independent streetwalker or to find her own previously undiscovered patch. Like anyone else, she had a right to eat and provide for her son if she was careful to avoid the invisible territorial lines that marked out whose patch was whose.

Leanne blamed her child more than gravity for her fading looks and sagging skin but loved him regardless. He was the purest thing in her life, and she would fight tooth and nail to make sure he was looked after. He was a constant source of worry, his big round face, too honest and open. He had come into the world giving. His affection for life was a light that burned bright for all, never diminished through time or the insults thrown his way. Leanne wasn't thankful for much but had reason to be grateful for his ignorance and saw his disability as a shield to his reality. She was his protector and mother, with a capacity for insults and violence that would put a navy to shame. For Leanne, the world was too real. Being the mother of invention, Necessity had made her look far and wide off the well-trodden path until she had found her place. Her patch. The zoo. And her son Anton loved it.

It had been overcast and grey, the threat of rain never too far away. The slim pickings still available looking for a discount had already left the streets and gone into places she couldn't follow, especially with Anton in tow. School holidays, the bane of the single parent. Seasonal trade and vacation care, the curse of every solo businesswoman, but what can you do? Unless she made some money quickly, the electric meter in their shabby apartment wouldn't last. The zoo was only a couple of bus stops from where they lived, and Anton loved animals which, if she were lucky, he could keep himself amused for hours. If she picked up a trick or two, it meant she had somewhere safe(*ish*) to keep him occupied.

What started as pure bad luck, wrong place, wrong time, had turned out surprisingly well, and she had landed on her feet or, more precisely, knees. She had tried to sneak in through the fence, telling Anton it was a big adventure, all part of the game they were playing. Fisher, the zoo manager, had caught them red-handed. But life's a deal, you take what you get and use it the best way you know how. Leanne instinctively recognized what sort of man Fisher was. Slovenly, overweight, clinging to the last strands of hair plastered over a greasy scalp, but above all else, an opportunist. A mirror to the zoo, managing it how he managed himself, out of shape and unkempt. She suggested there were ways in which she could pay the entrance fee in kind. *There has to be some kind of arrangement we could come to*, she told him, *he wouldn't regret it*. She was clean and safe and came with an assortment of flavored condoms. The bulge in his trousers sealed the deal. It hadn't taken long to set up an informal working relationship. She could ply her trade at the zoo, provided he was fully serviced whenever he felt like it, and he felt like it a lot. In return and a safe place to work, he introduced her to several friends and skimmed a little for himself, *a finder's fee*, as he put it, although he never considered himself her pimp, he came close. For her part, she got free tickets and a patch off the radar and was mostly left alone. The convenience suited Fisher's laziness, he didn't have to go far when the urge struck, sex on tap. Her looks may have been on the downward side of the hill, but she had only just started her descent. For Fisher, who had already made it to the bottom long ago, she was a step up. He was grateful for what he could get. He was cheap, and most working girls charged a little extra to compensate for his looks, it was a match made in paradise.

Their arrangement had been working well, the zoo had become a day-care for Anton when Mummy had to earn, and he seemed to have brightened considerably now that mum had a job at the zoo! Today was a good day. Two tricks down, and it wasn't even lunchtime, a quick hand job behind the burger stall and a blow job by the gift shop. She had left Anton by the penguin enclosure; it wasn't much of an exhibit, a concrete tank no larger than a domestic pool sunk into the ground. Visitors could look over the black metal railings and watch a tatty parade of penguins jump in from one side, swim to the next, hop out, waddle back and repeat. Social and fun-loving by nature, the birds had little to do but squabble and dive for cigarette butts thrown in by callous onlookers, but they hypnotized Anton. He saw what others didn't; the grace and beauty of their glide as they cut through the water and giggled at their Chaplain-like gait. His mother told him not to move; she was *working* somewhere. He had no idea what *jobs* his mother did at the zoo, but whatever they were, he knew they were important, as she would often disappear at a moment's notice to *work*. Still, he was grateful that whatever crisis she attended didn't usually take too long.

Unfortunately, the pool needed to be cleaned because of the cigarette butts, which meant the exhibit was closing. A thin, wiry man had announced to a non-existent crowd there were better exhibits elsewhere than an empty pool. Never one to question authority, Anton did as he was told. Besides, since his mother *worked* at the zoo, she no doubt would already know this, so Anton wandered off.

Leanne was *working* at the food court, her favorite haunt, or rather, at the back of the food court out of sight, hidden between two industrial bins. The manager of the doughnut franchise was taking his well-earned break before the midday rush. She knew how to bring him off quicker than the ambitious half an hour he paid for and wondered if he would be willing to give both her and Anton doughnuts on the house by way of a bonus if she did a good job. His stomach gently bounced on the bridge of her nose as she knelt, trying to ignore the smell of fried food, it was making her hungry, and it wasn't easy with her mouth full. Gently cupping his balls, she gave them a quick squeeze and inserted her finger in his anus simultaneously. He came immediately.

"Never had that done before." Doughnut man grunted, his ruddy face even more flushed than before, "maybe we could make this a regular thing," he grinned, "you make sure you come around for a house special, on me."

Leanne checked her watch, not bad for just over five minutes work, and dinner is already taken care of. "Maybe we will, maybe we will," she smiled, trying to sound coy and seductive while wiping her chin. Repeat business was always good for the pocket and now the belly. It made him shudder, maybe not too regular, he thought. Leanne didn't notice, her mind already drifting back to Anton and how much he liked the crispy creams with the extra frosting and custard.

It hadn't taken Anton long to get lost, and he was starting to panic. The crowds weren't particularly large, they never were at the zoo, but he felt confused and disorientated. He asked several people in uniform where his mother might be, but no one seemed to know who she was. He tried to explain she worked there, but they just laughed and told him to get lost. He wanted to scream, to start crying or hit something, but he didn't want to disappoint her. After all, it was his fault, he hadn't done what he was supposed to, and most likely, she would be angry. She never liked it, if she had to come looking for him, if he were a blubbering mess, it would be far worse.

"Are you lost?"

The question snapped Anton out of himself. Looking up at where the voice came from, he blinked into the sun. The man was a shadow, with his head haloed by the sun he resembled one the people featured in the big book he liked to look at when his mum was busy with her TV programs. They always looked like they were helping others. *He must have come to help.* Anton thought and felt his fears slowly side away.

"Are you alone?" Asked the man. Anton shook his head; he couldn't see the man's face, but his voice sounded kind.

"My mum works here. She'll be worried." Anton sniffed back.

"That's a coincidence." Said the man crouching down in front of him. "So do I, see." Adam pointed to the zoo logo on his shirt. "Do you know what she does here?" Anton shook his head. "That's ok. Can you tell me her name?" Adam gently placed a hand on the boy's shoulder, "How about we see if we can find out where she is? My name's Adam by the way. What's yours?" Anton didn't really want to tell the young man his name, his mother had always told him not to talk to anyone and was pretty sure he should have stayed where he was supposed to. But looking up at the young man, he figured that since they worked together, it would be ok if they went to look for her and slid his hand in Adams as they headed off to find where she would be working.

Leanne wasn't happy. Leanne was worried. Leanne was anxious, and Leanne was scared, which meant Leanne was getting angry. She didn't cope well with stress, she never had. It was the reason she flunked out of high school. She hadn't been able to get a job, let alone keep one, and why she took what she referred to as her *medicine.* The only precious thing in her life wasn't where he was supposed to be. Why had he moved? Had he been taken? She had said in no uncertain terms, "DO NOT MOVE FROM THIS SPOT." Why couldn't he do what he was told, life was hard enough without him making it worse. SO WHY THE FUCK COULDN'T HE JUST DO AS HE WAS TOLD? Her anger built with each searching step. She didn't have time for this, and time was money. There were people to service and medicine to buy. She also wanted to be home by four, her favorite soap was on, *The Blue Code*. Now that Maryanne was pregnant by Dr Jack, he wouldn't be able to marry her best friend Lacy, who may or may not be responsible for the death of Aunt Emma? Lacy was finally gonna' get hers. Leanne's imagination was in gear and had already left the driveway. The paranoia that accompanied her *medicine*, never too far away, began to curl its icy fingers around her spine. In her world, abuse, depravity, and deviancy were commonplace. She knew men who would pay big bucks for an opportunity to corrupt someone like Anton. Not on her watch, not this time, she'll find who took her boy and make them pay. No one fucks with Leanne Bonelle, at least not unless they pay first.

Anton was feeling better and was back to his happier self. It was odd that no one seemed to know who his mother was and doubly odd she never had to wear a uniform like everyone else. Maybe it was a secret *job*, and she was like a spy. If that was the case, then he'd just blown her cover and she'd be doubly mad. Adam was on his way back with two ice creams from the pretty ice cream seller with the black lipstick and funny hair. When they'd asked her about his mother, she'd said she had an idea as to who that might be but had no idea where she might be. When Anton had asked what sort of job she does, she'd found that very funny and started giggling and suggested they go and ask Fisher who was the boss. Maybe she wasn't a spy after all.

Anton was feeling confused about his mother, having made up his mind to find out exactly what she did, so that if he ever got lost again, he'd know where to go. In the meantime, he was happy to hang out with Adam. He knew a lot about the animals, and they all appeared to like him, especially the dangerous ones, which was far more fun. Adam told him they were his favorites, he certainly seemed to be theirs and had promised to show him the wolf. They stopped momentarily at the monkey house on their way. Adam kept him happy and distracted by the stories he told, especially how sometimes if someone in the crowd was nasty or mean, the monkeys would throw their poo at them. Anton thought that was hilarious and secretly hoped someone would be nasty today so he could watch. Of course, he wouldn't dream of doing anything unpleasant to a monkey, but he also knew that if you were prepared to throw a cigarette butt at a penguin, you probably wouldn't have a problem being mean to a monkey, so watch out. But much to Anton's disappointment, they left the monkeys to their excited chattering and eventually made their way to the timber wolf.

"She's my favorite," said Adam as he crouched down in front of the cage.

Anton was amazed at its size and how its eyes seemed to glow as it recognized Adam and walked towards them.

"What's her name?" Anton asked.

Adam had never thought to give her a name, he considered it demeaning for them both, taking a sense of ownership. It wasn't that kind of relationship. "I don't know, she doesn't have one."

"Can I stroke her?"

Adam considered it for a moment, it had taken almost two months for them to become acquainted, and it was only recently she'd allowed him to stroke her, he wondered what would happen if he let the little boy poke his hand through the bars, but then thought about how disappointed Shelly would be if he lost his job, "I'm not so sure that would be a good idea," he said.

Anton was undeterred and was about to reach out towards the wolf when they heard Leanne.

Fuelled by anger, one thought pounding through Leanne's head, driving her forward, *I'm going to kill him when I find him. I'm going to kill him when I find him.* Although in a place filled with dangerous animals, she had never once entertained the thought that there was any real risk as she watched on in horror as Anton began to stick his hand through the cage bars and screamed.

The noise was palpable and penetrating. Anton immediately withdrew his tiny hand. The wolf licked its jowls and glanced up at Adam who shrugged back. Relief turned to rage, quickening Leanne's steps as she surged towards them. Paranoia and anxiety mixed with a shot of aggression sent her brain into overdrive, any rational thoughts drowned out by the chaos inside. She needed the zoo and couldn't afford anyone or anything to jeopardize it, let alone feed her kid to it. "What are you doing to my kid?" She shrieked.

What few visitors that had been aimlessly meandering through the pitiful exhibits suddenly had something worth looking at, as Leanne rounded the corner full of fire and fury and snatched Anton by the wrist, far harder than intended, almost dislocating his shoulder.

"Careful!" Adam called out, instinctively reaching out to catch the boy before he fell. His concern was a trigger for a lifetime of anger. Reduced to doing tricks at the zoo to keep her and her son fed, housed, and clothed, and someone was telling *her* to be careful.

"Leave my fucking kid alone," she continued shouting, "I saw what you were doing," she turned to the crowd that had started to form for support, incensed by a whiff of pedophilia, "he was trying to feed my kid to the fucking dogs."

"I wasn't doing anything," Adam protested. Given her size, the blow was much harder than he thought her capable of, nor could he understand why? He had the situation under control and was looking after the boy, helping, doing the right thing, they even had ice creams, he had no intention of feeding the boy to the wolf.

Blinded by rage, Leanne couldn't see beyond the red mist that clouded her view; it was a look Adam recognized, although he would never tell Shelly. Leanne needed to hit something, someone. It no longer mattered why. All she ever wanted was to be a *normal* person, to live a *normal* life. This is what the world had done to her, and it wasn't fair. She'd never been given a break, someone else always taking her share and leaving her the crap, and now this! They had no idea what it took. No more. After years of living in a pressure cooker, the lid was finally off. No more. *Look at what you made me do, you did this,* she wailed at the world and the blows rained down.

Adam could only hear snippets of words and phrases snatched through the storm, though he got her intent. Adam wanted to hit back, catch her thin wrists, and bend them backwards so he could hear them snap. Drive his boot into her neck and twist her head so he could tear it free from her body. Instead, shielding himself from her blows, he felt time slow as he became aware of all things at once. The boy was crying and screaming, trying to pull his mother away. The woman, all twisted and ugly, a vitriolic spew of shrieking hatred, her spittle lightly splashing his face. He told the beast to stay away and focused on the child. Thank God for hands. Hands pulling, hands separating. The woman still kicking, pulled away, and held by the large man known as Jackson. Adam had met him only once, something to do with security, he would have been more at home swinging on a tire in one of the larger cages. The second pair of hands belonged to Fisher, who'd come running as soon as he'd heard the commotion. As a group, they were the most exciting exhibit at the zoo.

Leaning into Leanne's face, Fisher snapped at her and told her to *"shut the fuck up"* in no uncertain terms. He needed to disperse the crowd. Small as it was, people talk, and rumors start. The zoo, already on borrowed time, had no need to accelerate its demise, not to mention the few good things going on that didn't need this kind of attention.

"Ok, people, just a misunderstanding, shows over. But if you really want a show, we're feeding the Hyenas right about now." Fisher announced to the crowd, his grip tightening on Leanne's bony shoulders as he dug his thumb into her neck, she winced at the pain as it broke the fog and began to lift the clouds. "Are you fucking crazy?" He whispered harshly in her ear. "You stop this right now, or I'll feed you to the fucking dogs myself." Leanne recognized the menace in his voice and went quiet.

"I...I...I was only trying to help." Protested Adam, confused as to how something could have escalated so quickly.

"It's true mum," Anton whined, backing him up, "he was going to..." No one saw the slap coming or knew how Leanne had managed to wriggle herself free, but this time Anton had all the attention he could never want. Jackson grabbed her hands and pinned them to her back. Fisher leaned in closer so no one could hear him.

"You want to beat your kid? You take him home and you beat him there. But you don't come back here. Now, get your shit together and fuck off. If I see you around here again, I'll call the police. We're done here, you understand?"

Leanne jolted back, panic registering as the words sunk in. Surely, he didn't mean it, did he? Her jaw still ached from all the favors she'd given in the past. That had to count for something.

"I was just trying to help," continued Adam to no one but himself. "He was lost, there was no need to hit the kid."

"Help! I saw the whole thing, he was trying to feed my kid to that... that thing," Leanne shouted, pointing at the now receding wolf.

"I don't think she needs parental advice from a retard. She has one of her own." Grinned Jackson winking at Eve, the ice-cream seller, trying to share a joke she didn't find funny. He shrugged and turned his attention back to Fisher, "What cha' doing Fisher, messing around with a skank like her? I told you she was trouble. You need to get her the fuck gone before Frank gets wind of this. You know what he's like." Jackson said still holding onto Leanne as if he'd forgotten about her, trying to sound serious, which for Jackson was hard, given his peculiarly high voice for someone his size.

"He's no retard, you freak," Leanne snapped back, straightening up, doing her best to cling to the last vestiges of dignity. "I'm sorry Mr. Fisher, I was worried. I saw him, I saw him with my own two eyes, he had my little boy's hand through the bars of the cage and that thing was coming over to take a bite," she turned back to the crowd, appealing for corroboration, "you saw it, you saw what he was doing."

Fisher rolled his eyes as the crowd, unwilling to be drawn into an extended conversation with Leanne, began to look away. "Ok, ok, shows over, if anyone can give me their account, that would be helpful," he said, knowing no one would as they slowly began to drift. He turned his attention back to Leanne, "how about we just take a break for a while, eh? Let things cool down. It doesn't look like anyone else saw anything."

"A break!" Leanne snapped back indignantly, confused as to why she seemed to be the one in the wrong, terrified that her only source of income was about to be suddenly turned off. "I'm not so sure that would be a good idea, I think some people might be interested in where I've been working the past few months."

"My mum isn't going to lose her job, is she?" Anton piped up in between sobs. He didn't want to give his mum another reason to hurt him, "I won't do it again, I promise."

"Job?" Fisher asked. The last thing he wanted was anyone connecting her to him through the zoo. He also knew the sound of a veiled threat when he heard one. The police were bad enough, but if some of the pimps got wind of what he was doing, they'd make it personal, not to mention what Frank might say. Even Jackson and all his steroid-induced muscle wouldn't be able to help, just the thought of his name sacred him. Jackson was right. Frank wouldn't like the attention. *All good things come to an end*, he thought, or at the very least for a couple of weeks until the dust settled. He didn't trust Jackson not to say anything either, always looking for an opportunity to undermine him and look like the big man. "Maybe it's best you just go," he mumbled before nodding at Jackson, ignoring Leanne's pleading eyes. "Just get rid of her."

"Well, fuck you Fisher, you'll be sorry. You won't find anyone like me." Leanne called over her shoulder as Jackson manhandled her out of the zoo, Anton reluctantly following. Fisher watched her go in clothing that was too small, too tight, and far too inappropriate for daylight and felt a stirring in the loins. She was right, he wouldn't. *Why is there always someone waiting to fuck things up for me?*

"Mr. Fisher, I would never do that," Adam said, reminding Fisher he was still there, worried he may be the next person expelled from the zoo.

"You! You get back to work before I change my mind about you. You don't get paid to stand around gawking," he snapped back at Adam, who didn't get paid at all, but that was between him and the doc and their special arrangement. So far, the kid had proved to be comfortably lucrative; what had she called it? *Procedural integration*, a fancy way of saying free nut jobs for hire. The kicker being, he got paid instead! A tidy little side hustle he was keen to siphon into his own pocket. Adam may be from the funny farm, but he still represented hard cash to him. With Leanne gone, he'd already lost one source of income, he wasn't intending on losing another. Adam was lucky that he valued hard cash more, although he was starting to reconsider, maybe in a couple of weeks, he thought to himself.

Leanne shrugged Jackson off as he frogmarched her to the exit, clearly enjoying himself, doing his best to impress anyone who was bothered enough to look, no one did, no one cared. She knew she'd be wasting her time with a man like him, different if she was a boy with a tight ass, she thought. Fisher was predictable. She knew she'd be back, it was just time. Men like Fisher were driven by two things, what was in their pants and in their pocket. She'd be back, and when she was, she'd show that gormless idiot who took her kid a thing or two, and that was a promise. Claiming to be all innocent and such like, *I was helping, I got him an ice-cream,* she mocked. She knew the truth of him. She'd seen it, something in the eyes that can't hide. It had only been a moment and, yes, she could have been mistaken. Yes, it could have been her medicine or lack of. But it was there all right, something else looking back. Maybe for once in her life, she really had done the right thing and protected her son from something that was truly dangerous.

Commotion over, but still feeling rattled. Adam had been left on his own, even the ice cream girl had left. They all had better things to do. Not him. He picked up his bucket and shovel and went over the previous events, it had happened so quickly, he had only been trying to help, do the right thing, he would never have let the wolf take a bite. He closed his eyes and sighed, thinking about Leanne. A grotesque mask, screaming and spitting abuse through yellowed teeth. Hands hitting, clawing, and scratching, her thin body in stretched leathered skin pulled taught, fuelled by rage, neatly packaged in teenage clothes too small. He would have liked to have reached out and smashed her head against the bars of the cage and fed her to the wolf. He could feel his heartbeat quicken as he imagined strong teeth chomping down on a brittle neck, and something inside began to stir, a closed eye now open. He started on the breathing exercises Shelly taught him, through the mouth, out through the nose, count to three, and repeat. He could feel himself becoming calmer. That was not the way, there was the boy to think of. No matter how disgusting the boy's mother was, he had a right to grow up with one. She clearly loved the boy otherwise, why so angry. It was just a misunderstanding, after all, best not dwell on bad thoughts, he decided. The animal disagreed.

# 20.

Adam was sitting crossed legged in front of the wolf's cage. Bars on three sides, a concrete slab at the rear with an alcove cut into it, that was jokingly referred to as its lair. There wasn't much in the way of stimulation for the animal. Adam could sympathise, deprived of its natural habitat, instincts held in check. What had it done to deserve a fate like this? Although many of his memories from 'before' were clouded and hidden behind a wall Shelly had built, Adam still remembered the cold sterility of the hospital, and understood the relentless boredom of captivity. He reached out and carefully stroked the muzzle of the wolf, which had now flopped on its side close to the bars where Adam was. At least he could get up and move freely. The wolf could not.

His mind drifted back to the boy and the misunderstanding. He hadn't intended to scare anyone. He only wanted to give the wolf something to break the drudgery of the day. He guessed he had done that regardless of the outcome and smiled back, the animal closed its eyes and absently licked at his hand. It was just a misunderstanding, she wouldn't hurt anyone, Adam told himself, but his inner voice said differently. Misunderstandings *get you sent back*. Dr. Shelly would understand. She believed in him, if she didn't, he wouldn't be here, and he absolutely, positively, did not want to let her down. Although lately, she never seemed too bothered or interested in his day-to-day accounts, preferring instead to get him in the tank as soon as possible. He didn't mind too much; it was an important part of his therapy to keep his head clear of any unpleasantness, and it worked. But the headaches were starting to bother him, as were the dreams. She told him not to worry, they would eventually fade, but for now, there was no sign of that happening, they felt pretty damn strong. He continued to scratch, but the thoughts kept coming. *Who in their right mind would ever think to hurt a child?* Not him, *Then who? Her? You already know, who hurt you?* He didn't like to think like that and pushed the conversation to one side; he would never put a child in danger, let alone feed it to the animal. He liked the boy; his big moon face, all smiley, innocent and trusting, why would he want to break that? *His mother, however!* He shook his head, she was the boy's mother, and boys need a mother, no matter how unkind or unpleasant, and that had to count for something. *Don't you count for something too?* He told the voice inside to keep quiet, it was just himself after all, and he was the one in control.

"You planning on feeding anyone else to it?"

Adam quickly withdrew his hand, the wolf growled. Timing they say is everything. He had forgotten about her during the *misunderstanding*; she had seen everything. Did she think the same?

"I wasn't," Adam quickly got to his feet, "I wouldn't hurt anyone. I just...," *Just what?* He had wanted to talk to her ever since he'd started work at the zoo. But could never muster the courage to mumble more than a few words, *how much for a flake? Can I get two scoops?* or *extra sprinkles please*, hardly constituted a fully formed conversation. It was fair to say she intimidated him, her style and manner, self-assured and confident. He liked her look, spiky hair with angry red flashes of color. The contrast between her deliberately pale complexion and overly heavy makeup reminded him of some of the more exotic birds that still remained in the atrium. She cut an odd figure cycling the ice cream cart from one place to another, emblazoned with the brightly coloured logo of a drooling hippo clutching an oversized cone. It wasn't quite the opener he imagined, having to explain he wasn't intending on feeding any children to the animals.

"Relax. I didn't think you were planning on feeding anyone to it," she said, climbing off the bike. "How do you do that?" Adam looked confused, "stroke it like that, I mean, without it ripping your arm off?"

Adam had no reference points for a real exchange with someone he liked. Sure, he'd thought about her. Carrying out imaginary conversations, never believing he would have one, yet here he was. His chance to impress upon her what an interesting person he was and how, if she'd let him, would do anything for her. That he was worth knowing, that she would feel safe around him, that he was quite literally the hidden gem in the dirt. His former self was long gone and not at all scary that only he could hear the voices inside. Besides, she didn't really need to know about any of that. What business was it of hers or anyones for that matter? He looked over at the wolf, watching them both with interest and thought about something clever to say, instead coming up with, "I don't know. Trust. I know she won't hurt me, and she knows I won't hurt her. I'm not a threat."

"Hmmm," she said, "I'm not convinced. If I were to stick my hand in, I'm pretty sure I'd lose it and I don't want to hurt her either."

"But you don't trust her."

"I don't think it's just about trust. I've seen you with the animals. You have a knack, not everyone can do what you do, trust me I know."

Adam thought for a moment. "Do you trust me?'

"I guess. I mean, I don't really know you," she cocked her head to one side and thrust her hand towards him, "Eve. There, now you know me."

Adam takes her hand, it's warm and small inside his, and he likesthe feel of it. He lets it drop before replying, "Adam."

"No shit!" Eve blinked back, "how about that, Adam and Eve in the garden of paradise. How could I not trust you?"

Shelly has explained the finer points of social etiquette, and he wants to say something smart back but looking at Eve, has no idea what she means, *how could she not?* Because he has a piece of paper that states he's not a danger to society, he thinks, but decides upon, "Ok," adding, "you want to stroke her?"

Eve's eyes widen, "I don't know, I'm not like you."

*No one is*, he thinks. "It's ok, just close your eyes." Adam gently takes her hand, places it under his, and moves closer to the bars. The wolf pads its way over. "Trust me," Adam quietly says. Eve isn't sure who to. When the wolf is close enough, Adam reaches through the cage, the back of her hand pressed into his open palm. He moves her hand with his towards the wolf and lightly touches the soft hair. Guiding her fingers with his, she can feel the fur under her hand and the hot, warm breath on her wrist. One more tickle, and he withdraws both their hands. "You can open your eyes now," Adam tells her.

Eve exhaled heavily. She hadn't realised she'd been holding her breath and wanted to say something profound to mark the moment. "Holy fucking shit, that was un-fucking-believable," she said instead. It's enough. Adam smiled back, pleased he's made a good impression. No misunderstanding.

# 21.

Fisher is sulking in his office. Jackson followed him back, the big idiot could never take a hint. He'd just lost the best fuck he'd ever had and needed some alone time with his favorite websites. Muscle was all well and good, but Jackson's size seemed to be inversely proportionate to his intellect, the larger he got, the stupider he became. Fisher was convinced that at this rate, he would eventually end up with the intellectual capacity of a potato. At the very least he could keep him in a cage with the rest of the primates and charged a regular P.T. Barnum per view. Perched on the edge of his desk like the missing link, he wondered if Leanne's boy would grow up to be someone like Jackson, he doubted it, from what he knew, Downs Syndrome, kids didn't live too long, maybe that was for the best, after all, junkie whore mothers didn't live too long either. Jackson was an idiot, true, but had played a pivotal role in his arrangement with Frank, and Frank was loyal to his friends, and the first lesson you learn with Frank is. *You don't fuck with Frank or his friends* because Frank is one scary dude, and Jackson was his friend. They'd done time together, shared a cell. Fisher wondered if they'd shared a lot more than just a cell. It gave him cold sweats thinking about it, but those kinds of thoughts were stupid and dangerous and often led to stupid and dangerous jokes. He couldn't imagine what Frank would do if he ever found out. He'd heard the stories after all. Frank, *apparently*, had once skinned a guy alive, or so the rumor mill had it, such was his expertise with a knife. No, Jackson may be one big stupid irritating lump of muscle, but he was well connected and worth keeping happy. Fisher leaned back in his chair, opened the bottom drawer in his desk, and took out his bottle of Jack with two tumblers. It made him feel like a character in a 50's detective film, all black and white and cool as fuck. He'd wear a trench coat if it didn't make him sweat so much and look like a fool, especially in this heat. He slid a glass over to Jackson and held the bottle over questioningly. Jackson grinned and nodded.

"Why the hell not, you know I usually don't, least not until I've worked on my back and shoulders, that's the key, isolate muscle groups and push, that way you can really max out." Jackson squeaked, picking up the glass as he gulped the brown liquid down in one swallow, wincing for effect.

*Prick,* thought Fisher, he should learn to sip, savor, appreciate things more, instead he grinned back and slapped his bulging stomach, "My sentiments exactly." He burped and poured himself another as Jackson looked away before putting the bottle back in his desk. He really disliked the man, stupidity annoyed him, as did Jackson's relationship with Frank. It meant he couldn't boss him around, tell him what to do. He hated having to pretend they were equal partners, friends even, all buddies together. Besides, it was only a matter of time. The zoo due to close any time soon, they were just a pitstop before the knacker's yard. Those he couldn't find homes for would eventually be destroyed, too old and too expensive to keep. Sad really, but if he honestly gave a fuck, he would be out there looking, which of course, he wasn't. Instead, he provided an alternative service. An easy solution to a problem no one wanted, while making a little, *ok a lot*, on the side. As long as he kept the paperwork in order, everyone was happy, no one would come looking, with most of the staff let go, there was no one left to care. Not unless he gave them a reason to, it would be so much better for all concerned if the place just sank without a trace, never to be heard from again, go quietly into the night, they'd said as much. Fisher knew the advantages of being in the *'too hard to think about box'*. A situation he was adequately well equipped to explode.

"I forgot to tell you, Frank wants a meet," Jackson piped up, absently flicking through the contents on Fisher's desk, "he wants to check out the latest contenders, see what he's promoting."

Fisher didn't believe Jackson could read, let alone make any sense of the paperwork on his desk, especially upside down, yet it still irritated him, he shuffled everything into a pile to be forgotten about later. So soon! *Not unless he gave them good reason to. Fuck!* It was in danger of becoming a regular event, leading to talk, rumor, and best-spilled secrets. Ask anyone in the know, and they'll tell you, *a secret is only worth knowing, as long as no one else knows.* Like all commodities, the value of a secret depended on scarcity, and if Frank had his way, it wasn't going to be scarce for much longer. Fisher knew it was a waste of time arguing with the meathead opposite, and Jackson's tell-tale smirk already told him his opinion didn't count for shit anyway. "I'll talk to Higgs," he sighed reluctantly.

Jackson wrinkled his nose at the very mention of Higgs, it was Fisher's time to smile. Higgs was the glue that kept it all together, the man in the middle, the man who makes it all work, and Jackson hated him. He was the complete opposite, pale and unhealthy with questionable lifestyle choices. Just skin and bone, but smart. Smart enough to recognize an opportunity when he saw one, smart enough to keep his mouth shut and smart enough to make sure no questions were asked. He could dance circles around Jackson, most likely Frank too, but he was way too smart for that as well.

Their relationship had been a stroke of luck. The previous vet, a nosey parker of the highest order, had stuck his beak in one too many of Fisher's side *projects*. The idiot had *accidentally* locked himself in a cage with one of the more violent and unpredictable animals under his care. Fisher arrived in the nick of time, the man was saved, but alas, his arm was not, and left soon afterward casting aspersions of blame to people who didn't want to know, and so hurried along his exit. Higgs applied for temporary cover, or rather his daughter had, they came as a package. His lack of references and sporadic work history should have been a handicap, not so for Fisher. Fisher had a need, and after a few phone calls, was sure he'd found the right man for the job. When they eventually met, one look told Fisher all he needed to know, and when he'd caught him red-handed up to his elbow in the pharmaceutical cookie jar, it sealed the deal, and they entered an uneasy partnership. Secrets have value. Of course, it wasn't an equal partnership, but it was the kind of partnership Fisher liked. Higgs had access to the cookie jar whenever he wanted, enjoying a limitless supply of uppers, downers, psychotropics, whatever he wanted, and all manner of creative combinations he could cook up. Fisher, in return, had a *willing* accomplice that would pretty much do whatever he wanted, including forging the cause of death on certificates when required.

"Higgs will do what he's damn well told," grunted Jackson and slid off the desk.

*Obviously, he will, you oversized moron,* thought Fisher. "Higgs will do what he has to. Frank knows that. This is about doing it right, about being careful, smart. Dotting the i's and crossing the t's. Keeping everything above board, all nice and transparent. We can't afford to have anyone poking around, about anything. Frank knows that more than any of us, and as you know, the only thing that really connects us to Frank... is you!" Fisher let his last two words hang, hinting at Jackson's worst kept secret.

Jackson felt like he'd just been stung, Fisher was right, they had been cellmates, the ex-con network was alive, and well, it had to be, look after your own, 'cos no one else will. Besides, being an ex-con meant something, *it meant you were one serious mother fucker.* You did your time. You had a rep, and you had connections. The same connections that would drag you down if you let them. If you were smart, time in the joint was time well spent. College for punks. But ex-cons are protective of their freedom, and no one wants to go back no matter how rewarding an experience. "Meaning?" Jackson snarled, trying to hide his anxiety with menace and failing. He knew Frank wouldn't be happy if he knew about his little sideline but hadn't considered that Fisher knew, given how careful he'd been. *Most likely bluffing*, he thought, Fisher was like that, always digging around, trying to find some dirt he could use as leverage. It was true, he didn't like Higgs, but he was beginning to dislike Fisher more. Getting a little too big for his boots trying to be the big *I am*, all boss man and orders, but he was no Frank. Frank would skin him alive, but Frank would skin *him* alive too if he broke his number one rule, *Frank looks after Frank*, and no one gets in the way. At least for now, they all needed each other.

"Meaning we need to keep our heads down... all of us. Including you." Smirked Fisher, it felt good to have something in his back pocket on Jackson.

"Like you did with the hooker."

Fisher shrugged, "She's already a distant memory. But those punks I've seen you with, well... hardly what I'd call discreet." *Secrets have value.* He'd been meaning to talk to Jackson about it for a while, all it takes is one accident. Some white trash kid trying to bulk up through steroids dies of a heart attack before he's twenty, questions get asked. It doesn't matter why, it never does, once you appear on the radar, the blip doesn't go away.

Jackson flinched, he didn't like being told what to do, and he'd grown used to the extra income, but more than that, he liked the respect, his turn to be the big man, calling the shots. His customers maybe young, but they weren't amateurs and knew what they were doing, and his stuff was the real deal, it worked, his arms were living proof of that. "Just you look after yours and let me take care of mine. Savvy?" Jackson snapped back, his high-pitched voice undermining his own threat. He wished he sounded different, sometimes the side effects didn't seem worth it, he flexed a bicep, but then again!

"Relax. Your secret's safe with me. We're friends, aren't we? Just let me handle Higgs. I know how to handle him. All I'm saying is we don't want to attract unnecessary heat, not from Frank or anyone. You get me?"

Jackson got him alright, and if he thought he was going to get his fat greedy hands on his extra slice of the pie, he had another thing coming and took his exit cue, slamming the door for extra emphasis. Fisher smirked, it was only a matter of time before he reached out and skimmed a little from Jackson's pot. Drugs! Idiot, stupid but lucrative, God knows there's no shortage of those willing to destroy their bodies for vanity. He took out his bottle of Jack and poured himself a much larger measure now he was alone. Life was cozy, but Frank was a problem, too greedy, too volatile, too dangerous. How long could they keep things going? He had no idea. He suspected it wouldn't be too much longer, and he needed an exit strategy. Jackson could be the distraction he needed, set him and Frank against each other, and while they were busy having a dick measuring contest, he'd slip out the back without a sound. A couple more scores, and poof! Vanish on the wind like a bad smell.

Too bad for Higgs. Too bad for Jackson, maybe he still had a chance to hook up with Leanne once things settled, that would be good. He took a sip and turned to his favourite website, pantywhores.com, and considered locking the door to his office.

# 22.

The sun pulled its long shadows across the city like a blanket as it began to dip behind the horizon. Adam was on his way *home* from work, at least back to the hospital, home for now. The short fifteen-minute bus journey was as unremarkable to his fellow passengers as Adam was to them, but not for him. It gave him an enormous sense of well-being, no longer the outsider, an imposter acting a part, instead, he felt connected to the world and them, just another working stiff on his way home. The drudgery of life has its own reward, the predictability of familiar faces. The same people in the same seat, day in day out, occasionally exchanging consolatory nods, as if to say, *yup, here we go again, same old shit, different day.* He knew they were bored by the same old routine. Journeys spent wishing for excitement, anything to break the monotony, if only they knew. Instead, Adam rejoiced at the tiny differences. People crossing roads, children holding parents' hands, even the homeless with their blank stares were enough to find meaning in the ordinary. For him, he wished it was longer.

Today was different, today was a mixed day. The *misunderstanding* had rattled him, not because of the violence or the prospect he might not be allowed to return. It was because of the thoughts he'd had, not him personally, but the other him that lived below the surface, what *he'd* wanted to do. But then there was Eve. He wished she could have stayed longer or that he could have sounded smarter, had a better conversation, anything to extend the glow he felt. The people on the bus were all well and good, but she had seen him, really seen him. They shared a moment, and he had given her something she would cherish. She had said as much and told him they would be friends. He knew he had the wolf to thank, and he would do so later. No one noticed him in the feed area, no one ever noticed him until now. Maybe this time he would find her a nice juicy steak, she would like that. He tugged at his trouser leg, making sure the ankle bracelet he had to wear outside the hospital was covered. He was always careful to make sure it didn't show when he left the bus. He didn't want to scare anyone or make them feel uncomfortable and would always depart several stops before the hospital and walk the rest of the way.

By the time Adam arrived back, all he wanted to do was eat the leftovers in the cafeteria, watch some mindless junk on the heavily censored TV and lie down in his not so sterile white room, now that he had been allowed to hang some posters—provided the images weren't too provocative—which meant no scantily clad ladies, superheroes, comic book characters, movie stars, rock stars, rock bands, nothing too religious, sporty or political. All that was left were pictures of flowers, animals, or landscapes, and since some of the more easily stimulated patients could become aroused by animals, imagination doing the rest. Adam stuck to flowers and drawings of the zoo, giving his room a very peculiar look.

The hospital staff were always courteous to him when he returned from a full day's work, always asking the same questions, though never waiting for a reply. "How was your day? Did you have a nice day? Did you work hard? Have you made some new friends? Did you bite anyone?'

Adam always nodded and smiled back, they no longer heard nor cared what he said. He'd gotten quite used to this new ritual of asking one-sided questions that didn't require an honest response. It was a way of acknowledging him, he had been away, was now back, and no one had to call the authorities in between, rather than a genuine inquiry. All in all, very satisfactory. Because he had been doing this for some time, he was almost considered an *outpatient* or *one of them* and was therefore given certain concessions extending far beyond hanging a photograph of a plant pot on his wall. It was attitude, theirs and his. He felt respected, he was doing his bit, a nod from one working man to another. Even the male orderlies, who, as everyone knew, were there for security, would ask him about his day. The weather, if he had a girlfriend or not, and would sometimes share a joke, admittedly he mostly never understood their jokes but laughed along anyway. Life was good, and now he had spoken to Eve in real life instead of just his head, life was so much better, and who knows, when they next asked the question, *did he have a girlfriend?* He might surprise them all and say yes! The thought drew a smile across his face as he wandered into the cafeteria.

"You're late Adam. Did something happen?"

Shelly's voice startled him, although not unexpected, yes something happened, but he had no intention of telling Shelly about Eve, some things were meant to be private. It wasn't that he didn't appreciate everything she had done for him, that he wasn't grateful. He knew everything he had, everything he was, was all because of her. She made it happen. She had told him so herself on many occasions, and she was right. Had it not been for her, he would still be the pathetically weak man trapped inside the beast, sweating in a windowless box without hope or reprieve. He had changed in so many ways, and today she had finally given him hope. He felt like he had a future, and she was responsible for that. She was right when she told him he owed her everything, he did, but how long did the repayments last? Besides, he wasn't the only one who had changed.

She had become less interested in what he had to say and more interested in the tank. He had always enjoyed their little post-mortems of the day's events, who said what, when, where, and how it made him feel. They gave him the chance to offload and for her to explain some of the finer details of outside the interactions he didn't quite understand. Instead, preferring the tank. She told him the tank showed her more than he ever could. It was the tank that kept him as he was. It was the tank that held the animal in check. It was the tank he had to be grateful for, *all hail the tank!* He hated it, the loss of power and self-control. Becoming less than he was, sinking until he disappeared below a thick pool of emptiness. Turned into nothing, the animal ran riot. The tank terrified Adam. What it contained. What it represented. The unrestrained access to the darker part of who he was, and that darkness ran deep. Of course, he never fully remembered what happened in the tank, but whatever it was, he knew it was bad, the animal only slept when satisfied, and the headaches bothered him. He mentioned them to Shelly, casually at first, he didn't want to make them sound like a big deal, but she dismissed them out of hand and told him they would get better, they hadn't. It was just part of the process, she'd said, a small price to pay for freedom. It wasn't, they hurt. Like a scab on a cut, she promised they would fade. He kept the visions to himself, a brief glimpse of memory never had, a fragment too abstract to make sense of but frightening, nonetheless.

"You know how important the sessions are," Shelly continued. "Is there anything you'd like to tell me before we get started?"

"No… the bus." He looked down, avoiding her eyes, he wasn't late, she was just keen.

"I see." She could tell by his face there was something else. It made her want the tank more. "Time to get ready."

"I was going to get something to eat first, is that ok?"

"How about I get them to leave you something?"

"I'd rather not eat alone."

"And I'd rather not waste my time."

Shelly took a step back and cocked her head to look at Adam. To her, he wasn't the man he thought he was. He was still the lab rat to her, but she knew he was growing and developing in ways that still had the power to delight and surprise. He had come such a long way, but the distance to go was so much further, and they, she, hadn't finished, not by a long shot. Ever cautious, she let herself relax, she didn't want to frighten him, too much too soon. Smile, stay calm, be patient, what's half an hour even an hour, she can wait, it's not as if she isn't in control. "Ok, why not."

A wave of relief swept over Adam, a temporary reprieve, she was smiling. Today was a good day. Should he have told her about Eve? Maybe not just yet, besides he didn't have to tell her anything she always knew what was on his mind, just don't think bad thoughts and tried to tell the animal to do the same, *do me this one favor is all I ask.*

*We'll see,* it whispered back.

Shelly had a coffee while she watched Adam eat. Spaghetti in tomato sauce, followed by sponge and custard, no flavor specified, twice weekly, a staple of institutions world over. She found their conversation boring, more so than usual and was easily distracted, noticing the smaller, more insignificant things about her charge. How the sauce seemed to pool slightly at the corners of his mouth before he licked his lips, how the wiggle of a single strand of pasta became more frantic as he sucked it back. She noticed the grime beneath his fingernails and wondered how much he was ingesting. Just how much shit did he eat daily as he shoveled food into his face? He was in a cheery mood. She was glad but felt jealous, which annoyed her. *Just who is he to be so happy?* She checked her watch, enough was enough, the sponge and custard could wait, time to get ready, time for the tank, then she'd relax, then she'd find out what he's got to be so cheerful about.

To Adam the food was never good, but today it tasted fantastic, it was the same old, same old. Things never change in a place where routine is woven into the fabric of the day, but today, nothing could spoil his mood. Adam was happy to chit-chat about this and that but avoided the *misunderstanding* and his time with Eve. Preferring to talk about the sun, the grass, the animals. How they seemed so much more alive than the crowds, watching through the bars of a cage. Shelly was quiet, appearing genuinely interested in what he had to say, nodding in all the appropriate places, but even the most patient listener has limits.

Shelly abruptly pushed his pudding to one side. "Ok, done? Good, let's go."

She didn't wait for a reply as she stood and began walking, expecting him to follow. Taking one last look at the sponge, Adam had no choice. He never could work out what flavor it was supposed to be anyway.

# 23.

The body in the tank floats. The body in the tank is an empty shell. The body in the tank is nothing. Hanging lifeless but for the twitching muscles of the dead responding to a place elsewhere. A place that doesn't, can't exist, where memories are lies and the truth held hostage to fantasy. This is a place where dreams really do come true, and nightmares are your best friend. This is the place where the animal roams free and is king. This is the place where nothing stands in your way, where the rules are yours; think it, have it. You want it, take it. There is nothing you can't do. There is nothing that can't happen, and you will always, always win. You see the woman and child, a child held captive by the bonds of motherhood too strong to be deserved. The child pulls away, running towards you, and the woman's rage erupts. She lashes out but you have already changed, you have become the wolf. Her face is a mask of anger and spitting hatred. Her blows are feeble and easily caught, and you bite down hard, tearing at the flesh splintering bone. She screams and tries to run and the chase is on. She is no match for your speed or power. Powerful muscles carry you faster, one leap, one single bound and she's caught. Hands held out, protesting, pleading, food for famine as she tried to push you off. You draw back and give her your warm embrace, sealed with a kiss. Soft flesh gives so easily. Her taste is smoky, worn out, and used. She is sour, but the blood is sweet. Soon there is nothing left of the woman, broken bones, torn clothing, and ripped skin. You howl at the moon painted as the ruler you are, your world, your rules, wanting more. The glass wall, invisible and impossible to touch, a barrier to the real world.

Leanne Bonelle had waited until Anton finally drifted off to sleep. Thank God he was a deep sleeper and wouldn't wake until his body told him to do so, which by experience was usually no later than mid-morning. Her expulsion from the garden was too severe, she missed the animals, at least the ones behind bars, the others not so much. Fisher would come around, he always did, his needs were as great as her own, his appetite more so, they were made for each other. She had been careful in choosing her patch tonight, a rare part of the street that was free but still had traffic—sorry souls looking for a bargain. It was pointless waiting for a *client* if you were too far off the right track, certain areas had a reputation, and just like any other product on sale, customers preferred to buy at the market. Her only saving grace was the late hour. The night was kinder to her looks than the midday sun, the streetlights less harsh.

Leanne had been out for almost two hours with only a hand-job to show for her effort, she'd tried to upsell, but her stained teeth were something of a turn-off. She dug into her purse, stuffed optimistically full of condoms, and rummaged for her cigarettes, *fuck, only two left!* The night needed to get a whole lot better, or it's going to be a tough choice between smokes or food, and the smokes always won out. She could put up with Anton's moaning for a while, but the nicotine cravings were too extreme to ignore. She lit her penultimate and took a long hard drag, one of life's little luxuries. Stopping mid exhale, frozen and alert like a Meer cat, spooked by a noise that shouldn't be there. Friend or foe? Prey or predator? It sounded big, bigger than a cat, bigger than a dog, and dogs don't climb trees! Leanne walked into the light, she wasn't too far away from the zoo, maybe it was one of theirs? Then she heard it, a low guttural growl, a sound made in the belly of a beast, telling her she wasn't the only thing that was hungry. A sudden movement and the wet slap of feet. Was she being stalked?

"Someone there?" She called out. Her voice, small and distant, belonging to someone else, too weak to be hers, and so very alone. She stood straighter, she was tough, she was from the streets, she'd been through worse, *no one fucks with me unless they pay.*

"Hey, you want some of this?" She shouted into the night, bravado kicking in as she thrust her crotch at the night, sounding more like herself, "c'mon honey, don't you be shy, if there's someone there, you'd better not fu.." Interrupted. Her voice cut short by the hole torn in her throat, breath rushing past words in a hurry to escape, the un-screamed sound of a cry. Leanne's legs buckled under her weight as she crumpled to the ground, her strings suddenly cut. Instinctively she reaches up to stem the flow and plaster the wound, but the blood gushes out. Fingers too slippery, too wet to pinch the skin. Her scream, the harsh rasping of breath and gurgling of blood. It comes towards her in one last leap, who was it? What was it? A glimmer of recognition? Something familiar she can't quite put a finger on as her brain begins to mist and fail. She sees the teeth, storybook big, nice and sharp. Her last thought is for Anton,

*I'm so sorry baby, look at what I gone and did, I got myself killed. I really fucked up this time.* And then she was gone.

# 24.

Jackson, fresh from his shower, was sitting on the bench between the lockers of his local gym, a full-length mirror opposite, and can feel the wooden slats digging into his ass through his towel as he tried to get comfortable. But he hasn't felt comfortable ever since *he* showed up, and today hadn't helped. The new guy, the guy with the strange eyes. It wasn't a great workout, but then again, it wasn't the worst. Leg day. The worst, if he could, he would happily avoid it. But no way was he going to look like the clowns who just concentrate on their upper body, the ones that look like cartoon characters—huge arms, big buff torsos held up by skinny little legs. He shook his head. Not him. Was it because most mirrors were only waist-high?

Arnie was the man, he had it right, controlled use of steroids. Max out in the gym but concentrate on separate muscle groups, that was the key. Today his head wasn't in it, he'd grunted out his reps, squats, deadlifts, and leg press, hoping to push and squeeze his frustrations out like a turd. Usually, it worked, extreme exercise had a way of clearing the head, making everything right, especially when he looked at the result, but not today. Today he'd even had to drop a weight just to make it through the session. If he was looking for someone to blame, it would be Fisher. Fisher, the fat greedy fuck who was incapable of keeping it in his pants. If he hadn't been carrying on with the burnt-out whore in the first place, there wouldn't have been any commotion. He'd warned him often enough she was trouble, even threatening to tell Frank, of course, he never would, *he wasn't no squeal*, besides he had his own little sideline to worry about and Fisher was exactly the kind of guy who would sell his own mother if it meant getting out of trouble. If truth be told, he hadn't minded getting rough with her, she disgusted him anyway, especially when she tried to *come on to him* by the exit. He wasn't Fisher, he had standards. But he'd caught the way Eve looked at him, as if he was the one doing the wrong thing. He wasn't the one with the retarded kid! And now there was the new guy to contend with. *Eve and the new guy, Adam,* the thought kept popping into his head. She had always been a prick tease, he knew she liked him, he absentmindedly flexed his pecks and biceps – what's not to like? His reflection winked back. He'd often caught her staring, even the largest of regulation shirts, short-sleeved naturally, were too small for his arms. Her aloof attitude was as much of a disguise as her get-up, dressing like an 80's Goth lesso! She was just like everyone else, and just like everyone else, *was up for it*, whether they knew it or not. *Adam. Just what the fuck was his problem?* There was clearly something wrong with him, something he didn't like, something that made him uncomfortable; he'd seen it plenty of times in the joint, the vacant stare betraying nothing, ready to explode, oddly enough, he reminded him of Frank.

Frank. He'd met Frank in the joint, shared a cell, and although he was bigger, there was something about Frank that was far worse, something that told you; *you don't mess with Frank*, something in the eyes or lack thereof, humanity. He knew from his early years before he got into working out, it wasn't how big, or how tough you thought you were, it was about how far you were willing to go, and Frank was prepared to go places no one else would. Those foolish enough to take him on learned the hard way, often with a permanent reminder, and so he had become his right-hand man. Of course, Frank could take care of himself, but why get down and dirty when you don't have to. Frank the master manipulator; warm and generous, cold, and ruthless. But Frank wasn't bad, he just wasn't good either, in fact, Frank wasn't anything apart from Frank. But true to his word, he'd told him back in the joint he'd take care of him, and he had. Frank had fallen on his feet and taken over an abattoir with ties to the local zoo. It had been Frank that got him the job as a night security guard, no mean feat for someone with a record. Jackson knew he was just a pawn in a game he couldn't see, but he was happy, his parole officer was happy, and Frank was happy, happy days all around. All except Fisher. Jackson smiled at the memory, Fisher had been a grade 'A' prick from the start, playing boss man with the ex-con. But he was Frank's eyes and ears, and Frank had a plan. Frank always had a plan.

Frank had the inside information on Fisher and had exploited it for all it was worth, he'd known he was a gambling man with ambition above his station who liked to throw his weight around and ran a dirty zoo. Frank extended an invitation to join some bigger games where the real action was, with real players, and Fisher, greedy for both reputation and a bigger place at the trough, was only too happy to oblige. All Jackson had to do was to make sure he didn't forget the date. Frank set up a card game, all very casual, light, and none threatening, fixing the pack to make sure Fisher came out on top. Fisher naturally had a great time, convinced he was a card genius was ready for a repeat. After a few more games and a few more wins, Fisher was all buddy-buddy with his newfound friend and couldn't wait for the next game. It hadn't taken Frank long to get him exactly where he wanted him, in over his head gasping for air. The games always wrapped with happy handshakes and bets being squared off, everyone leaving the best friends. Everyone except Fisher. Frank had been the perfect gent, ready to wave any debt, even spring for an extended line of credit, but his price was high.

It was the perfect sting. In debt to Frank with no way out, Fisher had no choice but to come clean about his own little sideline to make his money back. Jackson sniffed; he would have rather taken a beating than invite the devil himself in. Frank already knew there wasn't much in town he didn't know, but like a vampire, he needed an invitation. The zoo had been on the rocks for years, an expensive relic of the past scheduled for closure to make way for a new shopping precinct. Fisher was caretaker to a graveyard, but ever the opportunist, had found a way to make it interesting, and by interesting meant profitable and was running a variant of the old cock fight, one zoo animal against another. Jackson had to hand it to him, the man knew how to skim. Fisher took door money and gave himself a healthy 15% commission on all bets. The fights were small but well planned. He even had a dodgy vet, Higgs, on hand to fudge the paperwork and patch them up. Frank was excited, he instinctively knew how big it could become, and the game changed overnight.

With Frank's contacts, they started to make some serious money — Fisher reluctant and scared shitless at first, quickly overcame his doubts by cash and lots of it. The operation moved to the abattoir, its benefits two-fold, they could house more people and dispose of the animals quickly with fewer questions. Jackson was promoted to head of security to ensure the smooth running of the operation and kept an eye on things. Expansion comes at a price, and he knew which ones to pay off. Life was good, but even he knew their circus had a limited shelf life, it was only a matter of time before someone talked or they ran out of animals. Jackson wanted his ducks in order. Cash available and ready to split at a moment's notice, it was just a question of timing. But you always want what you can't have. And what he couldn't have, was Eve. He admired himself some more, why wasn't she interested in him? He stood in front of the full-length mirror and let the towel drop. He was in great shape, lean and lumpy, bulges in all the right places. He stared down at his shriveled penis and gave it a flick. It wasn't the 'roids' he told himself, it was because the rest of him was so big, that's why it looked so small. He grabbed it by the shaft and squeezed, trying to imagine Eve naked and felt a slight twitch in his balls, he looked back down, much better, and tried to think of ways to get rid of Adam to win her heart.

# 25.

5.55 am, Shelly glanced at the time and stretched herself awake. She always beat the alarm to the morning and took a moment to enjoy the soft opening tones from *Also Sprach Zarathustra* by Richard Strauss. The slow crawl of a cello barely there, gradually joined by a double bass and the three rising notes of a trumpet, before bursting into an ecstasy of optimism as the orchestra enters, leaving an echo of anticipation to be filled by the beating hearts of the timpani drums. The dawn of a new age, science over religion, the beginning of the journey to meaning and enlightenment heralding the birth of the Superman. She had never considered herself to be something of a culture lover, not because she didn't believe in art, far from it, she could appreciate the link between the subconscious and conscious as illustrated throughout history, but because she never gave herself the time to. Strauss was different. She had gone to see Kubrick's *2001: A Space Odyssey* as a student and had marveled at the opening sequence, never realizing first-hand how powerful and emotional music could be, and subsequently embarked on her own journey of discovery and from then on, Strauss and her were seldom apart.

She swung her legs out of bed and walked towards the open window, the morning breeze puckering her skin to goosebumps. A dreamless night was always a good night, feeling refreshed and more alive than she had in a while. Her research was going well, Adam was providing her with a wealth of material to wade through and she was enjoying the abandonment as a passenger inside the mind of another, yet there was still a piece missing. Hopper. Hopper had been exposed to a depraved world on the brink of decay, the nefarious and degenerate, his company to keep. It was hardly a surprise he would eventually succumb to violence himself but battled against it, in the belief he was doing what was right. He was the good guy, they the bad. The lines had been drawn. It was black and white to Hopper, but recently they had begun to blur. Watts had been the catalyst, Adam the trigger, but she knew Hopper had stepped over it several times before, willing to give in to his darker self. She could imagine how exhausting it must be to keep everything locked up so tightly. Looking through the eyes of Adam, she felt there had been an intangible connection, a recognition of a shared bond, ethereal and incorporeal existing only in the perception of the psyche. She wanted to know what he had seen in Adam and if he had recognized it in himself.

It was a circle she was keen to close. Would Adam recognize Hopper after all the work they had put in together? For all intents and purposes, Adam was a different man. And what of Hopper, would he recognize the beast within and see beyond the veneer? Had she been able to exorcize the animal to keep it at bay, successfully separating it from Adam? And if she could, what of hers, was it still dormant, like Hopper waiting for the right opportunity to show itself?

Today was to be their third session, and although still early in their relationship, she felt they were beginning to establish a foundation of trust through her explicit approach to his actions by way of understanding and empathy, slowly building a bridge between them. Patiently listening to him describe the world he inhabited, how it made him sick to the stomach, how he felt he was unable to create real connections, instead preferring to think of everyone as guilty, that way he couldn't be disappointed. When she asked him of what, he'd told her it didn't matter, it was just a matter of digging. *We're all guilty of something,* he'd said, and believed it. His eyes stained by the grime of the city tainting everything he saw. He talked about Art, how he'd let him down, and the guilt he'd taken on. She nodded along, making encouraging comments, sympathizing when necessary. It was a delicate matter steering him towards her own goals whilst encouraging him to see them as his own. Hopper needed to feel he was in control, making decisions autonomously as she pulled the strings.

Insisting Hopper was placed on administrative duties as part of his treatment, something menial to keep him occupied and engaged Shelly was able to monitor his behaviour more closely. Explaining that left to his own devices Hopper would constitute a danger to himself and to others and that the department had a duty of care for its old soldiers. Most likely he was suffering from PTSD and if they abandoned him at this stage would be liable for a court case. The police department acted predictably as expected asking for her help, which she'd been only too happy to give, offering up practical suggestions on how to manage his behaviour. It had been her idea to place him on Missing Persons, giving him access to a variety of unsolved crimes she could use to her advantage. Since Adam's time in the tank, she had been experiencing some uncomfortably vivid dreams. She assured herself it had been nothing until she came across a news story, more of a by-line than anything else, of a prostitute that had gone missing close to the Zoo, which bore the uncanny sting of familiarity, however without a picture to go by, she shrugged it off as nothing more than coincidence, it had only made the news because of the downs syndrome kid she had left behind. Yet lurking in the back of her mind, a niggling seed had taken root.

# 26.

Shelly dressed quickly after her cold shower, a thousand pins landing on her skin, reminding her she was still alive. Bearable for only a few moments, she forced herself to stay under for longer when the splinter of memory broke into her mind like a shattered icicle. Indefinable as it was intangible, like the proverbial cuckoo, it didn't belong to her. She stumbled out of the shower, clutching at her eye, and held onto the basin too afraid to look up, unsure what she might see looking back, but there was nothing. The same clear green eyes looked back, her pupils black and empty, it was just her.

Sitting in her office waiting for Hopper, it felt less real, more like the ghost of a waking dream, so much so she doubted it even happened at all, and try as she might, couldn't recall what it was she had seen. She shrugged it off when she heard the knock at the door and readied herself for her new favorite patient.

Hopper felt like a contradiction. He didn't like the idea of having to go and see a shrink, it made him feel like a little boy being told off and sent to the headmaster. He considered himself, if not bulletproof, certainly strong-minded. Mistakenly thinking he had his shit together, the previous sessions reminded him that wasn't the case, yet to his surprise, more than anyone, had started to feel less like a failure and had begun to look forward to them. Then there was Shelly. He liked her. He liked her cold detached manner, he could imagine how it would put other people off, but not him, he never felt patronized or judged, and she genuinely seemed to *get him*. He liked her professionalism and her distaste for authority. He assumed to get where she was, she would have had to have fought hard, and he liked that too, and he also liked the way she looked.

"Jack, it's good to see you, how have you been?" Shelly shook his hand and gestured to the couch.

"Not bad, only beat up one person on the way over, so all in all, a good start, but it's still early!" Shelly smiled at his joke. He liked that too.

Hopper settled onto the couch, he'd grown used to the idea and considered it ironic. The initial pleasantries over, Shelly began to recount their previous session. They had discussed what she termed as his anger issues. To Hopper, everything was a trigger, he was a walking pressure cooker ready to erupt. She doubted it would take much to open the valve.

"Last we met, we talked about things that can act as a trigger for anger. What I'd like to talk about today, provided your willing, is to talk about the reasons why." Shelly began.

"Because people are irritating?"

"That's true, they are, but not always. Anger, in itself, is natural, often used as a survival mechanism to give us a boost of adrenalin to combat threats. The problem is how we manage it and what constitutes a threat. For example, you're at Starbucks, you're late, maybe you're on a meter, and there's only one person in front of you, but they're still trying to figure out if they want a latte with or without soy or maybe a cappuccino with caramel, and ordering for their colleagues back at work, then they forget the order and have to call in, and all you want is a black coffee. It's annoying, but it's not a threat."

"Sounds like a dick."

"Maybe. But why not? What's it to you? Why is it so important for you to get your coffee and not them?"

"Yeah ok, I get it. I'm the dick, not them."

"It's not quite what I would have said, but we have a choice when caught in the moment. We can take a step back and pause. Take a breath. It's ok to be annoyed and frustrated because you're not getting what you want when you want it, but what does that sound like?"

"You're saying I'm a child?"

*Yes.* "Not at all, but it's easy to rationalize our anger when we're not in the storm. Think of how many people go through a simulated training exercise, only to freeze when the real thing happens. We get caught up in ourselves, in the moment. What I want to know is what are you caught in? Anger is a symptom. It could be guilt, depression, feelings of abandonment, or a sense of loss, all leading to frustration. Often when we self-medicate with alcohol, our inhibitions are already lowered, and so..."

Hopper thought about how many bar-fights he'd had, he always considered them his own form of personal therapy, but he had to agree, any relief was short-lived, he was often consumed with self-loathing which he would numb with another drink and another fight and so on. "I get it, we act on whatever pops into our head?" He finished off for her.

"It's about control or lack of. Violence can be just one symptom of it, often stemming from frustration. Do you see how the loop works? What I'm interested in is how we take that control back. So that you're the one in control and not our darker self."

"You make it sound like we're two people."

"Perhaps we are, but I'm more inclined to think that we're a mixture of everything. What happens on the outside, as much as what happens on the in. Part of how we govern ourselves stems from learned behavior. Family, parents, friends. The things we see and do, how we react to them, how we've seen others react. All of it teaches us how to behave. So, for this session, if it's alright with you, I'd like to discuss your childhood."

It wasn't alright, and nor did he want to, but he guessed at some point they were going to get to it sooner or later. Hopper thought about his childhood, it hadn't been great, but then again, it hadn't been the worst. Some people had it tougher, and they came out the other end ok, although you never knew what personal demons haunted them on cold nights. He had grown up as the only child of a battle-weary street cop and a beat-down mother. His father, a strict disciplinarian, would lose his temper at the drop of a hat, and Hopper already hated he was following in his footsteps. He'd been celebrated for his heavy-handed no-nonsense approach, often doling out rough justice when he felt the need to, rather than clog the courts with misdemeanors that would result in a fine they couldn't pay, or jail time, which meant families would go hungry. His philosophy: why should the innocent pay when he could remind them there was a damn good reason to toe the line? If only someone had reminded *him*. Hopper had endured the beatings, *take it like a man*, his father would say, flexing his belt, only he wasn't a man. Worse when he drank, *worse when Hopper drank*. But it was different when his mother took the beatings, of course, his father was always remorseful, but the bruises angered him more, embarrassing him in public shaming him. As a child, Hopper hated him, he was a bully, and as a result, so was he. The end, ironically, had come by way of Batman. It was an apology toy, bought to assuage his guilt from one of his more severe strappings. Back in the seventies, the toys had been diecast metal. Hopper had loved it, a copy from the tv series he was obsessed with, complete with miniature figures and plastic bullets, although there was a lot to be said for the expression on the Boy Wonders face.

He had left it at the top of the stairs. Batman had been chasing the Joker to the edge of a cliff when he heard his mother shout. Abandoning the crime-fighting duo, he'd rushed to her aid. His father, already oiled with whisky, had turned his attention to the young Jack Hopper. It was unclear how they ended up by the stairs. The story they had stuck to was how his father had stumbled, he hadn't. No one walks backward with a belt in their hand. His mother had pushed him, she hadn't meant to do it, she had only wanted to spare the boy another walloping. A stagger and a stumble and a fall. The drink will do that. Had it been a cartoon, it would have been comical, but it wasn't, and it hadn't. A slow-motion fall. Retired on a disability pension, he lingered in their house permanently. Physical violence changed to psychological, as he became more demanding, slowly drinking himself to death *for the pain*. His funeral had been well attended. They had all said what a terrible shame it had been and what a great guy he'd been. It wasn't, and he hadn't been. Unless they were referring to how long he lived after the accident. Did Hopper blame himself? No, he did not. He had been glad. Joyous even, but his mother had shriveled, pickled by the guilt he never felt. Had it messed with his head? Too fucking right it had. He hated the idea of becoming the man he loathed, especially when everyone else hailed him as a hero. All except Art. Art was just a young cop at the time, but he knew and had taken an interest in the young Jack Hopper and did his best to make sure he didn't end up on the streets. Boxing, athletics, anything to channel all the anger and pain he felt all led to the police training academy, and here. Dr. Shelly's couch.

"Would you say your own childhood was a happy one?" Shelly continued, knowing it wasn't, "it's often where we find unresolved issues. Your file says your father was paraplegic, but also a policeman. That must have been hard. Do you remember what happened?"

*It was, and yes, I remember only too well.* "It was an accident, stupid really, it wasn't even on the job. He tripped and fell down the stairs, boring really."

*Liar.* "That must have been hard."

"We coped."

"Coping isn't living. Coping is existing. Doesn't sound very happy."

Hopper shrugged, it was a time and place he didn't want to spend too long in. "Like I said, we got by." *You have no idea.*

Shelly nodded and decided on another approach. "You know when we hide the truth for ourselves, it makes our life a lie."

"You think I'm lying to myself?"

"You don't seem to want to talk about your childhood."

"It feels a little predictable. Blaming everything on a shitty childhood?"

"You don't think it's reasonable to assume our upbringing has an effect on how we behave as adults?"

Hopper rubbed at the temples of his forehead. "I guess, I believe we have to take responsibility for our own actions at some point, we have to pay for what we did?"

"And what did you do, that was so bad?" Hopper blinked back, reminding Shelly of the proverbial rabbit in the headlights. She decided to change tack to keep him off guard. "Tell me Jack, did you always want to be a policeman?"

For as long as Hopper could remember, there hadn't been much else in his life. It never occurred that it hadn't been a conscious thought? He honestly didn't know, it provided the distraction he needed, but had he wanted to? "I guess so. After my old man ended up the way he did, I don't know, I just... did."

"There must have been a reason?"

*Guilt.* Hopper had wanted to show the world he wasn't like his old man, he could be better, only he wasn't. He'd manage to follow in his father's footsteps in more ways than one. "I guess I wanted to give something back."

"Why? You think you owed the world something? Your father, perhaps?"

"No," Hopper answered too quickly before composing himself. "No, I didn't owe him anything."

*We all owe our fathers something*, Shelly thought. "No? Why not?"

"Because he was fucking paraplegic." Hopper blurted out, "he didn't even know I existed." He could feel his irritation rising as he tugged at his collar. He'd managed to avoid thinking about his father for so long that he'd convinced himself the old wounds had healed. He'd been wrong.

Shelly picked at the scab, "which for a young boy would have been hard. What about your mother?"

"What about her, and please don't ask me what my relationship was like. It was fine and no, no Oedipal tendancies."

Shelly nodded and considered Hopper's defensive response without reacting. She was beginning to build a bigger picture of what drove Hopper. "She must have been busy looking after your father?"

*You have no idea what he was like,* "Yeah, I guess he kept her on her toes alright."

"But not much room for you."

Hopper felt raw, exposed. He felt sure Shelly could see beyond the flimsy stories. Hadn't it been his fault after all? But it wasn't guilt he felt, but anger.

Anger at his father, anger at his mother and anger at himself that he'd been too cowardly to finish the job when he had the chance. He'd been alone all his life and had spent a lifetime building a shell he thought would be hard enough to withstand the pain, one session with Shelly, and it had already started to crack. "There were kids who had it tougher than me, least I wasn't beaten every day."

"No, there is that." Shelly took off her glasses and smiled sympathetically, Hopper's answers were strangely illuminating, *least I wasn't beaten every day*, a clear reference that at some point he had. An unprompted topic suggesting he would have found it preferential to being ignored. A desire to wilfully be beaten was usually an indication of guilt of some kind, a need for punishment. She wondered about the accident but decided not to press on the cause, preferring to tackle the effect instead. "Jack, you said earlier you didn't know why you joined the force?" She waited for him to acknowledge her point. "Do you think it may have something to do with seeking approval or a way of dealing with repressed feelings? Do you blame yourself for what happened?"

*I knew it*, "No, I know it was an accident. I was just a kid."

"It would be normal if you did. Children often do, they put themselves at the center of the world, which ultimately leads to feelings of guilt, so they spend a lifetime trying to prove themselves worthy."

"You think that's what I'm doing, trying to prove I'm one of the good guys?"

"It's not out of the realms of possibility. When we repress our emotions or feelings, things we are unable to deal with, they can have a real physical effect. It's not just the job. Numerous things can trigger it, like something out of the ordinary. When we're confronted with something that questions our own stability, it can leave a footprint. We all have painful memories, Jack, things we'd rather not think about, but unless we acknowledge them and how they make us feel, they can fester and grow until the pressure gets too much. If they break free on their own accord, they're much harder to put back. It's a little like Whack-a-mole, you can stop one, but another will pop up straight away. Think about what happened with Michael Watts."

"You're saying, because I had a shitty childhood, that's why I beat up Watts?"

Shelly shrugged, "Maybe. It may not have been a conscious act."

"You're wrong doc. It was a very conscious act. I did it because I wanted to, I wasn't trying to repress anything, and if you ask me if I'd do it again. I'd say yes."

Shelly was impressed with his certainty, but he was wrong, "it's not about what you did, it's about what you didn't do. You could have had a psychogenic blackout, a loss of control, although uncommon."

"What do you think it was?"

"I think you need to find out what it is that you're ignoring. Your childhood is a part of it, but it's not the whole story. There's something else. Something missing. Watts was a barrier to doing some good, which presents a paradox. To do something good, you had to do something bad. You had to embrace a darker side. Perhaps we can start there."

Hopper thought back to the day he found the girl. He'd never talked about that night, what he saw, how it made him feel, what he wanted. No one had kicked up a fuss because the girl had been found and she was alive. *Take the win*, the guys in the force would say. But it wasn't a win, he'd seen something he couldn't forget. He'd looked deep into the abyss and found something he couldn't, wouldn't admit to, and no matter how many drinks or how many fights he had, it was always there lurking in the dark, mocking him. "Like someone standing on my brain," Hopper said, more to himself than to Shelly. "So, tell me, doc, how do I get them off?"

"You have to recognise who it is first, and then we can figure out why." Shelly eyed Hopper carefully, it was obvious that his need to atone was the driving force behind his actions. "Tell me, Jack, why do you think being a cop is so important to you?"

"Because I want to stand for something, make a difference."

It was a textbook answer, one that was rolled out on recruitment drives, but like all marketing statements, meant absolutely nothing. "Ok, and why do you think it's so important to make a difference?"

"Because someone has to," Hopper reflexively answered.

"And that someone has to be you?"

"It has to be someone."

"But why you?" Shelly pressed.

"I know what you're getting at, because I need to be seen as one of the good guys, because I never had enough hugs at home when I was a kid. I get it." Hopper felt irritated by their exchange.

"Do you? Because I don't think you do. None of us are good Jack and none of us are bad, we're a mixture of both. There's a part of us that wants what it wants and to hell with the consequences, but there's another part that weighs it up and makes a call. Yes or no, can we get away with it, what will happen if we get caught? Sometimes one side wins out. Sometimes, it's the other. Your need to be good, stems from somewhere," Shelly said, adding offhandedly, "do you have bad thoughts?"

*Yes, I have bad thoughts all the time,* he wanted to say. His internal struggle to do the right thing, to attain for what he might do and for the thing that lurked inside. "No more than most," he lied.

Shelly scribbled in her notes, Hopper hated it when she did that. "It must be hard," She began, more to herself than to Hopper, "to want to be seen as good. We all look for approval one way or another to know we have a place in the group, that we're valued. And now that's been taken away from you. It must be very frustrating." She paused for a while, allowing her words to sink in, "Tell me Jack, how do you see yourself?"

Hopper thought about his darker self. He'd had enough time to self-reflect, and he didn't like what he saw. Things he should have done, things he shouldn't. *How did he see himself?* Deep down, he wanted to say good, that yes, he was one of the good guys, defender of the weak. He lived by his own moral code and had a line drawn, he'd seen enough in his lifetime to know the difference between right and wrong, good and bad and he knew which side of the line he belonged on, but deep down he also knew which side of the line he wanted to be on. *How did he see himself?* He'd rather not say. "I don't know what you mean?"

"It's a simple question. If we're locked in a cycle where our sense of self-worth comes from someone else, how can we ever measure up, especially if that person is no longer with us?"

Shelly had a habit of letting her questions hang in the air, feeling no need to close the gap on any uncomfortable silence between the two. For Hopper it was different, he felt ashamed, worthless. He loathed himself. He'd tried so hard in the past to be what he wasn't. She was right, how can you ever measure up to a dead guy, especially one you killed. He wanted to tell her; he could feel the words lodged in his throat, ready to come out, that it wasn't guilt he felt but relief, a calming sensation. The guilt came from having the feeling not from what he did. Life on the streets had never been this bad, instead, he took the coward's way out, he wasn't ready, not yet. "What do you suggest?" He asked.

"I think we need to find the part of you that's missing," Shelly took off her glasses and carefully closed her note pad. "You want to be the good guy Jack, then be the good guy. Tell me about the Missing Persons, we could start with that."

# 27.

Tap
Tap
Tap
Tap
Delete, delete, delete.
Tap....tap, tappy, tappy, tap tap...tap, *fuck*, delete.

Hopper's session with Shelly had left something of a bad taste in his mouth. He either needed a fight or a fuck, and since neither were an option so early in the day, he'd gone back to the station. Stuck in the bowels of the building, out of sight out of mind, he was busy entering data for a newly acquired system. The department had decided to transition to digital several years ago and was in the process of upgrading. The new platform was cloud-based and would allow for instantaneous referencing, which was made possible provided it had the information to reference. Hopper had been given the task of transferring, uploading and inputting data, both old and new.

The improvements shepherded in a new age of policing, creating an army of remote AI bots set to scour the material in a heartbeat, a larger information bank meant better cross-referencing and, therefore a far more effective system. Doing away with the long, exhausting hours of police drudgery and the paycheques that came with them, overtime wasn't given up so easily. The aim was to streamline into an efficient, time-saving machine. To Hopper, it meant redundancies, less policing, and bigger loopholes for savvy lawyers to jump through. There was even talk of allowing the community to police their own neighbourhoods. Unfortunately, the improvements weren't working as well as promised. According to the resident tech, Dom Tolson, with whom he shared the space, there was a problem with the codecs and translation protocols, not to mention people didn't like change, especially when it hit their wallet.

Hopper was used to nodding along, tutting his disapproval, when necessary, as Dom continued to malign both developers and, as he saw them, the dinosaurs upstairs, which seemed to keep him happy. He could have been unraveling the mysteries of the universe, but as far as Hopper was concerned, it was a different language and one that he had no interest in learning, despite Dom's continued efforts.

It was the punishment from hell. In addition to transferring old records, Hopper had also been tasked with entering information from paper forms into the new system. Some of the older members of the force still resisted the idea of computers, braving some of the most incomprehensible handwriting he'd ever seen, bordering on illiterate. His lack of dexterity and banana fingers did little to ease the frustration he felt, and was grateful for Dom's help, who in return was equally grateful for the company and extra pair of hands. Had it not been for Hopper, Dom would have been consigned to the drudgery of doing it himself, but with several floors of tech incompetents, he was often called away to solve the common crisis of an unplugged computer. Hopper could think of worse people to share his space with.

Tap
Tap
Tap
Tap
Delete delete delete.
Tap....tap, tappy tappy tap tap...tap, *fuck*, delete, tap.

It was an unstoppable flow of people transformed to data, a new age of techno-wizardry and the infallibility of AI, no longer at the mercy of human error, only it wasn't. The bureaucrats who marshaled where dollars were spent, had abdicated all responsibility to the lie they'd been sold. As Dom constantly pointed out, had they allowed the right people to buy the right tools and do their job, they wouldn't be in the mess they were in. The right people being him. Instead, their decision-making ability depended on how expensive the restaurant was, the reps took them to, and the caliber of wine. It was his job, as it had been pointed out, to make sure it worked. It didn't matter if it couldn't, just as long as someone was bashing away at the keys, doing something *techy*!

"Enjoying yourself?" Dom asked, as Hopper continued to punch at the keyboard with his fingers, each tap unnecessarily harder than the last.

"This is bullshit," complained Hopper, "I can't even read half of this crap. There used to be a literacy test back when I joined, half of these guys can't even write!"

"What's bullshit is the guy on the second floor complaining his cup-holder no longer works." Hopper threw him a quizzical glance. "That's right, computers don't have cup holders! The old ones have disk drives. That's what bullshit is! Having to deal with these fucktards day in day out. Christ, it's the twenty-first century. I despair."

"You know it wasn't that long ago I was one of those fucktards."

"This is true. But you at least had the sense not to even touch your computer."

Hopper stopped typing, "Yes, but this, however, is worse than your pathetic attempt to trump me. You know why? Because this replacement of good old police work will eventually come back to fuck us in the ass. Allow me to explain, it's human nature to be lazy, and this will turn us into lazy fucking slobs who don't give a shit, and what's worse, we're going along with it, that's what the real bullshit is."

"Interesting analysis on the new system, but you are, my neanderthal friend, as per usual, wrong." As much as Dom hated the new system, he hated the prejudice Hopper's generation seemed to have against technology. As with all software, the biggest problem wasn't what it did, more so, how it was used. "Going back to, as you say, *good old police work* is why there's a litany of innocent people behind bars, because some lazy slob, sorry... *some lazy fucking slob* couldn't be bothered to check or cross-reference. You don't need to give a shit. You just need to be thorough. What's worse is how monkeys, no offense Hopps, are running this state-of-the-art piece of software, but I believe I win."

"None taken. I am proud to be considered a monkey by you and see it as something of a promotion. Besides, I thought you hated it?"

"Hate is a strong term, Detective Hopper. I hate the idiots who integrated it into our archaic system, I hate the idiots who sold it as something it's not and I hate the ignorance of people who think it can do everything. It can't. It's not a replacement. It's an adjunct." Dom fell into the chair opposite, although fifteen years Hopper's junior, he considered Hopper as his trainee. "Have I taught you nothing padawan? In principle, it's a great piece of software engineering, it's just the fuckwits who put it together for us. Had they asked..."

"Yeah yeah, had they asked you, it would have blah blah fucking blah. It's still bullshit Dom and you know it." Interrupted Hopper. It was a conversation they'd had many times before.

"No, no, no, my friend. Let me lift the veil from your eyes." Dom wheeled his chair next to Hopper and shoved him out of the way, and cracked his knuckles. In his element, Dom was a master, but like Hopper had been consigned to the lower echelon of operational duties because of poor social skills, zero tolerance for those he considered stupid, not to mention calling the Captain a moron, whom he also considered his intellectual inferior. Hopper, grateful for the help and company, knew it to be a shame, Dom was correct in his assumptions, he was far smarter than his superiors and should have been considered an asset. Instead, because of his dislike for authority and the chain of command, had been relegated to the basement, out of sight out of mind. It was one of the reasons they got on so well. For Dom, the police would be a by-line in an increasingly impressive CV, as he left for a more lucrative future, which Hopper encouraged, only to be replaced by a lesser version.

Dom continued to run his fingers over the keyboard playing his own symphony. "What this allows you to do," he continued, "is not only cross-reference, which is cool in itself, but it also lets you introduce your own set of filters through its learning algorithm, so the more you use it, the smarter it gets. That, my friend, is pretty clever. You use keywords to narrow the scope, which means you can reference anything by anything, the problem isn't how it works, the problem is the integration and building the data bank, which is why you're here." Dom punched the enter key, "and voila!" Dom wheeled his chair back as if he'd just finished a full tyre change in an F1 pit stop, arms raised in celebration and smug satisfaction waiting for the appropriate response at his handiwork.

"Voila what?" Hopper asked, with no idea what he was looking at.

In Dom's eyes Hopper never failed to disappoint. "You shitting me!?" Dom excitedly pointed to the screen. "There, voila there!"

"It's a map!"

"Jesus Hopper, how long have you been down here with me? You know I blame myself, I would like to say it's me, not you, but I'm afraid it is you." Dom continued, "A map is not just a tool of how to get from A to B or the graphic representation of an area, a map, or at least this map, is a geographic slice of socio-economic trends, shown in their respective forms, sizes, and relationships to one another." He waited to get a response from Hopper, "it's really fucking cool!"

Hopper sniffed, "it still looks like a map!"

Dom didn't take the bait, "Yes, I appreciate it still looks like a map, but you see here." Dom took the curser to a series of fields on the interface, "this is effectively your search criteria, by changing the filters you can introduce different overlays or even combine them. For example, I type in homicide and the map changes, the greater the density, the deeper the color, you can also view by stats but I'm guessing that's a waste of time in your case, it requires a further degree of effort." Hopper winced, "I type in aggravated assault, and we see our hotspots. If I were to add any unsolved crimes and cross-reference with places, people etc. we can narrow the field even more... See! Now that's real police work. Take your missing persons, no one gives a shit, right? Now given this is just a rudimentary test, since your still inputting data, but you can already see the hot spots." The map immediately changed, highlighting different parts of the city in a range of colors, "and if you were to do it by date...Voila!" The map subtly changed once more.

"What's this supposed to mean?" Hopper pointed to a cluster of dots in one area.

"At this stage, I suspect it's more to do with how much data you've put in... as you can see people go missing everywhere, but there's a greater skew towards lower socio-economic areas, which is what you'd expect. That's this area here," Dom said pointing to the screen. "What's also apparent in these areas is the lack of crime that gets reported, and in the case of MP's you'd imagine there's most likely a good reason to go missing. There's be a host of reasons; migratory, resistance to data through a cash economy, but all in all a pretty good indication as to where the problem areas are."

"In English."

Dom pushed his hair away from his eyes and sighed, "In poor places, people go missing."

"I could have told you that. So, you're telling me that given how many thousands, if not millions, but essentially a fuck ton of cash, the conclusion we have is that. There's a higher percentage of crime in poor areas?"

"You're simplifying. It's a trend. Trends are important. Trends come and go. You look, say six months ago." Dom's hands glided over the keyboard once more, and the screen changed, "the picture's different, it shows anomalies, six months ago less people went missing. With an anomaly, there's usually a reason why, in this case, most likely because you haven't entered in enough data, so it's skewed. But, it would usually mean an area of interest or a developing pattern in the real world." Hopper still looked confused. "Let's say you've just made a health drink, right? You'd want to know where to launch it. With this you can track everything that matches the same demographic, you can even cross-reference through anything that has a digital footprint, like Facebook, Insta or whatever. This means when you come to sell, you do so on a granular level and target only those who are interested, thereby maxing out your sales potential. Preaching to the converted in effect."

"Which is good for us?"

"In the case of your health drink, you get to save a shit ton of cash and let the market do the rest. It's about the application, it can be used as an identifier so that, you, the police, can monitor a potential hotspot before it gets out of hand. That's what's cool about it, it could be used as a precognition tool, instead, we have a monkey, you. No offense again. Plugging in data no-one gives a shit about!"

"Isn't that a bit creepy?"

"It's totally creepy, but cool as fuck. Like I said for it to really work, it needs a digital footprint or echo, like a smartphone. You can view any common threads by case, date, hair color if you like. If you were lucky, for instance, you could find out you have psycho targeting redheads in this area here." Dom tapped the screen, "Hell, it's even mobile friendly! You have a smartphone, right?" Hopper rolled his eyes, "Just checking. See, not bullshit at all, you can be all big brother in the field. Of course, you can't, 'cos you're stuck in here with me, but someone could."

Hopper leaned back in his chair and stared at the multicolored map on screen, a dark shape had grown through a derelict section of the city Hopper recognised only too well. The stain had the nagging familiarity of a place Hopper would rather forget, a place where a girl had once been abducted and the monster he had met.

# 28.

Nathan Moynihan, or Nate to his friends, was bored. Conscious of his age, he was at the awkward time in his young life, no longer a minor, not quite an adult, at least not in the eyes of the state. You still had to be twenty-one to buy a drink, but you could fuck at sixteen, get married at eighteen, and be welcomed into the joint with open arms for those unlucky few. Nate still had three months left to go. He, like many his age, couldn't see the point in the double standards, it forced 'minors' into unsafe practices, created a binge drinking culture, and gave overzealous cops an opportunity for an easy bust to pop their cherries. Although Nate wasn't too bothered, he didn't much care for booze or drugs, at least not the ones that mattered. He preferred a clean mind and a clean body, or cleanish. His drug of choice and that of his small gang was steroids.

He'd initially met Jackson at the gym he went to, Tiny's, membership courtesy of his mum, and had been working out for months but was frustrated by his lack of improvement. No matter how hard he pushed himself, nothing worked. He'd even devoted himself to twice daily sessions some weeks, but the only thing growing was his frustration. He'd seen Jackson around, he was one of the serious builders, often spotting some of the other guys, still big, but not when standing next to Jackson, they paled by comparison. At first, he'd been intimidated, but Jackson caught him staring and nodded a quick hello, and after a while, they struck up a conversation. Nate wanted to know how? How'd he do it? How'd he get so big? Jackson, never one to shy away from hero worship, was only too happy to pass on his knowledge, recommending split sessions, one for back and shoulders, one for chest and arms, not forgetting leg day, he also told him to think about his diet, or how to cram as much protein in his body to be more precise. Nate told him he'd tried the split sessions, was sick of drinking protein shakes, and couldn't afford chicken and steaks every day. He'd tried everything.

"Everything?" Jackson had asked with a sly grin. It was a moment that changed Nate's life. Jackson waited for a quiet time in the gym before showing him the ampules. Steroids, he'd told him, were the only real way to get big, but only when used properly, in a controlled way. Nate was keen, desperate. There was so much about his life he wanted to change, and now he could, with a little chemical help from his new friend. But the cost! Tantalizingly close but still out of reach. Jackson came up with the perfect solution. If he knew others who wanted what he had, all he had to do was make a few introductions and sell on, if he sold enough, he'd be getting his for free. It wasn't dealing, Jackson assured, it was more about providing a service. After all, no one was getting high. It was music to Nate's ears, there was no shortage of *wanna be* jocks, determined to get big, no matter what the cost. Instagram fame was only a few needles away. And so started a happy relationship.

Nate got big, Jackson got richer. Both getting the results they wanted, both comfortable with the exchange, and settled into an easy routine. The gym was too obvious to sell in, and was getting suspicious. They also maintained a strict zero-tolerance policy. They didn't have a problem with their clientele using, they just didn't want it happening on their doorstep. Instead, Jackson suggested the zoo. It was perfect, there were no disapproving side-eye glances or carefully pointed questions, and Jackson had the run of the place, including access to the security cameras, so he always knew who was around and who wasn't. It was foolproof.

In Nate's steroid-addled brain, he'd begun to see himself as something of a lieutenant to Jackson's Captain, drumming up business. He felt like he was part of something bigger, on the up, singled out for better things, finally getting the respect he craved by becoming a someone. A someone like Jackson. It was no secret he looked up to him, even dreaming about him on occasion, but he kept those dreams a secret, figuring they were just by-products of the steroids. He wasn't interested in naked workouts, not unless Jackson was, but for health reasons only. He liked girls, he told himself and anyone else that was prepared to listen, he wasn't like that. Over time, he'd even amassed his own crew, other spotty youths keen to advance their years unwilling to wait, looking for the shortcut. All steroid abusers, they resembled a group of unsupervised overgrown toddlers, moon-faced and bloated. Nate, as supplier, naturally assumed the role of leader, and they had started to make the zoo their permanent hang out, waiting for the opportunity to impress. He'd heard about Frank, but only whispers in the dark, about how bad-ass he was, and Nate so desperately wanted to be bad-ass himself. He'd always figured that Jackson had other things going on outside of the zoo, it was clearly just a cover—even Superman had a day job! Where else did he get the juice? Nate had talked it over with his gang often enough, too much time on their hands and not enough brain cells to spend it wisely.

Jackson watched them at a distance on screen, holed up in his bunker that was little more than a breeze block tool shed that he'd commandeered as his own security office, complete with an antiquated surveillance system he'd inherited. Jackson, king of Kong, the alpha male, lord over all he saw. On the desk in front of him, a display screen flickered. Low resolution black and white images of the zoo showed a matrix of different vantage points as captured by the closed-circuit cameras. Carefully positioned, he'd moved them around, making sure there were enough blind spots where he could sell invisibly but still had access to most of the zoo, especially where it counted, giving him access to a library of private moments and up-skirts, as well as being able to keep an ever-watchful eye on the toddlers and most importantly of all, Eve.

During his time at the zoo Jackson had collected a substantial library of footage for his own entertainment, he'd even uploaded a few to various porn sites just to see the reaction and view their viewing figures. Apparently, he wasn't the only one with a voyeuristic interest. He'd also found them far more useful than for just spying on Eve and had come to realize the value of being having eyes everywhere. Omnipresent and powerful, they presented opportunity, insurance, and knowledge. Opportunity to keep an eye on Eve, insurance against Frank and the knowledge of who was doing what and when. After all, all ex-cons know; never trust an ex-con. As much as he trusted Frank, he didn't and had even installed a camera out of sight overlooking the surgery, figuring it was his insurance if anything ever went south. Fisher, he trusted even less, an oily fish capable of slithering his way out of trouble only too willing to throw his grandmother under a bus if it helped him, and Higgs was simply just too smart for his own good and Jackson had no intention of ending up on one of his meat hooks. It was his way of staying protected, he had enough material on the tapes stashed back at his place to burn everything to the ground.

Nate didn't much care for animals, unlike the rest of his crew, who could remain entertained for hours by the antics of the monkeys. He found them irritating, one even had the audacity to lob its own shit at him after he'd flicked a cigarette butt at it. It had almost hit as well, which caused no end of laughter from the group. Had it not been for the bars he'd have leaped over and shown the scraggy-looking beast just who was boss. Instead, he'd settled for a heavier object, but all he could find was an empty coke can which he'd filled with dirt. It had missed and the monkey laughed even harder. He sulkily moved on, more annoyed than before, he wasn't meant to be the figure of fun, his posse reluctantly following. They settled in front of the solitary wolf. Mackenzie Valley Wolf. Canis

Lupus Occidentalis, the largest wolf breed in the world, Nate read of the plaque zip ties to the bars of the cage. If there was one animal he liked less than most, it was a dog. His mum had a dog. A cute little shih tzu with big wet sorrowful eyes and a fluffy white coat. He would swear blind she loved it more than him, she doted on it, obsessed over it, constantly feeding it little treats until it was almost as fat as her, which to his mind would be impossible, he'd wanted to flush it down the john. Whilst the rest of his boys watched the animal in awe, excitedly jabbering about Game of Thrones and what it would be like to have one as a mascot, Nate pulled the wooden stake off a nearby sign that read, keep off the grass, and jabbed it through the bars of the cage.

Adam had been methodically collecting rubbish, jabbing at the empty packets and coffee cups scattered across the zoo, spearing them with the metal spoke at the end of his pick-up stick before sliding them off into a large canvas bag loosely slung over his shoulder. To the casual observer, it looked like dirty work, but for Adam it provided purpose and kept him busy, giving him a sense of well-being to look back on the grounds he'd just cleared and was quietly thankful of the public's disregard for the grounds of the zoo. He had noticed the group of overgrown toddlers earlier when they were at the monkey house and considered saying something, but the alpha male had his own way of dealing with troublemakers. Adam wished the boy with the big moon face he'd helped could have seen it; he would have found it as funny as he did when the monkey shit almost hit the larger of the youths. He recognized them of course, he'd seen them around several times with Jackson, and, assuming since they shared the same physicality, they most likely shared the same personality traits, namely that of being an asshole, and decided to ignore them until he saw them at the wolf's cage.

Jackson knew he should have intervened when he saw Nate at the monkey house but instead had sat back to enjoy the show. He hadn't been disappointed. He felt like a producer of his own reality show. He had the power to decide what happened and what didn't happen and for how long. Besides, he liked the extra cash the steroids brought in and didn't want to scare any customers away. He also needed to project the right image. He'd begun to lose interest in them when he caught sight of Eve. She had been doing a roaring trade because of the midday sun and was wearing his favorite outfit, a loose-fitting black vest, which probably accounted for the line of young boys waiting to be served, and for once, she was on her own. He had become uncomfortably aware of the growing friendship between her and Adam and resented their time together. He assumed it was because she felt sorry for him, in the way one does a stray dog, but this was his opportunity.

It wasn't fair to hurt a dumb animal, but watching Nate provoke the wolf, Adam seriously considered taking the wooden stick off him and ramming it into his eye. "Hey," he called out instead, "stop that."

Nate turned to look at Adam, he'd been having a lot of fun, much to the nervous amusement of his friends, several of which who weren't really into torturing animals. "Why, what are you gonna do about it?" Was his predicable response. He'd been looking for something or someone to hit all day, and after sizing Adam up, didn't consider him to be much of a threat.

Adam didn't have a clear plan; all he'd wanted to do was stop them, and he had, and now their attention was focused squarely on him. The wolf was still snarling, teeth bared. Adam considered feeding Nate to it, but judging by his size, he'd have trouble squeezing him through the bars, *maybe one arm at a time*, his inside voice suggested. "I think you should just leave," Adam said, walking towards them, pick stick still in hand. "I don't want any trouble."

"C'mon Nate, lets go," one of the group said, already uncomfortable with the way Adam seemed to be staring at them. Nate, never one to back down, disagreed. He had a reputation to protect or at the very least develop, "You're kidding, you scared of a skinny little punk like him?" He turned back to Adam and the pick stick he was still holding, "And what d'you think you're gonna do with that?"

Adam looked down at his hand, he hadn't been aware he'd been holding it, now that he was, he was still considering his options.

Jackson was trying to impress Eve. The conversation he'd rehearsed in his head always went smoothly. He would say all the right things, interesting things, and she would laugh and ask him questions about how much he could lift. He would patiently explain that weight training wasn't the meathead activity people thought it was. It was about the power of the mind, discipline, and dedication. You had to think the weight up, as well as push it. It was all very Zen; he was actually a pretty deep guy! The reality, sadly, was always different. *Why the hell Eve couldn't just stick to the script!*

"Thought I'd come and check on how you're doin', been keeping an eye on you." Jackson had said with a swagger, wanting to say something cool, something that made him sound important, how he cared for her and would never let anything happen to her, at least not while he was around. But as soon as the words came out, he sounded like some creepy guy spying on her. Which he was.

Eve glanced up at the cameras, "Giving yourself a quick workout?" she said, balling a fist, shaking it up and down.

*Why did she have to be such a bitch?* Jackson thought as he tried to laugh at her comment as a good-humored joke between friends. "It's nothin' like that. I keep an eye on everyone, I was just... you know... letting you know, you 'ain't got nothin' to worry about with me around. Keepin' an eye on you is all."

"And that's supposed to make me feel so much safer?"

Jackson shrugged, "I'm just trying to be friendly. I would have thought someone like you could do with a friend."

"Meaning?" Eve folded her arms and shifted her weight to the other foot. She knew exactly what he meant. She'd known his type all her life, overgrown man-child, sulky and petulant at best. Dangerous and volatile at worst. Especially when they didn't get their own way, she decided she was no one's victim long ago. That Jackson couldn't take a hint only reinforced her opinion of him. She'd tried to be subtle, kind, flattered, even tried blaming herself, *it isn't you, it's me. Fuck that, it's definitely you.* She'd told him they could be friends, *not likely*, to let him down gently. Big mistake. She'd quickly realized that any attention was interpreted as some sort of come-on through his steroid-addled brain. All she had left was to rip the band-aid off in one go. But it made her uncomfortable. She didn't like being the bitch. Like the makeup, it was a disguise to wear from time to time. Sadly, it had become so comfortable she'd almost forgotten what it was like without it.

She was making him mad. It wasn't how the conversation had been meant to go. Instead, Jackson could feel the pressure building in his head. *Why couldn't she just stick to the god-damned script? Or at the very least, show a little gratitude. Wasn't he the one trying to do her a favor after all?* "Meaning nothing. I'm just saying it wouldn't hurt if you showed a little gratitude once in a while."

"Gratitude! You think I should be grateful that you're spying on me? What about the others you point your cameras at, you think they should be grateful too?"

Jackson was becoming aware of the queue for ice-creams and the extra eyes on him. He didn't need an audience to hear what Eve had to say and leaned in, his bulk dwarfing her, "I think you should watch your fucking mouth." Thankfully their exchange was cut short by the commotion at the wolf cage.

Nate had snatched the pick stick from Adam, who, keen to avoid confrontation, hadn't protested. His *other*, the one that lived inside, had slunk off embarrassed. The rest of his cronies had Adam pinned against the bars of the cage, as Nate jabbed at the wolf from between his legs, under his arms, hoping to provoke it into attacking and taking a bite out of Adam, the wolf instead snarled, and growled biting at the pole, not Adam.

"That's assault asshole," Eve screamed at Nate. She had been aware of the group of toddlers for some time and knew they were trouble, especially the larger of the group, and also knew the reason they hung out at the zoo. Jackson's not-so-secret sideline. She stormed towards them when she saw what happened, her arms outstretched, clutching her mobile as if it were a crucifix ready to ward off evil spirits. Jackson had no excuse not to follow.

Nate was having fun, of course, he had no intention of actually letting the animal take a bite out of the skinny guy, he just wanted to scare him, but so far, he didn't seem scared at all, it was making him mad, and when he saw Eve heading his way holding her phone out followed by Jackson knew he was in trouble. He nodded to his gang to let Adam go, "we were just having a laugh is all, no harm done, he's not even hurt."

"Is that so," Eve continued filming, "well, I saw the whole thing and have it in my phone, and this is going straight to the police."

"Police!" The word penetrated the fog in Nate's clouded head as he looked at Jackson for help, "You're not gonna let her call the police are you? What about..." He quickly stopped talking when he saw how Jackson was glaring at him.

"No one's calling the police," growled Jackson in a squeak, he didn't want Nate squealing to the police about their little arrangement, potentially fucking up his parole or worse, Frank finding out. He quickly turned to Eve, "just give me the phone."

"No chance, this is evidence, if I ever see any of you dickheads again, I promise you, this will not only go to the police but will end up on every social I can think of."

Getting the police involved was bad enough, losing his customer base was unacceptable, "and I said gimme the Goddam phone," he barked, snatching it off Eve.

Eve stood back open, mouthed as Jackson deleted the video she'd just taken. She knew she was powerless to get it back and to try to do so would only look childish. On the other hand, Adam had no such reservations as he made a grab for it. More surprise than anger prompted Jackson to lash out, nor had he intended to hit him so hard, but Adam still ended up on the floor with a bloodied nose. Eve quickly went to his aid. "You asshole," she shrieked at Jackson.

It was not the end Jackson had in mind. He was supposed to be the good guy, the one offering to be her protector, instead, he stood there feeling stupid, just like the rest of the overgrown toddlers. There was nothing left to say as Jackson flung the phone back at Eve, *why can't you just stick to the script*, "Your phone."

Nate was about to open his mouth when he realized the rest of his group had already taken the opportunity to slink away, and without backup, Nate felt naked. Jackson glowered at him, "don't, just don't." He didn't need to be told twice and followed on. Jackson had nothing left but his anger. Adam had become more than an itch, he'd become competition, and in Jackson's eyes, there was only one way to deal with competition. "I've got my eyes on you," he snarled, "and I'm every-fucking-where, get it?" He took one last look at Eve and thought about what could have been, what should have been, and abruptly walked off.

# 29.

Revisiting old haunts of the past was never a good idea. Hopper didn't need reminders of places he'd been. He had his own nightmares for that. His last session with Shelly hadn't gone the way he'd wanted, opening wounds he'd been happy to ignore. He wasn't missing, he was right here. Wasn't he? Thinking back to his childhood depressed him, some memories were just too painful, a past ripped away like a band-aid, all because of Batman. Had he been born in that moment? He wasn't sure. It was when the beatings had stopped, but the real punishment began, the tiny voice in his head telling him, reminding him, he was never good enough, it was his fault, he was weak and a coward and a killer. Had he spent a lifetime seeking forgiveness in all the wrong places when the only place he should have looked was himself?

There was a lot he held back in his sessions with Shelly, telling her what he thought she wanted to hear, he didn't want her thinking he was some nut job psycho. The irony wasn't lost, he wanted her to see the real him, beyond the mayhem and the crazy, but was no longer sure who that was anymore. *How do you see yourself?* She asked, and he couldn't answer. At the time, he hadn't really understood what she meant by, *find them find yourself,* and thought it more psychobabble jargon, the stuff shrinks say when they're out of ideas, things that make them sound smarter than their patients. But she was right, he had more in common with them than he cared to admit, like them, he was just another missing person no one could be bothered to look for. In his mind he'd always considered, you murder, you're a murderer. You rape, you're a rapist. You're a cop, you do cop things, but who was he? That he didn't know, without the badge, he was nothing.

Hopper didn't know how long he'd been staring at the map back at the station. There are some memories darker than childhood. It shouldn't have come as any surprise there was a higher proportion of red dots in the lower end of town, because sometimes it was easier to cut and run than face the music, and some people just didn't want to be found, it was as simple as that. Generally, there were more unresolved cases in lower socio-economic areas than affluent ones, and without evidence of a crime or a body they were difficult to process. Many went missing because of "personal" problems, dodgy financial commitments, unwanted child maintenance payments, or court requests and appearances were largely ignored. Dom had been careful to point out that since only a small percentage of data had so far been entered, the results would be skewed, painting a false picture. Hopper thought it odd he had gone to great lengths warning him to be careful, *it's easy to see patterns when you want to*, Hopper nodded along, *yeah, yeah I get it*, but he could still dream there was a serial killer on the loose, where's the harm in that, a guy can hope, right? But after an optimistic and enthusiastic start, Hopper had to agree with him, the weight of disappointment knowing Santa Clause and the Tooth Fairy weren't real, and serial killers don't turn up when you want them to, no matter how hard you wish.

He'd found several straight off the bat. Tony Marchushio; missing for several days. Hopper found him listed as a John Doe. His final hours were spent under a false name maxing out his credit cards before taking a swing on the rafters in his motel room by his neck. It had taken Hopper all of forty-five minutes to find Revelle Lemain. A quick cross-reference through the system found her on Facebook, *digital echo*. She'd been conducting an affair with a colleague from work who had been stupid enough to boast about his carnal good fortune online and helpfully posted a couple of pictures of them both in the tub! Many were stories with little difference, refugees from a life that wasn't worth living, abandoning ship, grabbing whatever life-craft they could before paddling to friendlier shores, and why the hell not? Hopper didn't blame them, no one gave a shit except the credit card companies, and they had insurance.

But Leanne Bonnelle was a different story. A pathetic and tragic waste of a life, all too familiar. Single parent, history of drugs, petty crime, soliciting blah blah etc. On the face of it, it was easy to pass judgment, a stereotype of the lazy criminal class, creating divisions where there were none. These people were different, see how they act? But dig deeper, and there was a real human story worthy of a sixty-minute special. Failed by an overworked system, doing whatever it took put food on the table for her and her son and a roof over their heads. No one goes on the game for fun. From what he could tell, she was an independent worker. But a whore without a pimp is, in many ways, more vulnerable than those with. Which meant she would have had to find a safe patch to work on that wasn't already claimed. Sex workers were just as territorial as any other jungle predator.

Her child, now *in care* of the state would be fed, housed, clothed, and abused. All her hard work gone to waste. It was a sad common story, but it mattered. She mattered. She mattered to him. Maybe because of his own lost childhood or maybe they shared a common history. Her red dot was in a place he'd been avoiding for so long. When Shelly told him he was still missing, he knew just where to go looking. He had lost something of himself when he had walked into that apartment, maybe it was time he tried to find it.

The building hadn't changed, thankfully Leanne's apartment was on the ninth floor, mercifully far enough away from the fourteenth. Hopper wondered if she had ever known who or what had taken up residence five floors above. He felt sure the stench would have traveled, but it seemed the ninth had its problems. As Hopper worked the lock, he could feel eyes on his back, all of which miraculously vanished as soon as he turned to face them. He was rusty with his picks but heard the satisfying click after several attempts and let himself in.

The interior wasn't what he expected and took him by surprise. The door opened directly to the living area, which was meticulously clean, unlike the rest of the building. The windows carried none of the grease smears giving clear, uninterrupted views of the city. Moderately furnished, there was a coziness he hadn't expected, soft furnishings and thick plumped cushions one could get lost in. An old widescreen tv dominated the far corner of the room, with the furniture arranged around it. There was a refurbished dresser populated with objects that carried only personal value, Hopper was struck by how many photographs there were of her son, from infant to podgy youth, he picked up the last, he still looked as if he were in single figures, admittedly it was difficult to tell with downs syndrome children. According to the missing person report, it was easy to mistake Leanne for a hard-cold street worker with an inconvenient kid. Her going missing could have been the best thing that could have happened. But you would be wrong. He was cared for; he was looked after, and he had been wanted. Leanne had tried. She had done her best with what she had. His mother wouldn't have just up and left.

The open plan kitchen, separated by linoleum, had been scrubbed hard enough to fade the pattern. There were no signs of roaches or any other infestation one might associate with such buildings, even Hopper had to admit, that in itself, was impressive. Even the fridge, its contents already beginning to fill the apartment with heady musty smell, reminding him the meter had finally run out, had been carefully stocked. The bedrooms painted a similar picture. Leanne's room betrayed little of her occupation, except for her "work" clothes, various sex toys, and an enormous collection of flavored condoms in a wicker basket. Her son, Anton's room, was small but compact, his single bed had clean sheets and the walls were covered with prints of various animals. His furniture was sparse, consisting of just a single chest of draws, on which his favorite stuffed animals were on display along with souvenirs and a roll of complimentary tickets to the Zoo, Hopper tore a few off. Leanne had given the boy the better room of the two, his had windows. The view wasn't great, but it let in what counted as fresh air in the neighborhood. Below was a maze of interlocking alleyways leading to cheap restaurants and sex shops, as well as similar high rises, interspersed with what would have once been playgrounds but had deteriorated into shopping center for narcotics. Further in the distance, he realized he could see the Zoo from where he stood. Given Anton's obsession for animals, he could imagine the boy staring out over the wasteland wishing for a better place that was only a short bus ride away. Hopper smiled; he hadn't been to the Zoo in years.

# PART 3

# 30.

There was so much more to say, but Higgs remained empty. Nothing prepares you for fatherhood. You find your way through personal experience. You were a child once; how hard can it be? You mine your past for precious memories but come up empty-handed. You don't remember because you can't, feelings pushed aside, squeezed out by the loss of innocence substituted by the dark muddy waters that come with age. First adolescence. Bringing with it a heady mixture of desire, want, and hunger. A cloudy brain yearning for things not yet learned only glimpsed. Then maturity, a change too soon. The heavy saddle strapped to thin shoulders ready for a rider, each one bearing down, the weight bending your spine. The expectation of responsibility that you were somehow 'ready' to take on more?

More things, more stuff. Stuff you're told you need to have. Stuff that reassures you and tells the world you're not a fraud. Older, more responsible. You need a job, a car, a house, a wife, a kid, a dog, a garden, a pool, neighbors, credit cards, tax bills, accountants, stress, anxiety, impotence, and gym memberships along with affairs and friends that act and think like you. Reminding you that, *yes, you're one of us, one of us,* only to be talked about and dissected later. A yardstick used to measure their life against yours, as you measure yours against theirs. Increments ticked off through possession and loss, all the stuff that makes you, you. A fake.

You think you remember what it was to be a child, to know the freedom of happiness, the joy of each and every day, and the possibilities that come with it? But the good memories fade first, leaving the stain of moments you'd rather forget. The ones that fucked you up and grew into long shadows keeping your life dark. You would think to avoid them, the pitfalls of your life only to stumble and create more. Foundations deep enough to build a life upon. Life can be like that. Retrospection is a cruel fucker, and not the teacher we applaud and thank for life's lessons learned.

There were so many things Higgs wanted to say to his daughter; how much he loved her, what she meant to him, how precious she was. How he felt when he first saw her come into the world, so tiny, so angry, and why not? Eve was late, it was warm and safe inside, she had everything she needed, why bother coming out at all? She had been induced, fourteen days late, the maximum time allowed before the bill had to be paid, beds made, and the room given an airing before the next guest appeared. She left pissed off, and arrived screaming and shouting, and closed the hotel down. Higgs always knew his daughter was going to be an only child, with a mind of her own, *she literally broke the mould that made her*. Intent on living life on her terms. No glass ceiling for her. He wanted to give her everything and made himself into the person he is today by doing so. If only he'd given her what she needed instead. Maybe they'd be a family. Maybe, she'd have a sister. Maybe mum would still be alive. Maybe he would have re-married. Maybe he wouldn't have been caught with his hand in the cookie jar. Maybe he wouldn't be an addict. Maybe, maybe, maybe. It wasn't how he imagined his life to be.

He had been both mum and dad and failed in both. Her mother died in a car accident, or more precisely from injuries sustained by the accident. Or to put it even more precisely, from the psychological despair she faced after the birth of her one and only daughter. Depressed and disheartened, she never fully got over the post-natal desolation of early motherhood. Without proper care and attention she began to disappear, consumed by the needs of another. Motherhood had not come easy; motherhood hadn't come at all. Neither of them was ready for parenthood, nor how demanding Eve would be. No one tells you how much work babies are. The human race would cease to exist if we knew the truth. Their tiny bundle of joy was a nightmare in a blanket. He had coped, she hadn't. He had enough love for them all; she didn't. He was working as a vet bringing home the bacon, so to speak, but it wasn't enough. Too tired to notice his wife was no longer there, replaced by a faded photocopy each day. Had he seen, he would have done something. But he hadn't, so she had. She had taken their car out for a mid-morning drive, sans baby, who had been left at home. He had gone to kiss her on the cheek, and she turned her face towards him, so he kissed her fully on the lips. He felt her warm breath mix with his own, tasting her damp open mouth. He recognized something once known in her eyes and went to work, ignoring the alarm bells ringing in his ears. He should have stayed and picked her up and wept together. He should have done so many things that he didn't, and so he left, and so did she.

The toxicology report said she was twice over the limit. He doubted she'd been drunk. When you're already numb, very little makes you feel. He knows that now, too many years too late. He became both mum and dad to tiny Eve. At first, there was so much help on offer. He was the charity project, the sad man with the unbelievably hard burden, *'how could she'* was mum's legacy, but as time went on, *'how could she not'* was his own. He'd had affairs, many, there's nothing so attractive as vulnerability. He'd fucked his way through friends, co-workers, friends' wives, and the ex-friends' wives, exhausting his supply. After a while, when his life didn't change, he became an old story, part of the past that should have had the decency to stay where it was put, the past. He could feel himself going the same way as his wife, disappearing from view. He needed something to make him whole and found it. The drugs were only ever meant to be a short-term crutch, but how can you stay away when the welcome was so good. He'd promised himself more times than he could remember that each hit would be the last. *This week, I'll stop this week, once a week is ok, it's just recreational,* but next week is always next week and since it's only Monday and the week has already started...you know the drill. Deprivation is no way to start a campaign. How many dieters binge before starting, *I'll start tomorrow, so tonight I get a free pass! I'll eat all the chocolate I can find in the house, then maybe the corner shop and the gas station or the 7 11... and then buy some more!*

You kid yourself you're in control, you're the exception not the rule. You can be a high-functioning addict, but as with all dysmorphic viewpoints, you don't see what everyone else sees. So what? You forgot to shave—the rugged look is in. So what if Eva didn't have her lunch? She wouldn't starve, there's food at home. So what the animal died? It was going to die eventually. So what the drugs in the cabinet don't match the paperwork? Who cares about bureaucracy? So what, so what, so what, and things begin to slide. Nothing prepares you for the bitter disappointment in your daughter's eyes. There were so many things he wanted to say, but "What are you doing here, checking up on your old man?" wasn't one of them.

There was so much more for her to say but found herself empty. Nothing prepares you for the day you stop feeling like a child, it creeps up and cloaks you like a shadow at dusk. Eve was old before her time, a parent to a father. She knew it had been hard on him but resented him for making it hard on her and had grown quickly bored with the succession of pretend mummies as a child, there for one night, maybe two. If she was really lucky, maybe a week before they left, before he scared them away. At first, she wondered if it had been her that drove them away, not pretty enough, not fun enough, not girly enough, too solemn, too sulky, too shy, too her.

She liked it best when it was just the two of them, with whatever animal or animals they were currently living with. They were her family, pets never owned but loved nonetheless. She could watch him for hours with a dog, a cat, a mouse, a bird, it didn't matter, come one, come all. All were welcome, sometimes he would catch her looking and would throw back a cheeky grin with a wink, often inviting her to help as they would stitch together some poor damaged animal. In those times, she saw him for who he was and loved him for it. Favorite moments spent with the broken, if only she could have fixed him. But daughters shouldn't have to fix daddies, they don't know how and can't. Their limited tender love is only part of the picture, there's a space that needs to be filled and Higgs filled it with whatever he could get his hands on. To be fair though, he had kept it hidden as addicts do, but even masters of disguise can only pretend for so long until the mask slips. Their lives became different, transient. He managed to keep working on and off, for places that couldn't afford the fees, they had even spent time with a circus, her favorite time, but even they, and circus folk are a forgiving bunch, had enough. They had wanted her to stay, a teary ringmaster with a weeping wife imploring her, but loyalties run with blood. What would he do without her? She couldn't leave him to his own self-destruction, she had her own to think about. They left the circus with an open invitation and a promise to return.

His medical training opened opportunities, inviting the more dangerous kind of animal into their home, to be patched up on the dining room table. Questions never asked, her father quickly developed a reputation as someone who could keep his mouth shut. Then there was the zoo. Her elation was short-lived and quickly replaced by suspicion – what kind of place offers a man like her father a job? A place with secrets, that's what.

It started out well enough, she was happy, he was happy. But something changed. Life became heavier, he even began to lose interest, becoming detached, indifferent. His hours changed, occasionally disappearing without notice, only to return with the additional weight of his secret. She knew he was using again. She recognized the tell-tale signs well enough, try as hard as she could to ignore them, she knew when the mask had slipped. It was only a matter of time. She prepared herself for the worst and made the decision to return to the circus, and if she went alone, then so be it. But the time didn't come, he stayed so she stayed, and an uneasy air became their oxygen. He began to fade, replaced by a hollow version of himself. Occasionally she would catch a glimpse, a brief reflection of who he once was, a familiar expression, a mannerism that was his alone. Too short-lived often replaced by something new, a look she had never seen before, full of self-loathing and hatred, one that haunted him. There were so many things she wanted to say, but "Why, should I be?" Wasn't one of them.

But that's how it was. Verbal ping pong, neither of them saying what they wanted to, both trying to score points with no chance of winning. There was no prize just one more step further away, *maybe this is how it must be,* thought Eve. Her only option was to keep pushing and pulling until the distance became so great, that the ties that bind would eventually snap of their own accord, blaming no one.

Higgs winced back. Eve had surprised him in the surgery, in truth he was glad to see her, he always was, but today wasn't one of those days, and no doubt she knew it. He was always at his worst in the days leading up to one of Frank's big nights and he knew it showed. He needed something to block the pain, the traitorous thoughts of how he betrayed his patients. The ones he'd sworn an oath to protect. This would be the last time, he promised himself, he just had to get through one more time.

"What brings you here if not to check up on me?" He asked, instead of, *I'm glad you're here, I've missed you and feel so lonely, but we seldom say the things we mean because the risk is too great.*

"You heard about that Asshole Jackson and his crowd of toddlers?" She deflected, instead of, *I wanted to see you, I shouldn't need a reason, you're my dad and I'm worried about you.*

"I did. I have one of their casualties with me at the moment." Higgs nodded to the rear of the surgery where the timber wolf lay sleeping before changing the subject. "I've told you before to stay away from them, why you work here is beyond me, when you could do so much better," he gently admonished, wanting to say, *please don't get involved, this place is dangerous, and I can't protect you, you need to stay away, it will kill me if anything happens to you.*

"Like you?" *Because I'm worried about you.*

"But you're not like me, Eve, you don't have to be here." *God forbid you end up a like me, there's still hope for you, leave before I take you down with me. This place is poison.*

It wasn't the conversation she wanted, Eve wanted him to run away with her, back to the circus, but then again, she never had the conversations she wanted. She let her hand drift from one stainless steel surface to the next, until she came to the holding pens where the sick animals dozed in a chemical sleep, heavily sedated. The area was designed to accommodate four animals at a time, but for now, held only two; the timber wolf and a cougar, their bodies gently moving to the rhythm of their heartbeats.

"I didn't think there was anything wrong with the wolf, what happened?"

"I thought you saw what happened. It has a puncture wound, most likely, it's infected. It was a rubbish stick, wasn't it?" Higgs said, shaking his head.

"But it'll be ok, right? I mean you have antibiotics and stuff?" Eve asked, her brow creased with worry, she was thinking about Adam.

"They're old. The conditions aren't great and what crowds we do get, seem to take enormous satisfaction in feeding them things they shouldn't. You know I once found a yoyo in a stool. I do what I can, which isn't a lot."

"You used to be able to do more."

Higgs sighed, that wasn't his job anymore. He didn't want his daughter anywhere near the animals, she knew enough to know which ones were sick, and which ones were weren't. These weren't. "I'll have to work late tonight." He said moving her away from the pens.

"Are they going to die?" Eve continued, she wasn't so easily distracted.

"I hope not," *one of them will, probably both.*

Eve watched the sleeping animals. She felt scared for them, very few, once admitted seldom left. "Maybe you can save them." She asked hopefully, *But I know you won't, you never do because something bad is happening here. I wish you'd tell me. I know you're in trouble and I want to help.*

*There's no saving these, the paperwork is already done.* "Like I said they're old, the place is falling down, we'll be closed before long." The way she looked at him was a dagger to the heart, he wasn't sure how long he could bear it. *I know and I feel shitty about it, but what can I do, I'm fucked! He would have preferred to say.*

Eve laid her cards on the table and hoped her voice didn't sound too needy, but all daughters need a father. "Then leave. We could just go, tonight. There's nothing for us here. Why don't we just take off? Back to the circus, no one would have to know. We've left before."

*Because they would, and they would hunt us down.* "And what about these?" He asked instead, "there isn't anyone else." He wanted to tell her the truth, he yearned for it, so much so it felt like a physical ache in his heart. Maybe now was the time and for the first time in a long time, he stood directly opposite his daughter, hands on shoulders, looking into her eyes, *say it, say it like you mean it, and there was so much he wanted to say.* "Soon. There are things..." He was interrupted by a voice outside. He glanced at the surgery clock; he was early. *Too late.*

"I'm not here to waste my time." The voice snarled, it was a cruel, harsh voice, laced with menace, a voice that warned all who were smart enough to listen, *I'm not like you, if you know me I will hurt you and I will enjoy it, and once I'm through I will think of you no more, so stay away lest you get crushed beneath my boot.*

For the first time in a very long time, there had been a clearing through the mist of bullshit that usually hung between them, and Eve got to see her father once more, albeit briefly. He was still there peeking out, screaming to be heard. He had become so small and tired and weak that he seldom appeared at all, but there he was, talking straight to the person he loved most, only he hadn't. There was something he wanted to say, but the voice outside did more than cut him off, it terrified him. Eve could see the fear in her father's eyes, not for him, but for her and she understood; any pain inflicted on her would be tenfold on him. "What things?" She quietly asked.

*Things you shouldn't know about,* he thought as the door creaked open. There are moments when time ceases to hold the properties it should, distending beyond boundaries as it turns to glue. Higgs was all too familiar with the distortion through his chemical romance, but this was different, this filled his stomach with cold stones. It was the first time Eve had seen Frank. Although smaller than Jackson, he was, by far, a more commanding presence, the room seemed to shrink as he entered. Like a black hole, his own gravitational pull sucked in the atmosphere and anything close enough to orbit. By comparison, Fisher, the runt of the litter, had been reduced to nothing more than a rodent scuttling between the legs of giants. Frank folded his thick arms, Eve watched the muscles slide and tighten as the tattoo of a cartoon bull with bloodied tusks and a hateful look in his eye held up a meat cleaver and seemed to wink, offering a promise of violence.

"Well, who do we have here?" Frank grinned staring at Eve, his voice sounding like boots on gravel.

"She was just leaving, so if you don't mind..." replied Higgs trying to usher his daughter out past Frank, doing his best to convey a sense of irritation he didn't feel to mask the fear he did. The last thing he wanted was Eve to appear on Frank's radar.

"Mind? I don't mind at all," replied Frank blocking her way still smiling, "so you gonna tell me or do I have to guess?"

"She sells ice creams, that's all Frank," Higgs said

"I don't see any ice creams, isn't she a little young for you?" Frank leered, "don't tell me she's a hooker? I heard there was a hooker working here," he caught Fisher's eye who quickly looked away.

"She's his daughter," squeaked Jackson, before quickly adding, "she's no one."

Higgs glared at Jackson, he'd never wanted to hurt someone so badly as he did at that moment and made a silent promise he would. "And right now, has somewhere else to be."

"Shame on you Jackson, she's not no one, she's family! I like that. I never knew you had family Higgs. That's good. Family keeps you straight, I'm sure you'd do anything for family, ain't that right?" Grinned Frank before turning his attention to Eve, already trying to think of ways to use her as leverage, "Can't say I see the family resemblance, but lucky for you, looks like you took after her mother. Must have been a looker. You got a tongue, sweetheart?"

Jackson cleared his throat, he knew Frank well enough to know he was never one to ignore an opportunity and would eventually find a use for Eve, if only as bait to be dangled in front of Higgs when it suited him and knew how she would react if she learned the truth of what they were up to at the zoo and why certain animals mysteriously became ill, never to be seen again. He may be an asshole in her eyes, but he didn't want to be seen as a cunt as well. Besides, this could be his only opportunity to redeem himself. "We're wasting time Frank. Just let the girl go." One look at Frank's expression told him he'd just made a mistake.

The room grew colder as Frank's grin grew wider. "Why, you have somewhere to be?"

"No Frank. Nowhere, I just thought."

"Thought what?" Frank smiled, it made Jackson shudder, "I didn't think you did that. Think. You taking charge now? Is that what you're telling me? I'm having a nice little chat here with...?" He raised his eyebrows at Eve, his dead eyes beginning to flicker with life and mischief.

"Eve." Eve said quieter than she wanted to and straightened up. She wanted to know the man her father was so terrified of, "and you are?"

"Frank. It's a real pleasure to meet you Eve," Frank said, grinning at Higgs. You see that?" He showed Eve the tattoo on his forearm. Thankfully the bull had stopped winking and pointed to the scroll wrapped around its torso, which read, "Frank's Place, Dying for a good time," in cursive script. "You see that truck out there," Eve looked out the window where Frank's truck had parked, it had the same grotesque cartoon painted on the cab, "that's me."

Eve couldn't help herself, she had a knack for saying the wrong thing at the wrong time, "is that in case you forget who you are?" She asked.

No one moved or spoke until Frank slapped his thigh and bellowed out a laugh cutting the tension in the room, "you are certainly Higgs's kid. He doesn't give a fuck either." He glanced around the room at the white ashen faces of Higgs and Jackson, "you guys need to lighten up. This little girl here has got more balls than all of you put together." The laughter stopped abruptly as it started as he turned back to Eve, "no," he said flatly, "it's for other people to remember who I am and what I do."

"And what's that then?" Eve asked.

"I make things disappear. Like a magician. Poof! I take care of all the dead things, and sometimes those that aren't." Frank winked. Eve was struck by the similarity between the expression on his arm and the one on his face.

"Like what, them?" Eve gestured to the animal pens at the back of the surgery.

"You sure do ask a lot of questions don't you. Maybe you should come round to old Frank's place and see for yourself? How'd you like that?"

"She wouldn't like it at all," Higgs interrupted, "and like I said she was just leaving," he shot Eve a glance like a bullet that said in no uncertain terms, *leave now*. Frank may be big, Frank may be violent, and Frank may be a dangerous psychopath, but he didn't scare Higgs. He was long past that stage. Frank could have reached out and snapped his neck in one swift move, and he couldn't have cared less. His daughter, however, was a different matter.

But Frank was having too much fun, "Tsk tsk tsk, Higgs, isn't that what they call helicopter parenting?" He waved his index finger in front of his face, "I'm sure she can answer for herself. What do you think darlin' you want to come for a visit?"

Fisher wasn't brave by nature but held self-preservation in the highest regard and recognized that the less people that knew about their little enterprise the better. Frank was wrong about Higgs, he did give a fuck. He gave a fuck about his daughter and would do anything to keep her safe, even if that did guarantee his silence. Unfortunately, it didn't work the other way. Eve was an unknown liability and was known for shooting her mouth off. He cleared his throat, "Jackson's right Frank," he said struggling to remain composed, careful to Jackson when it counted, "we're wasting time. She doesn't need to know anything."

Frank stared at Fisher as though he'd just stepped in something unpleasant and only just realized. "Fisher, who the fuck let you in here?" He grinned, as he turned back to Eve and winked, "there's always a kill joy in every crowd isn't there?" He said as he stepped aside, "maybe next time I come to collect."

# 31.

Jackson finally caught up with Eve by the now-empty timber wolf cage. She could hear Jackson's clumsy footsteps behind and wanted to run but refused to give him the satisfaction. The coldness she felt in the heat of the day cemented the dread she felt for her father, the weight of disappointment with each leaden footstep driving her further into the ground. She had hoped, prayed even, she and her father could have gone silently into the night taking nothing. She recognized the pain in his eyes, the deep resignation of his fate, and the shame he felt, yet he was still there for her despite everything. She remained staring at the empty space when Jackson's oversized hand grabbed at her shoulder. She had never considered herself as someone capable of harm, but if she'd had a knife, she would have gladly stuck it into his stomach and sliced. She detested him and settled with a swift kick to the shins.

"Don't you fucking touch me," she spat at him.

Jackson could feel the heat of her hatred radiating from her. The bee-sting in his shins told him how she felt. He gave her a little shake to remind her he was still the one in charge. "Stop it," he squeaked, "I was trying to help back there."

"Really! Then tell me what the hell that was all about."

"You're overreacting, it wasn't anything. Look, I know Frank probably scared you back there, he likes to come across all mean and shit, but his bark is far worse than his bite. It's just Frank being... Frank. He runs the abattoir, is all, Fisher probably called him, we've got two sick animals back there. You saw them. You've got nothing to worry about. I've got your back; I wouldn't let anything happen to you. You should know that."

"No? And what about Higgs? You got his back too?"

Jackson shifted his weight and leaned against the bars of the cage with a lop-sided grin, "I could."

"Meaning?"

"If you were a little nicer, I could."

Eve took a step back. Jackson repulsed her, "Oh, I see, a little you scratch my back, and I scratch yours."

Jackson, never one to read a situation, gave Eve a half-crooked smile, "something like that," he said as casually as he could and went to stroke the side of her face, thinking he'd finally found a way to get through to her. That beneath all the muscle, he was just like everyone else. Yes, he'd made bad decisions along the way, but he'd paid the price. He wasn't like Frank or Fisher, deep down, he was a nice guy, and it was about time she saw that. Life was beginning to look up, he thought, if she played along. He should have bribed his way into her heart months ago.

Eve slapped his hand away immediately, "what do you think you're doing?" She blurted, "you think a little blackmail is a turn-on, are you fucking mad?"

Jackson let his arms fall to his side. He was an ape, emotionally immature and prone to bouts of violence, but in his heavy-handed manner, had the best of intentions when it came to Eve whether she knew it or not. He hated the way she constantly rejected him. What the hell did he have to do to get through to her. "Christ Eve, why d'you have to be such a bitch? I'm really trying here."

"You just don't get it do you," she protested, "It's not about you. Just tell me what the hell that was about back there."

"I can't."

"So, there is something?"

Jackson wanted to shake her like a rag doll. His head hurt and he couldn't think straight, it wasn't what he meant. "There's nothing going on." He was beginning to raise his voice, "Christ Eve, ask your dad, he's probably the one that called Frank."

"You said Fisher did."

"Fisher, Higgs, it doesn't matter. We have sick animals, we call Frank, that's it."

"They didn't look sick to me."

"For fuck's sake Eve, leave it alone. This has nothing to do with you."

"Doesn't it? He's my father."

"And I've just told you," Jackson shouted back frustrated. He was drawing a crowd, he took a deep breath; he was getting angry. She was making him angry. It was her fault, if she'd been a little nicer, a bit more receptive, it wouldn't be like this. He looked away; he should have never listened to Fisher. It was about time he did his own dirty work, instead of insisting Jackson go after Eve and put her mind at rest, all he'd done was make matters worse, all because of her. He glanced around the zoo, glaring at the faces still watching them, eventually taking the hint and moving away bar one. He couldn't wait to be rid of the place. Frank had already told him there was room for him at the abattoir, but for now, all he had to do was sit tight and be his eyes and ears, he could do that, he thought and caught sight of Adam watching from a distance.

*Him*, Jackson wanted to go over and make him pay. He'd become something of a bad smell, always there when you least expect it, silently infecting everything in its presence. He blamed him for Eve's lack of interest, had he not come along, they'd be a lot closer by now. He looked at the empty wolf cage. He'd seen how friendly he'd been with the animal. Well, good riddance, he thought, at least he'd have that to look forward to.

"You just don't get it, Eve, do you?" He finally said, "I'm not the bad guy here. I'm the one trying to do you a favor."

This time it was Jackson's turn to storm off. He'd deal with Adam later, on his terms, when no one was looking. He'd show them, he'd show Eve, he would play the protector and savior, and in return, she would be so grateful she wouldn't look twice at a skinny little runt like Adam.

# 32.

The aviary is the least visited exhibit. Its position makes it hard to get to, located at the highest part of the zoo, situated on the outer rim overlooking the grounds. The site of an old quarry, the zoo was initially built in the excavated basin, limiting its growth, as it could only expand upwards along the sweeping rises that shielded the zoo on three sides. This proved not only costly but also structurally dangerous as it created something of a wind trap, which meant any plans for growth were quickly shelved, leaving it to a doomed future.

From this vantage point the whole zoo was visible, a microcosm of fake life. The distance hides the decay, it's only up close you can see how abandoned and damaged the zoo is. The aviary is a fitting metaphor and hides its disappointment well. From below, looking up, you would mistake the dome-like structure to be intact, a lasting relic of better days, encouraging the climb needed to take in the view, thinking the reward would be worth it, only to be disappointed. The netting and wire mesh surrounding the dome has long since degraded, and the metal framework, snapped and rusted, is held together by only the flimsiest of repairs. What once created the illusion of freedom now presents the opportunity for escape. The birds that do remain, remain through their own volition, conditioned to stay through a lifetime of disappointment. The more delicate and exotic, had long since been attacked and killed by stronger, less attractive birds, cannibalistic instincts driving them to a repository of easy prey, *it's funny how the murderous ones always know the way in and out.* It was where Eve came to think.

Eve saw her own life mirrored by those that stayed. She had once felt the idealism and promise of youth, the unbridled optimism born through a lack of experience and understanding of the world. She had gained both in too short a time. Was she the same as the birds, conditioned to stay within the confines of her prison, her freedom a painted illusion on a brick wall? *You can only butt heads for so long.* Like the birds, there were windows, shallow openings she could squeeze through and leave her life behind. The Jackson's and Fisher's of this world, the

Frank's all becoming smaller through distance, but there was still Higgs, her father. The anchor that kept her moored to the same spot. She knew he would never change, could never change, like the birds he was conditioned to stay, preferring the safety of misery over the unknown. Perhaps it would be better for them both if she did. She had never considered the possibility that, as he was to her, she could be to him. A weight around his neck that slowed him down. But there had been something else, something he wanted to tell her. She knew there was still hope. She had seen the fear in his eyes, and knew this time, he was in over his head.

The man called Frank scared her far more than she let on, she had been around enough predators to recognize one when she saw one, but he was different. There was more than just an underlying threat of violence, she expected that with a certain type, but behind his eyes was an absence, an empty pit where humanity should live, and he wanted it filled. She had the uncomfortable feeling he didn't care how. Beside him, Fisher and Jackson paled as amateurs, and as low as they sunk, she was sure they still had a line they wouldn't cross. Even Jackson in his muddled and confused brain, understood there was a fundamental difference between right and wrong. It was clear that her father was in trouble, but her choices were limited without knowing. She wanted to run, part of her wanted to abandon him to his fate, knowing if she didn't, she would be dragged down with him. These were the choices he had made, not her.

The sun was beginning to dip behind the ridge pulling its light behind, its shadow spreading like an ink stain, tainting everything it touched. Adam trudged up the hill, he could still make out Eve, a fiery halo lighting her up like a vengeful angel looking down. He had seen Eve arguing with Jackson by the empty cage; the wolf had gone, and he was worried.

It had taken him a while to find her, the aviary was the only place left, isolated, abandoned, and ignored. It was the perfect place to avoid the electronic eyes of Jackson, his cameras, both real and fake, didn't reach that far. "I was looking for you." Adam managed to get out in between breaths, "What happened?"

Eve, lost in her thoughts, hadn't noticed Adam trudging up the hill. "About what?" She asked, unsure if he was talking about her father.

"I saw you with Jackson by the empty cage. I thought you might know."

The wolf! Here she was silently panicking and fretting about the trouble her father might be in, and he was talking about the wolf. It was like asking if you'd left the stove on when the house was on fire. *I don't care about the fucking wolf, I care about my father*, she wanted to shout, but it was hard to be angry at Adam.

146

She'd come to know him in the last few days as an open book. Honest, caring, dependable, and above all, transparent, there were no hidden agendas, with Adam, you got what you saw, which for her was a rarity. Her world, built on fragile shifting sands, was eroding beneath her feet, it was good to have a friend she could depend on, "It's in the surgery," she told him.

Adam was confused, he'd been right there, he'd even checked to make sure the wolf hadn't been injured and gone back the following day after his session in the tank. He'd had a troubling night and woke with an uneasy feeling in the pit of his stomach, bad dreams hovering on the outer reaches of consciousness, something about teeth, and so he'd gone to check, relieved to find the wolf was fine. He'd shaken it off and as the day grew so did the distance between his subconscious and conscious state. He was no longer angry; the tank had done its job. He understood they were just bored youths who hadn't done any real damage, at least, not as far as he could tell. Although he would never venture behind the bars, he wasn't that stupid. "Why?" He asked, "you saw her?"

"That rubbish stick they had," Eve shook her head, she didn't want to be the one to tell him, but better her than anyone else, at the very least she could let him down gently, "it must have gone in, looks like it got infected."

Adam frowned, he could feel his heartbeat quicken, "is it bad?" He asked.

"I don't know," only she did know and wanted to prepare him for the worst. "Look, the zoo isn't set up for this," she said not wanting to blame her father, "it's old, like the animals," She waited for her words to sink in, "I'm sorry Adam, she may not be coming back."

"What do you mean?"

Eve didn't really want to spell it out, she sometimes felt like she was talking to a child talking to Adam, "Look, it's basically about money. In so much as, we don't have any. You've seen how many people come to the zoo. The cost of fixing up a wolf or putting it down comes down to profit," she shrugged, avoiding his eyes, "look around, we're not profitable. You can thank those assholes for that if you ever see them again."

"Is that what you were talking to Jackson about?" Adam could feel a slight throbbing behind his eyes as he clenched his jaw muscles.

"No. Yes, maybe. I don't know," Eve said, "it's complicated,"

"You like him?"

"God no!" Eve exclaimed, taken aback, "no, he's an asshole, what makes you think that?"

"He's always watching you."

"What, and you think I like the attention? Christ Adam, I thought you were better than that."

Adam winced, "I'm nothing like that," he said sulkily, *not anymore*, he thought. "I sorry. I didn't mean to.." he let his words hang, he had no idea what he really meant to say, how much he liked her, that he would do anything for her. He flicked at the ground, *then show her*, the voice inside said. "What will they do?" He asked, ignoring it, changing the subject.

"I don't know. Take it away," she shrugged, thinking of her father. She had come to the aviary to think, she had her own problems, and Adam wasn't helping. Looking at his open face, she wanted to tell him, to draw him in but knew how selfish and unfair it would be, after all how could he help, how could anyone. "I'm sorry Adam, I know you're not like Jackson or any of them. It's this place, it gets to you after a while."

"I can help. If you'll let me."

"There's nothing you can do," Eve sighed and stood, "there's nothing anyone can do."

Adam looked up, "I know people think I'm stupid. I'm not. I can do other things." *You can bite people*, his voice said, he mentally pushed it away, now wasn't the time. "There may be nothing I can do. But I know whatever it is, you don't have to do it on your own."

She wanted to hug him there and then and could feel the fissure of emotion seeping through, if she wasn't careful, she would give in and let the feelings take her. Instead, she steadied herself and took a deep breath. Adam deserved more than she had to give, especially now. How could she risk him as well? "I think maybe I do." Eve didn't wait for an answer and quickly headed off down the hill before Adam could see the tears boiling behind her eyes.

"Eve?" Adam called to no response, she had already gone, the conversation was over.

*Ha!* The voice inside laughed, *you're a fool, I told you, she doesn't really like you, walking away like that, she thinks you're weak, a pussy.* The voice, louder now and more insistent, gently chastised him, but was careful not to be too angry. Adam knew the animal inside only had his best interests at heart, but this time he was wrong, he shook his head. "You're wrong," he argued back. "She's not like the rest of them." *I'm wrong!* The voice was indignant, *am I? What about our friend?*

"What about it."

*You just going to let them take it?*

"No."

*I can help, I'm stronger than you, without me you're weak.*

"Without you I'm normal, just like everyone else. Dr Shelly told me so." Despite the heat of the day, Adam still shivered.

*I wouldn't say normal, sitting on a hill on your lonesome, talking to yourself. There's nothing normal about that. So what are you going to do?*

"You already know," said Adam and followed Eve down the hill.

# 33.

It was dark and uncomfortable, and Adam was bored. He was also hungry and was thinking about the menu back at the hospital. It would be scrambled eggs on toast with the obligatory sponge and custard. He thought about Shelly and if she would be worried and if she missed him, he tugged at his ankle bracelet; she always knew where to find him. He chose his hiding place well, he was used to being unseen, often going about the day unnoticed. He'd spent a good majority of his life living in the shadows, to be the invisible man was his nature. He had positioned himself in the crawl space beneath the surgery, concealed by shadows and overgrown weeds, impossible for even the most curious to see.

Night had come slowly, and Adam felt himself drift into an uneasy sleep full of wolves. Running with the pack, driving them on, chasing the kill, Adam was free. The bloated youth in front, gripped by panic and fear left a scent so strong, it lingered long after he'd gone. He was no match for the wolves, and they easily caught him. Surrounded by sharp snapping jaws, Adam stepped from the shadows, moving slowly, circling him, thinking of where to bite first. Even in sleep, he could feel his muscles tense, wound tight as a spring, and he leaped.

The heavy boots above woke him before he could take a bite, and he woke with a start, frustrated as the dream quickly evaporated.

"Let's get this over and done with." Adam recognized Jackson's high-pitched squeak immediately, "you sure these two are gonna cut it, it's a big crowd. Frank wants a performance?"

"They're not circus animals," scolded another voice he hadn't heard before, cold and distant, filled with disdain.

"You know what I mean," grunted Jackson.

"He won't be disappointed," the other voice snapped.

Jackson grunted as Adam heard the door close.

"You got money on them?" Fisher this time, his voice fat with greed. Excitable, dripping with avarice.

"No," the other voice said.

"Why not? You must have an idea which one's gonna win, you could tip the scales, give me the heads up," Fisher suggested.

*Which one's gonna win,* the words registered as a punch.

"No."

"No? You mean, no, you don't know or no, you won't? Which one?"

"Both."

"You know Higgs, you act all high and mighty. Just remember the part you play. You're just the same as me, you may as well get the most out of it."

"Just because I walk in shit doesn't mean I have to enjoy the smell," Higgs replied.

Adam could almost hear Fisher trying to think of something clever to say back, the best he could come up with was, "fuck you Higgs."

*Higgs.* It was a name Adam wanted to remember.

The door opened once more, "everything ready?" Jackson piped up, Adam, imagined him as an overgrown Micky Mouse, so mismatched was his voice from his body. "Then let's get them loaded. The truck's already here."

Adam heard more grunting as something heavy was loaded on a trolly and wheeled outside. From Adam's vantage point, a truck had pulled up outside the surgery. He crawled forward for a better look. It was a flatbed truck with a canvas cover stretched over a steel frame. A cartoon bull clutching a meat cleaver had been painted on the side. Above its head were the words, *Franks Place,* set in a semi-circle halo. Beneath the bull, the words, *dying for a good time,* were written on a red scroll in elaborate swirly text. Adam was quite impressed with the picture.

Jackson eventually loaded into the crates into the back of the truck, helped by the driver, a thick-set burly man with hair poking out of the back of his shirt on his neck, but sadly nowhere else, as Fisher and Higgs stood by ineffectively and watched. He had seen Higgs before and knew he worked at the zoo, he held what looked like a doctor's bag in his hands, and Adam assumed he must be the vet, *traitor,* thought Adam. *We'll remember him,* said his voice.

The burly man climbed back into the cab and waited as Jackson and Fisher climbed in. Higgs remained watching. "I'll make my own way there," he said.

"No, Frank said, you come with us," the burly man said, holding the door open. Higgs took one last look, locked the surgery, catching some movement below.

"Have you got a flashlight?" Higgs asked the thick-set man.

"We're wasting time," Jackson grumbled as Higgs took the flashlight and swung its beam into the crawl space. "What?" Jackson shouted.

The light cut through the gloom, highlighting abandoned webs' silvery threads and disused coke bottles. An empty needle caught in the glare winked back, reminding Higgs of better times. "It doesn't matter," he called back and climbed in the cab with the others.

"You're paranoid, Higgs. What were you expecting to find?" Adam heard Jackson ask from the back of the truck as he made himself comfortable between the sleeping wolf and cougar.

# 34.

Adam should have been back hours ago. Shelly watched the little blue dot on her screen and wondered where he'd gone. Of course, the responsible thing to do was to alert the authorities and say what? There was a killer on the loose, and she'd been the one to let him out. Only in the eyes of the law, he wasn't. Committed to a high-security institution for an indefinite term, he was hers to do with as she pleased. He hadn't been found guilty of anything; they hadn't found any bodies. She knew different. She'd taken a walk inside and met his other. She knew there would be questions she couldn't or wouldn't want to answer, not to mention the end of her career. She had acted alone, circumnavigating the usual bureaucratic processes. Instead, Adam's position at the zoo was a clandestine affair, an arrangement between her and Fisher. He had been only too keen to accommodate her offer of a cash arrangement. *Off the books.* Any reputable organization or individual would have asked why, she had been careful with her research to find the right one, Fisher had only asked, how much?

She was excited to see what memories Adam would bring back. Experience by proxy. Besides, he was never far away, the blue dot told her exactly where he was going as she traced his journey along the map towards the only building visible, the abattoir. She wondered if this was how generals felt sending their troops into the great unknown, it would be dangerous, but the end would be its own reward. Through him she had become intimately connected to the internal conflict between the id; the primal and instinctive part of the psyche, and the ego; governed by its own referee, oscillating between a learned moral construct and the sneaky compromise of acceptability or at the very least, what we can get away with. Since she had allowed Adam's id to run free within the safety of the tank and become acquainted with his unrestrained hunger. She found it addictive, the pleasure of abandonment, and it had grown. Yet outside of himself, he had become the very model of a lap dog, passive and eager to please. There were two sides to Adam, only one of which she liked, and it was growing stronger, she could feel it in herself.

It was the anger that lived inside Adam, that was the reason for his pain, as an act of survival, the id had broken free, pushing through the membrane of reality to become the driving force of his consciousness. She felt closer to the truth because of it but couldn't shake the feeling of disappointment. Adam had been a success in so many ways, but she wanted more. Hopper was different, he had found a way to forge his own moral compass, channeling his resentment and guilt into something worthwhile, but there was still a common denominator between them both. He had blacked out during his interrogation with Watts but like an automaton, carried on regardless. His id, like Adam, taking control. A desire so strong, not to exact the punishment he saw fit, but because he enjoyed it. There was pleasure there. Was that what she was missing? The notion of pleasure in its many forms, had she been looking in the wrong place the whole time? It wasn't why we do the things we do, it was why we don't. It was the pleasure of destruction. Buried deep, hidden from view, it was there. The seed that grew to destroy itself, the ouroboros serpent, destined to feed upon itself, only to be reborn and begin again. It went against everything we knew, consciously or otherwise, the need to become accepted, to become part of something bigger only to burn it down. It was there, stepping out on a high-rise resisting the urge to jump, it was there watching the storm hoping for the devastation it brings, it was there wanting to let go of the rope, just to see how far the fall went. It was there in every act of destruction. The contradiction of life. Was it the need to know how far our own mortality stretches, or because of a simpler need, the need to feel alive? The curse of conscious thought, hiding in plain sight. She had sought to learn if our nature was the result of a genetic imprint, a virus passed down through the bloodline, infecting generation upon generation of killers, and if not, was it then manufactured by our environment, shaped by our own hand mimicking God? But the longer she spent with the tank she had begun to realize the desire was there all along, what caused it to spiral beyond control was the artificial world created by our own arrogance, thinking we could go against nature. But nature has a way of biting back, Adam was living proof. She had watched Adam pinned against the bars of the cage and understood the release he needed, edging closer and closer until it spilled into his waking life, but not yet. She needed to taste what he had to offer, to know what he felt. Her hand absently drifted between her legs. The blue dot could wait, she could not, and readied herself for the tank.

# 35.

Inside, outside, upside, down.

The two crates almost fill the back of the truck. It's a tight squeeze for Adam, each bump in the road an alarm clock to the sleeping beasts. They can sense and smell each other; three wild animals, two in boxes, one free. Captivity is an aid to aggression. Once awake, they become quickly agitated, aware of their surroundings, or lack of, scratching at the splintering wood. Adam can sense their confusion and burning hatred; he feels it too. He thought back to Eve. He had wanted to show her, he was there for her, that he would never let her down, but the look on her face told him otherwise. Was it a mistake? It didn't matter, he was part of her journey, and she his, this one act sealing them together and he found comfort in that as they trundled along.

Finally, the truck began to slow. Adam had no idea how long or how far they travelled but someone watching does, he tugged at his ankle bracelet and thought about Shelly. Would she be worried? Call someone and send in the troops? He doubted it, all she was interested in was what's in his head, the dreams and bad thoughts. The things that keep him up at night are the things that lull her to sleep. Always tense before a session, her anticipation rewarded by the worst he has to offer. His trauma cold comfort as she pokes and probes, looking into the darkest corners, never telling what she may have found. He wished she could stop the drums, the pounding, or at the very least try rather than dance along. Tonight, if he made it back, he would give her something to jump to.

Peeking through the tarpaulin doors on the truck, they drove into what looks like an industrial compound without checkpoints. The packed forecourt is full of expensive-looking cars. A temporary canvas walkway was erected, complete with velvet rope barriers. Lit by torches, the entrance feels tribal, exclusive, and dangerous. Adam can see an impressive-looking man by the entrance wearing a gorilla mask, it does nothing to dispel the growing anxiety and the feeling this may have been a big mistake. He could argue he hadn't been in his right frame of mind, the animal disagreed, he had. Adam felt like a conscious passenger, unable to make decisions for himself, only along for the ride, the illusion of free will. As the truck turned towards the rear of the building, he took his cue, unsure if it was him or his other, who decided to jump, and rolled quickly out of sight, keeping to the shadows.

The rear of the building lacked the spectacle of the front, no lights or velvet ropes or heavy-set men in monkey suits and masks. Instead, it catered for the practical and functional, the wide roller doors already open, reveal heavy plastic drapes hung on runners like teeth to a greedy mouth. The truck stopped directly in front of a large man wearing a leather apron and white boots stained red. His arms folded over his barrel chest, Adam can see the tattoo on his forearm, it matches the painting on the side of the building, *this man is king in here*, thinks Adam, *this is Frank*. His face is lit by a wide grin, eyes burning like black coal sparkle in the headlights, but it's a dark empty light that devours everything it catches. Adam has never seen anyone quite like him, menace radiating outwards, but the voice inside tells he has, he only needs look in the mirror.

"Full house tonight," Frank shouts. "Get Higgs over here. I want these fuckers wide awake and ready to play," he jerks his head back towards the entrance when Adam can hear the nervous chatter of excitement, "give these cunts a show they won't forget."

Unseen and unheard, Adam makes his way in through an open window at the top of the building. Muscles fuelled by adrenalin, he scales the wall easily. Hidden amongst rafters and suspended walkways, he is surrounded by heavy chains and meat hooks, looking down from the best seat in the house. Below, the space is cleared of clutter, an octagonal cage takes centre stage surrounded by tiered seating platforms. Every seat is taken, each member of the audience wears an animal mask. Some have come in a group or flock wearing identical faces, while others prefer the higher apex predators, loners, or individuals. A nightmare picture of well-dressed demons that will haunt Adam for many nights and he thinks how pleased Shelly would be.

Inside the bowels of the abattoir, Higgs watches the animals nervously and thinks about Eve and his chance of escape. Frank, in his office, changes from slaughterman to showman. Fisher, always the nervous bird, fuelled by the prospect of easy money, anxiously and repeatedly bobs his head from behind the curtain and back again. Adam can just make out Jackson, cold stone, unmoveable like a sentry. A hush descends, followed by the immediate rise of an expectant cheer. A collective blood lust incapable of being silenced edges the crowd forward.

Harsh industrial lights burst on from above and quieten the noise. Frank, ever the showman, entered unseen, under cover of darkness, only to appear as if by magic. Head bowed; body posed to theatrical effect. It's the bit he likes. A blanket of silence descends as Frank waits for the respect he demands, deserves, needs. In his sharp white tuxedo, black tie, and polished shoes, Frank is a severe contrast to the dinner jackets and the blood-stained industry surrounding him, a red rose pinned to his waistcoat like a shot to the heart creates the finishing touch.

Frank is a born showman, he was always meant for greater things, to be noticed, to be seen, upfront leading the dance to a tune only he knows. He raises a champagne flute and drains it. "To the kingdom," he bellows and throws the glass to the ground where it smashes into a thin carpet of broken glass, the silence breaks, his toast is met with rapturous applause and cheering.

Frank felt like a king, it's a part well-practiced, he knows his script off by heart, refined over the years, imagining himself to be a student of evolution, subscribing to what he believes is the true meaning of the phrase, *survival of the fittest*. Only his version has an addendum. Gloria Gaynor would be proud to sing, *only the strong survive*, the strong, being, meaning, him.

"The predator lives in all of us," he booms, "but only you get to decide who you are. Are you weak?" He shouts above the rising cheers. *NO*, the mob screams back. "Are you prey?" A chorus of voices answers, *NO*.

"Are you sure?" Frank continues goading them to a frenzy. It was pantomime. He had them exactly where he wanted. They saw themselves as strong disruptors of society, breaking all the rules; otherwise, why else would they be there? But Frank knows. Frank knows their secret; he knows how weak they are. He hides his disdain well. His speech is for himself, not them. He is an audience of one, he'll let them share in the notion that they, like him, will call the shots, they, like him, are the ones in charge, but they, unlike him, are all wearing masks.

"No," he bellows, "you are not, we take what we want, we do what we want, and we do it to whoever the fuck we like!' He screams, and the crowd goes wild, happy to play along, stomping on chairs, shrieks, and whistles. Frank knows their buzz will last all night and for days after. Life will be better, sex will be better, every feeling amplified through gratification, decisions made without thought or consequence, impulses acted upon, until they meet someone like him, then they'll hide and go quietly back into their box. Frank is only too happy to take their money, they disgust him.

"But when all is said and done, we ask; do I have what it takes?" He baits the crowd. "Am I strong enough, tough enough, smart enough? Will my poison work, do I bite or claw? Who will you be tonight? Make no mistake, my friends, life is a battle. The jungle may have changed, but the rules remain, survival of the fittest... and strongest." Frank takes a moment to revel in the noise, his words carefully chosen. He eventually turns to the side and nods at Jackson. Lights flare on cue, chasing the remaining shadows.

"In one corner, we have the mountain lion, strong, fast, agile. Teeth and claws that would rip any one of us to pieces in an instant." The cougar snarls at the crowd, as it claws at the locked sliding door between cage and octagon. Frank smiles, *Higgs has done his job well after all* he thinks and nods to the opposite corner, the lights flash once more revealing its opponent. "Canis Lupus. The wolf. Vicious, with a bite that can snap a man's neck like a twig. A creature of myth and horror. Who will win? Both sit at the top of the food chain, both worthy adversaries, two rulers, who will survive? You decide, ladies and gentlemen. Place your bets.'

Adam's heartbeat quickens when he sees the wolf, he resists the urge to jump down, he has never seen a feeding frenzy but imagines this is what it must look like. Sharks on dry land ready to turn on each other for the sake of a few dollars. He feels the muscles in his jaw tighten, there's a part of him that would love to be amongst them, *not yet. Not yet but soon*, and can feel the monster scratching at the door, only this time he's happy to leave it unlocked.

Frank, lord of all he surveys, watches on, a keen student of natural selection. Believing it gives him an insight into human nature, God knows he's been exploiting it long enough. The greed, the insecurities, the need for control and power, and the self-loathing hangover that follows. How many in the crowd, he wonders, would give everything they had to be free, do they even know the meaning of the word? To be free from the spirit-crushing jobs they return to, back to the obligations of the profit margin, to bosses, clients, and trophy wives. What would they give to be free, be the man he is, and take what was lost, irrespective of price? That's what gives him the edge. Some might call it conscience or lack of. Frank calls it evolution. He raises his arms, calling for quiet, the frenzy dies down, the two unlucky animals' pace in what little room they have ready to spring, to bite and tear. Frank exits the ring, sometimes he would like to stay, and walks to his Cesar's viewing platform. Like so many before, he and he alone has the power over life and death.

"May the strong survive. Open the cages," Frank shouts for the last time.

It begins slowly, the cougar and the wolf circling one another, searching for a weakness, a moment when each can spot the moment when their guard is down.

The air is alive with a contagion of static electricity. Fear and excitement building, and against his better judgement Adam feels it too. He would like to tear into the mob and free those he feels closest to, instead, frozen by impotence, watches on. The voice inside tells him not to worry, to be steady and enjoy the show, he will get his turn. He knows it will not let him down and the knowledge of that alone is enough to comfort him as he watches the fight, feeling each bite and slash of claw as the blood begins to soak the concrete floor.

Higgs turns his back feeling sick; he knows how badly he has let himself down as a human being. He once believed he had a responsibility to the animal world, the privileged position of custodian, to care and maintain their charges, not to squander the privilege. He knows there will be a price to pay; there always is.

Fisher breathing hard is excited by the blood lust and the prospect of money. Money brings all the good things that aren't offered freely, money will get him Leanne back, or another one like her, money will buy him entry into a world he disgusts, he doesn't care, he knows the right price will buy a ticket. Once money changes hands, and the deal is done, it doesn't matter what *they* think of you, *they*, just like you, prefer money above all else, they can always snigger in the dark and they will. He doesn't care. Money brings power and status. Fisher licks his lips and thinks about his share; it's going to be a big haul.

Frank finds it hard to feel anything anymore and sometimes wonders if he ever did. He watches the animals and the excitement of the crowd, cheering on the brutality and cruelty of the fight. The emotion doesn't register because Frank's emotions don't register anything. His favourite part isn't the fight, although he enjoys a good blood bath as much as the next man, it's the crowd. He loves to watch, to try to understand. Will he? Can he ever be a part of something beyond himself? It's a question he's asked himself a thousand times before, and the answer is always, why would he want to be? What's the point, what is there to join? He closes his eyes and leans back, the noise drifts above him as his world turns black. This is his freedom, this is his power, why would he ever give it up? No longer caring who wins, the outcome will be the same, opening his eyes, the fight is in full throw, the snarling, the howling, the biting, and clawing. And as he looks up for the first time in a long time, he finally sees something exciting.

The noise is deafening, the roar of the crowd lost in the moment, the animals are one in a flurry of violence, each one biting, clawing trying to get the advantage. When it looks like all is lost, the cougar pushes its hind legs into the body of the canine and tears down, the dog yelps, stomach exposed, guts fall, jaws clamp, and life leaves forever. The cougar, itself badly hurt, continues to bite, and shake, until finally exhausted, it collapses. The crowd shrieks its collective approval. Higgs wants to be sick. Fisher tries to suppress the erection growing in his pants. Adam, high in the rafters, wants to scream, the pounding inside too loud to bear, ready to split his skull when two hands grab his shoulders and pull him down, a high-pitched voice he recognizes snarls,

"Enjoy the show?" And the world goes black.

# 36.

"Wake him up."

Jackson barely touched Adam with the cattle prod, but it's enough to send a jolt of pure pain through the mist of sleep, pulling him back into consciousness, but he's no longer alone. The other voice, the one that lives inside, closer now, telling him to go back to sleep, it's his turn now. Tempted though he is, Adam shouts it down through the pain, *not yet*, he tells it. *Then when? You'll need me soon enough.* It answers back.

Adam, tied to a chair, is in the center of the octagon, the crowd has gone, and he is alone with Frank, Fisher, Jackson, and Higgs. Frank leans closer, his face filling Adam's field of vision. "Who do we have here?" His voice is calm, measured, almost friendly. "Some kind of nosey parker, sticking his nose in where it doesn't belong."

Fisher can feel the panic rise, tying knots in his stomach rendering him mute. What the hell was he doing here? He was supposed to be back at the hospital, this wasn't part of the arrangement. He quickly glances at Higgs for help, who conveniently pretends he hasn't noticed.

"His name's Adam," grins Jackson, who can't believe his luck, adding, "he cleans up the shit at the zoo," and thinks about Eve and how nice it would be to have her all to himself. He gives Adam a sharp nudge with the toe of his boot, not hard enough to knock him over, but enough to make it sting. "The man asked you a question, stupid."

Adam, still groggy and disorientated, blinks at Jackson. He's sick of people calling him stupid. He thinks of the wolf and how it died and remembers why he's there and why he hates Jackson so much. He draws back his breath, collecting the phlegm at the back of his throat and spits.

The glob of spit lands on Jackson's leg, it's thick and ugly and mixed with blood, he doesn't want to touch it. Frank snorts with laughter. Jackson, embarrassed, reacts and swings his arm across Adam's face. The slap is hard enough to knock over the chair. "Did you see that?" He squeaks indignantly, "did you see what he did? He's not right. He's not right in the fucking head," and stomps away in a sulk, looking for something to wipe his leg.

Adam lying on the floor, still bound to the chair, head stinging from the slap, hears the animal. It's much closer, he knows it's coming and begins to smile, he can't help it. *Now?* It asks, impatient to get started. *Not yet*, he tells it, *but soon*.

Frank crouches down on his haunches to get a closer look at Adam, he's curious about the young man, not because he wants to know who he is, he doesn't really care. He wants to know the secret Adam is keeping and why the smile, and notices for the first time that his trouser leg has risen over his boot, exposing the ankle bracelet in the fall. "Well, well, well. Look at what we got here?" He grabs the chair pulls it back on its legs so their faces are level. "Adam, from the zoo!" Frank glances at Fisher, "Now," he continues, his voice still friendly, "you gonna tell me what this is?" He asks, tapping the hard plastic with his knife.

Fisher knows there will be questions, questions he can't answer. His mind, racing through possible outcomes, knows none of them are good. He takes a deep breath and gathers all the strength he can. "He's harmless Frank," Fisher said, looking at the ground, afraid to catch Frank's eyes, "he won't say anything, I'll.." he can feel the moisture drain from his mouth and finally swallows, "I'll vouch for him." He finally glances up at Frank, running out of things to say.

Frank is seldom surprised, but Fisher's unexpected display of guts makes him curious, "Oh, you can, can you? So what, you're the boss now?" Frank asks, smiling, "he must be from somewhere really special for you to stick your neck out like that, somewhere a lot scarier than me. Ok then, you tell me, how are we gonna deal with our little problem here? Because you know as well as I do, when you vouch for someone, that means you're responsible for him. He goes blabbing, and it's not him I'll be coming for," he said, twirling the knife in his hands, "You still keen to vouch for him?"

"I say we feed him to the tiger," Jackson grins at Adam, walking back from cleaning his leg, which now has a wet stain over it.

"It's a cougar," Higgs corrects, and no one's feeding anyone to anything. I didn't sign up for this."

Frank stops smiling, "you took the money, Higgs. What did you think you were signing up for? This isn't some fucking girl's guide club," he snaps, eyes suddenly flaring with anger. "What do you think this place is? I could mince him up so small, we start putting him in pies. This isn't some fucked up democracy here. I'm it. You got that. I'm the one who makes the decisions around here, not you."

"And the bracelet?" Higgs asked.

"We could cut his foot off," Jackson suggested, "take it somewhere."

"As I understand it these things track where you are. Isn't that the point."

"Yeah, I know genius. That's why we cut his foot off, duh!" Jackson was sick of Higgs constantly putting him down, if Eve wasn't his daughter, he'd do something about it. But she was, and he'd promised to look after her stupid old idiot junkie dad, she'd better be worth it, he thought. "Ok you got a better suggestion?"

"I have actually," Higgs said, rummaging through his bag, "I can give him a mix of gamma-hydroxybutyric and flunitrazepam. If I give him enough, he won't even remember his name let alone this evening."

Frank mulled the idea over. "You know that's what I like about you Higgs. Smart. You hear that Fisher, GHB, and a roofie, now that's what I call a solution. Something to take away his bad memories, either that or give him permanent brain damage." He laughed and lightly placed one of his shoes on the chair Adam was tied to, gently pushing it back so that it tottered on two legs, "what do you think Stickybeak? Sound good to you? You want to forget this ever happened?" He asked before giving the chair a final shove. "Tell you what, doc," he said, stepping over Adam, "Fisher and me are gonna have a quiet little talk, and he's gonna tell me all about him. Then we'll figure this thing out. One thing I do know is, this ain't no police bracelet; otherwise we'd be hearing sirens by now, and afterward. Well, afterward, I think we're gonna have a little more fun ourselves. How's that sound? In the meantime, Jackson, you just keep him safe and sound."

# 37.

Adam is no longer there. Adam has already slipped back, unseen, into the dark where he can watch from the safety inside. He hopes the other Adam will be alright, *don't worry about me,* he tells him, before breaking the surface, *this is going to be fun.*

The cocktail Higgs gave Adam was part benzodiazepine, part amphetamine with a light dusting of hallucinogenics designed to take the edge off. Adam, wide awake and wild-eyed inside the octagon, was struggling to focus on the faces of Frank, Fisher Jackson and Higgs, their features sliding between, making them almost indistinguishable from one another.

"Hey, nut job," Jackson called out, his voice drawn and oddly low, "how'd you like the show now?" He slurs.

Adam wasn't sure how he liked it at all, as the laughter echoed through the building.

"Open the cage," barked Frank, his mouth as wide as a shark with twice as many teeth.

Jackson moved to the other side of the octagon, leaving an echo of himself behind, hurrying to catch up. His laughter followed like an oil slick caught on the wind. He slid the gate open, and the cougar, reluctant at first joined Adam in the ring. Adam marvels at the size and color of the animal, pulsing with life, there is a glow surrounding her, and he is in awe. Behind her, the faces of Frank, Fisher, Jackson, and Higgs appear as mercurial stone, grey and dirty by comparison. He commits them to memory, knowing he'll be seeing them soon enough.

Frank watches on excited, in many ways, he envies Adam, this chance to feel alive. Fisher came clean about who he was, the threat of a private conversation was enough for him to piss in his pants, and he'd spilled more than his guts. Adam was on a day-release scheme from the local nuthouse. The bracelet was a legal requirement for safety reasons, keeping the hospital informed where he was. Frank initially found it hilarious, but as Higgs pointed out, if anything did happen to him, it would draw a lot of unnecessary attention to the abattoir, particularly why they were there late at night. It was the kind of scrutiny Frank was keen to avoid. Higgs had already come up with some bullshit story as a cover. The kid had already been seen hanging around the wolf's cage, so it made sense he would do something stupid when he found out it had been taken away.

Adam had hidden in the truck and tried to save the wolf by letting it out and was accidentally hit with a tranquilizer dart in the commotion, which is why he was so heavily sedated. He was lucky to be alive, even adding how lucky the hospital was that Frank wouldn't be pressing charges. Frank liked that bit, he had to hand it to Higgs, he was smart. It sounded plausible enough. Besides, who the hell was going to take the word of some nut job over him, and what's more, it couldn't be disproved, especially since the drugs would wipe his memory and the hallucinogenic would take care of whatever remained. Frank okayed the story but thought, why not make it real? So what if Adam ended up with a few scratches? It was his own fault; after all, crazy people do crazy shit!

Jackson was a little disappointed that Adam wasn't going in the mincer, although was still hoping he might get torn to shreds instead. Watching Adam circle the cougar, he couldn't understand what Eve sees in him. Soon it will all be over, he tells himself and thinks of his own story. He'll tell her how he tried to save him, how Adam went mad. He'll explain to her he was from the loony bin and wonders if she already knows. He doubts it, but then again, she's always had a soft spot for freaks. He shakes the thought from his mind, he knows she'll be upset, he's not that dumb or insensitive, but he'll be the one to comfort her and tell her, yes, he was there at the end. *Did he suffer?* She'll ask. Yes, I'm afraid he did, he hopes, but he will tell her different and remind her that it was his own fault anyway, and Higgs will just have to back him up; otherwise, his daughter could always find out what really happened. No, Jackson will tell her what a hero he was and how he tried to save him, and wonders if he should scar himself on one of his arms, just to add a hint of realism to the story.

Fisher feels sick. He gently touched the side of his mouth, Frank didn't have to hit him. He told him what he wanted to know, it wasn't a big deal. Hell, it wasn't his fault Adam had jumped in the van, and now what? He was somehow responsible for him! How was that fair? He's not like Frank and Jackson and wonders, *just how the hell did I get mixed up in this?* He already knows the answer. One look at his ever-expanding stomach would tell anyone the same. Greed. He wants more than he's owed, more than what's his. He didn't like Adam, and he didn't like his shrink; too full of herself, like her shit don't stink! But he liked the money. Was it worth it? It had already cost him Leanne, and he still missed her.

What else would he cost him? If he gets torn to pieces, he knows it would be bad, but isn't sure for who. Like Frank, he'll play the odds. Unlike Frank, he has no choice, and he begins to think of getting away, far away, and starting again. He already knows a guy who knows a guy, something about a boat.

Higgs knows a man is no match for a wild animal and an injured one can be even more dangerous. He had hoped the drugs would have been enough. Even if he remembered a little, it would have been more like a bad dream than a living memory. The worst that would have happened would be a headache for a few days. He hadn't gambled on Frank. He should have known better; the man was psychotic. More than that, he was a sociopath, charming when needed, charismatic and smart, unfeeling, and empty. Looking at his three associates one at a time he thought about the gun nestled in the bottom of his bag and wondered if he would be able to take them out one by one. Frank would have to be first, then Jackson and finally Fisher. He wished he was a better shot, would Jackson run at him if he hit Frank, if he only winged him, did he have it in him to finish him off? If he used it, he knew it would be the end. He could feel his heartbeat. No one was looking at him, all eyes on Adam. He wasn't sure if he'd ever get the same opportunity again.

Adam, who isn't, and the cougar slowly circle one another, maintaining a safe distance, neither willing to make a move, they both have too much respect for that. The injured and exhausted cougar wants only to sleep. She knows the last time she entered the cage, she was hurt, and didn't want a repeat. The animal before her poses no real threat and she senses something familiar but can't remember why or where. She looks beyond him, at her captors safely behind the wire mesh and snarls at them, they did this, and they should pay, she has no doubt that her and her companion inside would show them how.

Frank feels a little cheated. He had hoped for a show, something with drama, and blood and guts and gore. Something with tearing and biting, something to satisfy his own blood lust. The anticipation had been intoxicating, his mind playing tricks, so much so, he almost stepped in there with them. The reality less so. He watched the sad display inside the cage and picked up a cattle prod. Adam can't have all the fun. He thinks as he jabs at the cougar, giving her a little encouragement.

The pain is blinding and pushes everything from her mind, replaced by instinct alone and the desire to survive no matter the cost. The anger consumes her as she lashes out at the only target she can see. Adam on the outside watches through his chemical haze as Frank reaches in and drives his stinger home. He can see and feel her pain as much as his own. He knows the attack is coming, he can't blame her, it's what he would do, he darts to the side but stumbles. The cougar twists in response and comes at him once more. Jaws so wide, he can feel its hot breath and a fine spray of saliva. On the inside, Adam, transfixed by her power, wonders if this is how it ends. He will miss Eve, or at least the opportunity of her, but that's life, he thinks, or not.

Frank hadn't expected the cougar to move so quickly, nor did he expect it to be over in one bite. But bug-eyed, he's ready to enjoy it, until it's so rudely taken away. There is a loud crack and the animal folds, violently pulled away from Adam as if by a sudden yank of an invisible rope. For a moment, he's confused as to what might have happened, and had Higgs not had a gun might have done something about it, but the last thing he expected was for Higgs to be a good shot. Instead, he lets out a raucous laugh.

Fisher, slack-jawed, knees week pulled from his hypnotic state, finally exhales. He hadn't realized he'd been holding his breath. His jaw still aches and he badly needs to piss and worries he may just let go. Adam is alive, and he's grateful to Higgs, but it presents bigger problems.

Jackson feels the bitter taste of disappointment, he was looking forward to being the hero of his own story, watching Adam being ripped apart, not quite saving the day.

Adam on the outside feels the dead weight of the cougar as it falls. Frank is still laughing. Fisher, sweaty and red-faced, is clutching at the wire mesh. Jackson grins and menacingly draws a finger across his throat, telling Adam his days are numbered. Adam runs at the cage through his fog. He doesn't see Higgs load a second dart into his gun but feels the stab of pain when it hits him in the shoulder and falls hard. It reminds him of an earlier time at the hospital, and for a moment, thinks he may still be there. It's hard to distinguish reality from the tank as he fades into the blackness and joins Adam on the inside, who has been waiting for him all along.

*Hello brother*, he says, and he is pleased to see him.

# 38.

The body that floats is as always, a contradiction to its environment. Disconnected, yet tethered. A kite at the mercy of the storm wishing for the string to break. Dreams and memories real enough, carrying the frustration and impotence of the past. The desire to change is strong, overwhelming, and all-consuming until the animal becomes the host. Knowing no boundaries fuelled by desire and want, thirst, and hunger, twin agents of frenzy. It's tasted freedom and wants more, armed with bloody intent it follows on impulse. Protector, mother, father, saint, and sinner it will do what the man cannot and become the author of its own story, rewriting the mistakes of the man.

Nate needed a workout, Nate needed to expel some energy, Nate needed to hit something or someone. He still felt like an idiot. Abandoned by his posse, he was back to being alone. He'd been stupid acting that way at the zoo, he should have known better, but no one got hurt. He knew they'd come back, eventually when they ran out of juice and wanted more. Same with Jackson, it was all well and good getting on your high horse, but at some point, you have to come down. But then there had been the girl, *all dressed up like it was fucking Halloween.* She had it all on her phone and said she was going to send it to the police. He'd do time for sure, what would his mum do without him?

He promised himself he would be a better person and if the cops ever came calling, he'd sing like a canary and tell them everything. He quickly pumped out a few more concentration curls and felt better. The skinny little runt at the zoo shouldn't have been a problem, *I'm bigger than him after all,* he thought as he admired his biceps and made a silent promise that if he ever saw him again, he'd finish what he started, but next time it would be on his terms away from the zoo, away from prying eyes.

Nate had gone to the gym to see if he could square it with Jackson, explain the misunderstanding, and make it all right. He'd hadn't been back for some time, but time is a great healer as his mum would say. Everything would work out. She was right, the twin principles of supply and demand were hard to ignore, and no one was stupid enough to turn down easy money.

Mum had known something was wrong the moment he'd walked back in the house. *God, she disgusted him. Smothering him, trying to buy his love through sugar. What the fuck was wrong with her? Do some fucking exercise once in a while!* But he always felt bad when he had thoughts like that. He loved his mum more than anything, he just struggled to show it, besides there was a secret burning through his soul that no amount of '*juice*' would fix. He knew she'd found some of his magazines and tried putting them back in the same place she'd found them, but she knew, and he would rather she didn't. Maybe that was why she'd been making more of an effort lately, maybe she thought he'd need her support? *Good old mum! Stupid cow's always there when I need her.* He thought, smiling. Once he'd fixed things with Jackson, he'd fix things with her. He hadn't left on good terms, when she'd seen the gym bag she knew where he was going and they'd argued, he was pretty sure she knew about the steroids too.

But Jackson hadn't been there. He'd tried to make it seem less obvious, acting like it didn't matter, but the other guys at the gym had teased him about it, calling him *his boyfriend* and it bothered him. Not because he found it insulting, but because he knew he would be. He'd worked extra hard trying to push those thoughts away and his limbs felt heavy, he was pretty sure that Jackson didn't feel the same way, but it didn't hurt to think like that once in a while.

Alone and lost in his thoughts, Nate decided to walk back, preferring to shower at home, worried in case he popped a boner whilst looking at some of the other guys. Besides, it was a warm night, and the gym wasn't far. He still had his magazines to keep him busy and was beginning to feel much better, *a workout will do that.* Lost to his thoughts, the sharp sting between his shoulder blades caught him off guard as did the guttural growl behind.

Inside now outside, relished the thrill of the hunt. Tracking Nate had been easy, his scent thick and heavy, spliced with chemicals hung on the air like a vapor trail. Silently watching,

Nate gasped for air, unsure of what was happening, confused why he could no longer breath, as his lungs began to empty and fill with blood, the rising bitter metallic taste causing him to gag. He spat on the concrete, surprised to see more had pooled at his feet. He wanted to run, but his legs, too heavy to move, began to fold as his strength left him. Strong hands spun him around as he collapsed on the ground and in a moment, it was upon him. He could feel the warm breath on his cheek and noticed how the light from the streetlights seemed to dance around its sharpened teeth like jewels in the night. *Something in the eyes,* he thought as he felt the teeth sink into his neck above the collar bone.

# PART 4

# 39.

It's been hard for Sarah Moynihan. Being a single mum is a tough job, playing both mother and father to an unappreciative audience of one. There had been men in her life but none willing enough to stick around and play role-model to her son. Over time, she found her waistline inversely proportionate to the number of male friends she had until it ended up just the two of them, her and Nathan or Nate to his friends. *But two's company and three's a crowd*, or so she told herself. She compensated for an absent son with cupcakes with only the shopping channel for companionship. She knew she was driving him away, but couldn't help herself, she was lonely.

He was always complaining how she embarrassed him in front of his friends, although his friends never seemed to mind. They liked the sugary treats she fed them with. He told her that she should go to a gym, take up running, get moving, do something, anything, but above all else, stop eating. Did she disgust him? The thought of her at a gym made her laugh and made her sad. The stares, the judgement, and the stifled giggles. It was enough to drive her to the bakery.

Tomorrow. I'll sign up tomorrow, the best day for a new routine—tomorrow. It was different for him. A young man needed an interest. Bullied at school when he was smaller, more sensitive than others, some would have used other words, some did. Some said worse, but that changed when he started going to the gym. It had been her idea. He should have been grateful for that at least. Paying for his membership with her credit card, encouraging him to go at least three or four times a week, which had quickly turned to daily and later twice daily. He grew bigger, the voices got smaller until they'd been silenced and stamped on once and for all, kids can be cruel, but the payback can draw blood.

But that was then, and this is now, and now her sweet boy was gone. Change is gradual. You don't notice until you do. His face changed first. The angled chiseled looks he developed as a young adolescent had been replaced by a rounder, fuller face peppered with angry red spots. His well-defined and veined muscles became the fat swollen arms and legs of an overgrown toddler. Becoming moody and sullen with an irrational temper, he was incapable of controlling but always sorry for. He became secretive and paranoid. Old friends were replaced by newer ones. Ones that looked like him. Their tiny apartment became their hangout. They would immediately stop talking whenever she was around, but familiarity breeds content and after a while, she became invisible to all but him as she continued to feed them and started to know some of their secrets, she knew about the gym and she knew about a man called Jackson.

Jackson had quite the influence on her Nate, whenever he called, Nate jumped. If Jackson wanted Nate, Nate would drop everything and run. Nate was no longer hers. Nate was his, and she aimed to find out who *he* was. Perhaps it was jealousy that prompted her to go searching in places she should have known better. Systematically going through his room, she exhausted herself by creating a grid, allowing her to search all his nooks and crannies, combing through draws and cupboards, under the bed, carpet, inside books, bags, even testing the floorboards. Of course, she found his magazines, well-oiled semi-naked young men posing with unfeasibly large appendages. She certainly didn't remember the ones from her past being so large and felt the slight pang of sadness for a life never lived, mixed with her own selfish joy at the prospect of never having to share him with another woman.

She knew he was unhappy; she had her suspicions but desperately wanted him to confide in her. Maybe it was her, the saccharine-coated love she offered, too rich a diet, giving him a diabetic psychosis, or perhaps it was the frustration he felt for the unrequited affection shown to the models in his magazines. It didn't matter what she said, how she broached the subject, it was always the same, ending in a vicious argument that ultimately deteriorated to name-calling, generally him to her. But this time it had been different, this time he was really mad, and for the first time she had been worried he might actually hit her and that's when she called him *faggot*, and he hadn't been home since.

It had just slipped out she hadn't meant it. He'd been so angry. It had been so out of character. After several biscuits, she decided to search his room once more to see if it would yield any more clues. Hidden inside his mattress was something she hadn't felt before. After unzipping she pulled out an old plastic Walmart shopping bag, the logo worn thin. Inside was a rolled-up leather pouch, once unraveled revealed what looked like a doctors kit, a neatly packed syringe complete with spare needles and several plastic ampules, all tucked up nicely in their own little pockets. After more digging she found another bag containing at least thirty more vials of the clear liquid.

Drugs! She wasn't shocked or even surprised. Such a predictable disappointment for a mature teen. She wasn't an idiot. There had to be a reason for the transformation of Nate to the swollen doppelganger that had replaced him. It was always going to be chemical. It wasn't the usage that made her angry, rather the supply, he was still considered a minor, someone was out there making a tidy profit fucking up the lives of children. But at least she had a name to go on; Jackson.

She knew she was running a huge risk to go looking. It had only been one night since he had been back, but call it mother's intuition, she instinctively knew something was wrong. They'd argued before and he always came home. She would apologize and make him his favorite breakfast; he would pretend to be mad for a while, or at least until he tucked into his pancakes. But this was a first. His bed remained cold and unslept in and given how important his carefully stashed booty was, it was even more unlikely he would stay away.

Standing outside the gym, she steeled herself for what she was about to do. *Tiny's Gym*, a windowless brick square situated in a particularly charmless carpark. She was sure whoever had named it, thought the irony to be hilarious, or perhaps there was no irony intended and was a cleverly constructed private joke referencing the clientele's penis size. She'd heard the stories about steroid abuse after all, but judging by the images in Nate's heavily thumbed magazines, perhaps that was wrong as well. Nate had chosen the gym himself. She should have gone with him, checked it out, why he couldn't have chosen one of the more family-friendly franchises she didn't know. Some rubbish about it needing to be authentic and *real*, where 'serious' people went. It was real enough now, and Jackson was about to find out just how real it gets.

Still hoping she would find her son, too embarrassed to admit his newfound sexuality, perhaps he'd taken to this adventure on his own. She wished there were windows to peer through, to catch a glimpse so she could go home without him ever knowing. He would be mad, no doubt, but they would makeup. She would show him how much she understood, how supportive she was, and there would be shopping, lots of shopping. Having a gay son could work out for the best, she need never be alone again.

She took a deep breath and stepped through the doors. The gym, as alien as a distant planet, with a smell strong enough to eradicate any lingering trace of breathable atmosphere. As with any gym she could feel a thousand eyes sizing her up, noting weight and measurements, judging her by the girth of her ass, her character paraphrased to one simple word, '*fat.*' The front desk, manned by something she assumed had originally started out as normal, but over time and steroids, had morphed into something bigger. She recognised the moon face, adult acne, purple striations across the chest and shoulders as if the skin, barely able to contain the muscle, was about to split and burst. He nodded a grim hello with confused eyebrows knitted together, she doubted if he'd ever seen anyone her size let alone spoken to someone like her. Without taking his eyes off her, he slid the generic gym leaflet over. She smiled back and giggled slightly through a mix of nerves and apprehension.

"I'm not here to join," she explained as sweetly as she could and saw the monster in front of her breathe out and relax, the ruddiness from his face slowly fading.

"No? You just come for a look?" He asked, a sly smile creeping across his podgy face.

"No, I'm looking for someone. Jackson? Is he here?"

"Lady, we don't give out that kind of information, it's a private gym, our members are private. Understand?"

Sarah did indeed understand. Being fat didn't make you stupid. She continued to smile as she calmly placed two of the plastic ampules on the desk. Judging by the man's expression he recognized them immediately and swiped them off nervously, glancing from left to right.

"What the fuck? Put those away." He snapped.

"You know what they are?" Sarah didn't wait for an answer, "of course you do. I found these in my son's room, he's a minor, understand?" She gave the monster in front of her a moment to process what she was saying, before adding, "that means underage."

The swollen giant leaned closer, keeping his voice low, hissed back, "I know what a minor is. We run a clean gym here," Sarah raised an eyebrow as he continued, "wherever your kid got those, he didn't get them here, get it?"

Sarah, *got it*, she *got it* in spades, clearly, the steroid-addled junkie across from her didn't. She was the one in the driver's seat, not him. "Maybe, maybe not, but we'll let the police decide. You keep the samples, I have more, besides I'm sure you'll find a use for them." Sarah turned ready to walk back out.

"Wait," The giant protested, "what do you want?"

Grateful he wasn't as stupid as he looked, Sarah turned back to the desk. "Jackson, you know where I might find him?"

Twenty-five minutes later, Lenny had told her everything she needed to know over a cup of tea and some homemade flapjacks she'd brought along in case she got hungry, making her promise to keep his name and the name of his gym out of whatever it was she was doing. He also made her promise to drop some of the flapjacks off the next time she visited.

*He wasn't so bad,* Sarah thought as he ushered her out by the back door. Jackson on the other hand was about to find out why things finish when the fat lady sings!

# 40.

Midday and the world felt like it was on fire. Hopper tugged at his collar, it's a futile gesture and does nothing to alleviate the intensity of the day. Dry air in, dry air out, scorching lungs, and burning throat. It had been years since Hopper visited the zoo, and from what he could remember, not much had changed. The layout was identical to how he remembered it, as were the enclosures and cages, and, like him, were a relic from the past. Clinging to old school notions that animals were there for entertainment. It was a place out of time, without imagination and reinvention. Never able to compete with the introduction of the amusement arcade, the animals had no chance. Doomed to fail, how could they contend with the new wave of digital entertainment about to hit, bringing with it an onslaught of alien invaders from outer space and the maniacal drivers of Death Race. It was an unwinnable war for the precious dollar and one that sealed the fate of those already in captivity.

For Hopper, the zoo, and places like it were symbols of everything he resented. He'd visited it a few times, once with the school and a couple of times with friends. They, like all kids from their neighborhood, took great pleasure in terrorizing those less fortunate than themselves, aiming to put enough distance between them and the associations of hardship, until they grew bored and moved on to other more exciting activities. Ignored and neglected, the zoo had already begun to slide into the impoverished territory of the neglected.

Hopper didn't really remember much from those days apart from the anger he'd felt. He had been angry at everything; happy families making happy memories, young couples caught in the bloom of first love, even the content elderly with enigmatic smiles hiding a worthwhile life lived. All of it made him angry. It was the wholesomeness that irked him, even at a young age Hopper felt it to be a lie, life wasn't like that, at least not for him. Walking around the zoo he felt he had more in common with the caged animals than he ever had with the meager visitors. It was a depressing place set in a downward trajectory established a long ago. For a city that struggled to feed and house its population, how could it be expected to look after the raggedy inhabitants of the zoo? That's what Nat Geo was for, and given the number of empty enclosures, it looked like it was living up to expectations. Stopping by the Monkey house, Hopper counted five bored-looking primates lazily picking fleas off each other, resigned to a fate they didn't deserve, imprisoned for crimes they didn't commit. They stopped to stare back at Hopper for a moment before continuing, deciding he was far less interesting than the bugs. They looked how he felt, some bars are more obvious than others.

Eve watched Hopper from a distance wondering why a cop would be visiting the zoo, at least judging by his clothes, she assumed he was a cop, or was on his way to a fancy-dress party and had lost his way, although given his dishevelled appearance Eve decided he was coming back from one. Either way, his presence gave her reason for hope, perhaps someone had reported Jackson for being an asshole?

She had waited up for her father last night and fallen into a restless sleep dreaming of Adam. When Higgs did finally come home, he was in a peculiar mood, more so than usual. Unwilling to talk, morose and sullen, he turned to their meager drinks cabinet for comfort, which as she knew, was not his drug of choice, and polished off almost half a bottle of scotch, but at least it was good to see him trying! Concerned, she wanted to know what had happened, if anything was wrong? He'd laughed. Laughed so hard it almost brought on a choking fit. She hadn't found it funny.

*What's the joke?* She'd asked.

*I am*, He'd said, *I'm the joke.*

*Then what does that make me, the punchline?* She'd said irascibly, and on and on it went. Each one playing for serve in an unwinnable match. It was an easy routine to fall into. Years of disappointment had conditioned her to see the worst in every situation. But this was different. Usually their arguments needed two participants, this began and ended in a one-sided screaming match. He hadn't argued, just sat there, and took it, sipping his drink, absorbing it until exhaustion claimed her, his silence his guilt. Too tired and weak to protest, fatigue eventually claimed her, and he'd taken her to bed like a child, his child, and tucked her in. She asked about the wolf and about Frank, he'd told her not to worry, that everything would be alright and kissed her goodnight. She told him she didn't believe him and that she could help, if only he would let her. It had been the only thing that had brought a smile to his lips, and he'd mouthed the words, *thank you.*

He was gone by morning, and she was left with a hangover of discomfort and unease. She knew he would be at the zoo, preferring the company of animals

179

behind bars rather than in front. He had his moods, she'd grown used to them, retreating into himself until he could no longer be seen, and the pain became too much to bear. His lifeline came in the hollow point of a needle. She always knew when he was using and wished there was something she could do. It's hard when you know you're not enough, but knew she wasn't. How could she be when he turned elsewhere for comfort. He would eventually surface as if nothing was wrong, his demons washed out by a chemical rinse. It was in times like these she didn't know if she disappointed him, or him, her. She knew she wished for a better life and hoped he did too. One that was boring and normal, of drudgery and predictability, of complaining about problems that amounted to nothing; recycling, global warming, politics, and celebrities, because she had the luxury of a life that let her. Instead, she was faced with worrying if this time might be the time he OD'd, that this time he'd fallen so far there was no coming back.

She had wanted to see Adam and looked for him, she needed the distraction he provided, worrying about him, meant she stopped worrying about herself and Higgs. She needed something, someone she could fix, and Adam fit the bill. Disappointed he wasn't at the zoo, she had no one to ask. People deserve a day off, she told herself, it was nothing to worry about.

The ice cream stand was an oasis in the desert, Hopper had thought to get a feel for the place before asking questions and the heat was beginning to take its toll. He knew if you wanted answers, never go to the top, start from the bottom up, from people who had less to lose, where the distance wouldn't hurt as much when you fell. The girl selling ice-creams seemed like a good place to start.

"Slow day." Hopper smiled, doing his best to appear casual, pointing to the chocolate. Eve handed over a scoop without saying anything. "Is it always like this?"

Eve eyed him suspiciously, it was obvious Hopper was a cop, no one comes to the zoo in a cheap suit with shoes like that. Experience had taught her a distrust of authority, the police had agendas of their own, they didn't need hers as extra baggage. As much as she worried about her father, he was her problem alone, and one she didn't feel the need to share. "Three fifty. You a cop?" She asked.

"What makes you think I'm a cop?"

Eve made a face, "You really have to ask?"

Hopper frowned, "What's the give-a-way?"

She looked him up and down, "you. The shoes, definitely the shoes. The suit too. And the tie. Pretty much everything."

"And there's me thinking I'm undercover."

"You an animal lover then?"

"If I was, I'm not sure this would be the right place to go."

Eve knitted her brow together, "Enjoy it while you can. We'll be closed before long." Hopper raised his eyebrows, "making way for something more important," she continued by way of explanation. "I think they're gonna build a Walmart."

"Better air-con."

"Not sure the animals are as nice." She was already tired of the casual chit-chat, cops seldom engaged in conversation unless they were digging. She hated the way they would dance around a subject, thinking they're being clever, sizing the situation up, getting a measure of the person, it felt too predictable, lulling you into a false sense of security always trying to set traps.

Hopper nibbled his ice cream. "You worked here long?"

*Here it comes.* "A while. Why, someone die?"

*Probably,* "No, nothing like that, just routine. Tying up a few loose ends for an ongoing investigation," Hopper lied, he felt it gave him a degree of credibility, no one in their right mind goes looking for dead whores. He took out his mobile and brought up a picture of Leanne. "You ever seen her around? From what I know she used to hang out here. She had a kid," Hopper had considered taking one of the pictures of Anton from Leanne's apartment but decided against it, there was, after all, no reason for him to be there, and as much as he hated it, dead hookers still have rights. Still, it was clear from the photograph what his condition was, "Downs Syndrome," he added confidently.

Eve found all prejudice ugly and wrinkled her nose at the cop. *Typical thick cop*, she thought and felt less inclined to help. "I'm not sure, maybe if you could tell me what he looked like?"

*Typical righteous stuck-up bitch*, thought Hopper, giving nothing away, "Short brown hair, big round face. C'mon, help me out here."

"I remember him."

Hopper let out a sigh of relief. "Thank you. You remember the last time you saw him?"

Eve looked away and shrugged, "A few weeks, maybe, I can't be sure," she could, she just didn't want to be, at least not yet. The memory of Adam attacked by a skinny middle-aged woman dressed as a teenager was hard to forget. Besides, it wasn't her problem, she had bigger fish to fry, literally. "Why what's he done, from what I remember he was a sweet kid."

"He hasn't done anything. It's his mum I'm interested in," Hopper took out his mobile and brought up an old mug shot of Leanne, taken against the backdrop of black horizontal lines. The harsh light was less than flattering as was the smudged lipstick, she'd had better nights, that wasn't one.

Eve rolled her eyes, "yeah I remember her, poor kid, she's crazy. Hasn't been around for a while. What's she done this time?"

Hopper pocketed his phone, "I'm not sure, maybe nothing. I was hoping to find her, seems like she was a regular here."

"I guess you could say that."

"Oh? And what would you say?"

"She liked the animals," Eve shrugged, thinking about how much she disliked Fisher and was only too happy to use the opportunity to make him sweat. "Look, honestly, I don't know anything about her, if you're looking for her, my guess is that she doesn't want to be found. But you really want to know, why don't you ask Fisher. I think she might have done a few jobs for him now and then."

The mischievous twinkle in Eve's eye didn't go unnoticed, as Hopper asked, "and who's Fisher?"

# 41.

Hopper hadn't noticed the blinking light of the CCTV cameras, but the eyes behind the lens had noticed him. Jackson was supposed to be Franks eyes and ears, and he'd let him down once already. He hadn't known about Adam, but that was hardly his fault. Who lets crazies out to run around doing whatever to whomever? It wasn't an ankle bracelet Adam needed; it was a leash. They delivered Adam back to the hospital safe and sound, thankfully there hadn't been anyone there to kick up a fuss or ask too many questions. His regular doctor was unavailable and after Higgs had finished spinning his story, he even had the orderly thank him for not pressing charges. Only too happy to avoid any unnecessary paperwork, he'd taken him back without question, *no one needed to know, give the kid a break*, he'd said. Higgs explained the drugs he'd shot him with, may cause some temporary amnesia or a sense of disorientation, but no lasting or permanent damage, after a good night's sleep, he'd be right as rain.

Frank wanted Adam back at the zoo, somewhere he could keep an eye on him, he didn't seem to care it had nothing to do with any of them. So far, Adam had been a no show and now a cop had turned up. Had someone talked? Adam? It seemed unlikely. By rights the kid should have been scared out of his wits. But who's to say once back in the safety of the hospital, his shrink hadn't called the cops? They had a way about them. He'd even seen a shrink when he was back in the joint, they all had, it was part of the program. Worse than a priest, probing, asking questions no one had a right to, picking at scabs until they started to bleed, it didn't take long before you were pouring your heart out. Jackson had found himself sobbing into his hands on a number of occasions, not that he would ever tell. He would have loved to known what they made of Frank, did he ever sob? He doubted it.

Fisher seemed confident Adam's shrink wouldn't talk, saying she had as much to lose as they did, Jackson doubted that. But Fisher would say anything to squirm his way out of trouble. Jackson knew only too well how slippery he was, he'd even hinted about the steroids, just to make sure Jackson knew if he kicked up any trouble with Frank, Fisher had something tucked away ready to pull out at a moment's notice. *We've got to watch each other's backs, look out for one another,* he'd said, adding, *your secret's safe with me,* in case Jackson was in any doubt as to what he meant.

Jackson had been engaged in his favorite pastime when the cop showed up; spying on Eve. It felt like too much of a coincidence after the night they'd had. He'd talk to her later, hopefully she would have calmed down about Nate, at least Adam wasn't around to fuck things up. He'd followed the cop as best he could see where he headed off to next.

"Shit," he muttered under his breath as he watched the cop walk into Fisher's office.

# 42.

Fisher was holed up in the building he commandeered as his office, away from prying eyes. From the outside, if you didn't know better, it would have been easy to mistake it for the public convenience. If you didn't know better, the smell would do the same from the inside. The building, a flat-roofed single-story demountable originally intended to be temporary, had become permanent over time. There were two offices inside, the smaller one, had once been used to house the administration team in better days, pre-Fisher days. Now currently used as a dumping ground for anything that didn't have a home or Fisher could sell off on eBay, quietly pocketing the money. A shared corridor ran the length of the building leading to a tiny bathroom that hadn't been cleaned since the change in management.

Fisher had been pacing back and forth, fretting, expecting the worst. His natural distrust of people kept him paranoid. What if Shelly didn't keep to her end of the bargain? She had been as keen as him to keep their arrangement private, she, no doubt had as much to lose as he did, although people who moved in her world had a habit of sticking together, so perhaps not. It was different for people like him. People like him were thrown to the lions. Still, Adam had been returned in one piece and the drugs Higgs pumped him full of were sure to do the trick. As much as he despised the man, he sure did know about drugs. He considered making an early morning trip to the surgery for shared comfort and reassurance and maybe a little bullying to take his mind of things, but without Jackson it was difficult, plus Higgs's supercilious attitude was sometimes too much to handle. Better to handle the anxiety alone. He also knew it would pass; it was just time. In his experience, the greater the time between him and the event, the less real it felt. Mornings after were always a problem, he needed to keep his mind occupied. Had Leanne been around, she would have provided the perfect distraction, although after logging on to some of his favorite websites, he doubted it, even they held little interest and he'd given up after an hour or so. Thank God he still had the bathroom at the end of the corridor. His stomach had been doing backflips all morning, and the smell wasn't doing much to help his mood. Sooner or later, he would have to get the toilet cleaned, shutting the door, and opening the window no longer seemed to be an option. He glanced at the clock on the wall, it was the middle of the day, he was beginning to feel better. If something was going to happen, he felt sure it would have happened by now. He wanted to, needed to talk to someone about last night. Frank scared him, but last night terrified him. He had been excited at the time, the usual thrill combined with easy money, but the prospect of watching Adam ripped apart made him feel physically sick in the sober light of day. His stomach lurched once more as his sphincter contracted, he didn't think there was much left to evacuate and was about to make his way to the toilet when the door opened.

"You Fisher?" Hopper asked, poking his head round the corner, wrinkling his nose at the smell.

Fisher had never felt the need to release his bowels as badly as he did just then and sat down, trying to appear calm. "Depends. Am I in trouble or not?" He grinned, doing his best to make light of the situation as he started to sweat. "Who's asking?" He didn't like the look of the man in the cheap suit who stank of cop.

Hopper didn't wait to be invited; it had taken him all of two seconds to assess the man. Don't judge a book by its cover, unless it stank. He took out his badge, "Detective Hopper. Now's not a bad time, is it?" He asked not caring what the answer was as he flicked some dust off the back the chair opposite Fisher's desk before settling in. "It won't take long, just a couple of questions."

*Not Adam, please not Adam.* It took everything Fisher had not to ask if this was about last night, "I was actually on my way somewhere." Fisher began, but looking at the immobile Hopper decided against moving, nor could he trust his bowels. "As long as it doesn't." He shifted uncomfortably as the leather cracked under him. He smiled apologetically, hoping Hopper wouldn't mistake the chair for him.

"I understand you knew Leanne Bonnelle?" Hopper took out his mobile and brought up the mugshot of Leanne.

Fisher recognized her immediately, it was funny how the mind plays tricks, he remembered her looking better. "I wouldn't say knew her, but I know who she is. You mind if I ask what this is about?"

"No, I don't mind," Hopper said, as he placed the two tickets he'd torn off the roll in Anton's room on Fisher's desk, "these say complimentary, they're not regular tickets. How do you get these?" He asked, ignoring Fisher.

*From me,* "I'm not sure how she would have come to have those. I have no idea."

Hopper put the tickets back in his wallet, "I didn't say I got them from her," he was used to adopting a poker face, but with Fisher it was hard not to grin, this was going to be fun. He softened his tone, "let's start again. How well did you know her?"

"I didn't. I mean I'd seen her around. I felt sorry for her boy, you know how it is. A mother like that, I felt he could do with some cheering up, that's all. I gave her some tickets, so what? No crime in that."

"You knew her kid?"

"Like I said, I'd seen her around a few times." Fisher leaned forward conspiratorially, "I actually caught her sneaking in, that's why... you know, the tickets. I felt sorry for her."

"That's real nice of you." Hopper smiled, continuing his good-guy routine, "and what did she give you in return?"

Fisher frowned, "Hey, all's I did was give her some tickets. Nothing, that's what she did, nothing. Can't a guy do something nice once in a while without someone casting aspersions?"

Hopper nodded along, "I guess I owe you an apology then?"

Fisher shrugged, "no harm done."

"When was the last time you saw her?"

Fisher thought about Adam and his stomach lurched once more, "must be a couple of weeks, maybe less."

"Why's that?" Hopper asked, "something happen?"

"Happen? I'm not sure I know what you mean,"

Hopper leaned back, "Well," he said stretching his legs, "You know she was a hooker, right? As I understand it, she was working here, would have been on a good thing too. Nice and safe. No pimps, taking a cut. I don't get it, why would she leave? Not unless you asked her to leave. So, did something happen?"

Fisher winced, he hated cops. He hated the way they would tie you up in knots. He considered his options, if he told the truth, he'd ask about Adam and in no uncertain terms did Fisher want a cop talking to Adam. Who knows he would say? If he said he kicked her out, he would ask why. Of course, he could spin some bullshit story about how he caught her turning tricks and him running a family zoo, but again, too many questions. Fisher figured it best to play dumb. "Nothing that I know about. One day she was here, then she wasn't. That's all I know."

"Is that right?" Hopper asked, not believing a word Fisher said, "So you must have seen her on a regular basis then?"

"No, not really, what makes you say that?" Fisher could feel himself start to sweat.

"Well, I'm curious," Hopper started, he'd perfected the art of acting like the dumb cop after watching re-runs of Peter Falk in Columbo, "you just said, that one day she was here and then she wasn't, right? So, did you see her on a day-to-day basis or not? I mean, how would you know, that she was here one day and gone the next, unless you saw her regularly? But earlier, you said you hardly knew her, even though you gave her free tickets for her kid. You see how confusing that is?"

Fisher could feel the sweat running down his back, his sphincter felt like it could explode any moment, "There's nothing confusing about it," he began, but was quickly interrupted by Jackson.

"You want to tell me what this is about?" Jackson squeaked in his high-pitched voice.

Hopper craned his neck to get a good look at the man who'd interrupted them. He was enormous. Big muscles were impressive, though not intimidating. Hopper had met several individuals in his time that mistook size for ability, all of which had come to a rather unpleasant end by his hand, knee, head, and foot. Strength was nothing compared to someone willing to fight dirty. Hopper brightened. "You mind telling me who you are?"

"Not until you tell me what this is about?" Jackson glared at Fisher, who, if he could, would have slapped his forehead and shouted, *duh!* If he didn't sound guilty before, he sure as shit did now.

"Fisher's helping me out with some inquiries," Hopper reached into his jacket pocket and flashed his badge, "Detective Hopper, and you are?"

"Jackson. Head of security," he said puffing out his chest, "If there's anything you want to know, you can ask me."

*Moron*, thought Hopper, "Perfect, then maybe you can help me," he said as he held up his mobile, "Leanne Bonnelle. You being, head of security, I guess you knew all about her?"

Jackson breathed a sigh of relief, *nothing to do with Adam after all*, "What d'you want to know about her for? We kicked her ass out a few weeks ago."

"You mind telling me why?"

Jackson realigned his belt, "She was causing a disturbance. Part of the job."

"Oh?" Hopper winked at Fisher, who was currently staring daggers at Jackson, screaming telepathically at him to *shut the fuck up*. "How so?"

One thought must have gotten through as it dawned on Jackson not to talk about Adam. He folded his arms defensively and flexed his muscles. "You mind telling me what this is about?"

"I need to talk to her. I was hoping someone here might be able to help," Hopper said casually, "you said disturbance, what kind?"

"I don't know. A disturbance, it was no big deal," Jackson shrugged.

"But you still kicked her out, so it must have been a bit of a deal."

"Soliciting," piped up Fisher, thinking Jackson was about to say something stupid, "I didn't say anything at the time, because... I guess I just wanted to give the kid a break."

"Yeah, soliciting," Jackson agreed.

"Hopper raised his eyebrows, "You were there?"

"No, not exactly."

"So, how'd you know?"

"The cameras," Jackson explained.

"Ahh, the cameras. Of course, which is odd in itself."

"What's so odd about that?" Jackson was beginning to feel as uncomfortable as Fisher looked.

"Well, he just said you didn't know she was working here, but you just said you saw her on the cameras. So you would have known, because you would have seen her."

"I think that was her first time," Fisher interrupted cutting Jackson off.

"And then you kicked her out?" Confirmed Hopper, who was having too much fun to stop.

"That's right," said Jackson.

"Because you saw her on camera. You mind if I take a look at that footage?" Hopper asked, "could be useful, might show if she had a pimp or not, maybe someone was watching her."

"I don't think she did," Fisher said too quickly.

Hopper smiled back, "then all the more reason to take a look, a lot of pimps get squirrely when one of their girls goes independent, gives the others ideas. Sometimes they have to make a statement, if you know what I mean," explained Hopper.

Jackson and Fisher exchanged glances; it didn't go unnoticed by Hopper. "There's no point," Fisher said, "it's an old system, we record on tape and once a tape is finished, we just use it again. Saves money."

"That's right," agreed Jackson, he was thinking of the tape still in the machine that would have recorded Adam sneaking into the truck.

"Pity," Hopper nodded, wondering what was on those tapes, "could have been helpful, but shit happens," Hopper said as diplomatically as he stood, "I guess I've taken up too much of your time already."

"I guess it does, sorry we couldn't have been more helpful," Fisher said cheerily, thankful Hopper was about to leave.

"Oh, you were helpful alright, don't you worry about that, I can see myself out," Hopper waved them off as he headed towards the door and stopped. "One last thing, what makes you so sure she didn't have a pimp," he asked in true Columbo style, "I mean, how would you know?"

Fisher stared blankly at Hopper, his mind blank, "I don't know, it's just a guess."

Hopper shrugged, "lucky guess. Pity about the tapes though, real shame," he said as he finally closed the door.

Fisher waited for a moment before letting out a rapturous fart, and prayed it wouldn't stain. Jackson made a face, "Christ Fisher, what have you been eating, open a window. Make you nervous, did he?" Jackson laughed.

Fisher remained stony-faced. "You moron." Jackson's humor quickly evaporated, "why the hell did you tell him about the cameras? Are you fucking stupid?"

A foot to the left behind the closed door, Hopper listened to them arguing and shook his head, sometimes it was just too easy.

# 43.

"Fork."

"Spoon." Hopper answered too slowly. Shelly had already thrown several unconnected words at him, asking him to say the first thing that came to mind, *don't think about it, just react, there is no right or wrong*, but he'd struggled to find an adequate response. He felt distracted, his mind preoccupied with Leanne and the zoo.

"Knife." Shelly interrupted his thoughts.

Hopper paused; the word stab popped into his head. He didn't feel it was quite right. "Cut."

"Open."

"Locked."

"Missing."

*Dead.* "Found."

"Animal."

"Zoo."

This time it was Shelly's turn to pause as she scribbled some notes down as Hopper shifted uncomfortably in his seat. "Childhood."

*Lost.* Hopper shook his head, "I'm sorry Doc, but honestly, I can't see the point of this. You mind if we stop?"

Shelly put down her pad and took off her glasses, and gave them a quick wipe, it was a move designed to indicate a more casual, off-the-record, approach. It was *because* Hopper wanted to stop that made the session so much more interesting. The word association test, originally developed by Carl Jung to unlock the subconscious, was based on the notion that a single word can trigger past trauma, revealing hidden emotions and conflicts by injecting them into what appears to be an abstract stream of consciousness. Although the responses were important, as they had associations of their own, it was the time it took that piqued Shelly's interest. A normal reaction time was usually between one or two seconds. For Hopper, in some cases, it took almost nine seconds to come up with a response, indicating it was either because his mind was blank or elsewhere. "Something you'd like to talk about?" Shelly asked.

"Last time we met, you said I needed to find the part of myself that's missing. What did you mean by that?" Hopper asked, his mind still on the zoo.

"What do you think I meant?"

Hopper hated the way Shelly did that; every question returned with another. He could imagine how irritating she could be in real life;

*You fancy Chinese for dinner?*
*Why Chinese?*
*Can you pass the salt?*
*What is it about the salt that needs passing?*
*What do you want to watch on TV?*
*Why do you want to watch TV?*
*You fancy a fuck?*
*Why do you ask?*

And so on, a series of endless questions. Hopper sighed. There was a lot he wanted to talk about and a lot he didn't. Sometimes he recited lines he'd heard on daytime TV soaps just to keep the conversation flowing. Figuring Shelly would probably like to hear something like that, a lot of the characters seemed to be in touch with their emotional side, and he didn't want to disappoint her. But this felt different. He'd left the zoo feeling energized, a man on a mission and wanted to know if that's what she meant, although doubted it would be that simple. "If I knew, I wouldn't have asked."

"Ok, last time we talked, we talked about your childhood and your need for validation," Hopper winced, "we all need validation Jack, it's not unusual," she said casually, "it's about degrees. When it becomes obsessive, that's when it becomes a problem. I don't think you're an obsessive." She paused and threw Hopper a smile. "Yet. But let's say, for argument's sake, you join the police, do your training, and start work. So far, everything's good, no problem. Eventually, the things you see become too much, and it begins to taint your view of the world until you see one thing that's too much to bear, and you snap. What was it that made you snap? Was it a slow progression of things adding up, was it your childhood, or was it one thing that made you snap? Or all of them? There's no real answer, you have to decide for yourself, and until you do, that part of you will always be missing." Shelly paused for a moment. "I've read your file Jack, perhaps we can find something in there. Something that stands out?"

*If you're asking, then you already know, why don't you just say it?* Hopper thought, the memory made him queasy, not because of what he'd seen, but because of how it made him feel and buried it as quickly as it surfaced. "If you've read the file, then there's nothing to discuss, surely it's all in there." He knew how he sounded, petulant and childish, but so what, there were things that need to stay hidden. Even from her.

*What about the time you met Adam?* She wanted to scream, instead of quietly studying his face, looking for any tell-tale signs that might appear. Like a stone statue, he gave nothing away. She decided to change tack. "Then let's talk about the future."

"Do I have one?" Hopper asked sulkily, thinking what a buzz kill she was.

Shelly knew Hopper was trying to provoke her, but she had no intention of rising to the bait, "we all have a future, Jack, it's up to us to choose the one we want."

"Isn't mine taken out of my hands? I mean, I'm here, right?"

"Exactly. You're here. So you should choose."

Hopper stroked his chin and considered his options, if he were to continue his current trajectory, Shelly would have no choice but to write him up as irredeemable, unfit, damaged goods. She was right, it was his choice. She asked him before; did he want to be the good guy? No, he didn't _want_ to be, he _had_ to be. He needed to prove to himself he wasn't like the monster on the fourteenth floor, hiding in the shadow ready to bite with teeth that weren't your own. That no matter how tempting the black water looked, he would not step in and let the current take him. Did he want a future? Yes. But there was one he couldn't, wouldn't have. "I started looking," he began.

"Looking?" Shelly raised her eyebrows, encouraging him to continue, "you're talking about the Missing Persons?"

"Most were as you'd expect, drifters, losers that didn't want to be found. But there was one."

"Only one! Who?"

"She's no one."

"There's a phrase, *No one's no one to anyone. We're all someone to someone,*" she gently admonished. "Do you have a picture?" Thinking about the woman she'd seen in Adam's subconscious.

"Sure," Hopper took out his phone and turned it back on, Shelly had a strict rule of switching off all devices, hers included. It took a moment before the screen appeared and he was able to access his photographs, he brought up the image of Leanne and handed the phone to Shelly, "Why?" He asked.

Shelly took a long look at the woman, the badly caked-on foundation starting to flake under the harsh lights of the police station. The smudged eye shadow and heavily borrowed lashes looked more like bruises than make-up. Impossibly red lipstick overcompensated for thin lips that looked like they had been sliced into her face. Her neck and cleavage carried the weight of gravity through wrinkles and stretch marks betraying her age past the garish make-up and costume jewelry. She was a pitiful sight resembling a clown, but a clown she recognized nevertheless. Giving nothing away, she handed Hopper his mobile back. "Context." She said, "she looks familiar. I think I saw something about her in the papers. She had a child? Is that why she stood out to you, because of your own lost childhood?"

Hopper put his phone away, surprised he didn't remember any articles written about Leanne, "No one's gonna go looking for people like her," he didn't want to talk about the building.

"And you think they should?"

"Doesn't she deserve the same as the rest of us?"

"And you think by finding her, you may find the part of you that's missing?"

"I felt sorry for her kid," Hopper said, feeling defensive, "you think I'm wasting my time?"

"Not at all. I think it's a good thing." Shelly encouraged, knowing Leanne was never going to be found. "What have you found so far?"

"I went to her apartment." Hopper said, as he described the interior, "it wasn't what you'd expect, she tried. She didn't just up and leave her kid."

"You suspect something more?"

"I do," Hopper nodded, reluctant to say more.

"I sense there's a, *but*, coming?"

Hopper sighed, "It sounds crazy when I say it out loud."

Shelly smiled back, "look around Jack, crazy is what we do. Go on."

Hopper thought for a moment, worried how he might come across, desperate, deluded or paranoid at worse, hoping to see something in the shadows, looking for another chance to be the good guy. *Find the whore save the kid, find the whore save the kid*, adopt a new mantra for the right occasion; *save the kid, save the cop.* The irony wasn't lost on him, sitting in the shrink's office worried he might come across as nuts. "Ok," he said, taking a deep breath, *here goes nothing*, "I went to the zoo," he began.

# 44.

Sarah Moynihan reached the top of the steps leading to the police station. Sweating and out of breath, she paused for a moment for a much-needed break and lightly dabbed at her forehead, whispering a silent prayer for air-conditioning. Nate and the man she'd met at the gym called Lenny, were right; she should do something about her health and promised herself she would check the shopping channel for the right equipment as soon as she got back home. There were always images of toned good-looking models vibrating on the latest, get slim fast, equipment with minimum effort. She liked the look of the electro pads she'd seen, maximum gain, minimum pain. The idea struck her as unique; pads stuck to various parts of the body, would administer a series of electrical pulses, causing the muscles to spasm and contract, thereby exercising without moving. It was a smart and appealing idea she thought, as she popped a candy in her mouth and waddled through the double doors.

Greeted by the familiar smell of hot air and hotter bodies, a pungent mix of B.O., and the overuse of deodorant. It reminded her of the gym. Disappointed her air-conditioning prayer wasn't answered, she shuffled her way to the front desk, her nylon blouse beginning to lose its opacity as it stuck to her skin through sweat.

By the time Hopper returned from his session with Shelly, Sarah hadn't moved. Hopper caught sight of her as he made his way in, but didn't give her a second look.

Sarah struggled to her feet and yelled after him, "Detective Hopper?" Hopper stopped dead in his tracks, thinking it to be a joke. One look at the Sargent told him otherwise.

"Missing persons." The Sargent smirked back. Several officers had been waiting for this moment and had already begun sniggering,

Hopper doubled back and snatched one of the forms from the front desk before handing it to Sarah, doing his best to ignore the stifled laughter. "Hand it in when you're done." He told her flatly.

Sarah held a crumpled form in front of him, "do I look mentally defective?"

"Excuse me?"

"Do I look like I'm an idiot or a simpleton, maybe you think I don't pay my taxes, or is it you're just too busy finding all those missing people? Tell me, detective Hopper, you find many?'

*Me personally? Now that you mention it, none.* The job was getting worse. Missing Persons was bad enough, he didn't need the humiliation of having to deal with it in the open. "We have a system," he mumbled, conscious they were becoming the entertainment of the day.

"A system?" Sarah exclaimed in a voice that seemed too loud for her body, "and how's that working out? I've been sitting there for almost an hour. They said you'd be back forty-five minutes ago. I'm done filling out forms."

It was clear the large woman wasn't going anywhere and was prepared to keep going until she got what she wanted. "Perhaps we can go somewhere to talk?" Hopper suggested, lowering his voice, hoping she would do the same.

Unable to find an empty interview room, Hopper settled on the police canteen, it was the next best thing for privacy, people seldom ate there. At least they would be mercifully far enough away to avoid the insensitive stares from colleagues, keen to see how far he had fallen. His demeanor began to soften as they took one of the cheap Formica tables in the far corner of the room next to the vending machine. Sarah had three out-of-date twinkies and a can of coke, Hopper made do with a plastic cup of diluted black coffee. He took two sips before sliding it to the side and lit a cigarette. He offered Sarah one, thinking it might do her some good to become addicted to an appetite suppressant.

"No thanks," she managed to get out in between mouthfuls, "I gave up. Long time ago. Health reasons," she noticed him staring at the empty wrappers on the table, "I know what you're thinking, Detective Hopper. I'm no idiot, this is very stressful for me. I only have the one boy and I'm all he has." She glanced up at the no-smoking sign as Hopper used his discarded coffee cup as an ashtray. Sarah took a moment to compose herself, brushing the crumbs from her dress. "It's about my boy Nate. He hasn't been home in a few days."

It took Sarah almost two hours to go over the details of Nate's life. Hopper guessed she didn't have many friends and was possibly using their time together as a cheap form of therapy. She explained how hard it was being a single mum, her son's sensitive nature, and the feelings of guilt she had, given that she was the one who had encouraged him to get big. Hopper grunted in all the right places, allowing his mind to casually drift to back to his earlier session, wondering about the things Nate would be repressing when he was older. When she was finished, Hopper folded the Missing Person form. "Sarah," he began patiently, "Nate is almost eighteen, given what you've just told me I'm sure he'll come back eventually. The best I can do is enter his details into the system and wait for a match."

Sarah, brought her shoulder bag to her knees and began rummaging around, eventually she placed one of the ampules she'd found on the table. "I thought you might say that. I also found this. Someone's been selling drugs to my boy, and I'd also like to know who, but I can't ask him on account of him being missing. And him being a minor too!"

Hopper picked up the ampule between his thumb and forefinger. She was right, selling to a minor was a big deal, even if the minor was only a couple of months short of becoming an adult! "You didn't show this to the Duty Sargeant?" It was more statement than question, the penalty for supplying to a minor was four times heavier than an adult.

Sarah pursed her lips, "They didn't want to know, just told me to sit and wait for you. So here I am."

*Idiots,* thought Hopper. Several months ago, he would have done the same thing, he knew what it was to be on the outside looking in. He shook his head knowing he was about to disappoint her, "I know it looks bad, but honestly, it doesn't change much." Hopper let his words hang, he would have liked to do more, but he was already looking for one kid's junkie whore mother, he didn't have time to go looking for a junkie kid. Sarah Moynihan looked utterly crushed. Hopper decided to lie a little, just to lift her spirits, "Ok, I'll ask around, but don't get your hopes up." Sarah's face brightened, *a little hope is better than no hope,* he thought, "my guess if you've got these, then he'll be back. I'm assuming he was a member of a gym?"

"Tiny's. But you'd be wasting your time. I've already been. He didn't get them at the gym," Sarah took a moment to enjoy the look of surprise on Hopper's face. "What? You think I'm just going to sit on my fat ass watching TV? Besides, you turn up, what are they going to tell you? But me. Well... I'm just some harmless old fat lady."

Hopper was impressed, he could almost imagine Sarah Moynihan interrogating a muscle-bound freak. It would have taken guts to do what she did. He nodded approvingly, although it may have done more harm than good, "I'm not so sure just because someone tells you, they're not selling drugs to your kid you can take them on face value. If anything, you may have just tipped them off."

"Detective Hopper, at least give me some credit. Just because he didn't buy them at the gym, doesn't mean he didn't meet the person selling them there. I already know where he works. His name is Jackson, he works at the zoo."

# 45.

Knowing you're in a nightmare doesn't change the terror of it. The texture and emotions match those of the conscious world. Their mercurial nature the only giveaway as one slides seamlessly into the next. Built on a foundation of best-kept secrets, the door to the waking world remains shut. Hunted through the maze of life, through cesspits once called home he is taught the meaning of fear. Adam runs the corridors of his past, lined with doorways to his childhood holding demons at bay too terrifying to let loose, each one a distant memory of the pain and hurt once endured now forgotten and so he runs, no longer knowing who he is or why, unable and unwilling to break the locks.

There is a fog in his mind, a thick soup clouding his judgment. There is someone or something behind. He can feel its hot breath and the sting of spittle on his neck. Lungs burning, legs aching, he runs until he cannot, falling and tumbling into the blackness, arms flailing, grasping at the dark, desperate to stop the descent, he sees the face of the wolf and wakes.

*Did you see?* The voice asks.

*Yes.* He answers.

Shelly watched the nightmare inside, safely from the out. Adam had woken dazed and confused with no clear recollection of events at the zoo. It's not important, she will find her own truth through the tank. The tank gave her access beyond the subconscious, it also gave her control. Adam would remember only what she allowed him to, greedily keeping the rest for herself. She had seen what Hopper could not. He had told her about his suspicions at the zoo, searching for a hooker who was a dead end. Poor Leanne, a signpost to something bigger and nothing more, pointing him back towards himself. She knew she had to be careful and stay one step ahead, offering only tantalizing glimpses of what the future could hold, encouraging his journey to discover who he really was. She would become an architect of chaos to understand order and control, to know if our inner selves can surface in a waking state as it had once with Hopper and why?

His need to be good, a distraction to what swam below, too scared to embrace reality, rejecting himself in favor of a construct built on lies and guilt. Was the monster always there, patiently waiting for the door to open, or was it birthed through our own refusal to accept who we are? Our act of repression making it whole.

She had watched the brutality of the arena at the abattoir, and the aftermath of Adam's id, run free. The abandonment of release satisfying the rage within. He had torn and ripped what he had been unable to, leaving him complete and in control once more. His monster now asleep, hers now awake, she wanted the same.

# 46.

Jackson is in the security room at the zoo after hours. Doubling as his man cave, it's the place he feels safest. Alone with his thoughts—which he doesn't particularly like—his own thoughts bring him down; his own thoughts sometimes get *too much*! He sometimes hates himself for what he does, how he acts, and can understand why no-one else likes him either. He tells himself, *'he must remember not to be such an asshole in future'* and curses his voice inside, telling it to shut up because he knows it's right. Frank's told him often enough; he can be his own worst enemy. *The biggest threat to you, is you. Shit happens, get over it, regret never helped no one.* He knows he's right. Frank is like that, he's almost always right.

Jackson knew he should be at the gym. It kept him focused and according to his timetable, it was a chest and arms session, his favourite, but the damn cop had messed up his routine and his head and Fisher hadn't helped. It wasn't right, Fisher talking to him like that. He expected it from Frank, took it even, but he'd always considered it something of a joke, even if the joke went a little too far. That was just Frank's way. But Fisher! That was something else, he was lucky he didn't just tear him a new one then and there. He could do it; he just didn't want his hands getting soiled in the process. He was sure Fisher would bleed out something rotten other than blood. The cop had them both spooked turning up when he had, but hadn't asked about Adam, just Leanne. But then, *just like the big fat stupid idiot he is*, he cursed himself, he'd gone and ruined it all and mentioned the tapes.

It wasn't hard for cops to get what they wanted, twisting your words, taking them out of context, making you sound guilty or stupid or both. Using everything and anything they could as leverage, a word in the right ear, a promise, and a threat. God knows there were enough in the world willing to rat you out for the price of a coffee. Even Eve. As much as he liked her, he didn't trust her and trusted Higgs less, who knows what he might have said. Junkies are terrible liars.

The whole Leanne business could have just been a cover. Eve wouldn't have thought twice about throwing them all under the bus if it meant saving her father, but what did she know, what could she tell him? Higgs would be a moron if he told his daughter anything, not to mention how it would make him look. He'd find out sooner or later, right now he had other things on his mind.

He'd reassured Fisher there were no copies and the tape he did have was wiped daily—it was part of his routine. Promising him there was nothing to worry about, at least nothing for him to worry about, Fisher less so. He was the one with his own private tape collection, after all, his little insurance policy, now including footage of Adam slipping into the back of the truck. It was the only real evidence he'd been there at all, unless you counted the ankle bracelet, and from what Fisher said, it didn't appear too reliable. They should have listened to him. They could have dumped the body anywhere if they'd cut Adam's leg off. Frank was right; it was an abattoir. If you couldn't make someone disappear in a place like that, where could you? Still, it had been fun what they did. He had to hand it to Higgs, he'd pumped him so full of shit, he barely remembered his name let alone what happened and no one needed a reminder.

But the cop had made him paranoid asking dumb questions about dumb whores. He'd told Fisher so many times to get rid of her, she was bad for business, it wouldn't be long before someone started to ask questions, and some of the pimps he knew wouldn't take too kindly to a freelancer operating out of the zoo. Thankfully she was gone, he'd seen to that. But Fisher was a problem, he had no idea how long he'd been talking to the cop or what he might have said. The only way to deal with them was to stay silent. It didn't matter if you had nothing to hide, in his experience, if they wanted to find something, they would, even if they had to put it there themselves, anything for a bust. They may not be the brightest, but they were relentless, and once they got a sniff of something, they would just keep coming back for more, chipping away until you dropped yourself in, *just like he had.*

He'd been the one to give him a reason to come back, even with the cameras he couldn't be everywhere at once, and then there was Nate. Idiot Nate. he'd been expecting him to come by and collect his gear, but since what happened with Eve hadn't been back. Admittedly it wasn't such a bad thing, him staying away, especially with the cop sniffing around, but he missed the money. If he did come back, the last thing he wanted was anyone sticking their nose in his business, which is why he called Sammy the pick and changed the locks. He had to wait until he had the place to himself to avoid suspicion.

He'd considered decommissioning the cameras a few times, but after watching the footage, had been even more reluctant to give them up, there was power in being everywhere at once. He could watch Eve whenever he wanted, not to mention Fisher and Higgs. He'd become addicted to it, people were fascinating. He had a trove of goodies he wasn't prepared to delete, the oddities he'd caught, how people behaved when they thought they were alone, stupidly thinking privacy was a shield. If no one saw it, did it happen? When it's on tape it did. He'd even captured a few hours of Leanne hard at work with Fisher, which made for some particularly uncomfortable viewing. But blackmail was always an option!

Jackson ran his fingers over the control panel, it was an old school analogue system, big blinking lights, solid man-sized buttons straight from Darth Vader's chest plate. Power at his fingertips allowing him to switch from one vantage point to another. He slides from one side of the desk to the other even though everything was within arm's reach. It makes him feel a little like Captain Kirk or Han Solo in charge of his own command centre, eyes everywhere, the ever-present Jackson.

The system is fed automatically, once a tape was finished, another would be inserted in its place. He'd already removed the previous ones which he'd enjoyed back in the privacy of his apartment but had left a tape running as the system didn't work without one and was watching the world in reverse on double speed searching for anything worth keeping when some movement on the screen caught his attention.

A few weeks ago, Jackson had found an old sleeping bag with a few pathetic possessions bundled in an overstuffed laundry bag, precious remnants of a failed life. He knew once word got out the place was considered a haven for the homeless, they would be soon over-ran. Like rats, once a place was infected, it was hard to get rid of them. You had to send a message plain and simple, *you are not welcome here.* Jackson cracked his knuckles, some people never learn, maybe it wasn't too late for a workout after all.

Stepping out into the monochrome world of the zoo, Jackson was surprised to see how much it matched the image on tape. Once the sun had set, the moon drained the colour from the zoo, replacing it with a blanket of anxiety. With many of the animals being nocturnal, the zoo was far more active at night and tonight was no exception. Jackson made his way towards the now empty wolf enclosure where he'd seen the shadow. The homeless were a sneaky bunch, some looked harmless enough but looks could be deceptive and many were armed with homemade shivs fashioned from whatever they could lay their grubby hands on. While others who looked big, bigger than him, were all padding. Having to wear their possessions as a living wardrobe, either way, he would have to keep his wits about him and slapped the heavy mag light in his hand, it could always double as a bat.

Knowing he was taking a starring role in his own show, Jackson took a moment to grin at the camera, giving himself a quick flex for the archives. He wondered how he might look in action and was damn sure he would look good. Unfortunately, in typical fashion, once there, the intruder was nowhere to be seen.

"I know you're here." Jackson called out to no-one in particular, feeling slightly relieved the sound he made may have scared him off. Some of the homeless have mental problems, he thought, and didn't want to catch anything in case they bit him. "You're on candid camera, you moron," he shouted out, "you come out now, and we'll have a nice cup of coffee, sort this nice and easy, 'cos if I find you, it's gonna be the hard way."

The sound of Jackson's voice is as familiar as it is unfamiliar, as prey he's easy to stalk. Your memory is awash with what he did and you feel your blood rush and heart pound. Your turn now, no wolf to hide behind, no bars keeping him safe, you are free. He smells of sweat and the acrid taint of chemicals. You take your time and savor the moment.

Jackson was doing his best to sound threatening, but his high-pitched voice comes out a little Disneyesque. He likes to think he doesn't scare easy, being big is no guarantee of winning in a scuffle, it's about who's prepared to do what. He's not like Frank, he has limits but knows desperation has no ceiling and if he were honest with himself, the homeless scare him a little. They have the wild-eyed look of madness which makes them unpredictable. Part of him wanted to go back to his little den, lock the door and sit tight. A different part is trying to remember how big the shadow looked, *not too big* he thinks. He hears the wet slap of feet on concrete and the ragged breath of someone with asthma and begins to feel relieved. Hopefully, it's just an old man. It sounds closer, but not too heavy. Feeling a little better, he turns quickly in the direction of the footsteps hoping to catch the intruder in the heavy beam. Still nothing. The slap slapping of feet moves behind, and he has the uncomfortable feeling of being played with. *Fuck this*, he tells himself, *if they're that desperate to sleep in a cage, they can have it!* He'll be braver in the daylight and takes a few steps away from the noise. The soft slapping follows like a shadow and stops with him. Even the animals have quietened. Two more steps, two more slaps. He can hear the heavy breathing behind and knows once he turns, he'll put a face to the terror he feels. Gripping the Maglite, he takes a deep breath hoping he's faster than the stranger behind. In one sudden movement he spins, raising the heavy torch above his head ready to come crashing down.

It's easy. Hiding in the shadows, the night is a friend to dark deeds. You smell the fear, heavy with adrenalin it thins the blood and you know the first bite will be sweet.

Jackson hears the snap before he feels the pain as the bone in his arm splinters. Shards pierce the skin like thorns and the blood pumps like a fountain. He would scream if he could, but there is a hand in his mouth, long bony fingers flatten his tongue as it tugs at his jaw, and all he can think of is how salty it tastes as they reach further down his throat. He gags, panicking, tries to draw breath, legs kicking out. But he is held tightly, legs wrapped around his waist. It's strong, far stronger than him. *It shouldn't be* he thinks as he falls backward under its weight. The blackness from the night seeps into his vision, clouding the edges as he tries to breathe and sees the teeth. Jackson makes one last sound, a belching gurgle of a scream ripped from his lungs before it forms. Jackson draws a single breath through the newly torn hole in his throat as fingers probe and tear. He's dimly aware of the head now buried inside his throat and the slurping chewing sound as his life is sucked away.

# 47.

Adam was feeling good. The bus journey to the zoo had been no different from the many others he'd taken. He recognized the same faces but didn't know they were in their usual seats. He gave each one a courteous nod as if to say; *Hi there fella, same old shit different day, all us working stiffs together again. I'm just as normal as you,* they acknowledged his presence as he did theirs. Everything was as it should be. Routines were important, the hospital had taught him that. He had taken his place in the tapestry of life and been accepted. Only things *were* different. He couldn't quite put his finger on it, it was like asking someone to describe how wet water is, when they suddenly notice the tiny attributes that made up the things they'd known all along. How a single bead of water can resemble the purest of jewels or how it might stick on a glass, reluctant to move, before combining with another and another, gaining weight and mass until one drop can become a destructive flood. If Adam had been pressed to describe how he felt, he would have said, *unblocked.*

There were things he couldn't remember, but it didn't matter, Shelly had told him he had been in an accident. He'd been shot with a tranquilizing dart by mistake, but it had been nothing to worry about, it wasn't important, and if he couldn't remember, he guessed it wasn't. Besides, the voice told him *it could remember* but wouldn't say. In many ways he was glad the voice was back, he'd missed the company, though it had never really gone away, often sounding like an echo of his own thoughts, but this time it was clearer more distinct as if it were sitting next to him on the bus, still, it made him promise not to tell. When he asked why, it wouldn't say, just that it didn't want anyone getting in between them again. Adam thought about that and agreed.

He had gone to work as per usual, he had a list of things he needed to do each day, he liked his routine, and wondered about the day he hadn't been there, would it have made a difference, should he say something, tell Fisher he was back?

The voice told him, with a slight giggle there was no need, that he should *just keep shovelling the same old shit he'd been shoveling all his life, Christ knows there's enough of it to go round, Fisher will find out who's back soon enough.* Adam thought it a little unnecessary to be so dismissive of his job and wasn't one hundred percent he understood what it meant but shrugged it off. It was after all, nice to have someone else make the decisions for a while.

Eve had spent another restless night with her father, unwilling and unable to bear each other's company for more than a few minutes at a time. Slipping into the familiar roles of disappointed daughter, dead-beat dad playing verbal ping pong, scoring points off each other. She asked about Frank, the wolf, relentlessly picking at the scab until he eventually stormed out, leaving her alone, neither one having anything left to say. She knew he was keeping secrets. Something inside had changed. He could barely look at her anymore without getting angry. She wanted to know what she had done, why he was being so cold. He just shook his head and left.

It was another predictably hot day, the shimmering heat keeping the visitors away so that there was little to distract her from her thoughts. She needed to dilute her paranoia and share it with someone less tainted. She passed the empty wolf enclosure and thought about Adam. Their last conversation hadn't gone well, so caught up in herself, she didn't have time for him, and yet he was the only one who remained clean, uncontaminated by the stench of secrets. She had missed his innocence. He offered his help without condition, and she had carelessly tossed it aside. She felt like a fool when she saw him.

Adam enjoyed cleaning. The repetitious act and the satisfaction of watching the transformation unfold were hypnotic to him. It didn't matter if it was shoveling shit or scrubbing graffiti off a wall, it was all the same. The slow concentrated movements of the steel brush followed by the dunk and splash of soapy sugar water revealing a pristine wall beneath the words, *faggots suck dick here* and the accompanying number. Adam hadn't noticed Eve watching and only turned when her shadow cut across the wall.

"Eve!" Adam hadn't realized he'd forgotten her until he saw her. *Eve,* the voice repeated, *be careful,* it warned, *if you like her, you'll keep her away, we'll only hurt her in the end.*

*Never, she's a friend,* he answered back, although wasn't sure why she was looking at him like that? Had he done something wrong, was that one of the things he'd forgotten about? Was it the accident?

"Is something wrong?" He asked.

She wanted to tell him in a flurry of emotions, *Yes, something is badly wrong, with this place, with me,* instead of, "I was worried about you. Where were you?"

There were times when Adam wanted to tell Eve where he'd been, where he lived, who he was. That he wasn't like other people, *no you're not,* the voice added unhelpfully. Adam frowned; he didn't need a reminder. "You mean the accident?" He asked, embarrassed.

Eve shook her head, "you mean the wolf? That wasn't your fault."

A memory shard clicked into place as he tried to concentrate. There were fragments, like an exploded bomb, pieces of shrapnel scattered over the terrain of his mind, images glinting in the sunlight waiting to be put back together. The harder he thought, the more confused the images, abstract snippets, fragments swirling like colored paint in milk. *It's too much,* whispered the voice, *you're not ready.* It couldn't hold them as the swirls took shape. The flash of teeth, and the shot of a gun. *More,* he cried to his other, as the wall gave way. They came thick and fast, an amalgam of thoughts and images woven together in a fresco of what he hoped wasn't real. The memories were making him dizzy, as the ground began to open, he backed away, fearing he might be swallowed whole, but the animal inside caught him. *Not yet,* it told him and stopped the flow, *there will be time enough for that later.* Adam steadied himself, there was more to see than he had been allowed. But they had gone, the harder he tried to focus his thoughts the less they made sense. His throat was tight, and his chest hurt, he could feel the pounding in his brain as the memories moved beyond reach, sinking from view. But there was something else, a stain that had been left and the bitter coppery taste of blood that wasn't his own. He winced and spat out a memory that wasn't his and was left with the feeling that something bad had happened, something terrible he didn't want Eve to know. There was a part of him that had done something very wrong and as much as Eve wanted him to remember, he knew he didn't. "I didn't mean to get in the way," he finally said by way of explanation.

"Adam," Eve asked cautiously, concern registering in her voice, "what happened?"

Adam couldn't remember, not really. There was a wall of noise where his memory should be, he felt cocooned in ignorance tearing at the silk. *Help me* he shouted at his other. *Alright,* the voice told him. *I'll show you a little* and opened the door just a crack. "The aviary," he blurted out, looking up, "we were talking."

"I remember," Eve gently coaxed, teasing out his memory, "I was upset. You came to look for me."

"You told me about the wolf," a broken fragment joined another, and Adam caught a glimpse of himself waiting, watching the truck before slipping in.

"You were worried," Eve said, knowing Adam had already been infected by the rot, "Adam, what did you do?"

Adam knotted his eyebrows together, "I went to the abattoir," he said quietly as the bomb began to reverse, the wreckage slowly pulling itself together as if drawn by an invisible thread. He looked up quickly and locked eyes. In hers, he saw the desperation of a future eclipsed by a past, she still tended the flicker of hope kept alive by her not knowing. She reminded him of something Shelly once told him; there is a cat in a sealed box, you drop a knife into the box. Did the knife miss or hit? Until you open the box, you decide if it lives or dies. Adam knew he was opening a box as he reached out and took her by the hand, "they make them fight Eve, they make them fight."

# 48.

Hopper didn't believe in coincidence, it felt too close to fate and destiny. Both poor excuses for the weak-minded, an easy out, abdicating responsibility for poor decision making, or lazy police work. To him, the notion of a cosmic force governing our actions was as ridiculous as blaming Batman for his current situation. Even if, in some small way he still did. After his visit to the zoo, or more precisely after meeting Fisher and Jackson, he'd already decided on a repeat visit. Guilty until proven guilty was a philosophy he'd grown into, and in their case, he was sure he wouldn't have to dig too deep. After Sarah Moynihan left, Hopper conducted a quick search for the name Jackson and came up with multiple hits. Jackson it seemed, was a common name amongst the criminal fraternity. After trawling through several pages, he finally came up with a face he recognized. According to Jackson's record, he was low level muscle, what most would refer to as *the heavy*, usually brought in for that *extra* level of persuasion, never quite making it off the lower rungs of the career criminal. He'd served time for assault, assault with a weapon, extortion, supply and possession of drugs and surprisingly indecent exposure. Hopper laughed at the last charge and thought about mentioning it next time they met. Everyone has a trigger; it was obvious the muscles were compensating for something. Fisher on the other hand, didn't register and without Dom's help, who was spending less and less time in the basement, would likely remain invisible. There could of course, be a simpler explanation; he may not have entered enough data into the system, could have gone by a different name or most likely hadn't been caught, but doubted it was because he was innocent. He struck Hopper like his namesake, Fisher, and just as slippery.

Adam needed time to think. He was still unclear about the events and the order in which they happened. A continually changing pattern of shapes and colors morphing and colliding into one, tantalizingly present, always out of reach, no sooner had he focused it would drift and move out of sight like specs caught in the eye. He remembered the abattoir and the iron grip of Jackson. But the rest was still a blur. He told Eve what he could piece together, but none of it made sense, a waking kaleidoscope of humans with animal faces, of Jackson, Fisher, and Frank leering through a mesh wire fence. A fight between animals and the urge to bite. He from the inside, cheering himself on and struggled to leave until they became one in the dark.

Shelly had told him the work was important, that familiar surroundings and routine would help, and just like *his other* had promised, everything would return, *when you're ready*, she'd said. If he didn't know better, he would have thought her, and *his other* were having private conversations behind his back. He made his way to the wolf's empty enclosure, already littered with discarded rubbish of convenience. *She deserved more* he thought, and began to clean, hoping to find something he'd lost.

"You getting it ready for something else?"

The voice startled Adam, he had given himself over to the methodical hypnotic state of an automaton as he ran through the corridors of his mind. He had been thinking about the last time he was there. *He'll never bother you or anyone again*, his other had said, *how can you be so sure?* He'd asked and the voice had fallen silent once more. He squinted up into the sun, it was hard to make out who was talking, but the voice had an uncomfortable familiarity to it he couldn't place. *His other* inside squinted through the window for a better look and smiled, *you*, he said.

"Another," Hopper glanced at the sign still clipped to the bars of the cage, someone had scrawled a crude drawing of a penis over the information, making it hard to read, "wolf?"

"No," Adam said as he turned to pick up an empty burger carton, "I don't think so."

"No? Least it keeps you busy. Cleaning? There's a lot of empty cages, you gotta clean them all?" Hopper continued, "So what happened? To the wolf?" He asked smiling trying to sound light and casual, ignoring the uncomfortable feeling that there was something weirdly familiar about the young man, but he struggled to think from where.

"It died."

Hopper nodded, he guessed that's why some people work with the public and some clean cages, "You been here long. Not the cage, I mean the zoo?"

Adam held up his hand to shield his eyes, "a while. why?"

Hopper squatted down to Adam's level to get out of the sun and get a better look, "my apologies, Detective Hopper," he said as he put his hands through the bars. Adam frowned and reluctantly leaned forward stretching to shake his hand. Shelly had always told him the importance of good manners. This time Hopper was able to get a better look at the young man, but still drew a blank, his face was so unremarkable it made it more so. Unblemished like a mannequin, without a single mark, it was almost perfect except for the thin hint of a scar running down his left ear disappearing under his chin, "and you?"

"Adam," he answered feeling increasingly uncomfortable and wondered where he might have seen him before.

"Adam," Hopper rolled the name around in his head, searching his memory, but came up blank, "have we met before?"

"I don't think so," *Do we know him?* Adam asked *his other,* who had mysteriously gone quiet.

Hopper cocked his head to one side as if studying him, "Odd! I could have sworn... you know, you look familiar." Adam stared blankly back as he waited for him to fill in the gap. Hopper shucked off his curiosity, *it'll come,* he thought, he wasn't here for Adam, he had, as the saying goes, *bigger Fish to fry.* Hopper knew most cleaners he'd met were rendered inconspicuous by their occupation, the hidden eyes and ears or any organization, best kept secrets often ending up in the garbage. "Guess you must have one of those faces," he said dismissively, and changed the subject, "I'm hoping you might be able to help me, you know Edward Jackson right?" Adam nodded, "you ever see him with this kid?" Hopper took out the photograph Sarah had given him. In the picture, Nate looked much different, less swollen with a slight lop-sided grin and floppy hair.

If anyone had asked Adam what sort of person Nate might have been based on the photograph, he probably would have said, *seems like a nice kid.* Instead shook his head. "No," he said, quickly handing the photograph back, feeling slightly sick at the memory of him.

Hopper had always prided himself on his ability to tell when someone was lying, considering himself to be something of a walking polygraph. Shortness of breath, too quick to answer, too quick to look away, an unconscious touch of the earlobe, nose or mouth, take your pick, there were a thousand little tells. He stared at Adam for a while trying to get a read on him until he eventually looked away. *Liar,* "You sure? Tell you what, I have a better one." Hopper brought out his mobile to access the recent one Sarah had emailed him, "what about this one, he looks more like this?"

Adam barely looked at the picture, "No. I see a lot of people, I don't remember any of them."

Hopper glanced around the empty zoo, if Jackson had a little sideline going on, it was a safe bet Adam wouldn't want to get involved, especially given the size difference. He took out a twenty and folded it in half, "maybe take a better look," he said as he held his phone out once more with the note clasped between his fingers.

Adam glanced at the money and looked away, "I don't pay much attention to the visitors."

Hopper kept his arm out until it became obvious Adam wasn't interested. "I guess not." Hopper glanced up at the security cameras. He was an idiot, he should have been more careful, they were clearly visible to anyone watching. Adam was obviously nervous, and he'd given him more reason to be so. In his experience, anyone refusing a cash incentive meant that whatever Adam knew was worth more than he was prepared to pay. At least whoever was watching would come out of the woodwork soon enough. Fisher or Jackson, it didn't matter which, although he hoped it was Fisher, he'd be far easier to persuade, and he had no personal qualms of using Adam as bait. "You mind if I ask one more question?" Hopper asked as he brought up the photograph of Leanne and held it through the bars of the cage. "You ever see her around with Fisher, maybe Jackson?"

Adam felt the sting of a memory that wasn't his and winced, no, he did not want to tell the policeman what might have happened, *but you know don't you?* His inner voice sniggered. "I can't help you," he said shaking his head, "I have to get back to work."

"One last thing," Hopper reached inside his pocket and took out one of his cards, "you ever feel like talking. You call me. Whatever this is, I'll make sure nothing happens to you, you understand?" He said trying to sound plausible like a cop on a TV show. The truth being, the more loose ends someone had to tie up, the greater the chance of getting caught.

Adam reluctantly took the card and waited until Hopper was far enough away before ripping it into pieces and dropping them into his rubbish bag.

In Fisher's experience it was easier to meet the cops head on, rather than wait for them to come knocking, avoidance was the strategy of the guilty. Getting in first meant controlling the narrative, besides, it was easier to find out what they knew, whilst being agreeably helpful, *give a little, get a lot more.* He had been in what was laughably called the souvenir shop when he saw Hoper arrive at the zoo. He'd been expecting him back ever since Jackson made that stupid crack about the security tapes. Fisher had gone to the security office to keep a watchful eye on him, but to his surprise found Jackson had changed the lock. Knowing how much time he spent in there spying on Eve he wondered who else he'd been spying on, him? Secrets fed his paranoia, especially when they weren't his, but it had been his paranoia that had kept him safe all these years. Jackson was obviously hiding something, most likely where he kept his stash of steroids for the feeble-minded idiots who hung off him. It wasn't good enough, Jackson was getting too cocky for his own good, becoming a liability, thinking his relationship with Frank counted for something when he knew there was no such thing as loyalty between crooks. He could imagine Jackson trying to undermine him, blaming him for the cop, the two of them cooking up plans without him, making him the patsy when the time came. They hadn't counted on his knack for survival, he hadn't kept his nose clean all these years by accident. Fisher had been in tight spots before and always managed to slither his way out, seeing Hopper gave him an idea as to how he could get rid of Jackson, or at the very least, keep him distracted whilst he made his own plans.

He had been relieved and surprised to see Adam back so soon and without so much as a phone call from the doc, it looked like they'd swallowed Higgs's story. Without the opportunity to watch from a safe distance Fisher eventually caught up with Hopper as he finished his friendly little chat with Adam and was now walking briskly towards the reptile house in the hope of 'bumping' into him. *Fancy seeing you here*, would be his opening gambit and without Jackson around he was only too happy to throw him under the bus.

Jackson was a fool to leave him alone, after all he'd be the one talking to the cops, not him.

Fisher checked his mobile for the seventh time in less than an hour, making sure he hadn't set it to silent by mistake. It wasn't like Jackson to be a no-show, it had now been two days in a row. He guessed he'd initially stayed home in a sulk, but two days? Apart from the conditions of his parole, not that it mattered any, it seemed excessive even by his standards, now wasn't the time to cut and run.

The reptile house wasn't much to look at, a red brick arched building with inset glass cases exhibiting mostly snakes and lizards easily found in your own back yard if you bothered to look. Although there were several poisonous varieties from different parts of the world. Fisher's favorite, *Monty*, a large, red-bellied black snake from Australia, had already proved his worth several times over. In his most recent bout, he'd been pitted against a rattler, neither of which were considered aggressive unless threatened or provoked, and both had put on quite the show. Monty, ever the exhibitionist, had finished off the bout by devouring his opponent. Much to the applause of the crowd and the relief of Higgs, a full belly meant they entered a kind of food coma, making them docile and far easier to handle. The reptile house also had another advantage, it was air-conditioned.

"Detective Hopper," Fisher said breathlessly as he finally caught up. "Good to see you again, enjoying the exhibits."

"There's not really a great deal left to see."

Fisher nodded sadly as if it were a great disappointment rather than a relief, he was looking forward to moving onto greener pastures and was already talking to a cruise ship operator rumored to be a front for laundering money and drug running. They were looking for someone keen to look the other way and Fisher's C.V. was exemplary in that area. He shrugged helplessly, "what can I say, we can't compete with the entertainment of the day. We'll be closed soon. What about you, you have a particular interest in reptiles?"

"The ones I'm interested in, tend to walk on two feet, much like yourself." Fisher winced at the barb and moved into the open mouth of the reptile house. Hopper followed, it felt apt to be talking to someone like Fisher in his natural habitat and was hit by the thick musty smell and change in temperature, he couldn't imagine how bad it would smell in the heat, and wasn't sure if it was the environment or the close proximity to Fisher, but either way wanted out of there as soon as he could, "I was looking for Jackson."

Fisher stopped at the first enclosure, which contained a brightly colored frog. "I haven't seen him today, is there a problem?"

"You have any ideas where he might be?"

"The gym," Fisher suggested helpfully, "he spends a lot of time there. I understand it's called Tiny's." The frog hopped back into the merge foliage at the back of the case.

"He's not at the gym."

Fisher pursed his lips and blew, "perhaps if I knew what you wanted? I noticed you talking to Adam earlier, perhaps I could?"

It hadn't taken long for something to crawl out, thought Hopper, although he hadn't expected it to be Fisher. "How about the tapes? Given that Jackson's not here, we could watch them together, unless there's something you'd rather I didn't see? You and the doughnut guy spit roasting Leanne? Maybe charging a little extra?"

Fisher winced at the thought, it had only been the once, and Terry had promised not to tell. "If I could, I would detective. Unfortunately, I don't have access," he explained, relieved for once he could tell the truth, smirking.

Hopper didn't like being treated as a fool and cut Fisher short grabbing his tie as he shoved him backwards against the glass, "I want you to know something Fisher," he growled, "I want you to know how much I don't like you, and I want you to know how much I don't like liars." He leaned in closer invading Fisher's personal space, their noses almost touching, "how did you know I was here unless you were watching?" Hopper tightened the knot around Fisher's neck, as much as it disgusted him, he enjoyed the feeling of power, vindicated by doing good, it was an intoxicating mixture.

"I'm serious," Fisher wheezed in between breaths, "he changed the locks, I can't get in even if I wanted to, " he spluttered struggling for breath, "I saw you! I saw you talking to Adam," he protested, Hopper didn't ease the pressure. Fisher knew he had one more play left before he blacked out. Control the narrative, give him what he wanted, "drugs," he finally managed to cough, "is this about drugs?"

Fisher's confession took Hopper by surprise, and he released the tension on his tie. He knew he would be easy, but he didn't think he would be this easy, his disdain for the man grew, "go on."

"I had an idea that he might be selling. I figured there was a reason why he didn't want you poking around, that's when I found out. I was looking for you when I saw you with Adam, is that what you were asking him about?" Fisher rubbed at his neck, "You know, you could have just come to me?"

Hopper narrowed his eyes, "I thought you guys were tight?"

"You kidding? Look, I gave the guy a break, but tight?"

"So why did you?"

"My old man was an ex-con." Lied Fisher, the words tripping off his tongue adding to the musty smell in the reptile house, "look, I know his parole officer, I owed him, and I guess I wanted to give him a chance. I guess I was wrong." Fisher made a mental note to give Mick Sheldon, Jackson's parole officer a call, he knew he'd confirm his story. He was a regular visitor to the abattoir and Frank always made sure he was well taken care of, as he had. He'd even introduced him to Leanne, although for some reason he'd turned his offer down.

Hopper wasn't taken in for a moment, as he could recall, it had been Fisher he'd heard calling Jackson a moron. "You're a regular civic hero, looking after whores and ex-cons like that, a regular charity. And now none of them are here. Just you. On your own." He took out the photograph of Nate and pushed it into Fisher's face, "you ever see him with Jackson? You know he's a minor, so far things aren't looking good for you."

Fisher sighed heavily and shook his head, at least he wasn't asking about Adam, and he wanted to keep it that way, Jackson was an obvious sacrifice. "Ok yes, I had an idea, but honestly, I wasn't sure what Jackson would do. You tell me, what was I supposed to do?"

"You tell me," Hopper snapped, he felt close to losing control, he already had what he wanted, but guys like Fisher made his skin crawl. It was obvious Fisher would sell out his own grandmother if it meant taking the heat off him.

"I'm telling you now. Is that what Adam said?" Fisher stammered, desperate to know their conversation.

"You're very interested in what he had to say, you want to tell me why?"

*Shit*, thought Fisher, *this was going from bad to worse*, "I figured if he'd seen Jackson selling, he'd be too scared to say anything, I was worried, that's all. What if Jackson does come back and he knows you've been poking around in his business, who's the first person he's gonna blame?" Fisher noticed a shift in Hopper, *thank God*, "You get to go home, where does he go? Something happens to him, it's on you."

Hopper hated to admit it, but Fisher was right. If he found Jackson, he could blame the kid and sit back and watch what would happen. It would be as good as an admission of guilt. "I'll keep him out of it. You, I'm not so sure."

Fisher was a little worried he may have overplayed his hand, but the last thing he wanted was Hopper getting suspicious of Adam and finding out about Dr Shelly. He'd have to deal with Adam later once he'd been able to get into Jackson's 'office'. "I can look after myself," Fisher snorted knowing he couldn't but Frank could, "besides isn't that what you'd like? Drop someone in it just to see what happens?"

Not as dumb as he looks, grinned Hopper. "Ok fat man, today you get to breathe easy, but remember I'll be back, just keep that door locked, I don't want you or anyone else poking around in there, you understand me?"

"Of course. I wouldn't dream," Fisher said indignantly, there was no need for Hopper at call him fat.

*Of course, you would*, Hopper thought, expecting him to have the door open by the end of the day. Enough rope, he smiled as he left Fisher still pulling at his tie.

# 49.

Fisher breathed a sigh of relief when Hopper left. As much as he hated giving the police anything, he needed space and time to think and could feel himself losing control, not that he'd ever had it, but Hopper worried him. In his experience, cops like him were like a dog with a scent; they didn't give up easily until you fed them something. He doubted he would have long, but Jackson was stupid. It was likely he'd have kept his steroids at home, if Hopper went calling and Jackson was there, no doubt he'd run, making himself look guilty and if he wasn't, and Hopper was the sort of cop he thought he was, he'd find whatever was there, even if it meant breaking in. It was a win-win for him at least. Jackson was an idiot if he thought he could keep secrets from him, and a locked door didn't present any real problems. He'd give Jimmy the Pick a call, known for his ability to open almost any lock with a no-questions-asked attitude. He'd used him several times when he needed to find information or plant something. But he still needed to find out what Adam might have told Hopper. If Jackson had his stash at the zoo, he'd get rid of it before Hopper came back and if he didn't, at the very least he'd get rid of whatever was on the tape still left running in the machine.

Hopper's visit had unsettled Adam, *his other* knew far more than he was letting on and was keeping things from him. He'd never considered his past before, who he had been and who he was now. *It doesn't matter, his other* insisted, *all that matters is now.* He knew he was wrong. Hopper's visit had told him that. *We know him, don't we?* Adam asked, *he's not important,* he'd replied, *he'll only mess things up.* What things? *All things.* Adam was getting tired of the cryptic one-sided conversation; he was the one on the outside after all, yet he was the one in the dark. *His other* had a plan, that much was clear, but wouldn't tell him what it was, and there were still his missing memories and the abattoir.

He had just finished scrubbing off a poorly advertised fellatio service when Fisher waddled over, dabbing his brow with an overused handkerchief, maybe he would have some answers. *Maybe*, his other said.

"Quite the adventure you had." Fisher began, hoping to find out what he remembered, if anything. Adam barely acknowledged him. "I saw you had a visitor." Fisher continued, waiting for a response, *God*, he thought *if this is what he was like with Hopper, he would have nothing to worry about.* "Had a nice chat, did you?"

There was something about Fisher buzzing the back of Adam's brain, scratching behind his eyes, "What happened at the abattoir?" Adam's voice came out harder than he'd remembered. He was gripping the handle of the broom too hard, the knuckles on his hand turning white, *his other*, was close by, listening in.

Fisher didn't like the way Adam was looking at him, it was the same way some of the more dangerous animals that were left looked at their food. Jackson was supposed to be the muscle, he wasn't used to this part of the job, "I don't think that's any way to talk to me." He said, trying to appear friendly, "I was just making sure you're ok, after... it wasn't my fault you know. It was Higgs..." He let his voice drift, waiting for Adam to fill in the blanks. He didn't. "You remember the accident?" Fisher asked, "at the abattoir, we managed to get you out just in time."

Adam tried to focus, a flash of teeth and the memory of the cougar flashed into Adam's brain but was gone before he could hold on to it. "I'm not sure." He said more to himself than Fisher, *you will*, his other answered, *see.* The memory of Fisher, hands curled around the wire mesh, eyes bulging as he drooled open-mouthed, clicked into place without context. Adam shook his head, "You were watching."

"Not exactly, don't you remember, you tried to save the wolf, you could have gotten hurt. I helped." Fisher suggested, "Is that what you told the policeman?"

*He didn't help, his other* told him, *he tried to hurt us, both of us,* "He wanted to know about Jackson."

"And what did you tell him? Did you mention the accident?"

*There was no accident, there was a fight,* "I told him I hadn't seen him."

"And that's all?"

"What else is there?"

Fisher was glad for once that Adam was inside a cage, he couldn't be sure if the drugs Higgs had given him had worked, "there is nothing else. But just in case you think you remember something, maybe don't. Best for you and everyone else if you just put it behind you. Frank wouldn't like it, or your doctor. They'd send you back, you wouldn't want that would you?"

"No. I wouldn't," Adam said blankly, he was already thinking of something else, how Fisher might look without a head.

"No," Fisher agreed, "then let's just keep it between us shall we? No need to go telling tales is there."

*Absolutely not*, his other said, "absolutely not," Adam repeated.

# 50.

Jackson's address was in a part of the city that would, at one point, have been considered dangerous, but the signs of development and misplaced gentrification were everywhere, a bizarre mix of trendy cafés and hipsters, prepared to endure the pain of transition, hoping to turn a profit, while rubbing shoulders with *the street*. *Keepin' it real*, real enough to maintain a foothold on cheap rent through muggings, rapes, and break-ins. According to the file Hopper had pulled, Jackson's history was as predictable as it was uninspiring. In Hopper's eyes, people don't change, count the number of repeat offenders serving time, and even invented a term for them, career criminal. Which, following on from Hopper's visit to the zoo, found himself in front of Jackson's apartment banging on the door. It was clear no one was home. Fortunately for Hopper, the neighbors still had a habit of minding their own business. After several attempts to pick the lock, his frustration gave way to a hefty shoulder barge.

The door opened easily into a small hallway that branched out to a living room, one side dominated by an impressive array of weights the other, an open kitchenette. Separated by a breakfast bar with a high-rise splash back, hiding a piled high sink with unwashed dishes. Hopper ran his finger over the plates to gauge an idea as to how long they had been sitting there, the damp, sticky stains told him not too long, about two days. The cupboards were still full of powdered protein shakes, low-carb bars, and tins of tuna. Inside the fridge were more pre-mixed shakes and enough ready-made meals to see him through until the end of the week. A search of the bedroom found a pre-packed gym bag along with the rest of his clothes. Had it not been for the sour smell of the shakes, you could have been forgiven for thinking Jackson had just nipped out for some milk and would be back any time soon, which was still a possibility. But if Jackson had left, he'd done so in a hurry without taking so much as his toothbrush.

Like the zoo, too many things felt wrong. There was no reason for Jackson to have left in a hurry. A visit by the police could be intimidating but not to someone like Jackson. He wouldn't have been scared off so easily, especially after one visit, he'd either gone to warn someone or hide something. Fisher made a show at being surprised and disappointed, but Hopper wasn't so naive as to recognize when he was being played. He'd gone along to see how far he could implicate himself and in Hopper's experience, anyone keen to throw light on an otherwise darkened corner was doing so as a distraction. Jackson wasn't the only one with something to hide, but Fisher could wait, he was nervous enough to make a wrong move, and Hopper would be there when he did. A quick tour of Jackson's apartment told him he wasn't rolling in money. It was always possible he was just some low-rent opportunistic dealer trying to make an easy score on the side. A more careful search found the inside of the wardrobe to be smaller than the outside. After wasting time trying to find a hidden door or lock, he decided on using one of the dumb-bells, the weight alone was enough to take out the wooden panel. Hidden inside the false back was enough steroids to suggest he may have gone into business for himself. Jackson, finally moving up the ladder, he would have been a one-man walking trade show with no shortage of customers. Hopper had done some digging and been surprised to find out how popular they were. Young men intent on ruining their bodies long term for short term gain, the side effects, from what he googled were terrible. It wasn't just the moon faces and additional acne, or the shrunken penis but the powdering and loss of bone strength. Jackson was obviously supplying and had a small army of wanna-be's like Nate helping distribute, but he was getting them from somewhere. The connection to Nate was obvious, but Leanne? He wondered if she figured at all, but when he'd met Adam, it all seemed wrong. Fisher had been too keen to dismiss him out of hand and divert Hopper's attention back to Jackson, he'd even been willing enough to throw Jackson under the bus to keep him away from him. Too many things didn't make sense, he was missing something, something he felt he already knew.

Hopper flopped on the edge of Jackson's oversized bed facing the widescreen television that connected to an old-style VCR. Strange how he'd missed it earlier, he hit the play button, expecting, hoping for a throwback to eighties porn and not the grainy black and white image of the zoo. He quickly ejected the tape and flipped it over; zoo #42 was scrawled, in what looked like a child's writing on the side, he replaced the tape and continued watching.

The footage started with the usual boring scenes of a deserted and unpopular zoo but quickly jumped to the first 'up-skirt' closely followed by the next and so on. Hopper was disappointed to find that it was a clumsy edit of home-made amateur porn featuring hidden camera footage. The only break, extended clips of the ice-cream seller he'd met, before the next cut to a titillating shot of a G-string or the clumsy sexual encounter of teenagers looking for a quiet place to fuck. Leanne surprisingly made the occasional cameo, often with Fisher in tow. Hopper skipped past their scenes on fast forward, thankful for the poor quality, as he watched the back of her head bob up and down in front of Fisher's crotch, his trousers pooled around his ankles. It was no wonder he had denied any knowledge of her, it wasn't a pleasant sight.

Eventually, the tape came to an end, and he inserted another, as much as he wanted to resist the temptation to keep watching, he found them curiously moreish. Unsurprisingly it contained the same grainy footage apart from one scene that featured Leanne in a starring role.

The characters were easy to recognize, there was Anton, her son, with one of the zoo workers who unfortunately had his back to the camera. The zoo worker and Anton were by the wolf's cage, only this time it was occupied. The worker pushed his hands through the cage, Hopper half expected the wolf to bite it off, but was surprised to see it licking his hand. He was about to let Anton put his hand through the bars when Leanne showed up. Even without audio, Hopper could hear the verbal abuse she was screaming. It was straight from an old black and white keystone movie, comically exaggerated actions, until it took on a darker tone.

Hopper had built a picture of Leanne as something she wasn't. Watching her in action, he realized perhaps Anton might be better off without her wherever he was. Some people don't want to be found, and some people shouldn't. It didn't take long for the scene to escalate as Leanne raised her hand to hit the boy, now cowering behind the worker. It's a moment frozen in time as the young man catches her hand. Leanne can't quite believe what's happened and turns her attention to him, who now bears the brunt of her anger. She's an unstoppable and impressive force as she reins blow upon blow on the young man who, to his credit, thinks Hopper, does nothing to retaliate. Enter Fisher and Jackson, stage left. The comedy duo offer light relief as they try to calm Leanne down, dispersing the small audience that has now gathered. Jackson eventually plucks her off the worker as if she were nothing but a collection of twigs. Fisher waving his arms wildly like the villain in a Mack Sennett comedy, orders her away. Anton sadly follows behind as Jackson manhandles her out of frame with more force than is necessary. Hopper half expected intermittent graphic slates to appear complete with dialogue written in cursive script, *away with you and never darken our door again.* Overall, it's a badly produced comedy that's more unsettling than entertaining. There's something off that he can't quite put his finger on and rewinds to watch once more. Hopper can't tell if it's because of the distortion or the white noise or because of the frantic activity, but he can finally make out who the young man is, Adam. But what troubles Hopper isn't that he lied, but that he appears to be grinning. It's an expression he's seen before but can't remember where.

# 51.

Things change. Eve knew that intimately, all her life she had experienced change. Change in circumstance, fortune, and parents, but none so profound as the change in Adam. It was a loss of innocence she felt acutely. He had put together a badly made jigsaw hammering away at the pieces, so they fit. He had told her about the abattoir, about things that barely made sense, of animals fighting surrounded by beasts of the jungle, of squawking hordes come home to roost and of barking seals clapping their approval. There was a lot he left out; she wasn't sure it was because he couldn't remember or wouldn't. Parts remained hidden, misplaced with lost memories, swapped by something she no longer recognized. A glint in his eye she hadn't seen before, an accent to his smile, he had become someone different, and she wasn't so sure she liked the new Adam. He told her about Frank the showman, of Fisher and Jackson and of a man called Higgs and she had felt herself split in two.

In moments like these, she hated herself. When did he become her responsibility? It wasn't fair to be lumbered with the guilt of womankind, wasn't it enough to be named after it. She hadn't forced him to bite from the apple, he did it of his own accord and she was the one left to shoulder the responsibility. It was hard to shake off generations of conditioning, after all, we learn how to gaslight from the best in the Bible and call it virtue. She took on the blame, it had been her father, after all, she had been the one to tell him about the wolf, about Frank and the abattoir, had that been her motive all along? Eve, the temptress, Eve, the manipulator. *You knew what I would do, I did it for you.* The excuse of the male charade, and they painted the female gender as the weaker sex? No. She didn't need a protector and hadn't asked for one, yet felt the sting of blame, generations of guilt passed down from mother to daughter. Careful how you look, don't dress too provocatively, don't act like a slut. They can't help it, but you can. But her mother was long gone, yet her father had reminded her how much of it was her fault. She shook her head, he was no different, refusing to acknowledge his part, playing the defender pretending ignorance is a shield for the uninformed. She had wanted to see him when Adam had left but knew it wasn't the time for accusations. The pain too raw, blistered and pink. Instead, she had waited to collect her thoughts and was left with one simple question; had he fallen so far, he was beyond help?

Higgs felt like the coward he was, he knew this now. He had watched Adam with Eve at the zoo hidden from view and scurried away before he had been seen, too fearful to lock eyes, worried for what he might see, the cruel reflection of his real self. The part he wished would stay hidden, safe beneath the surface. He should have lived the lie he'd been given instead of letting go, preferring to use grief as an excuse, but he could no longer hide from himself and the truth. Living a life built on selfish avoidance, his only excuse; he caught the current early and liked it, the effortless pull of pleasure, how easily it came and how hard it was to give up. *Go with the flow*, what a joke.

He had spent the last few hours trying to make sense of where he was in life and how he could repair the damage. He could have stayed at the zoo, but the temptation to use would have been too great, he needed to see Eve sober and straight and find out what Adam had told her, his release would come later. She would be waiting and would want answers that required more than a diversion, she deserved more. More than him, he thought as he opened the door to a waiting daughter.

"I've been waiting for you," Eve said, her voice calm and measured. She wanted to avoid a fight; a shouting match was no way to get answers.

In moments like these, Higgs felt his life reduced to living through the prism of a sitcom. Eve, all grown up demanding answers from her wayward father, all she was missing was a rolling pin cradled in her arms folded tightly across her chest and a laugh track. The tone in her voice told him everything he needed to know. He sighed and went to pour himself a drink. They say confession is good for the soul but looking at his daughter and the hurt he had caused her, knew confession was a selfish act designed to shed responsibility and court sympathy. The weeping child, holding up the fragments of a broken cup. He thought of teary-eyed evangelists caught out, blubbering apologies live on TV, excusing themselves for being human, the greater the volume of tears, the higher the income as they apologized with one eye on the bank account, making sure their flock would acknowledge their weakness as an act of strength. *See I'm just like you*, they would weep, *only richer*, they would quietly add, before doing it all again. But not him. He knew he was the linchpin that held everything together, without him it fell apart. He had kept records, knowing this time would come, his destruction was her salvation. It was the only thing he had left to give, only he hadn't realized how hard it would be. Confession is not good for the soul; confession damns it to hell. He knew in his heart no matter how angry she would be, she always had the capacity for forgiveness. It's what happens when you hitch your cart to a junkie, you grow to love the drug of optimism and blind faith just as much as they did the drugs. The familiarity of the continuous cycle of' *I'm sorry, I forgive,* was far more comforting than the wrench needed to break it. As he poured his drink, hands shaking, he didn't want her forgiveness nor her understanding, he wanted her to despise him, to hate him, good riddance to bad rubbish, he deserved it. In the end, it would be easier for them both. He didn't want to argue, but knew he had to. "I'm sorry mum, I didn't realize there was a curfew," was his opening gambit. It was a weak opening, childish, but a glance at her face told him it had hit home.

"I saw Adam today." Eve struggled to keep her tone neutral, calm, and collected.

"And what did he say?"

"He told me about the abattoir, I was hoping you'd be able to explain."

He took a long swallow of his drink and refilled his glass. He wanted to tell her so badly, but knew she would try to do the right thing, be the moral compass he couldn't. It wasn't fair to let her shoulder the responsibility of them both. Instead, he would discredit Adam and tell her the truth about him. He knew the drugs he had given Adam would distort his memory, his recall disjointed and fluid as a dream. "There was an accident, he tried to save the wolf. He couldn't." Higgs painted a different picture, an accident born through stupidity on both parts, he took on the blame but not the accountability of his actions. He was trying to help and by doing so put his life in danger.

Eve remained unconvinced, "he told me something else," she let her words hang, saying it out loud made it real and she wasn't ready for that just yet, "tell me it's not true, tell me something else, tell me anything," she was shouting, the look on his face told her everything she didn't want to know, "I want you to explain to me why there are less and less animals," she could feel the sting of tears roll down her face, she hadn't wanted to give so much away, but in truth, she was scared. Scared he'd finally got himself into something he was unable to get out. She knew she was as much as an addict as he was, but her addiction was to what could be, what might have been. All she wanted, had ever wanted was for him to be a dad. Her dad. It should have been a simple request, to be the man who would be there to comfort her when dates went wrong, to keep her safe, tell her she was grounded, and admonish her for wearing the wrong sort of clothes. She wanted a father who would eventually become embarrassing but loveable. To have a man to base every other man on, someone to stroke her hair in the dark of night and tell her it was going to be ok. But it wasn't. The man she wanted had gone, and she should have known better. He had silently slipped into a vein when she wasn't looking. The tell-tale signs were always there to see, had she bothered to look.

Ashamed of what he had become, Higgs avoided her eyes, "sit down Eve," he asked, looking at his shoes, "I'm going to tell you something, and I want you to listen carefully. It's important."

Eve listened patiently as her father told her about the hospital and repeated the same lie, he told her not to trust Adam, that he was dangerous. She didn't need to replace one broken man with another. She needed a life away from him, away from everything. He told her how he could never change, that she was a burden of responsibility he didn't want or need and when he'd finished, he watched her sob quietly into her hands.

"We could leave," Eve finally said, shoulders shaking, "it's this place, all we have is each other, why can't you see that? If it's so bad, why can't we just go, we've done it a hundred times before." She knew she was pleading, it wasn't the way she wanted to show herself. "It'll get better, I promise."

It was a promise that wasn't hers to make, but she was right. It would get better, but without him, he shook his head, "you should go," and slid a piece of paper over, a phone number from happier times, "they would take you back, but not me." He already knew what he had to do, and to do it needed Eve as far away as possible.

"So that's it then?" Eve asked, "this is how it ends?"

Higgs looked at his daughter for what he knew would be the last time, but hoped it wasn't. She would never know how badly he wanted to take her in his arms and tell her what she meant to him, that without her his life was as empty and hollow as an unused kit. She mattered, God how she mattered. She would never know the strength it took not to cry with her and tell her how sorry he was, that, yes, she was right, they could leave together, the two of them against the world as it always was. But they would find him, Frank would find them both, and what then? She would never know how much he ached and how much he will miss her, that he was willing to go to the gallows in her place. "Yes," he finally said, "this is how it ends. What else did you expect? I'm sorry Eve, there's nothing left to talk about, you should go," and for one he told her the truth.

# 52.

The flashes of memory were only the threads of a bigger picture Adam was struggling to knit together. It was like watching a topsy turvy film, full of jump cuts of unrelated scenes placed in the wrong order. He remembered the journey, the abattoir, animals fighting and crowds cheering, but every memory was like sludge weighing him down. He had disappointed Eve and so badly wanted to please her, he would have done anything, *you already did and look where that got us*, his other said. He disagreed, she was closer now than she had been before and that was because of him, the way she had looked at him, her touch, she needed him as much as he her. He wanted to tell her everything, *his other*, told him she wouldn't like it when she found out. *Then show me*, he'd asked. *No*, he'd sniped back and disappeared in a sulk, leaving Adam to re-arrange the bits himself.

There were other things he couldn't remember, things that had never occurred to him to ask, who he was and who he had been? Who was the policeman asking questions? There were specters and ghosts behind every corner, ever present, never there. Shelly had always told him they didn't matter, that the future shaped him, she was the one that called him Adam. Her first. His mother. His *real* mother. There had been something in the way Hopper had looked at him, something he knew, but he looked as damaged as Adam searching for himself through the lives of others.

There was only one place he could go. He couldn't remember the moment when *his other* started talking, he had always been there but had moved from the shadows and come calling, and when Adam asked *why, why now?* He would only tell him because he needed him, *don't you remember?* He would ask, knowing he couldn't. And now he was in the tank floating in the dark.

Shelly had been excited to see him, although she tried to hide it, asking about his day, who he met, what they said, how he felt, all the while making him promise not to miss anything out. It had been his idea to go back in the tank and she had agreed readily, greedily and waffled on about repression and a whole lot of other stuff he wasn't interested in, nor did he care, he just wanted his memories back.

"How are you feeling Adam?"

Shelly's voice, everywhere and nowhere, he felt her rather than heard her, it gave him the disconcerting feeling that she had entered and was now part of him. A parasite, milking his brain, is how he had begun to see her. He tried hard to shake the thoughts from his mind, she would know, she always knew, it was annoying she would never tell, nor would *his other*, no matter how many times he asked. *I'm protecting you*, it would say. Adam shook his head, *No*, he told it, *you're protecting you, not me*, and for the first time realized his *other* was anxious. Knowledge is power, if he knew everything, then why would he need him? *I'll never let you go*, Adam promised, *we'll always be together*.

*You won't like what you see.*

*I'll take that chance.*

*You'll blame me.*

*I won't, show me.*

Their conversations in the past were often one sided, Adam playing passenger to a hidden driver, always grumbling about how ungrateful he was, *after all I've done*, his other would say, *and this is the thanks I get!* But this time was different, this time there was the stab of jealousy, this time he had Eve.

*You like her better than me?*

*Of course not.*

*You'll leave me when you see.*

*I will never leave you. We'll always be together.*

*Promise?*

*Promise.*

"Adam?" Shelly's voice cut into his thoughts, interrupting him.

*How rude*, his *other* said. "I'm ready." Adam replied, and thought about the last conversation he'd had with Fisher, '*what happened, it wasn't my fault. It was Higgs,*' he'd said. Higgs, Adam rolled the name around his memory, there had been something about a gun.

The faint clicks and hum of the mechanics inside the helmet cause Adam to tense, an automatic reaction to a fight he can't win, a puppet controlled by a God in a lab coat. Eyes pinned, he knows what is coming but still feels the shiver of intrusion, violated by *her*. What she sees, she would never say, his legacy, the nightmares he tries so hard to forget, visions of terrible things and terrible deeds he wished would sicken him but do not. This time is different, this time he is a

230

willing participant ready to dive and retrieve his precious memories. He knows the routine, he's been through it so many times, but never like this, and as much as he hates it, there is another part, *his other*, who is trembling. He feels the sink of the needle and the warm spread of hot oblivion, he falls, drifting back away from the light as the static changes and *his other* takes his place.

For *the other*, the world is different, he is different, his is on the inside wishing to be outside, but this is real. Borders are changing, a shift in density and a blurring of the lines. Inside is where he lives. Inside is the world he controls that holds no surprise. He does what he wants in the way he wants. Inside he is king, all-powerful, no repercussions here. Today is different, today is not the same, a bird in a gilded cage, a comfortable prisoner, is still a prisoner after all. He has had a taste of the outside, the unpredictability of a world unknown. There are things that will surprise and amaze, he knows this now. *His other*, his now more conscious self, wanted to know. He could have shown him and avoided all of this, but why take away the fun. He will tear down the curtain and show him everything, he already knows how he will react, the guilt, the sorrow and the sadness. Consumed by what is right, still trying to keep her happy. He will play the game and show them both what they want and paint a world so brutal, violent, red, and vivid it hurts to look, that they will never want reality again.

He is the one in control and he's not going back without a fight. No longer prepared to sit in the dark, patiently waiting for his time when there is so much more to be had and he knows this, this is his secret, and he wants more. No longer a whispering voice in the darkness, easy to be pushed down buried so deep he's only allowed to play in the prison of *his* mind. Not anymore, he's been out. The inside on the outside, and he's not going back without a fight. He will do what needs to be done, the slashing and the tearing and the biting and the ripping. He will rise he can feel it, the other Adam has left the door open, the key in the lock.

# 53.

Like all addicts, no matter what the drug, there is an unspoken knowledge of the damage being done, junkies are weak, but not stupid. An acceptance of what could have, should have been, had it not been for the monkey on your back. Sadly, the desire to stop is never as strong as the desire to keep going, unless caught in the thrall of the drug of choice, only then do you have the strength to stop when it's too late, or at least until the effect wears off and the cycle begins anew. Higgs knew the trick to stopping is to stop, but like all good addicts, there is loyalty to self-destruction. A swan song thinly disguised as self-control, the comforting friend saying, *just one last hit, then I'll stop! One last cigarette, one last joint, drink, line, pipe, one last piece of chocolate cake, I'll stop when I'm out, when it's done. I bought it, it's stupid to waste it!* All good convincing lies designed to keep moving. The dichotomy of life; to love what hurts us the most, love life, embrace death, ask any thrill seeker. Higgs knew he would never, could never give up. He wasn't as strong as Eve.

Had he ever had doubts about his course of action, he only had to remember her disappointment. Doubt used to be his bedfellow, his constant companion, the voice in his head telling him he wasn't good enough to be a husband, brave enough to be a parent, and he knew the voice was right. He'd always kept two sets of records, one designed to conceal and falsify building lie upon lie, the other told the truth. It had been his insurance policy, his way of protecting her, though he never thought he'd have to use it. The voice of doubt still nagged at him, telling him it wasn't time, nudging him towards the shiny cabinet where all the goodies were kept. *Still time for one more*, the voice told him, and he so badly wanted to agree. Eve would get over it, he lied to himself, knowing she wouldn't. It was an effort no-one would know, but he managed to resist the call, there was just too much to do. He had two letters to write, one to his daughter and one to the police. Without Jackson, Fisher had been jittery, and was liable to make a mistake. He already knew there was a cop poking around asking questions. Eve had given him a name; Detective Hopper. All he needed was to give a little nudge in the right direction, and if he was smart, he'd be able to follow the trail he'd left.

The first letter to Eve was far harder than imagined. How much easier it would have been to write what convention dictates when one is about to exit from this world; to say how sorry he was, how he had envisaged a life so much cleaner and brighter and how much he loved her. The last part was true, but had he loved her more than anything else in the world, he would have stopped using long ago. That devotion was for reserved for his chemical buddy and close friend, the monkey. Did he love her more than life itself? Of course, he did, he was about to prove it, but life played a cheap second fiddle to the demands of his real mistress, no matter how hard he tried to kid himself, and so he launched into a course of action that would cost him his and spare her hers.

Instead, he told her the truth; he was weak, and while he loved her more than life, he loved drugs more. Life, he told her, had been made dull. It was his fault and he owned it, but without the accompanying ecstasy, he couldn't face the drudgery alone. Drugs may be a life lived through an empty promise, but the journey was bliss. He hoped she would appreciate the honesty. It was because of love, she needed to be free of him, free enough not to look back, free enough to not waste time mourning over a man that hadn't existed for some time. He loved her enough to tell the truth. He had been a terrible husband and worse father, he had died in the crash that killed his wife, her mother. Despite him, she had already become far more than he could have given her and would be far more without him. He could no longer bear to be the grinding stone that would drag her down. He wanted her to remember him as he was, an addict devoted to what he loved the most, so much so he would never stop, forgettable as a stiff breeze, was how he should be remembered. He loved her more than life itself but not as much as heroin.

It felt brutal but needed to be convincing and final, he didn't want her to go looking, if he was to save her, the cut needed to be clean and surgical. They would come looking for him, not her. Together they were a target, alone he could disappear without a trace. He would become the fantasy of a father she never had and told her to enjoy life without him, he needed time and space and urged her to trust him. Once it was over, he would come back a different man. Over time he had managed to save a substantial amount. The money he'd made didn't matter, it never had and had always felt uncomfortable, but unlike Judas, he wouldn't scatter it from a tree, he would use his to do some good. He'd never been able to spend it without drawing too much attention to himself and his needs were basic, contained in a glass case at the surgery, if he was lucky, he would OD, if not he would be gone by morning.

He separated the money into neat little packages and, by using one of the zoo guides, marked out where her inheritance was hidden. Purposeful and with meaning, he went from one empty enclose to the next, the irony wasn't lost on him, and hoped that the ghosts of the animals who once inhabited the cages would protect her. The animals he'd let down over the years squawked and growled at him, he deserved their scorn, he had betrayed them most of all. Under the silvery moon, he dug and hid three packages, a total of sixty-three thousand, more than he imagined, more than he was worth, it seemed a fair exchange. The money would be enough to give her the start she would never have with him. By the time he was finished, he felt exhausted, *not yet*, he told himself, *but soon*, he added the cheap map of the zoo, detailing where to find her inheritance. One job left; it was time to deliver the second letter.

# 54.

Hopper was watching the same monotonous footage he'd seen earlier at Jackson's apartment in the comfort of his own. Knowing the neighborhood, knowing he'd broken the law, and knowing he'd broken the lock on Jackson's door, it wouldn't be long before the neighbors came a-picking, or someone became suspicious. He thought it best to take the entire collection, including the VCR with him. If he had to go back a second time, the place would be picked clean, he could also use the break-in as a reason why he was in possession of them. Hopper felt himself getting bored, although he grudgingly had to admit, the 'up-skirts' had a certain illicit quality to them, but over time, even the copulating young couples lost their charm. Like most porn, the more you watched, the more desensitized the experience until the background became more interesting than the action, there's only so much to take before the curtains or quality of the furniture begin to catch your attention, but he'd kept watching anyway.

Hopper's diligence and tenacity paid off several tapes later when he saw Nate shuffling over to the wolf's cage, the same one Adam had been cleaning. It was a mindless act of cruelty driven by boredom. Hopper shook his head, disappointed on behalf of his mum Sarah. Parents will always blind themselves to the true nature of their children, shouldering the blame themselves or happily dumping it back on society.

*"It's not his fault, his father left. He needs a role model. He's misunderstood, bored, if only there was something for kids to do, it's the computer games they play, too much sex and violence on TV. It's my fault, your fault, anyone's fault but theirs."*

All of it bullshit. Hopper found the lack of accountability as ugly as the act, sometimes more so, the unwillingness to recognize that sometimes, an apple grows bad on the tree. Nate, it seemed, wasn't the sensitive child she had once known, replaced instead by a sadistic bully intent on harm, keen to inflict pain on those smaller and weaker. Hopper understood it too well, resentful and angry at the world, ready to lash out at anything and anyone. He knew better than most, *we all have shit to deal with, you don't get a free pass because you swallowed some.* How had Shelly described it, Whack-a-mole, repress one thing, and another would pop up, but there was no guarantee with what might take its place. There were success stories, people who had dug, clawed, and pulled themselves out of their situation against all odds, channeling their pain and hurt into something positive. These were the heroes that Art celebrated; Nate was not one of them. There was no reason, no excuse that Hopper could think of, that drove Nate to torment a wild animal safely behind bars. He gritted his teeth, if he did find him, he'd be only too happy to have a little one-on-one time before he returned him back to his mum.

He wasn't the only one. He had to hand it to Adam. It was a brave move to confront Nate and his crew. Hopper would have preferred it if the tape had audio, but he could guess at the exchange. It didn't take long before Nate had Adam pinned against the cage bars as they tried to provoke the animal into attacking him. Curiously the wolf avoided him. It was only the intervention of Eve that stopped them. Arms outstretched, holding her phone out like a modern-day Van Helsing, the only thing missing was a wooden stake.

Jackson wasn't far behind. After an angry exchange, he snatched Eve's phone, no doubt to delete any record of what happened before handing it back. It was clear that Jackson didn't want anything compromising his customers. He understood why Adam had lied and made a mental note to ask the ice-cream seller when he went to the zoo looking for Jackson. As interesting as it was, it still didn't explain Nate's disappearance.

Hopper spent half a bottle of bourbon and the best part of the night scrubbing through the tapes, looking for something other than the homemade voyeur porn. It wasn't until the last video he found something else. It was a familiar scene he'd watched several times, but it hadn't struck him as odd until now. Every six weeks or so, a truck with the words, *Franks Place* would pull up outside the surgery, usually at night, and loaded with crates before driving off. Nothing unusual, unless you considered the time. Hopper thought about the drugs he'd found. Jackson had to be getting them from somewhere. Although Fisher didn't strike him as the drug-dealing sort, he was also far too keen to throw Jackson to the lions to keep him occupied. No, something else was going on, something he'd seen but hadn't recognized.

Another man would occasionally feature, but not always. Not quite as large as Jackson but more imposing, he carried with him an air of menace that managed to bleed through the grainy footage of the CCTV footage. A quick google search told him why, *Frank's Place,* was an abattoir situated on the fringe of the city limits. As Hopper knew, the stain of death wasn't so easily washed off. But what made this trip different wasn't the time of the collection, nor was it how agitated Fisher appeared alongside the fourth man, whom Hopper assumed was the zoo vet, but the dark shape crouching in the shadows watching. Once the truck began to move, the figure, cloaked in darkness, moved quickly and slipped in, under the tarp, unseen by anyone other than Hopper.

Hopper had to hand it to Adam. He was full of surprises.

# 55.

The duty Sargeant eyed the disheveled man in front of him suspiciously, junkies weren't hard to spot, and he'd had a gut full already and he'd only just started the night shift. He glanced at the clock on the wall, six hours before he was relieved. It was getting past midnight, the time for lunatics and miscreants and by the look of the man, he was bang on time. The first round of drunks and prostitutes wouldn't be far behind.

Higgs had tried his best to appear normal, but the itching under his skin wouldn't stop. His paranoia was riding shotgun and was doing its best to take control of the wheel. He'd tried to shake it off on the way over. There was nothing worse than a drunk overly articulating words in a pathetic attempt to impersonate the sober, he felt the same way. He took a deep breath and handed over the crumpled package, his hands beginning to shake. "I have something for a Detective Hopper." He said deliberately and slowly, the uniform didn't move, "it's important," he blurted, raising his voice more than intended.

"Name?"

Higgs could feel the sweat run down his back. He hadn't considered they might like to know who he was, "tell him... tell him a friend dropped it off. From the zoo." The officer grudgingly took it, gingerly holding it between thumb and forefinger. "Please make sure he gets it." He knew his voice sounded less sure now that people were looking at him. Bravado gone, all that was left was a weak husk unable to look the officer in the eye. He didn't wait for a reply, he'd done his job and desperately needed fresh air and something to calm his nerves, he was at risk of passing out.

Sargent Potts didn't know Detective Hopper but had already decided he didn't like him. He had no reason not to but felt his best chance at making detective was to go along with the crowd, and the crowd disliked him, so he did too. Looking at the greasy package left by the junkie with the bad attitude, he placed it on the side of his desk and shook his head. He didn't run a delivery service or take messages, it wasn't part of his job, he wasn't a glorified receptionist in a neatly pressed uniform. Detective Hyde had been Hopper's partner and shared enough stories, not necessarily to him, but since he was in earshot at the time, considered himself included as much as the rest of the room and joined in the laughter, ignoring the odd stares from some of his colleagues. Hopper, by the sounds of it, was incompetent and a loose cannon. He was also on administrative duties, so whatever was in the package wouldn't be of much importance. Potts tugged at his collar, he was hot and tired, and wanted to move on from the night shift. Helping idiots like Hopper wouldn't do him any favors. They were meant to be straight shooters, follow the rule of law. You might not like it, but it was all they had. In his opinion, it was what separated us from them. Ignore it, and you were just like the animals outside with a badge, it was an abuse of position and power. Yes, he would deliver the package to Hopper as well as an earful and was busy making up the conversation he would never have when the double doors crashed open.

*You could set your clock by them,* he thought as Candy Caudell, the first of many, was led to his desk to be formally charged, only to be let out in the morning, never to be followed up. He couldn't remember the number of times she'd been booked and charged with soliciting. So many they were on first name terms, and he'd taken something of a shine to her. Maybe they could work something out if it ended up being a slow night. It's easy for files to go missing. Sadly, it wasn't, and he watched his opportunity slip through his fingers as more and more *Candy's* were brought in. Paperwork growing by the minute, so much, it eventually covered the package he'd already forgotten about, when it slid off his desk onto the floor, he didn't notice. There was always tomorrow night, he thought as he watched Candy escorted to the holding cells. He was sure he'd see her then.

# 56.

A body floats its mind elsewhere. The zoo, that abattoir, of animals and crowds of fights and killings. Images swirl through the mist, ethereal in nature demanding form. Visions of the id fill the screen as the body jerks and twists. The id doesn't forget, nor does it forgive. The id takes what it wants without remorse and pity. It's spent too long in the dark, constrained by construct governed by others. Now is its time to run free. Now it's time for others to know the full extent of its liberty as it rises and breaks the surface. The id is free and knows what it must do.

# 57.

Higgs closed his eyes, savoring each rush. Ants dancing a feel-good dance tingling his spine, keeping the conga line moving, past the brain stem where they stop and party some more before heading onto the salubrious venue of the thalamus, flicking the brain's reward circuit into overdrive. Better than sex, the release more potent than anything he'd ever felt. He'd always excelled at science and as a qualified vet, knew how to mix the right cocktail for the right occasion for the right high. Slumped in his surgery, eyes half-closed, the part of him that counted, elsewhere, partying on with the ants. He'd done his job, been the responsible parent, one last party, and he'd make his excuses and politely leave by the back door, but in the meantime, inner Higgs was going to have a fucking good time! He deserved it, especially after the night he'd had.

In his mind's eye, Higgs was the man he always wanted to be, he'd done the right thing, he told himself. After all, he wasn't such a bad guy, unbound by convention, unfettered by clumsy expectation, he was free. Life could begin again. The music that wasn't there played loud to the beat of his own biorhythms, why can't life be like this all the time, he thought, as a rush shivered from the top-down pulling at the edges of his mouth, a happy grimace, head snapping back as he rode the wave. But reality has a way of crashing the party when you least expect it, the sound outside was like an anchor, shot through the fog dragging him back to reality. He opened his eyes with a deep breath as he came up for air and the world swam into place. The technicolored disco had momentarily been replaced by the dull greys of the surgery, and he was back, but no longer alone.

Higgs knew the biggest problem with habitual drug use was the accompanying paranoia that went with it hand in hand, and in his current state couldn't be sure if the noise he had heard was real or imagined. Jackson had a nasty habit of turning up when least expected. He was an idiot. The thought hit him like a punch to the groin, he'd stopped to congratulate himself, but in his hurry hadn't considered the surveillance cameras. Was he out there waiting for him? He waited, listening to the silence of the zoo. Imagined. His mind playing tricks, there was no one out there, he would have noticed as he'd buried his treasure. He shook his head, paranoia. It wasn't real, until it was, and he heard it again, only closer.

It was outside, the unmistakable sound of someone trying to remain hidden. With his buzz still alive and kicking, he knew he was on the downslide, if he wanted to, no scratch that, needed to get back in, he'd have to punch his entry card and make a new batch otherwise the ants would shut the door for good—at least until the next time, but for the moment his senses were on high alert, and he grabbed the nearest scalpel.

Clutching the steel bench for support, Higgs made it to his feet. The sound was closer, circling him. An animal on the hunt, but unlike any animal he'd heard before, a low growl, an agitated snarl, not Jackson after all. An escaped animal perhaps? He was sure he'd made sure all the cages he'd entered were secure when he left. Had he been so careless? He felt oddly relieved, he could deal with that. This time louder, coming from above. Whatever it was it was, was now on the roof, and whatever it was certainly wasn't Jackson. Higgs stepped towards the door, the edges faintly glowing, and grasped the handle. As he swung the door open, the zoo was lit by the colors in his mind, an incandescent garden of paradise. Doctor Timothy Leary once said, drugs are a gateway to God. Higgs had never allowed himself the pleasure of total abandonment until now and knew he was right. The animals were singing, praising. His emotions hit as one. He'd never seen anything so beautiful. A tsunami of feeling knocked him off his feet. He giggled to himself, the music getting louder. The sounds of the night. How could he have been so stupid that he was ready to give it up. He finally knew what he must do, he would wipe the slate clean, his love for Eve wasn't the disposable commodity he thought it to be. He made the choice to live and be the better man. The trip wasn't over, it was only just beginning, he was the journeyman and in control, he felt ecstatic, elated, and closer to the animals than he'd ever been. His epiphany would last and carry him through to the next day. He would bring it down, but he wouldn't burn with it, he knew he could change. Eve had given him the strength to do so.

Caught in the thrall of this new direction, he heard the scratching of feet on metal and looked to the roof. It was too late. He had been a fool to think redemption lay within the barrel of a hypodermic needle. Silhouetted against a brilliant moon, his demons had come to claim him, and in the midst of his chemical fog, could only think of little red riding hood, *my Granny...how big your teeth are, how big your claws, how big your...* he stopped thinking when the blood supply was abruptly cut off from his brain as his head was removed.

A crimson shower of red mist sprayed the floor. *The Other* drank its fill, the burnt copper taste of blood heavy on its lips.

# 58.

Shelly felt alive and refreshed, better than she could remember. She was seldom excited by her patients, often finding them routinely boring and predictable. While she recognized their past trauma and understood why they ended up in her care, she offered little or no sympathy. It's not that she wasn't big on empathy, far from it, she considered herself to be highly empathetic, often identifying with the thoughts and feelings of her charges, especially Adam. It was more the expectation of cause and effect. *Do this and that happens.* There was an obviousness to it all, Adam and Hopper were different. By eradicating Adam's identity, she had created a blank canvas and built an arena allowing his id to run free in the hope she could satisfy desire brought on by impulse and reflex, developing a deeper understanding of who we were at birth, if our behavior was congenital or a series of outfits knitted together by experience and place? How much of us was really us? Did we even exist at all? How much was retained before it became repressed, before *fitting in* became just another survival instinct? Inside and outside, a confused contradiction between the twin pillars of right and wrong. Each one a construct of acceptability. What was right in one society wasn't always right in another. We weren't so much products of our environment but rather adaptive beings that would bend and shape to fit. Right or wrong, there was no nature vs. nurture, only a precarious balancing act on the high wire. Tilt one way, and you compensate by a tilt to the other, which meant yet another swing, a continuous oscillation between acceptance and rejection like the pendulum of a grandfather clock. The tank offered stability and freedom from the lies we told ourselves. She had come to believe; the greater the repression, the greater the pressure, until it eventually ruptured, as it had for Hopper. We were living onions. Peel one layer to discover another underneath and another and another. Life was plugging the holes in a dam. No sooner had you plugged one hole than another would spring up elsewhere.

Shelly knew Adam had already met Hopper, the tank gave her a rare insight into not just what he did, but how he felt. She had known Adam as the beast, a product of his past. Her challenge had been to deconstruct and rebuild one brick at a time. Cause and effect managed within the safety of the tank releasing his pressure. But Hopper was more than just an echo of the past, he was a connection to Adam's id, his primordial self. She needed to know how robust the dam wall was and if the tank was successful. But Hopper could give her more. As much as Adam was on the inside looking out, Hopper was on the outside looking in. She was curious to know if he been able to see beyond the veneer of Adam's construct or if he had remained hidden? Would they become the catalyst for each other, a reminder of how it was to abdicate responsibility, to give in to the id? How much of Hopper needed to be peeled away before the real person was finally exposed. She was excited to find out.

Hopper didn't like the smell of hospitals, even the private ones where they change the flowers every day and use scented soap in the toilets. It reminded him of dead witnesses, of turning up late and Art's dead wife. He also had conflicting feelings about Shelly. He wasn't so sure he liked the extra company riding shotgun inside his head, probing and snooping in the dark, hoping to catch a glimpse of the 'real him'. As far as he was concerned, you got what you saw, and that's all there was, unless guilty, and everyone was guilty. There was so much he wanted to tell her and so much he couldn't. He wanted to talk about Adam, and why he had developed an itch behind the brain he couldn't scratch, he wanted to talk about why he'd lied about a missing prostitute, a steroid-addicted kid, but most importantly, he wanted to talk about the zoo.

Shelly had planned to keep her session with Hopper informal, she wanted to know him better and for him to drop his guard. She wanted to tell him so much, especially about the zoo and keep him pointed in the right direction, but needed him to think it was his idea all along.

Hopper knocked and opened the door to her office. "Jack, I thought we might spend some time in the garden," Shelly beamed at him, hoping to catch him off guard in less formal surroundings, "it's such a beautiful day, what do you think?"

Hopper didn't think it was a good idea at all, the day was hot, and he had been looking forward to the air con. "Sure, why not?" He smiled and followed her out.

Shelly gave him the briefest of tours on route to the garden. An endless series of corridors sparsely decorated with low budget attempts to humanise and minimise the sterility of the hospital. A potted plant here, a picture there, punctuating the long white walls with pretend humanity and failing miserably.

No matter how hard or how often the staff referred to the place as a *'care facility,'* it still screamed the word, *Institution*, or worse. Along several of the longer corridors, the wall space had been allocated for artwork produced by the inmates. Primitive and childlike daubs that did little to elevate the mood. Shelly reminded him they were referred to either as patients or clients, not inmates. Hopper asked if any of them were free to go, she just grinned and didn't answer. Hopper took a moment to look at the disturbing self-portraits staring back through blank eyes. Eyes full of doubt and uncertainty, delivering a chilling message; *no matter how bad you think your life can get, trust me, if you're on this side of the wall, you're doing better than me!* He shivered and caught up to Shelly, past the rec room where a small group had gathered to watch TV behind a caged mesh. A young man in brightly colored dungarees was on screen acting out a bizarre scene on an improvised airplane of cardboard boxes to a captive audience of bright and colorful fluffy toys. Wanting to break the silence, Hopper asked *what sort of programs are the inmates, sorry patients, allowed to watch and who controls the channel changer*, praying someday it wouldn't be him. Shelly told him the playlist was mostly limited to children's programs and painting shows, nothing too confrontational or disturbing. Hopper glanced back at the TV. Without sound, the scene was bordering on manic.

They moved on past the empty dining hall, Shelly occasionally nodding at colleagues they passed on the way, it's a small gesture that renders Hopper invisible. He doesn't care, he's doing his best to copy her professionalism, to remain neutral and calm, to show her that he remains unmoved by what he sees and resist the overwhelming urge to run screaming back the way he came, not a good look in a mental institution. Every attempt and gesture of normality a reminder, *there is nothing normal in this place.* Plastic tables with plastic flowers bolted to the floor. Souvenirs of a world now closed off, reminding their long-staying *guests* they are no longer welcome in it. The people in here are not going to get better, the people in here are systematically and institutionally being torn apart and are slowly disappearing along with the rest of their memories.

The gardens were a welcome sight, the heat, a relief to the frigidity inside and the scent a gentle reminder the world doesn't smell of lemon wash. Hopper gulped it down as if coming up for air. Shelly passed him a packet of cigarettes. "I thought this was no smoking?" He asked, taking one, thankful for a thread of normality.

"It is. Perks of the job. Anyone asks. I'll tell them it's a strategy designed to put you at ease." *Which it is*, she shrugged, "there was a moment back there, I actually thought you were either going to pass out or start running," she laughed, keeping the mood light, "It's easy to forget how unsettling the place can be when you're here all the time. Frequency normalizes I guess."

"I'm not sure I could ever feel normal in a place like this."

"You'd be surprised, we adapt, we learn to live with what we have, to fit in. It's a human compulsion to want to be accepted no matter the situation. On the other hand, you could consider it something of a litmus test as to how you are, depending on how you behave. I'm sure we'd make you comfortable." Shelly winked. Hopper wasn't sure if she was joking or had already picked out a bed for him. She took a long pull on her cigarette and leaned back exhaling, watching the smoke drift upwards. "It's a filthy habit really." She said more to herself than Hopper. "Desire governs logic, I guess."

Hopper nodded, unsure of what she meant and took a drag himself, feeling more relaxed, thinking if anyone saw them, they might mistake them for colleagues or just a couple of friends having a smoke together. It's a nice fantasy, "it's a tough addiction," he agreed, although he's not sure he's talking about the cigarettes or the fantasy.

"Not really. It's willpower, the addiction is minor in comparison to the habit. It's the ritual that's hard to stop, that and the voice in your head. I don't stop because I don't want to. I enjoy it. But is that me talking or the little voice? If I rationalized it, I know it's bad and should stop, but I don't. Besides, you give one thing up only to substitute it for something else. It's the same with repression."

"Whack-a-mole, I know, you said it before."

Shelly nodded, "it's good to see you're paying attention, and what has been popping up for you lately? What did you find at the zoo?"

Hopper shifted uncomfortably; he wasn't sure if she would see his investigation as little more than paranoid delusions. In their last session, he mentioned Leanne and Shelly had encouraged him to go looking in the hope he would find himself. He'd found a lot more. It wasn't uncommon, in his experience, most people had something to hide, all he needed to do was lift the lid and shine a torch. We all have dirty little secrets we'd like to remain hidden in the shadows. His philosophy had always been *guilty until proven innocent*, of what it didn't matter, if he went looking, he'd find it. This was no different. There was something rotten at the zoo, of that he was sure, but he was struggling to connect the dots and find the common denominator. Drugs? It seemed likely after hearing about Nate, but it didn't *feel* right. His meeting with Adam told him that, along with the tapes. His search for Leanne had escalated into something more, perhaps that had been Shelly's idea all along, but doubted she would be overly enthusiastic to hear about breaking into Jackson's apartment, not to mention stealing the contents. He decided to keep that to himself, at least for the time being. Instead, he thought it best to test the waters before jumping in, "I'm not so sure, something, I think."

Shelly leaned closer, she knew he was being deliberately vague, she needed him to trust her. "Isn't that what you detectives like to call a hunch?" She asked, trying a softer approach, "tell me Jack, what do you think a hunch is?"

It was far more than a hunch he was feeling, but decided to go along, "a feeling, I guess, when you just know. Experience?"

"Exactly. It's almost the same as knowing when someone is looking at you, even when you have your back to them. It's actually called gaze detection, and it's not, contrary to belief, a form of ESP. The truth is less interesting. Our brain picks up signals, subtle shifts in the environment, things that tell us what to expect, whether to expect a threat or not. It's part of our survival mechanism from our more primitive selves, it keeps us on our toes. Your hunch is the same. You might *feel* something's off because it is. Not because you're excessively intuitive, but because you already know something that your brain hasn't made sense of. It's a puzzle that needs to be put together." She knew she was breaking every rule, becoming an enabling to his psychosis, but what was the phrase, *you can't make an omelet without scrambling a few brains!*

"And you're saying I have all the pieces?"

"I don't know. If you tell me what you know, perhaps I can help put it together in a way that makes sense, or at least help you see it clearly. What did you find Jack, when you went looking?"

Hopper nodded, it made sense what she said, "they're hiding something. At the zoo I mean. Leanne's not the only one who's gone missing." Shelly arched her eyebrows, encouraging him to continue, Hopper sighed, "you mind if I have another cigarette?" Shelly passed him one and took another for herself, "there's another kid," He started, "not really a kid, big bloated steroid user, I found out where he was getting his drugs from."

"The zoo?" Shelly asked, thinking about the swollen adolescent tormenting the wolf.

"A guy who works there, Jackson, another meathead."

"Have you spoken to him?"

Hopper shook his head, "I can't find him."

"Did he know you'd found out about the drugs?"

"No. He didn't. That's the point. I only just found out. The kid was reported missing by his old lady, but I didn't know any of that when I met him. He didn't strike me as the sort to get spooked so easily."

"Perhaps you made an impression?"

"It wasn't that. I had nothing."

Shelly knew he was stalling, "there would have been something. What did you talk about?"

Hopper ran his fingers through his hair, it was hot outside in the sun. He would have preferred to stay in her air-conditioned office. The more he tried to think about what he knew, the more elusive it became, "nothing. I went to see Fisher, he runs the place, an oily son-of-a-bitch if ever there was one. I wanted to talk to him about Leanne, but here's where it gets interesting. I said Jackson was a meathead right? He comes barging in, all worried about what we might be talking about and mentions the CCTV cameras around the place. That's when I become interested."

"I didn't know there were cameras there. Did you ask to see the tapes?"

Hopper grinned, "That's another thing, these two slime balls get all coy and defensive and won't let me anywhere near them. It's almost as good as an admission of guilt."

Shelly was as excited as Hopper, he wasn't the only one interested in the tapes, "what do you think's on them? Evidence of him selling the drugs?" She suggested, trying to sound naive.

"I think Jackson's stupid, but not that stupid. There's wasn't anything like that on them."

*Wasn't?* Curious choice of word, thought Shelly, as it dawned on her, "you've watched them?"

It wasn't often Hopper jumped without looking. She was right; the pieces were right there. He just needed to know how they fit together. Fisher had been so keen to get him off the scent he was prepared to throw Jackson under the bus. "I have," he began, deciding against telling her how he managed to become in possession of them, figuring, if she didn't ask, he wouldn't have to tell. She didn't ask. "There's not much to look at, a lot of it was Jackson's amateur homemade porn, up-skirts stuff like that. Weird shit mostly, I can see why he wouldn't want anyone else watching." He let his voice trail off, still deciding on whether to mention Adam.

Shelly knew if that was all there was on the tapes, it would have been unlikely he would have even bothered to mention them, let alone how he came to have watched them, "you're stalling Jack. I can sense a *but* coming, what else was on the tapes?"

"There's a truck from the abattoir that turns up, usually late when everyone else has left."

Shelly could feel her excitement building but remained calm. She knew she had the advantage, having already seen what Hopper had, although from a very different perspective. She enjoyed staying one step ahead, enjoying a spectator's seat from the corporate box inside Adam's head. Knowledge by proxy. "That doesn't sound unusual in itself. There must have been something else," she said, keeping her voice measured.

Hopper hadn't intended to give so much away, but he had to admit, it felt good to offload. "There is. At first, it didn't make any sense, I just put it down to coincidence. But you said it yourself, if it feels odd, it's probably because it is. There's someone else who works there, Adam. He's picks up the rubbish, cleans the cages that kind of thing, I showed him the photographs of Leanne and the steroid kid, thinking he might have seen them with Fisher or Jackson."

"And?"

"It was weird, I knew he was lying at the time, little give-aways, that sort of stuff, but there was something else about him. I guess you could call it a hunch or whatever you called it, gaze detection? I don't know, maybe I'm seeing things that aren't there, trying to make sense of it. But he's on the tapes with them. Why would you lie about something like that unless you have something to hide?"

Shelly was impressed the connection between them was still there, she nudged Hopper further along, "if, as you say, there were cameras at the zoo, perhaps he would be worried someone might see him talking to you, Jackson for instance."

"But Jackson's gone, at least for the moment. It's not that, and if he was that scared, then tell me, doc, why would he hide on the truck?" Hopper shook his head, everything he found took him somewhere else, he felt sure Adam was the key, but had no idea of how or why. The zoo had become a pandoras box of unanswerable questions, "You think I sound crazy?" He asked half expecting her to come back with, *do you think you sound crazy?*

"There could be lots of reasons," Shelly said, knowing it to be true, but there was only one, "Why don't you walk with me." She said, standing, "I'm sure you've heard of cases where people swear blind, they've seen the Virgin Mary's face in a piece of toast or wallpaper," Hopper looked confused, "They're not really there," she reassured him, "but we see them anyway. Of course, our brain is tricking us into seeing something that doesn't exist, I think we can accept that the Virgin Mary, if she were to appear, it wouldn't be in toast. I would assume she would have more style than that, but there's nothing to say that the face you see hiding in the bushes isn't real. It's called pareidolia. It's the brains' way of making sense of the outside world when something doesn't make sense. Our mind's way of connecting the dots. It works the way it does through our need to survive, like gaze detection, another throwback to our primitive selves. It could be showing you something dangerous, warning you to stay away, but then again, it could be just toast."

"So what should I do?"

"You follow the truck."

# 59.

The abattoir was visible for almost half an hour before he reached it, a solitary blot on a flat lunar landscape. Had Jack Hopper been a superstitious man he would have turned around long before he reached it. He had considered going back to talk to Fisher or Adam. Fisher clearly didn't have a high tolerance for pain, he wasn't so sure about Adam, something in the eyes. Besides, what if he lost control and had another seizure like he did with Watts? Nor did he want Fisher an opportunity to give whoever was at the abattoir the heads up he was coming.

The landscape, seldom picturesque on the city's outer rim, seemed to die the closer he got. A sparsely populated terrain, peppered by the skeletons of dead trees, rigor mortis roots clutching the ground, holding them vertical. They seemed to lean in and whisper, *'Go back, everything dies here.'* Hopper felt his skin prickle with sweat through the car's air-con and shivered, the only thing that grew out here was paranoia. He eventually past a garish looking sign pointing to the abattoir, *Franks Place, always open,* and turned down a single lane road. He could already hear the squeals of the reluctant guests as he drew closer. Temporary but final accommodation, no need to book, plenty of room for all. The building grew out of nothing as it loomed into view. A charmless concrete block with a holding pen to the side where the animals wait impatiently, agitated, and uncomfortable, not so dumb they don't recognize the sounds of their own drifting out from the one-way entrance through hanging plastic teeth.

The first thing to hit Hopper as he walked through the doors was the noise; *this is what hell sounds like.* Several workers cast suspicious glances his way, continuing with their work whilst managing to keep a watchful eye on him, *they don't get many tourists.* He made his way to the killing floor, the belly of the beast, where the animals entered in single file ushered into a maze of steel fencing. Hard looking men in leather aprons and rubber boots perched on the railings like carrion crows, oversaw the slow and steady march, only too willing to help the more reluctant by the liberal use of a cattle prod. The end of the maze fanned into separate channels, each one offering the promise of a more permanent exit, where heads were locked in place by a sliding bar, like modern-day stocks. The worker on the other side would use a high pressurized bolt gun, that would deliver a single shot accompanied by a high-pitched hiss. The animal would collapse immediately, its brain scrambled. Each cow was then hoisted by its hind legs high above the blood-soaked arena and transported through another set of plastic doors to be skinned and eviscerated. The proficiency of the system was impressive as it was terrifying, it took a special kind of man to work in this environment, thought Hopper; the ability to shrug off so much death was not to be taken lightly.

Hopper was directed to Frank's own personal killing booth at the far end of the room, he felt sure word had already reached him well before he did. Set apart from the rest, it contained a variety of long knives, a steel pick and a few things Hopper had never seen before but was confident enough to recognize instruments of exit when he saw them. But it was the heavy-looking sledgehammer, stained a deep red through overuse, that caught his attention. Hopper could feel Frank's eyes on him, watching with a level of curiosity usually reserved for the creatures locked in place. Hopper pulled himself together and gave the man he already disliked a curt wave. Frank grinned as he put the compressed gun back on its hook and picked the sledgehammer, he swung it high over his head in a well-practiced arc and gave Hopper a quick wink before bringing it crashing down on the head pinned in front of him. The cow's head exploded on impact. Hopper wanted to be sick as the animal crumpled and lay twitching on the other side of the gate. In a highly skilled and well-practiced manner, Frank lifted the locking bar and fastened the beast's hind legs to the lowered hook before hitting the single red button. The chain clattered as the carcass was lifted into the conveyor above, to continue to the next stage of its journey. It took a little more than ten seconds.

Frank swaggered towards him, hand extended, a wide murder grin spread across his face flecked with blood, the bull on his forearm scowling back. Hopper took his hand; strong muscled fingers enveloped his and he felt like Frank could rip his arm from his shoulder if he wanted. He was big, bigger than he appeared on tape. Unlike Jackson or Nate, Frank's muscles were practical; formed and sculpted through heavy labour and a hard life, his forearms rippled as did the bull who seemed to come alive at the prospect of violence. Hopper looked down at his hand, now stained a dirty red.

"Looks like you got blood on your hands," Frank said, as he handed Hopper a red stained hand towel hanging from a hook. His voice a deep gravelly drawl as he eyed him up, "you get used to it," he grinned. "So now we're blood buddies, you mind telling me who you are?"

Frank already had a good idea who the man in the cheap suit was and had been half expecting a visit. As good as Higgs's story was, it felt contrived, too thought out to be real. He wondered who spoke first. Adam? He doubted it. Higgs had given him enough drugs to knock an elephant over. His doctor? Fisher? Higgs even? At the end of the day, it didn't matter, he'd find out who in his own time, and have fun doing so. In a way, it was a gift, life was becoming boring. It was what people like Fisher could never understand, it was a game. It wasn't about the winning or the losing, it was how you played, and now they had a new player.

Hopper flashed his badge, he already knew they were already past introductions, "Detective Hopper. Nice place you got here. Yours?"

There were many things Frank was proud of, his rise through the ranks from hired muscle to businessman, in particular the gambling ring, but above all else was the abattoir. As much as he enjoyed the thrill of easy money, he'd found, quite by accident, a legitimate occupation suited to his personality and had become quite the businessman in the slaughter trade. Initially, like the zoo, the abattoir had been on its knees. The previous owner had put it up as collateral to cover some bad debts, who, over time, had mysteriously disappeared, not before signing the operation over to him. Left with a debt-ridden business he knew nothing about, he'd kept it operational as a money-laundering service for several organizations he'd previously done business with. However, the competition withered and died once word got out, and the abattoir started to turn a profit. His inherited connection to the zoo had given him a base from which to work and provided a means to keep the money clean, not to mention he had some skilled workers who produced a quality product. "Names on the sign," he said with a real sense of pride, "but you already knew that, otherwise you'd be a dog shit detective, no offense, just saying how I see it. So, what brings you out here, Detective Hopper, you boys having a barbecue back at the station?"

Contrary to the wide-open space, Hopper felt claustrophobic and hemmed in, surrounded by so much death and violence the abattoir was the epicenter of brutality. He swallowed hard and considered going vegetarian, "is there somewhere we can talk?"

"Why not." Smirked Frank as he replaced his hammer and motioned to one of the workers not to send any more animals his way, "I'll give you the nickel tour."

Thankfully for Hopper, the initial violence eventually gave way to cold expediency and productivity. Even Hopper had to admit he was impressed at how a single animal could be so quickly broken down from the execrable to the edible, making certain sensibilities weren't offended with the end product.

"We got it down to almost 30 seconds." Frank boasted, as they came to the end of the production line, "course, we have to be careful when we skin them, the shit don't end up on the meat, that can cause real problems. We slow it down, make sure we do it right, nothin' left to chance. You can take a few steaks home, or you one of them pussy whipped bleedin' heart vegetarians believing in animal rights and other fucked up things that 'ain't got no place on Gods earth?" Frank didn't wait for an answer, he didn't seem the kind of man who was particularly interested in a two-way conversation. "You don't look like one, although for a while back there, you could have had me fooled," he continued, grinning. "Can't stand them myself. Un-natural conceited fucks, all high and mighty thinking these here animals got feelings! Next, they'll be demanding the vote, imagine that? Flood capital hill with even more bullshit. Although might be a little more honest, ain't nothin' more honest than this place. Doesn't solve the shit problem either, most likely they eat their fair share, bet you've eaten some shit in your time, you being a detective and all. Hell, we all have to eat a little shit sometime, 'ain't that right?" Frank bellowed out a laugh making sure Hopper recognized the cue to laugh. He didn't. Frank frowned.

"I understand you know Jackson pretty well?" Hopper shouted back.

"Used to," Frank shouted back, "shared a cell back in the day." Frank enjoyed the look of surprise on Hopper's face, "I got nuthin' to hide, detective. I did my time, besides, you'd find out soon enough, you come all this way, thought I'd save you the trouble. What's he done?"

"I was hoping you might be able to tell me."

Frank gestured to the rest of the workers who were now eyeing Hopper with obvious disdain. "Look around, detective. Most of the guys here are ex-cons, but I don't hold for no funny business, you come here, do a day's work, get paid. That's it. You fuck up, you fuck up on your own time, not mine. I ain't my brother's keeper." Frank stopped walking and turned to face Hopper, "but someone, anyone coming around here casting aspersions about what we do, now that would be just plain foolish. They'd better be sure as shit, they have something more solid than a gut feelin, ain't gonna end well if they don't. Jackson's a big boy, if he's fucked up, then he pays the consequence, ain't nuthin' to do with us."

Hopper wasn't so stupid to understand a veiled threat when he heard one and, looking around at the hard faces watching, knew how careful he had to be. He didn't want to play his hand so quickly, as keen as Fisher was to roll on Jackson, he felt the least he could do was return the favor. "And Fisher?"

"What about him?" Frank asked, already thinking he was the weak link. They had moved past the evisceration stage and were now in a chilled room where the workers had changed into what looked like white raincoats with shower caps and had just walked through a bloody storm. "Deboning," Frank shouted, explaining the next process. "We cut em up and sell em on, let me get you somethin' for your troubles." Frank nodded to a portly man with forearms the size of a cow's leg. He sliced off a large steak without taking his eyes off Hopper. Frank wrapped it in butchers' paper, blood already beginning to seep through. "Least you know it's fresh," Frank said as he handed it to him.

"Fisher told me Jackson was selling drugs, did you know about that?"

"Drugs!" Frank stopped walking and appeared genuinely surprised. "Like I said, I run a clean place here." Frank narrowed his eyes, "Is that what this is about? What else did that fat fuck say?"

Hopper shrugged, he didn't want to give too much away, preferring instead to stir the pot and see what happened. "So how does it work? Fisher just calls you up, and you come running?"

Frank didn't like the tone in Hopper's voice, "I don't come running for no one. Look around, 'ain't no secret to what we do here. We kill things. Someone tells you different is out and out lying. You have something on your mind detective, you spit it out."

They reached the end of the tour, finishing at the rear of the building, where some workers were currently loading one of the same trucks Hopper had seen on the tape. "You go there a lot?"

Frank shrugged, "when they need me."

"Looks like they need you a lot."

"They call, I come. That's it. It's all signed for, I got the receipts if you'd like to check. Like I said; I ain't got nothin' to hide."

*We all have something to hide*, "By Fisher?"

"Higgs. He's the vet there. You ask him." Frank was becoming uneasy, he'd been a gambler his whole life and knew when to bluff and when to show. He saw himself as an expert on human nature, picking up tiny signals that told him when someone was bluffing and when they weren't. It wasn't the hand you were dealt, it was how you played it, especially when the marc opposite was holding the winning hand. Desperately trying to contain their excitement as they pushed the table to raise the stakes so they could clean up. It was obvious someone had been talking, otherwise why the visit, and by the looks of Hopper, he thought he was holding a full house, waiting to catch Frank in a lie. But Frank always knew when to call. A guilty man is a man with something to hide. "This about our little stow-away?" Frank's admission hit Hopper like a rubber bullet. Pleased with the reaction, he continued. Stick with the story no matter how implausible was the lesson he'd learned moving up the ranks. The first person to crack would take the heat. "Like I said, we ain't got nothin' to hide. If that's what you're here for looks like you wasted your trip."

Hopper had been waiting to play his hand when the time was right. He was disappointed to lay his cards out so soon into the game. "You want to tell me what happened?"

Frank snorted. "Not much to tell, you ask Higgs. Some kid from the zoo hides in the back of my truck. Goddam vegetarian has a hard-on for one of them animals. Thinks he can save it. I mean for what? We're doing them a kindness, quick and painless. You want to spend your life in a cage. I done it, trust me, here's the better place. Kid tries to cut it loose, nearly gets himself killed in the process."

"And you saved his life," Hopper said, not bothering to hide the sarcasm in his voice.

Frank starts laughing, it's an unnatural sound, like the devil himself rattling the bars on the cage. "Not before Higgs hits him with a tranq dart, dumb asshole was aiming for the wolf, but he's such a bad shot and he hits the kid, goes down like a dead weight. But we got him out in the end, not that he'll remember much, them darts have enough shit in them to drop an elephant. It's lucky he woke up, let alone remembers his name. You ask Higgs. He'll tell you. Caused all kinds of pandemonium. Kinda funny really."

"And you can confirm all this."

Frank arcs his arm back towards the abattoir an elaborate gesture, "be my guest, you ask around. They'll tell you same as me."

Hopper felt sure they would, by the time he reached the zoo, Frank would have been able to call ahead making sure everyone stuck to the same story. It still didn't explain why Fisher and Jackson had been so reluctant to let him see the tapes. He was missing something, hiding in plain sight, he was just too dumb to see it. Frank's story sounded plausible but too convenient. Adam was still the key. He'd seen something he wasn't supposed to. He just needed to pry the truth loose. "And the kid, what would he say?"

"Who the fuck cares! He was pumped so full of drugs I doubt he would even know what time of day it was." Frank sniggered before abruptly changing his tone. "You know we don't hold with trespassers here," he said quietly, his voice slow and deliberate, full of menace, "you ask me, he got what he deserved." Frank leaned a little closer, "but he didn't say shit, did he?" Holding Frank's stare was hypnotic. Hopper seldom felt like prey trapped in the darkness of his eyes. There was a deep void, an emptiness looking back, waiting to be filled. "I thought not," growled Frank, before looking away, releasing Hopper now that the threat had gone, as he adopted a more neutral tone, *not Adam then*, "too embarrassed, I guess. Look, as far as I know, the kids got mental problems. I was happy to let sleeping dogs lie. No one got hurt, not really. Who told you, Fisher? Worried about his little arrangement with his shrink?"

"His shrink?"

Frank began to laugh, "he didn't tell you that? He's from the God damned funny farm."

# 60.

Valeria Perez lived a modest life with her son, Alexander. It had been just the two of them for almost four years, long enough for the memory of Alex's father to fade into a fantasy she could invent herself. Never one to deprive her son of anything, she had decided long ago not to rob him of a father and manufactured an alternative reality to the one she had lived. The one where he beat them because he; drank too much, took drugs, lost at gambling, lost his job, was bored, blamed his wife for... everything. Instead, Alex's father, the pretend version, had been a noble, loving, hard-working man, and had he survived the car accident, he would have been the positive role model Alex could look up to. It didn't matter it was a lie. The fantasy did just as well, if not better.

Alex was six today. Six years of joy. Six years of having someone to love so intensely, the reward, knowing life counts. He gave his mum purpose and pleasure; she was his world and she his. She loved their tiny one-bedroom apartment, small and cosy, cheap to heat in winter, stifling in summer. Fortunately, they were on the twenty-third floor, high enough to keep the windows open and catch what little breeze floated through the city. They were small complaints though. Valeria had a steady job cleaning at the hospital and was doing well with her online course, at the end of the year she would have completed her IT degree and moved on to something bigger, she'd already contacted HR at the hospital about transitioning into a better position and to her surprise had found them supportive and encouraging. Life was good and six years was something of a milestone. Alex was doing well in school, had good friends, and loved animals. As a special treat, she had decided to cash in some of her vacation days and take him to the zoo. She heard it was closing, part of her was glad, it wasn't a great place to keep animals, the other part, however, knew it was the last chance she would have to show Alex the sort of animals they could only ever look at in picture books. Travel wasn't in their future, even after she secured her much-prized IT job. A better house, nicer neighborhood all took precedent.

Originally, she wanted it to be a surprise, but unable to keep it to herself, had told her son a week before his birthday. It meant that everyday held a special significance as the slow countdown began. It was an exquisite form of torture for them both and drew them together even more. Finally, the big day arrived. Alex could barely get his miniature sneakers on he was so excited, and to be fair, neither could Valeria. The day had started well, a cloudless brilliant blue sky, a slight drop in temperature made the day bearable, the bus arrived on time and had two empty seats next to one another. Only happy smiley people were on board, who seemed to share in their excitement.

The city passed in a blur until they reached their destination, they were the only ones to disembark. Valeria was grateful, she didn't like crowds and they entered the zoo without a wait. After a quick pit stop to the toilets, Valeria decided to buy Alex an ice cream. Even the girl selling them, who at first glance looked slightly fierce with her spiky black hair and heavy eye makeup, had been only too happy to give them both ice-creams, and for free. For free! On account of it being Alex's birthday and them being so deserving, something about the zoo should be paying them. Valeria hadn't caught the rest, but whatever it was she had said, it didn't sound suitable for Alex's ears. Valeria didn't care. They had a free day together and were eating ice creams, it simply didn't get better than that.

The monkeys were a treat. Alex found them comical, enthralled by their movements, Valeria didn't share his excitement and saw them as old and boring but was happy to go along with the ooh's and ahh's for his benefit. She knew the stories they would tell each other later that night would involve scenarios that didn't happen. After the coolness of the reptile house, she could feel herself flagging as they stepped into the heat once more, the bigger more exciting animals had already been packed off to better places or at least so she hoped. However, there was still enough to keep a small boy entertained and he almost doubled up laughing along with the hyenas. Insane manic giggles filled the air as they buried their snouts and tore at the carcass inside their enclosure. A quick glance at her watch told her it was still early. She had been hoping to catch some of the animals being fed but considered it too early, she assumed each routine would be different for each animal, although the sign at the front did say feeding time 3 pm. Odd as it might be, it didn't seem to bother the hyenas much. Valeria had once read somewhere that the laughter of a hyena wasn't a reflection of happiness rather a response to agitation or attack. During feeding time, they would often claw and nip at each other to get a mouthful of meat. Valeria couldn't help it; she found their laughter infectious and laughed along. It was only when one hyena, who, after hearing a particularly hilarious joke, stopped to screech, and giggled a warning the rest of its pack to stay away, in hindsight Valeria wished she'd listened harder as it paused to lick at the bloodied stump of a hand.

Back in his office, Fisher could have sworn he'd heard the screams from there.

# 61.

Hopper could still hear Frank's laughter echoing in the back of his mind long after he'd left the abattoir. He would have liked to have rammed the steak, now staining the passenger seat of his car a deep red, down his throat and wiped the stupid grin off his face with the butt of his gun. *I have nothing to hide*, Hopper shook his head, he'd heard the same phrase spoken by so many, the promise of a guilty man cloaked in arrogance, believing they had outsmarted the cops too dumb to see what was right in front of them. If experience had taught Hopper anything, it taught him that it was impossible to hide everything. There was always a weak link, the wrong word said in the wrong ear, a contradiction in a well told story, or a misplaced object giving up the tiniest of secrets ready to trigger a domino effect until the whole thing fell over.

Hopper knew by now Fisher's phone would be running hot and was curious to know who he would find the more intimidating; him or Frank. He felt sure Fisher knew what Frank was capable of, there was an emptiness to the man he'd seen too often, a darkness as thick as quicksand ready to reach out and pull you under. Frank was scary, true enough, but Fisher didn't know how far he would go. He could always refer him to Michael Watts.

Hopper had been on his way to see Shelly, there was only one *funny farm* he knew of, the same one he went to once a week, when he heard the call. Shelly would have to wait, if she knew something, why didn't she just say, rather than send him on some bullshit errand? Maybe the body that had just been found at the zoo might throw up some answers. He screeched to a stop in the middle of a busy intersection, almost causing a pile up, before making a 'U' turn and driving off in the direction of the zoo, to the sounds of horns blaring and angry voices advising on how to drive.

By the time Hopper arrived at the zoo, uniformed officers were already keeping reporters and public at bay, as onlookers and freelance photographers scrambled to record something worth posting. Hopper, as much as he hated social media, wasn't so ignorant he didn't understand the value of original content. He hadn't been the only one to have heard rumors of colleagues selling 'on the scene' images to the latest news crew as a supplementary income. Once an image had been disseminated online, there was no stopping it. The gorier, the better, such was the appetite and demand of the hungry social beast. The number of likes and shares would soon muddy the waters. News stories tainted by conjecture and conspiracy. Unfounded ideas designed to turn a dollar and improve subscription numbers would take precedence over anything resembling truth or fact. Everyone was looking for an angle, truth be damned. Real truth didn't matter. The only truth that did, was the one that drew the greatest applause. Fake news! Fake life. By the time the facts were known, no one would care, people moved on, there would be something bigger and better to look at. It was inevitable, the same reasons as to why no one gave a shit about the Leanne Bonelle's of this world, it wasn't because they weren't newsworthy, but because they weren't salacious enough.

Hazard tape was stretched across the Hyena enclosure to preserve what they could as they packed away the remains. The animals, who'd now been deprived of what was once a tasty treat, were now locked inside a separate pen, pacing backward and forwards, eyeing the interested crowd as one might a fresh dinner.

Detective Hyde recognized his old partner looking over the railing, trying to get a better look. "Hopper! What are you doing here? You think this might be one of yours, or you just come for a look?"

"Any idea who it might be?" Hopper asked, ignoring Hyde, he still hadn't forgotten how useless he was in the field.

Hyde shook his head, "Not a lot left for a visual ID. We're bagging the remains to take to Morty's. You? That why you're here?"

Hopper shook his head, keen to talk to Fisher and Higgs. He also wanted to know if Fisher had opened Jackson's shed yet, he assumed he had, "no idea."

Fisher felt sick. Open sphincter kind of sick, too scared to eat, too scared to talk. He'd always considered visitors an unwanted inconvenience, they got in the way, and he didn't need the distraction. Frank had called earlier, his voice cool and calm, resonating with unspoken threats of what might happen if Hopper ever showed up again asking questions. He hadn't accused Fisher of talking. He didn't have to, it was clear from his tone of voice what he thought. Fisher, in his interminable style, desperate to deflect any blame, had started blabbing about Jackson, talking too quickly without thinking. About Jackson's little sideline selling drugs, how he was taking too many risks, how he'd told him it would only be a matter of time before someone took an interest. Jackson was the real reason

Hopper had been poking around the zoo, not him. Frank quietly reminded him about his connection to the hospital. Explaining that since Jackson hadn't been seen or heard from in a while, he hadn't been the one doing any talking, which left only two, and given that Hopper didn't seem to know who Higgs was, it was a simple matter of subtraction, leaving only him. *All roads lead back to you Fisher*, he'd snarled, *this is your mess, you clean it up, or I will*. Fisher didn't need it spelling out what Frank meant. It was too unpleasant a coincidence that a body had turned up, but Higgs hadn't. He was worried that Frank may have already started cleaning house already, and he was the only loose end remaining.

He needed time to think. Word spread fast in the busy cycle of online news and social media, and the place had never been busier. Morbid curiosity brought in the crowds, a chance to say, *I was there*, did the rest. A person had been eaten at the zoo. What better reason to come, a reminder life was precious, *don't get too close, you might just get eaten!* Good advice, he was already too close, time to go. Between the body being found and the police turning up, Fisher knew he had only a small window of opportunity to turn the cameras off and remove the tape. After his conversation with Frank, he knew, if it was Higgs, the Hyenas were currently digesting, he wouldn't have wandered in alone. Someone would have had to have helped him in, and whoever it was would be preserved on Betamax forever. All he had to do was hold his nerve and he might be able to leave in one piece now that he finally had leverage.

Fisher had already been interviewed by the police, along with a handful of others, none of which were of any help. Detective Hyde, asking stupid questions; *had someone left the enclosure open? Have you any idea who it might be? How would someone fall in? Did anyone have access?* So far, no one had mentioned Higgs, so he hadn't either. There was no reason to. Had they asked him, he would have said honestly; he didn't know where he was, he had no idea of the intestinal working of a Hyena. However, they did ask about the cameras, looking for a quick resolution. Fisher had played his part, bumbling his apology, embarrassed that Jackson, their head of security, was the person who usually dealt with them, but since he'd gone AWOL, no one had bothered to maintain them. There hadn't been a tape in the machine for some time. Besides, with cutbacks and the limited budget he had, not to mention the zoo was due for closure, the cameras were now mainly for show. Hyde had been disappointed, but what could he do? Without Jackson, there was no one to contradict his version of events. Fisher could have said anything, and he had. Offering up his own explanation that might account for the John Doe in the Hyena pen. They'd had a problem with the homeless for some time, poor lost souls looking for somewhere safe to stay, there was a strong possibility one may have wandered in by mistake. Hyde had nodded along, agreeing the city did indeed have an issue with the homeless, and it was getting worse. He was only too happy to have an easily digestible ready-made scenario handed to him on a plate, knowing it would take time to identify the remains and possibly never would, depending on if they were already in the system. Like him, Fisher hoped that Higgs had managed to keep his nose clean, but what did he care if he hadn't. It was a strange way to suicide.

By now, Fisher had the remaining tape securely hidden away, his own insurance policy, and given the interest, he knew how valuable the footage would be. He could always sell to the highest bidder once he'd made a few copies, by which time he'd be long gone, traveling light on the open waters, out of Frank's reach and the long arm of the law, just a little too short. He could imagine how much a network would pay for exclusive rights to see someone eaten alive. Frank was right, it was in all of us, the desire to seek out destruction, even better in the safety of your own home, especially if it came with a warning, *some viewers may find the following footage distressing*, it all helped to attract more numbers. He was still thinking about how much he could make when the door to his office slammed open, and Hopper walked in.

"Who is he?" Hopper snapped; he was in no mood for games.

"Who? The body? I have no idea."

"Don't play dumb Fisher, you know exactly who I'm talking about."

"Do I? Look around, Detective, the place is crawling with cops, how should I know who you're talking about? Is this still about Jackson? Did you find him?"

There weren't many people Hopper liked or had time for, he could count his friends on the remaining hand of an amputee who'd recently lost several fingers and a thumb. But there were some people he held a particular disdain for, people like Fisher. Unctuous by nature, he wore his character on the outside. Bad breath, bad body odor, bloated, sweaty, greasy, wheezy Fisher, as ruddy as the freshly cut steak sweating in Hopper's car. The rational part of Hopper's brain told him Fisher couldn't help the way he looked, it was a prejudicial response to get angry at him based on appearance, but Hopper was far from being rational. He stepped around the desk and grabbed him by the collar.

Fisher was never good in a physical confrontation and went weak at the knees, sliding to the floor, ending up between Hopper's legs. "Get up," Hopper snarled, repulsed at where he landed as he hauled him back up by his tie. "You better start talking."

"Or what?" Fisher wheezed, his mind already racing. When Hyde had interviewed him, whilst he had been the perfect host, he had also taken the opportunity to ask a few subtle questions of his own. "I know all about you, Detective Hopper. Missing persons, isn't it?" Fisher registered the surprise on Hopper's face, it was good to hit a home run. "You think I didn't ask? You're not even supposed to be here."

"You're right, Fisher, I'm not," Hopper said as he straightened Fisher's tie, pulling it tight so that Fisher started to cough and went a deeper red. "That's why you're going to help me. What did they tell you about me? They tell you I put a man in a coma? From what I understand, he'll have to piss and shit in a little bag for the rest of his life, he'll never walk unaided again, and you know what else? I liked it. I liked doing it." Hopper jerked Fisher to his feet and slammed his head against the window, leaving a greasy smear, "you think they'll help you? They won't, they'll just let me do my thing, and when I'm finished, they'll come on in, all disapproving and shaking their heads, and then they'll ask me what I found out. If you're smart, you'll avoid that."

Fisher wrenched himself free from Hopper. "I don't have to tell you shit," he coughed, "if I'm smart? What about you? How did you know about Adam and his little trip to the abattoir? I didn't tell you. It wasn't Adam, so how'd you know?" Fisher grinned, it was look that not even a mother could love, Hopper thought about Leanne and how she'd earned her money servicing Fisher, he hoped she'd been well paid. "You've already seen the tapes" Fisher said triumphantly, "what d'you do? Go to Jackson's apartment and find them there. Isn't that breaking and entering? If I'm smart?" He repeated, thinking he had the upper hand, "you think your tactics intimida.."

Fisher didn't get to finish what he was saying as his nose ruptured. Hopper hadn't planned on it, hadn't even thought about it. Like Nike said; *just do it*, and he had. It was like a reflex, a sneeze even, something beyond his control, sure he'd wanted to but hadn't intended to act. He looked at Fisher clutching his nose, blood seeping through his fingers and had the odd sensation he'd been elsewhere for a moment. This time he made a conscious decision to hit him again. "How about now? Do my tactics intimidate you now?" Hopper asked, pleased to finally get some relief as he wandered over to Fisher's desk and picked up the glass paperweight.

"Look at what you did to my fucking nose," Fisher stammered in between gulps as he backed away, his eyes nervously fixed on the paperweight in Hopper's hand. "Look, we can sort this whole mess out. There's no need for violence."

Hopper disgusted by the blubbering wreck of a man, no longer cared, "Oh I think there's is."

Fisher breathed a sign of relief as the door to his office opened. "Jack?" Hyde asked, surprised to see his old partner standing opposite a bloodied Fisher holding a paperweight.

"He fell," grumbled Hopper as he walked out, taking the paperweight with him.

# 62.

Eve remembered the boy with his mother. They had walked up chattering enthusiastically, in the way excited people do, expecting everyone to feel the same way, drawing in bystanders by their energy. Every comment, every exhibit, every decision made, no matter how small or ridiculous was, at that moment, all part of the fun. Vanilla or chocolate, sorbet or ice cream, nothing decisions made crucial, because in the end, it matters. They were together and couldn't be disappointed, the sun was out, and they were at the zoo, what could be better? Their mood was infectious, it was the boy's birthday, and Eve had given him an extra scoop refusing to take their money. She liked and envied them, their obvious closeness and shared delight made it a day to remember, and she wanted to be a part of that. Life was good, it should stay that way for as long as possible, and for a moment it was. She was someone else, working in a place somewhere else, basking in their happiness, lapping up the warmth.

It *was* a day to remember. She had so badly wanted to be a part of it, and now she was. She heard the screaming from the other side of the zoo. People came running, mobile phones at the ready. The story had already been posted by the time the police and ambulance turned up. She walked past them on her way to the surgery, her pace quickening with a sense of dread. They were both huddled together under a tinfoil blanket, no more warmth, no more happiness, instead a shared memory each of them would rather not have. He would remember his birthday long into adulthood, more than most thought Eve.

*It's this place,* thought Eve. It was a con, a sepulcher that promised so much more, delivering only decay and poison. A final resting place for all who entered, animals and people alike, clean on the outside, dirty on the in. As bright and as strong as the sun was, a coldness had begun to grow inside. She had seen Hopper and prayed that the body, or what was left, belonged to one of the people he was looking for; Nate, the inflated toddler, or even better, Jackson. Both preferred outcomes over what she suspected. She ran to the surgery, dread spurring her on.

The quiet greeted her long before she opened the door. The absent sound of her father confirming her worst fears. She recognized his *kit* first. The tools used to stamp his passport for a short trip to paradise. Typically, her father was so careful to pack away any evidence of his drug use, not today. Cabinets remained unlocked, and papers left out unattended. While he lived a messy life, she had known him meticulous in the surgery. Had it not been for the silence and the empty water bowls, she would have been convinced her father had stepped out for a moment and would return any time soon. The chill she'd felt earlier had spread to her loins and thighs and moved to her chest as it filled her with a sense of foreboding, cold icy fingers pinching her heart. She knew he was never coming back. What had he done? The remnants of *one last time* were everywhere. She began looking for clues, something physical and real that would contradict her assumption and suspicions. They had separated on the worst of terms. They had argued before, each one raising their voice, but this had been different, final. His clothes were already gone as was the tell-tale sign he had moved on. His most prized possession, a photograph of her mother, the only real thing he cherished. And then she found it. She should have seen it straight away, hiding in plain sight along with discarded papers and several drafts of the same thing. The brown manilla envelope addressed to her.

Like everyone else at the zoo, Adam had watched the commotion and excitement build. A body had been found. A body had been eaten. Part of him was horrified at the discovery, but another part, a growing part had been as excited as the snap-happy social hunters. He wanted to see for himself, curious as to how much had been left, but when he saw Hopper, he knew better than the join the onlookers hoping for a glimpse of gore. Instead, he'd gone looking for Eve. He wanted to tell her what he knew, how the pieces had fallen into place, but visions of something else skewed his memory. He remembered the cage, the screaming and the animal faces jeering him on. But he also remembered other things, darker things, things he would rather not share.

Eve tore open the envelope. Inside were two sheets of paper. A photocopied aerial plan of the zoo turned treasure map. Higgs had carefully drawn three red x's at specific enclosures with a brief annotation of what to look for. The second sheet was his goodbye. She could barely read to the end her eyes were so clouded by tears. It wasn't so much a confession but an account of who he was, stripped bare. He told her she would never be far from his thoughts as long as he wasn't thinking about drugs. He told her he was an obstacle to her happiness, that she would be better off without him and so he had left, and told her not to come looking. Inside he wrote everything needed to push her further away so she could begin her life again, this time without him and provided the means to do so. He told her everything, the abattoir, his involvement, how it started. The roles they all played Fisher, Jackson, Frank, and even Adam. He told her how he felt, his shame and embarrassment, the realization he was her burden. He didn't want her forgiveness, nor did he want her compassion or sympathy. What he wanted above all else was her to know the possibility life held without him. He told her the wheels were already in motion and not to do anything to disrupt his carefully laid plans. She had a part to play. Her part was to wait. Wait until such a time she was ready to collect her inheritance. He would be long gone by then.

Adam found Eve outside the surgery, or rather she found him. He could feel himself tremble as she walked toward him. He caught the tears in her eyes and felt ashamed. *This is a mistake and you'll be sorry, his Other* told him. *This has nothing to do with you*, he answered, telling it to be quiet, he hadn't eaten anyone. He was, like her, a victim of circumstance, collateral bit players in a story that wasn't theirs, and she felt the intimacy of shared misery. He looked thin and vulnerable, his arms tightly wound around his body, hugging himself because no one else would, and she thought about the contents of the letter and what he had been through. Her fear turned to relief, she couldn't save her father, but she could save him.

"Eve," Adam began his voice a nervous whisper. He could feel his words already failing. He wanted to tell her everything, who he was, what he'd seen. Scared his confession would be too much to bear, *his other* pushed him forward, *tell her.*

Eve broke the moment and reached out. "I already know," she whispered back, drawing him to her. Nothing else mattered. It was enough. Instinct took over, and they folded into one another, holding so tightly, afraid to let go, fearing if they did, they would be swept away by events. All they had was each other.

# 63.

Hopper felt dizzy, running around in circles chasing ghosts. Par-ei-do-lia, he rolled the word around in his mouth before spitting it out, this wasn't some trick of the mind, seeing faces in shadows. He would have preferred to spend more time with Fisher, perhaps moving on to Higgs, but with so many police around and now Hyde, it was all he needed. Art had taught him long ago, when everything begins to crumble, ask the dead. A body had been found and facts don't lie.

Morty's was the mortuary where they stored the bodies of John Doe's until cause of death had been established. Named after the resident forensic pathologist Dr. Leonard Mortimer, not Mortuary or Mortician as some of the younger detectives assumed. Art had been the one who had first commented on the coincidence between the names and started calling the place *Morty's*. It had been a running joke between the two men for as long as Hopper could remember until eventually, it stuck. Hopper had known him ever since he joined the force, he was old school, cut from the same cloth as Art, everything was done by the book, which in the world of fast-food detective work was frustratingly reassuring and had a slightly affectatious way of speaking, making him sound more like a professor and less like a police pathologist.

Morty had already laid out the remaining pieces on the stainless-steel bench in the center of the room, arranged in their relative positions, there was more than Hopper had first realized. The head was still missing, although there was a section of neck and shoulder still intact, several ribs, no intestines, one forearm, one hand, a partial pelvis badly cracked, left thigh, two kneecaps, right calf, and one foot, all heavily chewed. Morty was still puzzling over a tray of indeterminable leftovers when Hopper walked in.

"You sure he was that tall?" Hopper asked.

Morty didn't look up and tossed over a small jar of vapor rub. "He?"

The gel was used to disguise any odor coming from the remains. Hopper smeared it over his top lip and blinked, the sharpness of the menthol cut straight through his sinuses, as he peered at the remains, "not many women I know have calf muscles that hairy."

. "Perhaps you're not as worldly as you think, detective. You should experiment more, expand your mind. I thought you were better trained. For your information, I have a cousin who would put this one to shame. Now, if you'd mentioned the pelvis?" Morty finally looked up, "I heard you were currently residing in the metaphorical sin bin Detective Hopper, is that not so? To what do I owe the pleasure?"

After spending time with Fisher, the company of cadavers and Morty was a welcome reprieve. At least their stories were discernible.

"Can't I visit an old friend? I brought you a bagel."

Morty peeked over the half-rimmed glasses he wore, combined his overly animated grey eyebrows that were in dire need of a trim, it gave him the look of a mischievous animated character. "Bribery and corruption still alive and kicking I see, good to see some things don't change. Salmon and cream cheese, with capers?"

"Of course."

Mort squinted at Hopper, "Dill pickle?"

"Naturally."

"Must be important for you to go to all that trouble, how exciting. You get it from the deli on the corner?" Hopper tutted and tossed the still warm bagel over. Mort caught it and shook his head, "a dangerous move my friend, it could have been a nasty waste."

"Don't kid yourself, you'd still eat it," Hopper produced two coffees, "triple shot skinny cap with caramel."

Mort happily took the coffee and unwrapped the bagel taking a deep breath, "hmmm, you must want something pretty bad detective."

"I'm amazed you can smell anything through that crap," said Hopper referring to the vapor rub.

"You're kidding, I don't use that shit!"

By the time Morty had finished eating, Hopper had caught him up on recent events, grateful for the distraction. Marty let out a solid burp and drained the last of his coffee. "I'm impressed Hop, it's been twenty minutes and you still haven't asked me what it is you came here for. Now that I'm all lubricated let's consider the foreplay over, and you tell me why you're really here? I'm assuming by the expediency of your presence, the answer lies in front of us. N'est-ce-pas?" Morty asked, nodding to the remains on the steel bench. Hopper had heard he was planning on moving to France once he retired, which by all accounts wasn't far off, and had taken to peppering his conversation with little phrases much to the frustrations of his colleagues, which only encouraged him further. "As you are already acquainted with forensic pathology, you understand that it's only recently been delivered, leaving me to deduce, you're either extremely keen or some after private insight ahead of the pack? De Quoi s'agit-il? If you want my professional opinion, I can tell you two things. Il est mort, and you're right, it is indeed a he."

Hopper glanced down at the remains. There wasn't much to go on and knew that getting any information from Morty before he'd had time to conduct a thorough examination would be like asking the Hyenas who they had for dinner. "You think the Hyenas did all this?" He asked.

Morty slapped his thigh and let out a laugh, "and now we get down to it. That's the story. A man fell into a locked enclosure. It sounds improbable but spend some time on YouTube and you'll find it happens, it must be where your old partner gets his information from. But not you?"

Hopper grinned, he knew how Morty saw Hyde and would relish any chance he got to embarrass him, "I'd rather listen to the experts than guess."

Morty waved his forefinger in front of Hopper, "tsk tsk tsk Hopper, appealing to an old man's vanity."

Hopper shrugged. 'I'd rather trust you than youtube, but if you prefer, I can take his word for it.'

Morty hopped off his stool. He was a good six inches shorter than Hopper, but his round frame compensated for his lack of height. He slid his glasses down over his nose and began prodding the remains with the tip of his pencil. Hopper noticed the end had been recently chewed and winced. After a few moments, Morty swapped his glasses for a pair with thicker lenses magnifying his eyes to almost double their natural size and leaned in closer. Hopper relaxed, he knew once the old pathologist found something that caught his eye, he wouldn't stop until the cadaver gave up its secrets. Hopper listened intently to his running commentary, knowing it wasn't for his benefit, but his own.

"Not being a zoologist, tu comprends, I'm not overly familiar with things like this, however, I did look up Hyenas once they told me what was coming. The tear marks seem consistent with what I've read, powerful jaws capable of chewing through bone. Interestingly, a pack of hyenas can consume a fully grown zebra in approximately thirty minutes, so our friend here wouldn't have taken too much trouble. What is interesting is that they tend to target the soft areas first. Around the stomach, groin, moving literally from the inside out. Once the intestines muscles have been eaten, the carcass is usually broken up amongst the pack. Often seen as carrion eaters, they rely on others to do the killing which they'll then steal." Marty quickly looked back up at Hopper to make sure he had a captive audience. There was no point in showing off unless you had someone to show off to. Satisfied that Hopper looked suitably impressed, he continued, "in this case, however, it appears the reverse is true."

"Meaning?" Hopper quickly asked, regretting the interruption as Morty frowned at him.

"Instead of the inside out, death was most definitely from the outside in. Not unusual though, if they were the ones responsible. But..." Morty's voice trailed off, "odd."

"Odd? What's odd?"

Morty looked up with a puzzled look, "the force of a hyenas bite is approximately one thousand pounds per square inch, that's a powerful bite. It will go through bone no problem, which is consistent to the removal of the extremities, hands feet, that sort of thing as you can see here." Morty prodded at the remaining foot, "bitten clean though, you see the bite?" Morty poked at the edge of the remaining foot. "But around here, and you'll forgive me as there's not much to work with, it's different." Morty prodded at the remains of the neck and shoulder. "The bite marks around the neck are torn, same with the shoulders. Very different."

"You mean a different animal?" Hopper asked, trying to make sense of what Morty was showing him.

"Possibly. But Hyenas are pack animals." Morty answered more to himself and noticed the exasperated look on Hopper's face, "this is purely conjecture. I'm not telling you anything concrete, you understand?" Hopper nodded, "some of the bite marks here and here," Morty continued to prod, "they're not the same. Not the same force, much, much weaker. There's a lot more tearing. It looks like another animal ripped open the neck and the Hyenas did the rest, but what's odd, and again this is basic research, so I'm not saying anything conclusive."

"I get it Mort, just tell me what's odd?"

"Hyenas are bullies. They hunt in a pack. For instance, if a lion makes a kill, it's not uncommon for a pack of hyenas to steal the carcass. The lion won't attack because there's more of them, strength in numbers. But as I understand it, the enclosure was closed?" Hopper nodded, "then there you have it. It would imply another animal made the kill, outside of the cage, and then thrown in after. There's also the pressure of the bite which is most peculiar."

"You're saying he was killed first, then tossed in with the Hyenas?"

"I'm not saying anything, if you catch my drift?"

"I'm sorry doc, you have to give me more than that." Hopper was feeling hot, a tiny voice from his past was mumbling something he chose not to hear.

"You can see here quite clearly. The bite itself is like a contradiction," Morty pointed to a clean bite mark between where the jaw should have been and the clavicle, "the pressure is enough to penetrate to skin, even to the extent of tearing, but it doesn't have the same purchase." Morty straightened his back and groaned, "for example, when we eat, the mandible is hinged at the rear when the greatest pressure is, but is only used to grind, ultimately we depend on our hands to put things in, right? A dog or a hyena has a long snout, a mouth that extends outwards making it more practical, so the bite has a larger radius with greater pressure." Morty flattened his hands together and began to open and close them as if they were hinged at the palm, "see? Whereas we're limited because only our bottom jaw moves up and down, but perpendicular to the top jaw, with less purchase." Morty held up one hand and balled an open fist, as he began moving his thumb up and down so that it created an improvised mouth. "Pathetic really, all we're good for is chewing. If you look closely, you can see the penetration, but the rest is tearing as if it's been pulled open, it's inconsistent to the rest of the wounds."

"You have any idea what would have made such a bite?" Hopper could feel the sweat through his shirt as the hair at the nape of his neck stood on end and a chill began to spread through his stomach.

"I'm not a zoologist Hops; honestly I wouldn't have any idea."

"Try one," Hopper didn't mean to sound irritated, he knew his friend was doing his best, "I'm sorry Morty, I just need a break. Anything would be a help at this stage."

The older man took off his glasses and gave them a quick wipe, he was approximately six months off retirement, conjecture was one thing, guesswork, something else entirely and he prided himself on an otherwise unblemished record, never one to give in to pressure from the ranks, and God knows they tried hard enough. He perched on the stool next to the steel bench and sighed. "Ok, think on this. Before special effects and green screens, studios used facades, they were inventive in a very real and tangible way. They looked like the real thing and for all intents and purposes were. But no substance. They weren't, it was just enough to fool the audience. That's what this looks like, a facade, it looks like someone has gone to the trouble of making it look like something it isn't, knowing the Hyenas would do the rest. It's just an opinion, but When you think about it, it's actually rather clever."

"A man did this?"

"That's not what I'm saying. I'm not saying anything, you understand. Are we clear?" Morty replaced his glasses and waited for Hopper to nod. "Good." Satisfied, the older man continued, "these are animal teeth, but I'm not sure they belong to whatever it was that made the bite."

Hopper could feel a fissure open at the back of his brain, as the floor gave way and repressed memories, he would rather not revisit swam back into consciousness, and he remembered who or rather what Adam reminded him of when he'd seen him grinning in grainy black and white, although it seemed impossible it could be the same person. The face may have changed, but the madness behind the eyes remained the same.

"Hops? Jack, are you ok?" Morty asked, but Hopper had already left.

# 64.

Hopper had left Monty's in a rush, unable to bear the weight of memories that had come crashing through, visions of things he'd rather forget; larger than life teeth set inside a mouth they didn't belong, and only just made it outside before he was sick. He could still taste the burn of stomach acid mixed the menthol catching at the back of his throat.

Logic told him it couldn't be true, his mind playing tricks, seeing things that weren't there. A nag that wouldn't stop, for his own sake, he had to be sure. He'd never been given a name but, after a quick search of old case files back at the station, eventually found what he had been looking for. Tagged as a John Doe, he had been sent to the hospital for surgery. Why, was a mystery to Hopper, an absurd notion of rights. He should have been left to die, instead had been patched up to be locked up, and almost disappeared without a trace, caught in the system, locked inside a labyrinth of bureaucracy complex enough to stay hidden. No one had given him much thought after the shooting, except for Hopper and what he'd seen behind those eyes. He'd chased his thoughts away with binge drinking and fights, it lasted three days before Art found him. Hopper didn't remember any of it, but that had been the general idea, some things are best forgotten. He had woken with the worst hangover of his life and prayed he'd done enough damage to his brain cells to make it permanent. Thankfully his mind was clear. Bad thoughts gone, replaced by others. He always knew they would come back, eventually. They always did, but late at night in different shapeless forms, at a time when they could be silenced with a clink of ice and a generous measure of bourbon. After a while, they stayed buried, pushed down into a deep dark well with a heavy steel door never to be opened.

Art noticed the change. Too quick to temper, too fast with his fists, running towards danger, the more violent the better. Art the philosopher. Art the observant. Art the ignorant. He didn't know, how could he? He'd asked his old friend about the nightmares and told him back way back then he should see someone, but

Hopper said no, insisting they weren't that bad. The last thing he needed was someone finding out how much he liked them. After the surgery, he had been discharged to a high-security institution and been forgotten about, destined to live out the rest of his life sucking on Jell-O in the comfort of a padded cell.

*I'm sorry we can't give out that kind of information over the phone.* The disembodied voice at the other end said when Hopper called. Receptionists, an above-ground Cerberus guarding their particular hell, under the misguided delusion, were somehow helping by not. He told them he had been the arresting officer and was following up on a cold case, and yes, it had been a while ago, and no he didn't have a name. It didn't matter, for the kind of information he was after, he would need a signed court order. Even the new computer program couldn't work its magic without a name. He was sure everything was connected, disparate strands from an unwound tapestry, if only he could stitch them together. Nothing made sense, his world twisted into knots. The more he thought the worse he felt until the bottle was almost empty.

He'd woken early and abruptly, the morning sirens of traffic reminding him what was and what was not, thankful for the mundanity of the day ushering in the normal. Dressed and showered, last night's dreams swimming between two states of consciousness, unsure which one was real now relegated to the dark, safety catch on, securely locked away for another time, he felt saner and safer. The greater the distance between him and them, the less important they seemed to be, barely there, vitreous memories drifting like specks of dust behind the eye, only ever seen from the peripheral vanishing from view when looked at directly. Had he over-reacted? Shelly had told him the more we repress, the harder they come back and that anything can trigger. He was still playing Whack-a-mole, but a slither of last night still clung to him like smoke from a bonfire, and he'd driven to the high security psychiatric institution that had been Adam's last known address.

Hopper turned into the carpark of a thankfully characterless white block. He found the lack of architectural features reassuring. Without knowing what to expect, his mind had been playing tricks on the drive over, a nightmare gothic expanse, and asylum from the horror movies of old? Instead, he entered a cool, institutional government building. It could have been anything and he could have been anywhere, a library, a records office, the exterior betrayed nothing of the interior. The floor-to-ceiling windows bathed the entrance in soothing light. The glass railings of the mezzanine above with their heavy traffic of bodies clutching manila files felt encouraging and helpful. Until he spoke to the receptionist, who told him it was impossible for him to see anyone in charge without an appointment, Hopper considered taking his gun out several times through the conversation, instead citing obstruction as a possible crime, of which she would be charged and arrested unless she picked up the phone. It was probably more to do with her desire to be rid of him than the threat that prompted her to contact Dr Conner.

Conner spent another thirty minutes explaining how the patients under his care, although wardens of the state, were still entitled to the same courtesy that would normally be extended to any other individual. He took great pride in his smug attitude, especially when it came to patient-doctor confidentiality. If he allowed any Tom Dick or Harry with a badge to walk in, it would no doubt open the flood gates. The *indefensible pinned on the undefendable* he'd said in a well-practiced voice. Hopper wondered how long he'd been waiting for an opportunity to use a line like that. Conner smiled benignly at the prickly receptionist, who almost swooned at his ability to put a thug like Hopper in his place. Hopper nodded in all the right places, making encouraging noises, all the while his hangover getting worse, the pounding brought on by the incessant droning of Conner's little speech. When he was finished, Hopper smiled and told him, *you can't blame a guy for trying,* it was a good hook. Male camaraderie, bonding over red tape and played his second hand. "There was one other thing I wanted to talk to you about." Hopper began and asked if he were able to get his professional opinion on a case he was currently working on, *it would be a great help to get an insight on how the mind truly works,* he'd fluffed. *In private,* he'd added whilst scowling at the receptionist for effect, *for security reasons you understand,* he'd said. Conner nodded, of course, he understood that some things weren't meant for the ears of untrained mind, and his inflated ego led the way.

Once inside the safety of his office, away from the security cameras and prying eyes of do-gooders who afforded better rights to assailants than victims, Conner positioned himself behind his large wooden desk with a deep purple leather inlay and flipped open his laptop. "Perhaps you can fill me in on some of the details," he asked, fingers poised at the ready over the keys, hoping to progress his career. Hopper snapped the laptop shut, trapping his fingers inside and leaned forward. Conner squealed.

The pounding was getting worse, it had taken Hopper less time to confirm what he wished he hadn't than to listen to Conner's speech. *Yes, he remembered the patient. Yes, he had been a difficult inmate. Yes, he had been signed out over a year ago, and yes, he remembered whose name was on the discharge papers.* He described her as a particularly cold individual, hostile and unattractive, not at all the way Hopper would have described Dr. Shelly.

279

# 65.

Fisher's nose still throbbed and had rolled two separate sheets of toilet paper into little balls before inserting them into each of his nostrils. Usually, he resented the intrusion of the police, but on this instance had been grateful for Hyde's interruption. From the look in Hoppers eyes, he knew he would have told him everything, anything and more. Fisher didn't consider himself to be a coward, but his natural aversion to pain also meant he wasn't prepared to take a beating for anyone, not even Frank had that privilege. If Hopper asked about his favourite position with Leanne, he would have gladly demonstrated as long as the paperweight remained on the table and not his head.

Hyde had dropped by to see Fisher as a courtesy to let him know that although they were leaving, the body had been packed away and the enclosure taped off, a couple of uniforms would remain behind as a precaution only. As Hyde explained, they'd had instances in the past where curious morbid onlookers would try to steal a souvenir, disturbing a crime scene for personal gain. Fisher, through his broken nose, had acted suitably shocked, agreeing it _was_ disgusting how some people behaved, wishing Hyde would hurry up and fuck off, as he was desperate to look at the tape to see how valuable it might be.

As much as Fisher's nose hurt, in the end Hopper had done him a favour, providing enough of a distraction that Hyde was more concerned about the reputation of the force, or perhaps just himself, that he hadn't even bothered to ask what Hopper was so interested in and why the beating. Preferring instead to focus on whether Fisher might want to consider pressing charges. Of course, he'd graciously declined, stressing it had been a terrifying ordeal never-the-less, all the while making sure Hyde knew how understanding and sympathetic he was to the police. Hyde had been so grateful he'd even let slip they'd had problems with him before in the past, and that this might be the very straw that broke the proverbial donkey's back. Fisher had reluctantly agreed, some people shouldn't be on the force, he'd said and Hyde had simply nodded along.

Hyde was the kind of guy Fisher could get along with, lazy, risk adverse, looking for easy answers. He'd been only too happy to go along with Fisher's suggestion of a homeless man, it made sense and meant no one had to waste time investigating something that was right under their noses. By the time he left, Fisher had laid it on so thick, he half believed it himself.

Back in what used to be Jackson's private domain, now his, Fisher swiveled in the black leather office chair. With the door locked, he felt safe, in control and was already regretting his decision not to press charges, maybe it wasn't too late to teach him a lesson. It wasn't just the beating, he didn't like the way Hopper talked to him, as if he was nothing, scum, a piece of shit stuck to his shoe. He cleared his throat and spat into his handkerchief. He couldn't help how he looked, overweight as a boy with hygiene issues, he'd never been popular but knew how to ingratiate himself. Never liked but always there. He provided a service, people like him did. You may despise and even hate him, but he had what you wanted, and Fisher was prepared to go places no one else would. Hopper had spooked him sure enough, but what did he really know? Jackson sold drugs. Adam had gone to the abattoir. So what? He couldn't tell anyone anyway and now it looked like he was out of the picture. He had nothing and who was there to tell? No one was listening anyway. Fisher was feeling good. He was in the clear and Hopper had managed to do it all to himself.

He'd waited patiently until he was sure it was safe. The two remaining officers didn't present a problem, had Leanne been around, she could have even made a few dollars on the side, there were worse ways to spend a night. Fisher considered rewinding back and forth to see if there were any more upskirts he could spend time with, but decided against it. Time enough for that later. He rubbed his hands together and wished he'd remembered some popcorn as he hit the play button.

Forty minutes in, and Fisher was already scrubbing forward double speed, hoping for something interesting. Eventually, Higgs appeared on screen by the surgery, this was going to be fun, Fisher thought as he settled in. The day began as usual, boring even, it was only when he reappeared at night when the zoo was deserted with a bag and shovel, Fisher perked up. He watched intently as Higgs made his way around the zoo, going from enclosure to enclosure, where he would dig a hole and bury a small parcel. He made three trips in all, and by the time he was finished, the bag was empty, and he returned to the surgery where he stayed. Fisher scrolled forward past the static frames until Higgs re-emerged from the surgery in a very different state. Gone were the secretive and furtive glances over his shoulder and the bird-like twitches, replaced instead by an exuberance Fisher had never seen before, especially where Higgs was concerned. It was a tragi-comic sight watching Him jerk around to an imaginary beat, too enthralled to notice the figure watching in the shadows.

Fisher's first thought was that it might be Frank, come cleaning after all, and if it was, he had the insurance to keep himself safe, maybe even make a little money on the side. It was like watching a pantomime, everywhere Higgs looked the shape moved on, he almost wanted to shout, *'he's behind you'* and scream *'watch out'*, as he helplessly watched Higgs peering in empty corners. Sanitized by the monochromatic cameras, Fisher was relieved he wasn't watching in color when the figure lurched at him from above. Mercifully the tape ended, and Fisher was spared the rest. He rewound slowly, feeling his legs tremble and his breath quicken hoping to reveal the identity of the murderer, but it was too dark, the footage too poor. He stared closer at the screen and wondered if it was a trick of the light or a distortion of the frame, but he could have sworn he could see teeth.

# 66.

Shelly was in a session with one of her favorite patients, Ryan Devall, a permanent resident suffering from Disassociated Identity Disorder, when she received a text message that Hopper was in reception demanding to see her. Hospital policy was never interrupt a private session unless it was an emergency. Even then, as his therapist, Shelly had the option of accepting or declining based on her professional opinion. She already knew Hopper had been to the institute where Adam had been discharged to her care, she paid a monthly retainer to one of the male orderlies to keep her informed. She was excited at what conclusion, if any, Hopper may have come to, and as much as she regretted cutting her session with Ryan short, she told reception to keep Hopper there and she would be down presently.

Hopper felt like an idiot, a dog chasing its tail. She had warned him, people start seeing things that aren't there, wishing they were, he just never expected to be one of them. But hadn't she been the one encouraging him? Feeding his paranoia, pointing out the phantoms in the wallpaper and he'd gone along with it. Wanting something to believe in, and wanting someone to believe in him and what had he found? A missing prostitute whose kid was better off without her, an ex-con selling steroids who'd ran at the first sign of trouble, a pampered and smothered kid confused about his sexuality with an overbearing mother. And at the center of them all, Adam, a festering boil burning at the back of his brain ready to burst. He felt violated, used, and abused but didn't know why. He needed a straight answer, direct and truthful, none of the usual ambiguous psychobabble spun in previous meetings designed to confuse, always sounding good but on reflection, empty. Her specialty, hollow words that meant nothing.

Even from her distance, Shelly could feel the heat of his anger radiating towards her. It was an expected moment, and she was well prepared, but she still needed to tread carefully. The wrong word in the wrong place would ruin everything, carefully laid plans gone to waste. Without Hopper, there was no Adam.

"It's him, isn't it?" Hopper asked, the calmness of his voice already beginning to crack.

"Not here." Shelly said, dispensing with the unnecessary courtesy of *hello* and *how are you?* She already knew.

Hopper followed Shelly to an almost deserted cafeteria. Bathed in harsh fluoro lighting, the ambient music that floated in the background did little to soften the clinical nature of the room, Hopper was relieved the multi-colored furniture wasn't bolted to the floor. Since the servery was closed, Shelly returned with two coffees from a vending machine. Hopper took a sip and winced, it tasted identical to the coffee back at the station.

"I'm sorry, it's the best I can do on short notice, we can go to my office if you'd prefer," Shelly glanced around as it were the first time she'd been there,

"Here's fine," grumbled Hopper, already hating it, knowing how Sarah Moynihan must have felt. "No more games. Who is he?"

Shelly considered for a moment of stretching out the conversation, playing dumb, *tell me who, who is?* But the time of games was long gone. "You know who he is Jack, you've always known."

"I need you to tell me."

Shelly sighed, "His name? I don't know, there weren't any records."

"Stop it. That's not what I meant, and you know it. Look me in the eye and tell me." Hopper was aware he was raising his voice and had already attracted several glances in their direction.

"I am telling you, but you're not listening. He's not the same. The man you knew. The man you shot. He died that day. Adam is different."

"Nobody changes that much. How? How is it even possible?"

"Facial reconstruction. A psychological wipe. He has no memory of his past."

"You sure about that?" Hopper snapped back. "There's a dead guy on a slab, or what's left of him that tells me different."

"They're already saying it was a homeless man, an unfortunate accident."

"But we know different, don't we?" Hopper shook his head, "Why? Why me?"

"Because you were the only real link to his past. I needed to know."

"And now you do, and so do I." Hopper stood, his chair sliding out behind him, crashing to the floor. A couple of male orderlies made their presence known, Hopper turned towards them, his anger flaring, "what the fuck are you looking at?" He snapped, waiting for an opportunity, any opportunity to relieve the pressure building behind his eyes.

Shelly reached out and touched his hand, "Jack. It wasn't him." She kept her voice calm, reassuring, knowing how important a tactile connection was to diffuse a situation, "this isn't just about him. This is about you. You asked me why, sit down and I'll tell you."

"And why should I believe anything you have to say?"

Shelly let her hand slip and stared back into her coffee, it was a calculated posture designed to indicate vulnerability, "sit down," she said quietly, Hopper didn't move, "please," she asked doing her best to appear defenseless. He grudgingly picked up his chair. "Thank you," she said smiling, she knew how crucial manners are in times like these and took a deep breath, it was time for a full disclosure. "You remember the Barbie Doll butcher?" She asked, "it would be over thirty years ago, I doubt anyone remembers his real name anymore, just what the tabloids used to call him."

Hopper had heard of the Barbie Doll Butcher, who hadn't? Responsible for the murders of several women. He had cut them up and swapped their body parts around before re-stitching them back together. He'd entered police folk law and heard there may even be a film in the making. The thought made Hopper shudder. "You going to tell me he's one of your patients? Where does he work, a day care center?"

Shelly remained composed. "I guess I deserved that. No, he's still dead." She'd spent a lifetime studying the subtleties of body language, a downward gaze, when and when not to make eye contact. A shift in body posture, a subtle touch of the face, all designed to illustrate an uncomfortable sense of embarrassment, she was on full display. "His name was Richard Lister Shelly," she began, "he was an accountant. Small local businesses. He was, what the papers at the time called, unremarkable." Shelly knew it was the normal everyday details that had the power to shock, not the big things, but the small. The things that people recognized in their own life, it helped normalize and bring the horror home. She glanced up and caught his eye, making sure she had his attention, she did. "I'm grateful no one remembers his name, I'd thought of changing mine so many times, but it's all I have." She paused for effect, letting her words sink in, before adding. "He was hated by everyone but me." Pause, look up, moisten the eyes, "I loved him. He was my father."

Her admission was like a dull thud to the stomach that sucked away Hopper's remaining anger. In a moment, Shelly had gone, a smaller frightened girl had taken her place. He couldn't pinpoint the moment she transformed. Never once had he considered she might have a past. People enter our worlds as fully rounded human beings with no history that's of any relevance to us. She'd once told him;

we suppress our darkest thoughts and dreams at our own peril. No matter what we do, they come back to haunt us in ways we never saw coming. It's why we make the choices we make, but he'd never stopped to think why she made hers. He wanted to say something deep and profound to articulate the dismay and sympathy he felt having to grow up with such a heavy burden, but all that came out was a whispered, "fuck!"

Shelly nodded, "Fuck indeed Jack, not the response I was going for, but I'll take it." Shelly noticed the corner of Hopper's mouth twitch and she knew she had him. "Here's not the place Jack. But I'd like to explain, properly, if you'll let me."

"Ok, then I think we're gonna need something stronger than coffee."

# 67.

The bar was only a short walk from the hospital, it reminded Hopper of his favorite. His favorite being a bar that sold alcohol. The standard myriad of assorted colored liquors that no one ever asked for, provided the backdrop to an otherwise unremarkable drinking den. The actual bar was a gally, long and narrow, providing support for several disconnected drinkers, grateful for the poor lighting. The bell above the entrance rang as they walked in, no one gave them a second glance as they took a booth by the far corner along the back wall. A single fixed table light with a green lampshade had been bolted to the center of the table, Shelly absently tested it, it reminded her of the recreational rooms back at the hospital. To the side of them on the wall were hung black and white photographs of past film stars with fake autographs dedicated to anonymous names of unknown recipients. Clark Gable, thanking Steve for all the good times, while Monroe acknowledged the vicissitude of her life and praised Mack for being a constant in the tumultuous waters of fame. *To Mack for always being there*, except when it counted, thought Hopper. None of it real, as fake as the wood paneling and patrons, but hopefully not Shelly.

"This your regular hangout?" Asked Hopper as he came back from the bar with two Bourbons.

"I've never been here before in my life!" She grinned. It was a good idea to have a drink beforehand, break the ice, it would make it easier in the long run. Once Hopper had been warmed by the alcohol and the edge smoothed off, she would show him the tank.

"So. Your dad was a murderer?" Hopper began, his previous compassion frozen over, maintaining the frost between them as he sipped his drink. "That's why you became a shrink?"

Not the best opening line Shelly had ever heard, but smiled nonetheless, she had no intention of swapping stories. The bar seemed to have been designed for post-coital regret, and she intended to keep her wits about her as she nursed her drink. "You could say that" she said, allowing herself a quick sip. "Like all of us, there were two sides to him, all I knew was the father I had, he was kind, caring and protective. There was only ever the two of us." She noticed Hopper grimace, "I know, given what happened, I've often thought about what happened to my mother. It was a conversation we never had, nor did I want to." She shrugged, "to me was the perfect father."

"Except he cut people up." Hopper reminded her.

"Except he cut people up," Shelly repeated. It was clear he was still angry and looking to score points. Shelly allowed the hurt to show, she would allow him that at least, "I realized I never knew him. Not really. He's what drove me forward, I wanted, had to know why. What was it that made him do it? A chemical imbalance, a deep-seated sense of resentment towards women? There was a need there, something buried. I eventually came to the realization that perhaps I was looking in the wrong place." Hopper arched his eyebrows, "we spend our lives trying to fix things that are broken. You've said it yourself. There are some people out there you can't fix. It's in them, maybe it's in all of us. But what if we could separate that part of us?'

Hopper sat upright and finished his drink, "you think allowing psychos to run riot out there is the answer? Like Adam? For fuck's sake you even gave him a name."

"It's not what I meant. I thought if I could understand Adam, I would be able to understand my father. You know what Virtual reality is?" Shelly asked, changing tack.

Hopper nodded, he'd heard some of the academies were using it to train recruits, to give them a firsthand experience of what to expect, he considered it laughable. In life, there was no reset. "Murder is real enough."

"I've always thought it an odd term myself," Shelly continued, "Virtual Reality." She turned the words over in her mouth like a boiled sweet. "There's nothing virtual about it, the mind doesn't register the difference between real and imagined. If you could do whatever you wanted without repercussion, would you do it? Michael Watts, Adam. Me? Imagine how liberating that would be."

Hopper considered for a moment how he'd sexualized Shelly in the past and brushed away the thought. "Isn't that what separates us from them. It's what makes us different. That's the point, isn't it?'

"Is it? Isn't that what brought you here. You couldn't. Does that make you just the same?"

Hopper clenched his jaw, he wasn't the same, he'd spent a lifetime proving it, "careful doc," he warned.

"What? What will you do? Beat me, beat someone else? There's a rage inside that needs to be let out. If I make you angry, who's to say you won't take it out on someone else. Think of the cases of domestic violence, a man gets laid off and goes home to beat his wife because he's angry. What if there was way to let it out? You remember the game Whack-A-Mole?"

"Because people get hurt," Hopper couldn't believe he was having a conversation about letting himself go, he'd wanted to so many times.

"That's not what I'm saying. Take Adam, I knew if I could separate that part of him, I could find out which is in control. I couldn't tell you about Adam, no more than I could tell him about you."

"So, you sent me there as a Guinea Pig?" Hopper asked, "You used me, and now there's a dead guy at the zoo." He shook his head, "I need another drink," and slid out from the booth.

Although the bar was still quiet, it had begun to fill and were fewer gaps between bodies, making it harder for Hopper to wave the bartender over. He hadn't meant to shoulder the man next to him, who'd already been there for several hours and was deep in thought about why his wife was such a *cheating bitch* and why wouldn't she give him a blow job like they did in the films he watched? He already had his glass to his lips when the jerk next to him rudely shoved him to the side as if he wasn't even there, spilling his drink, making him look foolish, and at these prices, liquor don't come cheap. Marv, the bartender had already warned him about picking fights, but this was an unprovoked assault, and God knows if his wife wasn't going to pay, someone else was. Here he is minding his own business and some asshole comes up and shoves him! Not even so much as a howdy-do, let alone an apology. "Mind where you're fucking going asshole," he growled at Hopper, praying he'd say something stupid back. It was all the excuse he needed to get Marie Lou out of his system.

Hopper hadn't realized he knocked the man, glancing at Shelly, he'd thought about this moment for so long, going out for a drink, taking her home, doing what normal people do. But not under these circumstances, although looking at her in the subdued lighting, he could still appreciate how attractive she was and didn't think smashing a glass into his neighbor's face would do much to ingratiate himself to her, no matter how much he wanted to. He considered her words for a moment, *if you could do whatever you wanted, imagine how liberating it would be*, he had to admit, right now, it would feel pretty damn good. Instead, going against instinct, he swallowed his pride, "sorry pal, my mistake," he mumbled as he got his drink and slid back into the booth.

"I know you think Adam is responsible." Shelly continued as if he never left, "but I'm telling you Jack. It's impossible. I would know."

"How? You said yourself, you never knew your father, and look at what he did. You don't know Adam any more than I do. That's what you shrinks don't get, you think you can get inside someone's head, you can't, in the end it's just us and them." Hopper knew how inelegant he sounded compared to her as he tapped the side of his own head, but he figured at least he made his point.

"And what if I could? More to the point, what if you could?"

"You owe me another fucking drink." It was an unexpected interruption that caught them both off-guard as the man from the bar slammed his glass down on the table. It was clear he wanted more than a refill. "I said you owe me another.."

Hopper cut him off, happy to oblige, "I heard," he snapped back, he could feel his adrenalin beginning to pump, "and this is a private conversation." Shelly looked back and forth between them both, excited at the prospect of watching Hopper in action, *coming for a drink was a good idea*, she thought, eager to enjoy the show. "So, if you don't mind," Hopper said flatly, meeting his glare. Shelly was impressed at how willing Hopper was to escalate the situation.

"What did you say to me?" The man continued. Shelly doubted he was deaf but recognized the courtship for what it was and was sure Hopper would deliver the appropriate response in return, something along the lines of, *you heard*.

"I asked you to leave and now I'm telling you." Hopper didn't disappoint.

"And I said you get me another drink or how about I take this one." The man swiped Hopper's drink and swallowed in in one gulp. Shelly could barely contain herself; she couldn't have designed a better experiment to illustrate what she was trying to explain and thought about how to use it to her best advantage.

"Excuse me," Shelly began, diverting the attention away from Hopper, "perhaps I can get you that drink."

The man from the bar looked at her as if she'd suddenly appeared. "Perhaps" he said, mimicking her, "perhaps you can suck my cock while he gets my drink, how about that?" He leered, impressed with his clever comeback. He usually only thought of the right thing to say hours later and considered this something of a result.

Shelly noticed the shift in Hopper's position as he balled a fist, "Jack," she said, gently touching his arm to get his attention. "I don't need a knight in shining armor, and I'd like to remind you, you are still on suspension," She turned her attention to the stranger from the bar, picking up where she left off. "Though I am curious," she began, "if that approach has ever worked for you? I suspect not, which leads me to believe you have an ulterior motive that isn't all bluster and posturing."

"You what?" The man snorted, knitting his eyebrows together, he wasn't expecting a conversation, it wasn't how things were meant to be, there was a protocol for this sort of engagement.

"Meaning, you actually have no intention of it ever working, I think if it did, you'd be terrified and wouldn't know what to do, it's a response designed for rejection. The question isn't why, but who? As much as you'd like to fight my companion, my guess is you'd probably be more interested in fucking him first. So. Perhaps." Shelly spat out, "maybe you're asking the wrong person."

The man from the bar looked from Hopper to Shelly and back again, "what did you just say to me?" He growled, confused, still trying to remain threatening.

"I think she just called you a fag," Hopper added helpfully.

He leaned in closer to Shelly and dropped his voice to sound more menacing, "then how about we go outside, and I'll show you just how much of a fag I am?"

Shelly shook her head and folded her arms. "No. It's not going to work. You've done it again. If I say, *yes, ok let's do it*, you'd have to resort to some violent pseudo sex, like rape, because ultimately you don't really like it, and no-one wants that, so I'm going to decline and say no. It's not much of a choice, is it? If I go outside, you're no longer a fag, but a rapist. At least in here, you're just a fag." Shelly put her fingers to her lip as if considering the conundrum, "Or would you rather be a rapist?"

Hopper smirked, as much as he wanted to release some tension, he had to hand it to Shelly, she was doing a great job on her own. The best he could come back with was, "you watch your mouth, you fucking bitch," before returning to safer ground and turning his attention back to him. "What are you smirking at? You so pussy whipped you need her to fight your battles? I still want that drink." The man grunted, pleased to be back on track with how these things were meant to go.

Hopper shifted in his seat, as entertaining as her comments were, it was out of character, she was playing a very dangerous game. Guys like him don't back down. He was keen to diffuse the situation before it got out of hand. In a different time, he would have acted differently, "you're right, my fault and no harm meant. Let me get you that drink." Hopper reached for his wallet.

Shelly was disappointed, she had hoped to watch Hopper in action, intent on using his anger against him. She still had one more trick up her sleeve. Hopper, lived by a code, a code that kept him in the right and everyone else in the wrong, even though she was the provocateur. She decided to take the risk and gamble he would still do his best to act as protector, it the role he'd developed for himself, "no, allow me," she said as she poured her own drink over the man's head.

The man felt something cold on the back of his head, it took a moment for his brain to process what had happened. He'd never felt anger like it, under normal circumstances, he would never hit a woman, or at least one he didn't know. But this was different, she'd insulted and embarrassed him, he wasn't sure if anyone had been watching, but if they had, he had been made to look a fool. He would have preferred to say something clever, but no one looks clever or sounds it with bourbon running down their face. It was a knee-jerk reaction, an in-built reflex, hit and ask questions later, he hadn't even realized he'd drawn his arm back until Hopper caught it.

Shelly had been prepared to take a hit for the sake of science. But Hopper was too quick and grabbed the man's wrist pinning it behind him and slammed the stranger's head into the table as he quickly withdrew his gun, pushing it into the side of the stranger's face. "You should have taken the drink," he snarled between gritted teeth. Shelly almost clapped.

"Jack, let him go." Shelly said, "I think it's time we left."

"You heard the lady. I don't want no trouble." The stranger managed to squeeze out, his face firmly on the table.

Caught between wanting to finish what Shelly started and knowing when to leave, Hopper reluctantly let him go and followed Shelly out.

# 68.

It's a strange thing to be bonded by violence. Shelly could understand the camaraderie of gangs. A shared experience ran deep. They had laughed about the incident at the bar as if it were a big joke, not what it was; a dangerous and deliberate escalation of anger designed to provoke Hopper. By the time they reached her lab, he'd almost forgotten the reason he was there.

It was a set straight from a sci-fi movie. A large tank dominated the center of the room, beneath which heavy cables snaked across the floor, making their way up the walls to the helmet suspended above, hung like the head of a sleeping insect. "What is this place?" Hopper asked.

Shelly had taken him to the annex at the rear of the hospital, explaining the building was initially used for the more experimental treatments in the past. Hydrotherapy being a particular favorite of the time. Patients were submerged in freezing cold water, bringing them perilously close to drowning, after which, if they survived, would be pronounced cured of their madness, unless extra sessions were needed. It was mercifully abandoned, giving way to electrotherapy. Fortunately, the building was far enough away so that the rest couldn't hear the cries of the patients. "I'm sorry about the Gothic overtones," Shelly called out from behind a control booth, turning the equipment on, "there's not much I can do I'm afraid. I'm lucky to have the space."

Hopper was studying the tank as the lights one by one were switched on. Although grudgingly impressed, he was still surprised by Shelly's behavior in the bar earlier, "are you going to tell me what that was all about?"

"How did it make you feel? Angry, violent?"

"I wanted to take him apart, you should have let me deal with him, but what I don't understand is why, why provoke him like that?"

"It wasn't him I wanted to provoke."

"Me?" Hopper asked incredulously, "why?"

"I wanted to prove to you how this works. You asked me earlier how could I possibly know about Adam? Unless I was able to get inside his head? What you're looking at, is effectively that." Shelly caressed the side of the tank, "it's an immersive virtual reality tank, it taps directly into the subconscious, through this, I can see not only what Adam does, but what he wants to do." Hopper still looked blank, as pleased as she was, it was also a little frustrating to dumb it down, she was impatient to get him in the tank. "Think back to the man in the bar, what you wanted to do. Do you still feel like that?"

"It doesn't matter much now."

"You think when we shut out those impulses, they just go away? They don't, they get repressed, pushed down, if you're lucky you might get an ulcer or a headache from time to time, maybe some extra heavy baggage. In the case of the man at the bar, I guarantee someone will pay for my actions."

"Little irresponsible, don't you think?"

"We need to blame someone for when things go wrong. Unlucky if you're in the firing line. Like you. Convenient for a society that keeps us repressed in the first place don't you think? My point is, no matter what we do, our true self bubbles to the surface regardless. What if I told you that some of the greatest minds of the twentieth century harbored some pretty twisted secrets of their own? Aristotle once said; *There is no great genius without a mixture of madness.* I know what Adam was, and what he is now, and I know what he's seen. This, all of this, allows you to act out those thoughts, to live them as if they were real. It allows that part of you to run free without repercussion. Can you imagine how liberating that would be? You wanted to know how I know. Because I've already been inside Adam's head. It couldn't be him." Hopper looked unconvinced, "if you don't believe me, why don't you test it for yourself?'

"You mean get inside his head?"

As tempting as it was, Shelly resisted the urge to drop Hopper in at the deep end, there would be time for that later. "I was thinking you. I'd like to show you how it works before we move on to that." Hopper eyed her suspiciously, "what's the matter Jack, don't you trust me?"

# 69.

Hopper had come a long way and as much as he didn't trust her, he wanted to. Shelly was full of surprises, the incident in the bar had thrown him and as much as he hated to admit it, he would have loved to finish what he started. But he needed answers and knew at least for the moment this was as close as he was going to get. Thankfully there was no need for him to submerge himself inside the tank as she had developed a new prototype, a simple VR headset that could be used in the same way.

"You're telling me, whatever I think gets recorded, so you see what's in my head?" Hopper asked dubiously, "you sure you're ready for that?"

"It's far more than that. Whatever you think exists on a conscious level, what this does is tap into your subconscious, our primordial self." Shelly said, strapping Hopper into a chair, "for your own good, in case you start lashing out," she explained, as she attached several electrodes to his chest, "precautions, we don't want you having a heart attack."

"One last question," Hopper asked, "how will you know if it's worked?"

"Think about the man at the bar or anyone else for that matter and how they make you feel. Think about what you'd like to do, the rage you feel. Keep it close, and when it's done. We'll talk again." Shelly stood back, admiring her handiwork and slipped the headset over him. "I'll need to give you a sedative to help you relax," She didn't wait for an answer and jabbed the needle into the base of Hopper's neck.

Hopper didn't like needles at the best of times and was grateful he couldn't see anything through the blacked-out visor. The warmth spread beyond the sudden burn of the needle, moving down his spine, across his chest, meeting at his groin before gathering speed, enveloping him in a cocoon of embryonic stasis. He wanted to talk, to ask where he was as the world drifted away and he was lost floating in a black sea of nothingness. No longer existing, he no longer cared.

Surrounded by emptiness, he had the curious sensation he had just been somewhere but couldn't remember where.

Shelly decided to start him off gently as she bent forward and spoke into the microphone, "Jack, I want you to concentrate on the light in front of you, can you do that for me?"

Hopper didn't hear the voice as much as felt it, inside and outside. Soft and protective, he would have done anything for the voice and noticed, for the first time, the burning flickering light in the distance, the more he looked at it the larger it became until it was everywhere. *That was easy*, thought Hopper, pleased with himself, *ask me something else*. The voice obliged, "go back to the bar, can you do that for me?"

Images began to shimmer and take shape as the bar materialized around him. Hopper felt himself begin to split, he became a contradiction of participant and voyeur. The Hopper he knew ordered a drink and looked back at Shelly, an exaggerated cartoon of herself, both beautiful and cruel. It felt natural to see the world through his own eyes, passenger and driver, beast, and man. The scene played out as before. Hopper knocked into the stranger at the bar and returned to the booth where Shelly was waiting. The Shelly in his mind was the same but different, inhabiting her own paradox. Distant yet sexually alluring, he had turned her into a femme fatale. Their conversation was muffled, a vague recall of dialogue, bad actors pretending to speak. The stranger arrived on cue, bigger than before and more menacing. Shelly poured her drink over his head. As before, the man drew his hand back. Hopper caught it, twisting it behind his back. This time the bone splintered. He drew his gun and pressed it into the side of the man's face, but unlike before, pulled the trigger.

The head exploded like a ripe watermelon. Shelly assumed Hopper had firsthand knowledge of a point-blank gunshot. It should have been the end, but always curious, Shelly was greedy for more. She leaned into the microphone once more. "Jack," she began, "take me back further, show me who you really are."

Colors and images swirl and form as Hopper's life goes by on fast forward, a drunk driver on life's highway, barely in control. There are beats to his experience, moments in time seen through the parallax of the subconscious, events that shaped his future self, small by nature, big by implication. The chain reaction of *if only*, guilt and regret. The batman car, a step too low hidden from view. The shame gulped down, swallowed whole, composting ready to grow, self-blame, self-loathing. His passenger always there, dormant waiting, urging him on in the dark, quick to anger, quicker to act. Inside a gnawing hunger desperate to claw its way out. Inside on the outside and its need to be free, ready to purge.

And then there was Adam.

A moment in time. The exhilaration and thrill of seeing what life could be like, to let go and give in, no more pain, no more pretending, no more restraint. The purity of truth and the freedom it brings. Hopper looked to the animal and understood the secret they keep. They are both the same.

Shelly has always known it to be a turning point, a defining moment for Jack Hopper, to be confronted by something he is but refuses to be. From that moment on, every action, turn, and decision has been a barbed spike, a thorn to remind him of who he is not. Adam opened the door; the animal came to visit and never went home. Everything after is a struggle. The savage beating of Michael Watts, giving in, separating, brutality giving way to abandonment. Shelly, her breath quickening through excitement, urged him on, "more," she whispered.

Hopper shows her the zoo and Fisher. She can feel his rage through the screen as he tears and rips through the man. The fury of Hopper is different to Adam, anger born from guilt is a harsh searing pain that requires an outlet, his release is euphoric and total. There is no Hopper, only the animal. She sees herself through the eyes of the animal and begins to understand. It's always been there. She's tried so many times to find it, looking on the mirror hoping to catch a glimpse of the beast inside, worrying, fretting, will she, won't she? But seeing it for the first time reflected in the eyes of Hopper she finally come face to face with her own monster and the id inside.

# 70.

Hopper floated back into the conscious world from the cradle of somnolence, ending what felt like a deep hibernation, and for a moment forgot where he was. Refreshed and newly conscious of his body, he felt straight off the assembly line. He couldn't remember the last time he woke up feeling this good, muscles taught and strong, connecting to sinews and tendons allowing his body to move as one. He pushed himself back into the mattress, tensing, making himself heavy as he exhaled, slowly bringing himself back to the surface as he sucked in oxygen. He was more than awake, he felt alive.

He could hear the slow rhythmic breathing of a body lying next to him asleep. Shelly. Disconnected memories hung over him, swirling in the mist. He had been angry but wasn't sure why. They had gone to a bar, something happened. A man. An argument. For the life of him, he couldn't remember what it had been about, something stupid, unimportant, and uneventful, nonsense. There had been a disagreement of sorts and the man had reacted badly. It had been wrong, he knew that much, it didn't make him feel angry or sad or ...anything for that matter. There was nothing, no reaction, no feeling, just an emptiness where something had once been. The more he tried to capture what it was, the quicker the hole closed. He rolled over, Shelly had her back to him. It should have felt strange being with her, it didn't, but he had no idea how he got there. He wanted to wake her, ask her what happened. He thought about the zoo and Fisher, there had been something he wanted to know. Something important about tapes, he couldn't remember, but did he really care anymore? A body had been found at the zoo, some poor homeless man who'd wandered in by mistake, the animals did the rest, *pity*, he thought.

He needed to piss and carefully eased his legs out of bed so as not to disturb Shelly and padded barefoot to the adjoining bathroom collecting his clothes on the way. Closing the door behind him, he slid his hand over the wall until he found the light switch and the room blinked into life. Small, utilitarian, and basic, he appreciated the simplicity and practical nature of the design, *a marvel of modern architecture to have everything needed within such a small space, toilet, washbasin, and shower*, he thought as he leant over the tiny sink and caught sight at his reflection, a man he wasn't sure he knew. He still didn't feel like himself, but that wasn't such a bad thing, he wasn't sure how much of himself he liked anyway. He splashed water over his face trying to make sense of why he was there. His reflection was a familiar stranger, momentarily out of sync like a badly dubbed movie. Every movement a delayed echo, he blinked this side of the mirror and watched as he blinked on the other a moment later. He remembered Shelly said there would be side effects. A shard of memory slid into place. Side effects. He had wanted to know about Adam, but he already knew. Another memory fell, he had gone to the hospital to find out, Shelly signed him out, she'd always known about their connection, his connection. She had been playing games the whole time. He should have felt angry, he didn't, the same void he'd felt earlier was still there. More memories began to flood his brain, they showered him like needles in the wind, each one a sudden jolt. She had wanted to prove her experiment worked, to show him that once a desire had been exorcized in the tank, it wasn't possible for it to happen on the outside. Need gone. Satisfaction guaranteed. He thought about the man in the bar and how there was nothing left, about Fisher, the zoo. Her. But she had been wrong, he knew that now. In him she had seen his desire. Their sex had been vicious and brutal on the inside, it had also been vicious and brutal on the outside. He checked his back in the mirror and had the scars to prove it.

He could feel himself syncing back together as one. She had told him the machine would record his thoughts, desires, and actions, allowing him to be the animal inside his own head, and she had opened the door to let him out. He had told her the only way to know someone was to take a walk inside their head, and now he could. He had wanted Shelly in the tank, but his desire had broken through to the outside. If it was true for him, then how would it be for Adam? He had known Adam as the beast and needed to know if he took what was on the inside, out?

It wasn't the first time Hopper had left a woman sleeping as he quietly closed the door, Shelly heard the soft click and opened her eyes. The room opened to a narrow corridor which led out to the lab. Hopper was surprised to see they were still in the same place, although had no recollection of leaving. He saw the headset where they had left it, she had been the one to take it off, she had been the one to lean forward and kiss him, biting his lips, drawing him in. It had been her; it had always been her. Had she been right? When he thought of her, he felt no desire. Yet still needed to know.

The screens had been left on, the machines still humming. He remembered how obliging she had been, showing how the system worked, giving him the grand tour, proud and boastful of her achievements. But her vanity paid a price, how easy it would be to slip inside Adam's head and know once and for all, the cost of his secrets the entry fee. He found the drive marked Adam easily. She had left it out, unaware of Hopper's curiosity and need to know. Although he considered himself as something of a technical luddite, Dom's influence had paid off, as had her instructions and he connected the drive to the main console. He made himself comfortable in the chair, no need for straps or injections as he gingerly put the headset on, he only needed a quick look.

It felt different this time. Hopper, surrounded by darkness, was acutely aware of where he was. He was in the lab, in the chair and having second thoughts. Did he really want to see and feel what Adam did, a small voice told him yes, whilst another argued no. The headset had been designed to block out sound as well as vision, and he didn't hear Shelly approach. Inside, the darkness gave way to static, and Hopper felt himself shrink. The needle and burning sensation he'd felt only a short while ago was the only give-a-way he was no longer alone, no longer in control, but as the warmth spread through his body, he stopped caring as he entered the psyche of another, Adam. His body and mind no more belonged to him than the world in which he entered as the door shut behind, locking him out of the real world.

Shelly had been lying awake next to Hopper, waiting for him to take the bait. Watching his id, she had felt uncontrollable arousal and abandonment wanting to become him, to devour him and know the part of him that lived inside. She felt so close to the tank and the promise that it offered, her anticipation was almost enough, almost, and she had given in to her own lust, knowing she would revisit herself through Hopper. See herself as he did by becoming him. But she needed him to understand first. Adam lived within them both. Like her, Hopper would experience the essence of him and become whole. She would give him everything and more, so that he would understand. He was the last piece of the puzzle. He wanted to know what Adam had seen, experienced and now he would, he would become him. The events of the zoo were nothing compared to the joy of release. He would bite and tear his way through Adams memories and make them his own. Bonded together by the tank and their shared id.

# 71.

Frank was working late. He liked the silence of solitude that death brings; it helped him think. He knew what he was, a self-aware sociopath is rare, he has an emptiness that reminds him every day. He doesn't see himself as part of the world or indeed part of anything. The people he knows have no special meaning or connection to him, it is the urge to find some satisfaction that drives him forward. There is a gnawing hunger he feels in the pit of his stomach and knows the detachment he feels isn't normal, they told him so when he was a child. He used to mimic the emotions of others to blend in, but after a while he gave it up, why bother trying to part of something he despised? Instead, he grew to love his difference, it allowed him to do the things others couldn't.

But Frank has a problem and being a high-functioning sociopath isn't it. It's the boredom he feels. It makes him feel dead inside. There are times when Frank longs for an end. The drudgery of the day is a trigger, his enemy the monotony. He'd worked for organizations, who's disregard for excitement left him cold, striving to put things in place so the money-making machines ran smoothly. He was the reason they did, his reputation for not caring, a disposition towards violence meant he was always looking for an excuse, people seldom gave him one, but it left him emptier than ever. Money was of little interest, if he needed it, he would take it. It was the stimulation he craved. He knew things were coming to an end, he could feel it. The detective had come to find the scent, he wouldn't be the last. It didn't matter, things end.

He heard about the body at the zoo, it sounded like something he would have liked to have seen and his mind drifted back to the kid who sneaked in. He had balls doing what he did, it took guts. It was a shame Higgs had spoilt the fun, but it gave him an idea. The reaction of the crowd was far more than he could have imagined, there was an appetite for his kind of fun.

The police would be crawling around the zoo by now, he could imagine Fisher blubbering, spilling his guts to the detective. He would be ready to sell his soul if it meant getting himself off the hook, *too bad fat man there's a hook with your name on it right here*, he thought and wondered how he might look without his skin. Higgs didn't bother him so much, if Frank had a soft spot, he would have had one for him. There was something about Higgs he came close to liking. Whether it was his anarchic nature, his *couldn't give a shit* attitude or true disdain for life, but Frank felt a kind of solidarity with the man. He certainly had a death wish, what junkie doesn't. Why else pump yourself full of poison? Unless like him he needed that little extra to make him feel, anything. When it all came crashing down, he would be quick, merciful, he owed him that much. Fisher less so.

The carcass in front of him gently swayed on its hook, still fresh enough to bleed, he could skin and gut a full-grown beef cow in under 30 minutes and have a steak frying on the hotplate in under forty. Frank licked his lips; he was getting hungry. Fisher would get his turn soon enough and wondered what he would taste like if it was him on the hook, too much fat. Sour, rotten meet, he grimaced as he lopped off a hunk of fat, when he heard the soft wet patter of bare feet. He spun the knife in his hand, had someone come looking for trouble? He hoped so.

"Someone there?" He asked the shadows, not expecting a reply, save the clink of chains and the slapping of someone running. A wide grin spread across his thin lips. "You gonna' stay in the shadows or you ready to come down and talk this through?" And by *'talk'*, he meant cut, slice, kill. His voice was met with silence. "I know you're there. I can hear you, you dumb fuck. You come down now and you tell me what you want." Perhaps the kid had come back looking for revenge, he was ballsy enough, "the longer you stay up there, the worse it's gonna get."

That was a lie, it couldn't possibly get any worse, he already had an appetite for slaughter and once he minced the hunk of meat on a hook and whoever it was that was stupid enough to come calling together, well, he was pretty sure they'd taste the same, who knows this could be the start of a whole new business venture. Sweeney Todd did it, why not him?

Quick feet, heavy above, were circling him, keeping to the shadows, waiting and studying, ready to choose the right moment. Frank followed the sound, knife in hand, ready for a kill. "You playing games? That's ok, I like games."

A loose chain swung down as his answer. A heavy hook arcing past, followed by another and another. Frank ducked and weaved his way through the swinging chains. "Is that all you got..." The last remaining chain swung down behind in a pendulum motion and caught him between the shoulder blades taking his breath away. Gasping for breath, he spun around feebly trying to grab at the hook sticking out of his back. He could feel himself weaken as his lungs filled with blood. He was drowning. He was drowning in himself and is angry this is the way it's going to be. It's not fair, he thinks, all he wanted was a fight.

Gurgling and thrashing, arms flailing, Frank is hoisted high into the waiting darkness like so many dead cows before him. Unable to scream, he now belongs to someone else, he's their puppet now. Clutching at the air, every movement a helping hand to gravity, sliding him further onto the hook until one last jolt pushes the point through his chest as the chain connects to the rails in the ceiling. Blood splashes the floor filling the drains. Frank's eyes begin to defocus and mist, *it shouldn't be like this*, he wants to shout. Suddenly his body jerks forward as the chain begins its journey along the conveyor system, pulling him along like a fairground ride. He swings through the plastic doors to where he has skinned so many beasts and starts to giggle with what little breath he has left, crimson foam bubbles down his chin as he finally comes to rest and his attacker steps forward holding a knife.

Had Frank been able to draw a breath, he would have laughed, a twisted hand reaches forward and buries its fingers into his neck, fingers clasp and squeeze. A mile-wide smile of twice as many teeth comes in for a kiss. Frank dies silently laughing as a piece of him is bitten off, *it's important to keep a sense of humor* he thinks, as his world is switched off.

# 72.

As Hopper slipped back into consciousness and his own body, he became aware of three things; his body ached when he moved, he was drooling, and the floor was hard. He could taste it; the floor. A cocktail of vinegary detergent and ground-in dirt. He was lying face down, his left arm twisted beneath had gone numb. He rolled over onto his back, balling his hand into a fist and out again, pumping the blood back in. He blinked away what was left of sleep and took in his surroundings, trying to process where he was, he'd never seen the building from the floor looking up, he seldom fell, he was lying in the center of the ring at *The Circle*. He managed to prop himself up on his elbows and then to a sitting position. He was naked, his body streaked with blood his shoes were gone. He quickly searched for injuries.

"It's not your blood." The voice came from behind. Art was sitting hunched forward on the first row of the benches sipping from a large mug, he had another cup on the seat next to him, the steam catching in the morning sunlight as he offered it to Hopper. Hopper could smell the coffee from where he sat. "I tried waking you, but you were dead to the world. All I could do was get you a blanket." Art continued, his voice slow and measured.

Hopper wrapped the blanket around his shoulders and hobbled to where Art was, taking the seat next to him, grateful for the mug of coffee. Cradling it in both hands he took a sip. He could taste the bourbon, Art's own special brew he used to call it. Hopper liked the familiarity of it, it was the only thing he did like. He was grateful to wash away another taste lingering on his tongue. They sat in silence for a while, neither man talking, Art figured if his friend wanted to talk, he would do so in his own time. Hopper had nothing to say, his mind blank, he would have preferred it, if Art could fill him in on how he got there. "What happened?" Hopper asked.

"I think that's my line. If you mean, how'd you get here? I have no idea. You tripped the alarm. I found you lying in the middle of the ring. Like I said, I tried waking you. That's all I got. Don't you remember anything? You want to tell me who's blood that is?"

Hopper rubbed at his temples and tried to concentrate, but all he could come up with was the early stages of a headache. He took another long swallow, almost draining the cup.

"Go easy." Art cautioned, Hopper could hear the concern in his friend's voice, "must have been one hell of a party."

Hopper finished his coffee, hungry for the last dregs, "you got another?" He asked, handing it back, Art swapped it with his own.

In Art's experience, the vague excuse of, *I can't remember what I did last night*, was a poor shield from embarrassment. Most of us can, but would rather not. Blackouts were reserved for the serious hard-core drinker or alcoholic, Hopper still considered himself the former, Art was beginning to think the latter. "Slowly," he said as he topped up the mug with another splash of bourbon from his hip flask, "take a hair of the dog that bit you and we'll figure it out together. No rush. Let's start at the beginning, you got up, you got dressed. What did you have for breakfast?"

It was a familiar technique. Hopper had used it himself several times, although never expected it to be used on him. It was a tried and tested method used to bring back memories from traumatized witnesses. Reboot the day, starting with the basics. Where did you sleep? Did you tie your shoes? What tie did you put on, why that one? Who did you see, what did you say, what was on the news? What did the killer look like? Hour by hour, little by little, rebuilding the day. As much as it irritated him, Hopper knew it was in his best interest to play along. "I had a ham and cheese roll, lightly toasted from the bakery on the corner. Too much sauce, there always is, they never get it right." Art nodded back encouragingly; the answers always lay buried in the details. Hopper knew the drill, he didn't need the additional questions, "I was wearing my dark grey suit, it's old, needs cleaning, but so does the other one. Makes me look like a cop." Hopper shook his head struggling to connect the day's events and glanced at the bleachers surrounding the ring. He recoiled in horror as squawking animals out for blood suddenly filled the seats.

"Jack, what was it?" Art was troubled, he hadn't seen his friend for a few weeks, normally it wouldn't have mattered, Hopper was known to go AWOL from time to time, usually surfacing several days later slightly worse for wear with a stupid grin on his face that lasted weeks, not this time. "What did you just see?"

The visions had gone no sooner had they appeared, Hopper shut his eyes, he could still hear the crowd cheer. "Animals, crowds of them. It doesn't make sense. I didn't see that, that wasn't me."

Art nodded along, *if it wasn't you, then who was it?* He was already out of his depth, "maybe we should call someone Jack, your doctor. How about that? What's her name, Shelly?"

Her name was like an ice pick behind the eye, opening a fissure in the brain, "She knew," Hopper said quietly to himself, as the memories, drawn together by an invisible thread began to click into place. "There was a body at the zoo. I remember."

"I heard about that; they're saying it was some homeless guy. You were there?"

"I went to see her, to tell her about Adam. Confront her, you understand?" Hopper continued lost in his own world. Art was convinced that although Hopper may have seen something, whatever it was may have triggered a breakdown, he'd seen it before, colleagues who refused to acknowledge the job affected them more than they let on, as if it were a sign of weakness.

"It was there, right in front of me," Hopper continued, more as a stream of consciousness, "I should have known. That's why I went back." There was something else, something tugging at the veil. "The tank," he blurted out triumphantly. "I saw, I saw it all. It was him Art, it was always him."

"Who? Who are you talking about?"

"He never had a name. Not before." Hopper stopped abruptly, an image cleaved its way in, brutal, vicious, and achingly familiar. He looked down at the blood on his hands. He needed to know if the memory belonged to him. He looked up at Art. "I need clothes."

Art knew better than to argue with a psychotic. Hopper ended up back at his place for a reason, the last vestige of sanity reaching for help, and he didn't want to spook him. Instead tried to buy some time before he did something really stupid. "I think you need a shower first."

Hopper eyed him suspiciously, "no funny business Art."

"No funny business Jack." Art promised.

Under the hot spray, the flashbacks came abruptly, real, and precise, as convincing as his own, but he knew they weren't. He punched at the side of his head, careful not to alarm Art by the scream buried in this throat. *Get out of my head,* he wanted to shout, *no,* they mocked. Suddenly the memories came at him in a torrent. The abuse as a young child, *not his,* the dead junkie mother, *not his,* the crucifixion, *not his,* the snarl and the razor-sharp teeth, *his?*

It was a lifetime of hurt and pain injected at speed, he could feel the tears well behind his eyes and he knew what it was like to be beaten to a bloody pulp. Innocence stripped bare with only the comfort of cruelty to hold. He understood the need to tear at the world, to bite back. He remembered the abattoir and the fight. The screaming crowd baying for blood, hidden behind faces that no more belonged to them, than the memories did to him. Yet he knew and could almost taste the desire for revenge, an insatiable appetite driving, pushing him forward, he clenched his teeth, he could feel himself slipping, it wasn't real. But a voice inside his head told him it was, the voice that had always been there, often ignored, no longer the silent passenger, *they're all dead. You know what you did.*

By the time Hopper finished showering, he felt split in two. Part of him. The rational part wanted to drive him home, take control, rest. Talk to Shelly. The other part didn't. The other part wanted to take a gun and start shooting. The other part wanted to see what he had done.

Art laid out the spare clothes he could find in his friend's size, from the disparate collection of uncared-for clothing and cobbled together an outfit more appropriate for a clown. An eclectic mix of brown brogues, slightly too short green trousers revealing bright yellow smiley-faced socks, a brown, yellow and orange speckled shirt with a two-tone disco collar finished off with a blue lightweight cotton jacket.

"Are you fucking kidding me, this is the best you got?" Hopper asked, scratching his head, "I can't wear this."

"It'll do for now. I don't think it's safe for you to be on your own right now. How about I call your doctor?" Art suggested.

Hopper stared at his reflection, he looked ready to book a permanent room at the hospital, one that's nice and padded. "I'll need your gun and car keys Art."

"Maybe we should just wait a while until you calm down."

*Wait?* Hopper's alarm bell began ringing as he carefully asked his friend what he started to suspect, "what did you do Art? Did you call someone?"

"You need help Jack. This isn't normal. I just think it's better if you just take some time, maybe we can talk some more."

Hopper nodded, he wasn't angry, he knew his friend had his best interests at heart, no matter how misguided they were. He couldn't possibly explain what he knew or had seen. But as much as he understood why Art wouldn't give him the keys or the gun, Hopper felt disappointed and hoped he would understand.

Art didn't see the punch coming. Hopper not only had the advantage of surprise, but he also knew his friend had a glass chin. A swift uppercut with the palm of his hand was enough to jolt his head back, momentarily stunning him. When connected in the right spot, the blow often resulted in a swift knockout, Hopper had enough experience to be pinpoint accurate and his friend crumpled like a dead weight. "Sorry pal, it's for your own good," Hopper told him as he gently placed a cushion from one of the chairs under his head. It didn't take him long to find what he was looking for; the keys were in a drawer under the counter, the gun taped beneath. Art's car of choice, an original Ford Mustang Mach 1, 69, naturally black, what else? Hopper turned the keys, and the car responded immediately with a low guttural growl. Hopper checked the magnum chamber, pleased to find it well-oiled and fully loaded, and tucked it in the waistband of his trousers.

# 73.

Have you ever had a dream so real, so utterly convincing, that when you woke, the panic of guilt gripped so hard it squeezed out the doubt? Hopper had to know. He had to know if it was real, any of it. He could feel memories that weren't his sliding over his own, morphing into one, telling him they were. He had looked behind the curtain and torn down the world. Behind lay an ugly reality he wanted no part of. Seeing through Adam, he felt what he felt, and wanted the same. Worlds merged into one, but what scared him more than anything was how much he liked it, *they got what they deserved*, the voice told him, and he agreed. Hopper had never felt as alive as he did now and was reluctant to give it up, but the squirming in his brain, the smaller part of him still resisted, struggling to be heard, told him it wasn't real. The other voice laughed back. He had to know.

He was speeding, gripping the wheel, grinding his teeth, it hadn't been him in the cage, but he knew the pain and anger, and the gratitude to Higgs repaid by a quick death. Leanne Bonelle, standing by the streetlight, he remembered her smell, the choking perfume that made him gag and her skin like paper, easily torn. Jackson at the zoo, ripped and broken, the metallic taste of his blood. Big baby Nate turned inside out. There were others too many to relive. The pounding in his brain was getting louder, wave after wave washing out the bad thoughts, bar one. Too raw and too fresh to be anyone else's other than his. Panic gripped him as he pressed his foot down.

Hopper reached the abattoir quickly, Art's 76 Mustang growling under pressure as images of Frank twirling in the darkness filled his head. He stumbled out of the car and headed towards the main building. A commotion had grown by the entrance as Hopper fought his way in. Untethered chains swayed in the breeze, bringing back unwanted visions of a hook slicing through the air hitting its target. He remembered Frank's frustration trying to reach the hook, his back too broad, the hook too high, the splash of blood as he was lifted high on the conveyor system. Behind the greasy plastic doors, obscuring a truth Hopper didn't want to know, the shape of a carcass still hung. Hopper knew better than to hope. Hope was a lie for the desperate, but he'd never hoped for anything more in his life. A force beyond his control took him through. He didn't want to see the split body of Frank, stomach torn open below the point of the hook, intestines hanging out gently swaying with the motion of the body. He didn't want to see the hole in his neck where his throat had been ripped open or the sightless eyes filled by flies that had started to buzz.

Fisher had come looking for friends, the zoo had been closed, the shadow of propriety had finally fallen across its doors, it was doubtful it would ever re-open. He'd tried to reach Frank by phone. He was nervous, alone, and had come looking for help. No Jackson, no Higgs, and now no Frank, *soon no Fisher*. Oddly grateful for the abrupt severance of their engagement, but without anyone to rely on, he was on his own which in turn made him anxious as hell. He didn't believe in coincidence, Frank had plenty of enemies, if someone was out to get them, he would be next, but he could hide, and he could disappear and with the right amount of money, he'd never be found. Who was he anyway? He wasn't important. Jackson and Frank were involved in things beyond his league. He was a small fish who dared to play in a bigger pond. The police had already warned him not to go anywhere and started to ask difficult questions that needed answers. Hyde, it turned out, wasn't as dumb as he looked and had begun to question the popular theory of whose body had been found at the zoo. He wouldn't, of course, not without the money, and Higgs had been kind enough to tape his treasure map for him before he'd ended up with the Hyenas. Poor Higgs, it was a secret he would keep to himself, what evidence there had been, was now destroyed, and when the police eventually found out who the body was, he'd be long gone by then.

Fisher watched Hopper back out of the killing shed, followed by an angry mob, and could hear the commotion from where he stood. They wanted to know who he was and what he was doing. It was only until Hopper brandished his gun they got the message and left him alone, several had already taken his picture, but judging by what he was wearing, there didn't seem much point. If Hopper had been to blame, Fisher wanted no part of it and scurried off to his car before he turned his attention to him.

*It wasn't me, it wasn't me.* Hopper wanted to scream at the men pointing their accusatory fingers at him. One of them recognized him from his earlier visit, convinced he was back to review his handiwork, had picked up one of his tools along with several others who were only too willing to serve up some retribution before the police arrived. Ex-cons had their own code. *We take care of our own*, and he knew they did. Thankfully the cold comfort of the .45 told them to back off, and they quickly obliged. He caught sight of Fisher from the corner of his eye. He knew there should be some rage left in him, but Fisher was a clown living on borrowed time. The man was already dead, he just didn't know it.

Fisher held up his hands in surrender, looking at the cannon in Hopper's right hand, "this has nothing to do with me," he pleaded, more so by reflex.

"Put your hands down, fat man," Hopper growled, brandishing the gun, "I know who it was." He shook his head as he took out the keys to Art's mustang. Shelly would have known. *Save the girl, kill the monster*, his old mantra. Shelly had been the monster all along, hiding in plain sight, pulling the strings. He opened the door to the Mustang and slid in behind the wheel. Fisher was still hovering, waiting for answers. Hopper started the engine, he almost felt sorry for him, "you all died the moment you stuck him in that cage, you were just too dumb to know it."

The comment caught Fisher off guard, not so much because he had found out about their operation, but more so by his cavalier attitude. It made him nervous, and if Hopper was right, then he needed protection, "wait," he protested and latched on to the window lip of Art's car, "I need protection," he panted, running in step with the car, "we can cut a deal," he managed to say before the car accelerated and Fisher was left in the dust on his belly.

Hopper laughed out loud as he thought about a memory that wasn't his and what the future had in store for Fisher, "it's too late, none of it matters any more", he shouted at the quickly receding figure of Fisher in his rear view mirror.

# 74.

Shelly had intended to wait. Anticipation, it has often been said, can sometimes be better than the real thing. It's why we do the lottery, why we go on blind dates, the dream of possibilities governed by imagination. Infinite variations of a brighter future, one in which you dictated terms. But in the end, when reality sets in, the end is, no matter how fantasized, wanted, or hoped for, is inevitably the end.

There was power in knowledge, and Shelly had looked forward to this moment since she first stepped foot inside Adam's head. She had watched Hopper experience the real side of Adam and understand the unbridled joy, the ecstasy of abandonment. To be alive without constraint, giving in to the animal inside. It was who we were. Outside was the construct, a facade to be torn down. The truth, far greater than she could have imagined, needed to be lived through. Who we are, who we pretend to be, was a bought-in lie, a pretence built to withstand a paradox we'd been sold and greedily gobbled up, usurping and corrupting the defining qualities that make us who we are, that in the end, suppressed them.

She wanted to know the truth of Hopper, it had been intoxicating to watch him grow, to feed off his anger and frustration. She couldn't wait any longer as she stepped into the tank, the gel warm around her body as she submerged and placed the helmet over her head. She would know what he knew, do what he couldn't, and become herself through him. In the distance, a white light burned, and she willingly swam towards it.

# 75.

Hopper knew, he'd always known, his vision once clouded by cataracts now clear. He didn't hate Adam for who he was or what he did, he understood him. Circumstance hadn't made him only released him. The Adam he knew, the one that lived in the shadows, had always been there, protecting, caring, a constant in a life built on sand. The Adam he knew had been a rock, repaid by neglect. The other Adam, the one on the outside, the weaker of the two had tried to ignore and separate, pushing the inside away as he were nothing, meant nothing. It hadn't made him angry, it made him sad. Alone, lost in his own despair, he took on everything the world had to give, shielding the other, his other. But Shelly opened the door, and all the anger, hatred, and rage had walked out and metastasized into something real. It stepped into Hopper when he stepped into it, and they became one. Did she know? He guessed she did. There was a window to the mind of Adam, who he was and what he wanted, but to really know the man, to understand in the way Hopper did, she would have done the same. Always one step ahead, pulling the strings from both inside and outside.

*Save the girl, kill the monster.* The monster was Adam. The monster was Shelly. The girl was Eve. He had planned to confront Shelly before, and she had turned him into Adam. This time would be different. He was the monster now, and there was no going back, opened, and unleashed. He knew what he had to do. There was no line, no code, fabrications built on paranoia, guilt, and fear. Without them, he was free to act, he had been a fool to believe in a system that didn't, wouldn't return the favor.

He already knew where he was going. He'd already been there. Adam had planned to meet with Eve and leave. She didn't know, couldn't know, the Adam she would be leaving with. Hopper had searched for a clue into what Adam intended to do once they were free, but the future was uncertain. Adam was two, both inside and outside, constantly switching drivers, but Hopper knew there was only room for one passenger inside. *Save the girl, kill the monster.*

# 76.

Art had made the call shortly after he had woken with a stinging headache and fat lip. Betrayal didn't sit comfortably as he spoke to Captain Blake. He'd wanted to omit the detail about the gun, it wouldn't have taken him long to find it, armed and dangerous, would be how he was seen, but Hopper had taken away that choice when he'd knocked him out. He had taken Blake at his word that Hopper would be given every opportunity to hand himself over, and yes, his doctor would be the first person he would contact, but it still didn't sit well, being an ex-cop, he knew how easy it was for tensions to escalate, all it took was the overly anxious twitch of a finger to change someone's life forever.

Blake tried calling Shelly, but she remained unavailable, he'd left several messages, it was up to her to get back to him. He'd been true to his word and *made an effort*, in his mind, it was enough. He'd entertained her odd requests throughout her sessions with Hopper, extending beyond what was necessary. Keeping him on missing persons, giving him a babysitter in the form of Dom. Agreeing to regular updates, even to the extent of constructing a map according to her specific instructions, he'd passed that one over to Dom. Thankfully he'd soon be rid of them both. She'd handed in her report several days ago, recommending Hopper for complete psychiatric treatment under her care. He'd signed the section papers that morning when he'd heard about the abattoir.

A body had been found hanging from a hook in the early hours of the morning. He had been informed of Hopper's visit the previous day, and an earlier call confirmed his suspicions. The description matched what Art had told him. He'd also mentioned the likelihood he would now be armed and dangerous and should be treated as such. Hopper had long been a stain on the department, had it been up to him, he would have wiped it clean years ago. Hopper was a dangerous relic, living in the past. He'd been relieved he hadn't been able to talk to Shelly, the last thing he needed was some *do gooder* shrink getting in his way. He didn't blame her, she was only doing her job. No doubt she had done her best with what she had, but the result was always going the be the same. He'd seen it before, a look, a change in demeanor, good cops going bad. Balking at a system they'd once vowed to uphold, beaten and hamstrung by bureaucrats who knew nothing of the job. The disappointment and anger of knowing you were drowning in shit, and no-one to throw you a lifeline. The best you could do was stay afloat, and Blake had watched many good guys sink, but Hopper wasn't one. He'd always been bad, something in the way he enjoyed the job a little too much.

Enough was enough. Forensics had been and gone and lifted enough prints to tell him what he knew. His last conversation with Shelly had been awkward at best. She'd explained that Hopper had invented a fantasy world that ran parallel to the real one, but in his, he was able to make connections where there weren't any and warned that Hopper was in a particularly fragile state of mind. Blake didn't care, just as long as Hopper was no longer his problem. His problem was where to find him.

# 77.

Waiting by the gates, waiting to get back in.

Eve on the outside, wishing she was in.

Eve felt like her namesake, trying to get back into the garden, tainted and ruined, taken over by snakes, poisoning everything in their wake. Grey rotten fruit and the animals mad as hell. Her life felt no longer tethered, anchored by who she was and her circumstance. Higgs, gone. She had heard about the homeless man, a nagging thought told her it was a lie, but one she needed to believe in. The police were asking questions, she knew once she got involved, there would be no escape.

She still had the note; his one act of kindness soured by truth. She had done what she could, neither excuse or blame, he was what he was and what he would always be, beyond saving, self-aware of his own shortcomings as a father, man, and human being. She was all he had and all that mattered, to protect her he would give her up. Had he loved her? Of that, she was sure, in his own way, but did he even know what love was? She remembered a line immortalized in song, *if you love someone set them free*, it's a line from a popular novel that was always misquoted, the second half often forgotten. The actual line is, *if you want something very, very badly, let it go free. If it comes back to you, it's yours forever.* Higgs was never coming back, she knew that. His love was a distortion through a glass syringe. Junkies don't love, there isn't room, all that's left is an all-consuming devotion to the one thing they need above all else. She was tired of trying to compete with something she would never match. Hers was a bleak future of disappointment and tragedy if she stayed. His; a mix of euphoric highs and unbridled rushes until it wasn't, when the darkness came and swallowed him whole.

The letter provided detailed instructions where the money was and asked for two things in return. Forgiveness. For him to be remembered as the man he was and not the man she would create by wishful thinking. Secondly, under no circumstance should she ever come looking. She could do one but not the other, he was her father after all, if only he could have found it in himself to forgive the man he'd become and move on to a better life, but she knew that was impossible. She had a choice; without knowledge and proof he could be where imagination took him, alive or dead, it was up to her. She decided on life, a future fiction where he would meet a kind soul who would take pity on him and be his ultimate redemption. He would show her hidden talents, saving a precious animal, cementing his role in whichever community he landed. They would grow old together. He would rediscover the world anew but would always be romantically pulled back by the dark secret he kept hidden; his daughter, the one he ran from to protect. His melancholy would be his attraction, dark, brooding, mysterious. He would be Bruce Banner reinvented, man of mystery, always running, a loner of magnitude. His Hulk, the addiction he tried so hard to escape. He was to become the central character in so many stories, reality was never as attractive.

Eve kept herself busy writing fantasies in her head, watching the skies darken, fat, heavy clouds ready to burst and wash away the past as she waited for Adam. They arranged to meet tonight, the heat giving way to a sudden chill that ran through the streets and sucked at the moisture in the air. Their plan was simple; meet, run away. They would find the money, blood money she knew, *but fuck it*, animals died for this, and still no one cared. She waited for the police to leave, watching green clouds rolling in, knowing the storm was set to take away anything they hadn't. No one noticed her, the skinny girl huddled by the entrance, she'd been invisible most of her life. It would be easy to sneak in, she knew the zoo's secrets so well, her second home.

Adam had changed, felt more so than thought it. It had been his final session in the tank with Shelly; so keen to get him back, prepped and fully immersed one last time, her expression reminded him of someone he'd once known, his past self or rather the other him, the one that lives in the dark, the one that got out. Inside the tank, he laid to rest everything he was, exorcism over, and the demon purged. He had torn, ripped, bitten, destroyed everything, everyone in his wake. Exhausted and spent, there was nothing left to give, and Shelly knew; the discarded husk sucked dry, she had already moved on. No one cared or noticed as he left. No longer wearing his ankle bracelet, he had jumped the walls without effort, his new life beckoning he never turned back. Shelly had what she wanted, all that was him, now hers.

The sight of Eve quickened his heart as he ran towards her. Their meeting, fuelled by longing, a giddiness reserved for love-struck teenagers. Temporary at the best of times, it wouldn't last long, they didn't have the luxury of time to fully enjoy it. There would be time enough later.

# 78.

The heatwave had finally broken, harsh angry rain, impatient to hit the ground, had turned everything to swamp. A blanket of water so thick it was hard to see through had come crashing down, drenching Fisher as he dug. Why so deep Higgs? Who were you expecting? Dirt turning to mud, he scraped the ground, the hole filling with a dirty brown soup as quick as he emptied it. Fisher on hands and knees doing all the dirty work, *as per fucking usual*, he mumbled under his breath. *Fuck 'em, Fuck em all, fuck the animals, fuck Frank, fuck Jackson, fuck Higgs and most of all fuck Adam and that snooty bitch Shelly*. He was on a roll, why should he be the one to bend over and take it? All his life, he'd been used, people thinking they were better than him, taking advantage of his good nature, thinking he was dumb, well *Fuck Them*, he was outta' here. He wasn't so dumb as to keep the cameras on, wasn't so dumb as to know exactly where Higgs had stashed his loot, wasn't so dumb as to know when to cut and run.

*You all died the moment you stuck him in that cage.* Hopper's comment rattled him, not because he knew, but because he didn't care. Fisher was running against the clock. It was time to get out and leave it all behind, *it had been fun, hadn't it? For a while, crocodile.* King of his garden, his own private paradise, overgrown and ready to crumble. His only regret, Leanne wasn't around to share it. He'd liked her more than he let on, didn't even mind her dopy kid. It had always been a business transaction, but fate has a funny way of bringing people together, he knew she had felt it too. He may not be much to look at, but who's kidding who here, she would have been grateful for his attention, especially now he'd be able to provide from them both. He was smiling. Thinking about Leanne always made him happy, the optimistic possibilities were endless. Once the dust had settled, maybe he'd try looking for her. Why not? Didn't he deserve some happiness? And if he couldn't, there would always be another Leanne, he pulled at his crotch, *time and place Fisher, time and place.*

Finally, he hit something other than mud. Putting his shovel to one side, he wiped away the dirt revealing the blue straps of what looked like a child's backpack. Greedy fingers scratched and tugged as he slowly exhumed the bag, it came away with a sucking plop as Fisher sat down on his haunches and unzipped it. His hard work had paid off. Several bundles of notes had been tightly bound together in plastic wrap, keeping the notes nice and dry, it took a lot to resist the urge to count it there and then. Excitement getting the better of him, digging up another man's treasure was just like fucking his wife or daughter, and he thought of Eve. He never could understand what Jackson saw in her, probably because she resembled a boy from behind. He gave a little chuckle. Despite the rain, he was in a hell of a mood, a cash windfall will do that to you.

"Where are you? I'm coming for you. This ends, you hear me. This ends now."

Hopper's voice cut through the rain like a serrated knife. Unexpected and desperate, it sounded too close for comfort. Fisher could hear the anger and finality in his tone as he called out for Adam. Fisher muttered under his breath; the zoo was beginning to come alive with the commotion Hopper was making. He weighed up the possibilities of making a run for it but doubted he would get far, preferring instead to settle on the lesser of two evils; he would just have to wait it out and crawled to the back of the cage where it was dark. Grabbing the bag, he zipped it shut. No sooner had he managed to make himself comfortable than he heard the wet slap of what sounded like feet. Praying for invisibility, he made himself still and held his breath. He first felt rather than heard the hot steamy panting from behind. Thick with excitement, it warmed the back of his neck. He was no longer alone.

# 78.

*Save the girl, kill the monster. Save the girl, kill the monster.*

Hopper's mantra pounding in his like the beating of a drum, his well-known chant, his mantra, hunting down a killer. He heard the sirens, distant at first growing louder by the second, and knew they would be here for him. It was ok, he would be the bait and lead them to Adam. He needed to find the girl first.

Adam and Eve were huddled together inside a cave. There was a hole where the money should have been. They heard Hopper's voice, "he's coming for you, isn't he?" Eve asked. "We should go. Are you disappointed about the money?"

Adam shrugged. He had all he needed, Eve and their freedom. Money had no meaning for him, he found the attraction strange. Life was about so much more. It served no purpose but to obscure the truth.

Hopper was moving quickly, his gun held tightly, and was surprised at how familiar the zoo felt, its secrets and hidden spaces now known to them both. *Save the girl kill the monster, save the girl kill the monster,* his mantra, his purpose, keeping him sane, a clear direction, but the voice kept asking *why?* Wasn't he the monster after all?

Blake was in, Hopper was out. It wasn't enough to simply, *let him go.* Men like him needed to be an example. This was a new order, a new shiny white system, out with the old in with the new. Hopper would lead the way, one last desperate act of negligence caught in the act. It was almost too good to be true. His prints had been all over the abattoir and the remains of Frank. Fisher, the snitch, the kind that always has a plan, confirmed everything Blake now knew as fact. Hopper, no longer fit for active duty suffering from acute delusions brought on by PTSD, living in a fantasy world, The Zoo and Abattoir, with him at the center playing hero. Shelly's account read like fiction. Once the courts were finished with him, she could have him for all he cared, and good riddance.

Hopper passed the surgery, a bloody memory that wasn't his poked at him from behind, making him wince. The beast was close enough to hear a forgotten but recognized sound. Like a moth to a flame, he ran towards it, praying he wasn't already late.

Blake heard the shouts and gathered his men as they moved in.

Hopper was outside the enclosure Fisher was in. He knew before he heard, before he saw, the connection they had was strong enough to extend beyond space. They were brothers now, a part of him had taken up residency inside Hopper. You can't take a walk inside someone's head without keeping a little for yourself. He could hear it, the soft low growls and hard breathing coupled with the enthusiastic tearing of gristle. He peered into the shadows and raised his gun. "Face me." He shouted into the shadows.

Fisher's head came to an abrupt stop at Hopper's feet. It rolled onto its back, lifeless eyes and a twisted grin looked up and mocked him. Hopper wanted to laugh, scream, and howl at the moon. He found it hilariously funny, knowing it was wrong didn't stop him instead it made it worse, *face me*! He raised Art's gun one more time, who should he point it towards, himself? Possibly!

"Put the gun down."

The voice was an anchor shot through fog, pulling him back to sanity. Blake's voice sounded artificial, robotic, filtered through the megaphone. Hopper couldn't look, the last thing he wanted to do was put the gun down.

"He's inside," Hopper shouted over his shoulder, "I've seen what he's done."

"It's over Jack, we know about the abattoir." The robotic voice of Blake shouted back. "We know it was you."

"That wasn't me." Hopper protested.

"Jack, your prints are everywhere, give yourself up, put the gun down, lie on the floor, you know the drill. There's no need for anyone to get hurt."

Hopper felt sick, violent, and vivid memories came back in a flash, edited highlights of Frank still stuck, still alive, still angry, swaying on a hook. Frank had dared him to do it, as he opened him up and took a bite. *It wasn't me*, he protested but knew it was. He had watched Frank cutting into the carcass of an animal, giving him ideas, and swung the chain, catching him like a fish, drawing him upwards so he could watch the life fade from his eyes and to be frank, Frank enjoyed every minute of it.

"That wasn't me," Jack screamed into the night and raised his gun. A single shot rang out through the zoo, startling the animals. Neither Adam or Eve looked back as they left the garden. Hopper fell. His world caught in slow motion as Blake's bullet cut through his shoulder, shredding the muscle from behind. But the image lit by the flash of a gun, bright enough to freeze the back of the cage, burnt into Hopper's mind. Shelly was laughing. Their eyes met for the briefest of moments, the flicker of recognition, and they both knew they had met long before the zoo, back when the man thought he could keep it at bay, back when the monster was out. But the monster was strong and had found someone else to wear, and he knew that the monster had even worn him, back when the monster met Frank.

Inside.

Outside.

Upside.

Down.

# 79.

They have been on the road for several days now, the city behind them long gone. Never bothering to look back, living by their wits. Eve loves Adam, and Adam loves Eve, but the thing that lives in Adam isn't quite so sure. He keeps that to himself. He knows how to keep it asleep in the dark. Shelly showed him how.

Jack Hopper floats. His body, supported by wires monitor every movement and twitch inside the tank. There is nothing on the outside he wants or needs. His life is on the inside now. He is the monster and, for the first time in a long time, feels free. Inside he can run, fly, break, smash and tear. Inside, he will rewrite his world, his past and bite down and chew on the gristle. He will rip the world apart. Inside he is king, master to desire, servant to none. His hunger drives him on, his mantra pushing him forward, *eat the girl be the beast, eat the girl be the beast.*

Shelly is on the outside looking in. She's happy for Jack and wants to feed his Id, she needs the freedom he offers and can't wait to be inside once more.

# The End

# Acknowledgements

Writing isn't a sprint, it's not even a marathon, it's a slow climb to the top of a mountain with numerous wrong turns, crevasses, potholes and potential landslides. But if you get to the top, the view is worth it.

In my quest to scale 'mount novel' there are always sherpas that come along when you need them most, and I owe them a huge thanks for their support, humour, and words of encouragement, especially when that little voice in the back of your head is telling you, you've made an enormous mistake and should never ever, under any circumstance give up your day job. You know the one, we all have it. The trick is to either ignore it of get the help of some trusty friends to shoo it away! Firstly, I'd like to thank my amazing wife, Katrina. You are the absolute best, I know people say stuff like that, but you really are. This would not have been possible without you. You've put up with me going on and on and on about this book for so long, and never once told me to forget it. So much so she was the one who suggested I write it as a novel and for that I'm eternally grateful, not to mention her wit, humour, support, love, and help. I'd also like to mention my two boys, Angus, and Luke. Whether you guys know it or not you've been a huge inspiration, the chats we've had, even the suggestions you've put forward all helped. You both have an amazing sense of humour, unbridled creativity and have turned into wonderful young men whom I'm immensely proud of. Trust me boys, if I can get this finished, there's so much more you're capable of!

I'd also like to thank Ken Atchity and Sam Skelton from Story Merchant for their support and encouragement. They were the first people who believed in this book outside my tiny circle of friends and family and gave me the self-belief I needed to get it finished.

Finally, I'd also like to thank some close friends who were kind enough to read the early drafts and pass on their thoughts and comments, John Walton (mate I still can't believe you read three drafts of it! So grateful.) Andrew and Dani Holman, (thanks for the breakfasts, Andy) and Adam Royle—your notes were invaluable! You've all been brilliant; I cannot begin to tell you how much it means when someone agrees to give up their time to help. Thank you all.

One last thing. If anyone out there is thinking of writing or starting a self-initiated creative project, please don't let the negative inside voice inside win. It's a battle, I know, but one you can win. On a more serious note, mental health is a serious issue, it's one that makes my heart bleed for people out there who are suffering in silence. Please get help if you need it, trust me, having that conversation works.

Thanks again and much love.
Kev

Made in United States
North Haven, CT
14 May 2023

36574683R00200